BRITTANÉE & JENNI
NICOL

Summer People

MONHEGAN, MAINE

Summer People © 2025 by Brittanée Nicole and Jenni Bara

First Edition June 2025

Illustrated Cover Design by elenbushe_art

Formatting by Sara of Sara PA's Services

Editing by Beth at VB Edits

contents

Playlist

HAVE A LITTLE FAITH IN ME - SYML
LOVER OF MINE - JOHN VINCENT III
SLOW HANDS - NIALL HORAN
RIPTIDE - VANCE JOY
MAINE - NOAH KAHAN
CRAZIER THINGS - CHELSEA CUTLER,
NOAH KAHAN
MESS - NOAH KAHAN
MESS IT UP - GRACIE ABRAMS
HOME - GOOD NEIGHBOURS
LITTLE LIFE - CORDELIA
BURNING DOWN (JOE JONAS) - ALEX
WARREN, JOE JONAS
COLD LITTLE HEART - MICHAEL
KIWANUKA
TROUBLED WATERS - ALEX WARREN

MONHEGAN, MAINE

dedication

To starting over as many times as it takes to get it right.

content warning

Content Warnings: This book contains discussions of sexual assault of a minor and death of a parent.

Fisher

Chapter 1

"I'VE ALREADY READ TWO CHAPTERS." I pop the bookmark into *Miracle on Maple Hill* and set it on the nightstand next to the pink sphere my nine-year-old niece calls a moon lamp. Tucking the pink and white quilt around her little body, I say, "It's bedtime, sweet pea."

She should have been asleep thirty minutes ago. My job isn't going to wait much longer. At this point I only have twenty minutes to get into the airline's system and back out before I miss the deadline.

"Night, Fisher," Sutton says as I pull her door shut.

With a long exhale, I hurry to my office. I've just slipped my headphones over my ears when Bing flops his big golden body down on my foot. My dog has been with me long enough to know that once the headphones are on, nothing short of banging his nose against my leg over and over will pull me out of the only place I've ever been truly comfortable.

I jiggle the mouse, and the computer comes alive. Time to move.

Eighteen minutes later, the three black boxes on my screens are full of green code. I've got it. The poor sixty-two-year-old mid-level IT idiot never stood a chance.

Not against someone like me.

I shake my head.

Thanks to the lax IT department and the network's vulnerability to a blind command injection, I easily bypass the authenticator and run a command on the router.

Basically, I unlock it myself and step right in. Damn, I'm good at what I do.

I drop in a few lines of script so the bug will run. And it's done. They're officially fucked.

Once I've backed out, I sit back and toss my headphones onto the desk.

I may not be good at many things, but I'm damn good at this.

Me: It's done.

Libby

Chapter 2

"THE PLANE IS *BROKEN*?"

The flight attendant forces a patronizing smile. "As the captain said, we're having a maintenance issue, but the plane is *not* broken."

"But I still have to get off?" I eye the champagne he's holding. The champagne I ordered. I want that champagne. No, I *need* that champagne. This is the beginning of my new life. At least it's supposed to be. And yes, I'm aware that I haven't yet left my old one. Nor can I just miraculously not be *the Elizabeth Sweet*, especially at LAX, where I'm currently taxiing on the runway.

If we could just get in the air, things would be better.

I would be better.

I should have flown private like my dad suggested.

"Yes. We're required to deplane because the person who approves maintenance concerns is on vacation."

A hiccupping laugh escapes me. "That's absurd."

"Yeah, man, that's crazy," the guy across from me says.

The flight attendant locks his jaw and glares at me. I was the first to question this ridiculousness, but one by one, the passengers in first class are getting rowdy.

"You're telling me a commercial airline doesn't have a person on

3

hand to approve a maintenance problem when the guy goes on vacation?" the man in front of me jeers.

"It's actually a female," the flight attendant says, chin lifted but eyes still narrowed to slits in my direction.

I'm not the one who made the misogynistic comment. I'm not sure why he's acting like I did.

"I say we all just stay on the plane. You can't make us get off," the sexist guy adds.

A low chorus of cheers breaks out, and I sink back into my seat and brace myself. It's more likely that the flight attendant will throw the champagne at me than let me drink it.

I let out the breath I'm holding when he turns, champagne flute in hand, and explains as calmly (patronizingly) as he can why we cannot, in fact, refuse to get off the plane.

I'm already grabbing my bag from beneath the seat and standing. "How long until we can leave?" I ask, pulling out my phone and checking the time.

My father arranged for a helicopter to meet me in Boston. He'll be really annoyed if I miss it. It's the only part of my new life that I let him have input in, and if I screw it up, he'll only want to meddle in other ways.

He's less than pleased that I'm leaving LA and doesn't think I should be running like this. Maybe if I told him the whole truth, he'd understand. But if I told him everything, I don't think I could handle the fallout. Not right now at least.

Later. Once I've become the new me.

The flight attendant sighs. "The earliest they can be here is twelve."

"Midnight?" someone behind me snaps.

I nod. Right. Definitely need another plan. It's already nine p.m., and with the time difference and flight time, I was already cutting it close.

While the rest of the first-class passengers argue, I slip past the angry man still holding the champagne flute. Head lowered, I don't stop until I'm standing across the desk from the gate agent. Turning on the charm, I rest an arm on the Formica between us and lean forward.

Before I can speak, her eyes light up. "Aren't you—"

"Shh." I put my finger over my lips. "Let's not draw a crowd."

The woman nods. "Of course. How can I help you, Ms. Sweet?"

At least my fame is good for one thing. "I need to book a first-class ticket on a direct flight to Boston, and I need to land by six a.m. so I have time to catch my connection."

Nodding like a bobblehead, she gets to work, her fingers flying over the keys of her computer. Her head tilts once, then again, this time her nose scrunching too. "Not possible."

My stomach sinks. "I'm sorry, what?"

She still has that smile on her face. The woman is giving me bad news, yet she looks as cheerful as she did when she first recognized me. "It seems our entire network has gone down."

"Your entire *what?*" Teeth gritted, I lean over the counter so I can see her screen. That doesn't sound like a maintenance issue.

I blink at the computer, then at her. I can't make any sense of what I'm seeing.

The smile she's still wearing is starting to look strained. "I can get you on another airline—"

"Excellent. Thank you."

She takes a breath and readjusts her smile, this time with much more effort. "But there are no first-class seats available that will get you there direct."

Closing my eyes, I accept that I'm going to have to give in a little. "Fine. Then I'll connect. What time will I land in Boston?"

"Oh, no. I mean there are no first-class seats available on any flights that get you to Boston tonight."

I nod. It's more like a bouncing of my head as I accept the inevitable. I won't act like a princess. I'm no longer that person. Coach is perfectly fine. All I want is to get to the island to start my new life. It doesn't matter how it happens. *Everything will be fine.* "Okay. Just put me wherever you can fit me."

"Oh, we thought we'd have the whole row. Hunny, you're going to have to take the baby. We have company."

With a steadying breath, I survey the last row, where a couple is seated, one by the window and one at the aisle, along with their crying baby.

A glance in every direction tells me that this is the only open seat, as the gate agent told me repeatedly as she booked the flight.

I will not call my father and ask for help. I will not call my father and break down.

I can do this.

"She's very cute. I'm guessing she's tired," I say, trying to affect a sense of calm. They're the ones with the screaming child. It's got to be stressful.

"She doesn't sleep," the mother mutters as she slides into the middle seat beside her husband. Then, as I settle beside her, she leans over and says, "I hate flying. Always get sick. Do you think you'll need your puke bag?"

Fuck. My. Life.

Fifteen hours later, my Uber driver, who smells like marijuana and dirty socks, rounds the corner into Boothbay, and relief like I've never experienced before washes over me.

I missed the helicopter my father arranged by fifteen minutes, one of my bags was lost, and I haven't made arrangements to get to the island, but just the sight of the ferry has my eyes stinging with emotion.

The last time I was here, I was just a little girl. Six years old and excited for the summer ahead and the time with both of my parents.

I know now that my father took that summer off because he and my mother knew it would be her last.

As I step out of the Uber and inhale the dewy spring air, I can practically feel my mother standing beside me. Her phantom presence is the reminder I need to straighten my shoulders and change my mindset.

She would have handled today's string of nightmares with nothing but grace. I don't remember a lot, more like snapshots of who she was, but she always wore a smile.

With that memory in mind, I force one onto my lips, thank the driver, who hands me the suitcase and carry-on I didn't lose, and head across the street toward the ferry.

Two steps off the curb, I jump back, narrowly missing the car that swerves around me, horn blaring.

"Watch where you're going, lady!"

My entire body sags. So much for Maine hospitality. I shake off the negative thought, look both ways, and continue forward. I will not let one person's bad attitude get me down. I'm almost there. I can see the ferry...*pulling away from the dock.*

"No! Please, wait!" Dragging my suitcase behind me, I rush forward, waving my hand in a pathetic attempt to get the ferry captain's attention.

It's no use. The boat gives a loud blast of the horn, and then it's spinning away from the dock and toward the horizon.

"You will not cry. You will be fine." My words are a little less certain this time, but I've made it this far. I can hang on to my can-do spirit for a little longer. When I get to the cottage, I can scream into my pillow, but not a second before that.

As I approach the blue booth with a cheerful puffin and a smiling whale painted over the open window, another fragment of a memory flits through my mind—my mother, father, and me standing outside this very booth, huge smiles on our faces.

I take it as a sign and inhale all the positivity I can as I step up to the attendant. He's got gray hair, a toothy smile, and ruddy cheeks.

"Hello, sir. I need a ticket for the next ferry to Monhegan Island."

"One ticket for ten a.m.? Yes, ma'am." He turns to the relic of a computer on the counter.

"Oh, no," I say with a bright smile. "I need one for the next ferry leaving today."

"You just watched today's last one leave," he replies, like he didn't just steal my last bit of hope.

My stomach sinks. "That can't be possible. It's only three o'clock," I force out, voice cracking. "Doesn't anyone need to get there for the weekend? There isn't a late Friday night—"

He shakes his head. "Nope. The only boat going out to the island tonight is the one that'll pick up the trash."

I slap my credit card down on the counter. "I'll take it."

He frowns. "You'll take what?"

"A ticket on the"—my voice wobbles—"trash ferry."

"Oh, that wasn't an option. I was just telling you—wait, aren't you that—"

I launch my upper body over the counter and grab the man by his suspenders, tugging him closer. "Listen, I need to get to the island. It's a necessity. I need to disappear. Yes, I'm that girl. The one who spent her childhood and the entirety of her teenage years on *Grady Party of Two*. Yes, they killed my character off via drug overdose. Yes, everyone says I'm difficult and demanding, and I know I'm not helping my cause right now, but I need you to get me on that boat. I flew ten hours—in *coach*—next to a woman who got sick *three* times while her kid screamed bloody murder. I missed my helicopter over to the island after I swore to my father that I could do this on my own. I can't fail at anything else. I just...*can't*. I'll do anything—*pay anything*—just, please, get me on that boat."

The man blinks and swallows, fear haunting his gray eyes.

I drop my hands immediately. "Sorry, I'm so sorry." Head hanging, I turn away. Oh god, I can all but guarantee that the media will catch wind of my location within the hour and news of a supposed mental breakdown will run rampant.

They wouldn't even be wrong.

For once.

"Well, ya coming?" a gruff voice calls.

Blinking back tears, I zero in on the man in the suspenders. He's on this side of the counter now, fingers gripping the handle of my suitcase. "Just tell Cank that you're my friend. They'll take care of ya, kid."

Relief washes over me with such intensity that it knocks loose the tears I've been holding back, and now I really am crying.

"Oh no. Don't do that." He reaches into his pocket, produces a grayish-looking tissue, and pushes it toward me.

Unable to be rude to someone who's being so nice, I take it. Crumpling it in my hand, I try not to think about how long it's been in his pocket or whether he's used it before.

"Come on, now. We've got garbage to pick up. Just ignore Gus. Kid's a bit weird."

Who's Gus?

Before I can voice the question, a gaunt-looking guy in a very dirty shirt with grayish teeth smiles at me.

Yeah, I'm going to ignore him.

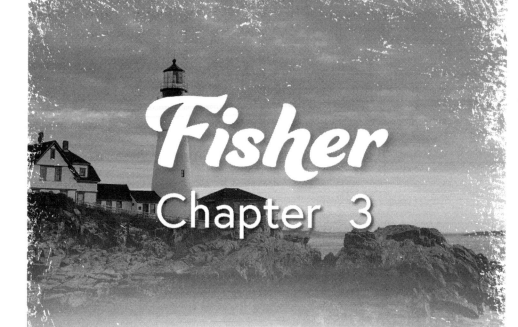

Fisher

Chapter 3

"DAMMIT, BING," I mutter as my golden retriever once again leaps from the passenger side of my truck before I stop. One day the dog is going to hurt himself.

Maybe.

Okay, fine. Probably not, since I have the *only* car on the entire pea-sized island. But a handful of residents cruise around on golf carts. And I'm setting a bad example by allowing my dog to fling himself out of a moving vehicle.

"Don't listen to your daddy." Cank sinks to his knees, and the dog races across to the old wooden planks of the dock, straight to the man who always brings treats.

As a dog with no shame, Bing flops onto his back, legs splayed, begging for tummy rubs.

The moment I slide off the seat and step onto the dry-ass dirt we call a road, a gust of cold salt air lifts my hair off my forehead. Shoulders lifted, I tuck deeper into the collar of my coat, hiding from the evening chill. "You're not going to be able to stand back up, old man."

His arthritis is always worse during the change of seasons.

Cank's chuckle turns into a cough. "Careful there, Fisher," the old man warns as I step onto the dock, my boots thunking heavily. "You're heading over the hill yourself."

Like hell I am. Though it feels like I've been back on this godforsaken island for a lifetime already, and maybe I'm feeling every one of my years, but I'm only thirty-four.

With one bare forearm against his denim-clad knee, he pushes himself up. Damn, I don't know how he does it. Even without the ever-present New England wind, it's barely fifty degrees, and yet the old man is decked out in his token welcome to the island uniform. White shirt and overalls. Man swears he's never cold.

He's got his signature butt-ugly floppy hat on too. As it flutters in another gust of wind, my eye catches on the new patch front and center.

A low chuckle rumbles out of him. "Do you like the puffin? Blue picked the spot."

Blue. I should have known. Only the island's oldest and most inappropriate resident would insist the patch be stitched on in a way that makes it look like the bird is doing unmentionable things to the damn whale patch.

"Kids see that," I grumble.

"Yet they won't think what you do." He rubs his beard, covering his smile. "You got to live a little, Sheriff. You know what you need?"

I huff. I know exactly what he thinks I need. Cank believes a happy man has three things. A boat. A cold beer. And a warm woman.

That might make him happy, but not me. I *have* a boat—that I don't want—dry-docked in the yard. And women are too much damn work. All day, every day, I'm surrounded by people calling my name, needing something from me. I don't need to add a person who comes with a honey-do list.

The beer? Yeah, if I'm lucky, I'll find myself one of those today. The island's brewery is just starting to crank out the spring season beer in preparation of the Memorial Day rush, so a Balmy Days ale is calling my name.

If I get to meet up with my buddy Wilder and his niece Lindsey for the Boston Revs game later, I might actually get an ice-cold brew. The likelihood depends on whether the fog burns off and the satellite can pick up the major league game.

Some days I miss the hell out of Boston. Scratch that. Every day I miss Boston.

"Save your breath, old man. Just because you're happy as a cow in crap with your wife and *Glory Days*"—I tip a chin out to the water, where his boat is moored—"doesn't mean I need either of those headaches."

"Mind your elders," Cank teases. "Sutton's not helping tonight?"

"It's way too cold for our sweet pea." My niece, whom I've been raising since my brother and his wife died three years ago, is even less acclimated to Maine winters than I am, even though she's never lived a day of her life off this island.

"Too bad." He shakes his head. "She'd have been excited about the new gossip."

I wave him off before he can start. Gossip flocks to the island like gulls in summer. I have no interest. I'm only here for the supplies on Cank's boat. The position of sheriff of Monhegan comes with some not-so-traditional duties. Making deliveries being one of them.

I glance at the boxes that need to be delivered to the inn and the small island grocery store, considering how I want to arrange them in my truck. When I catch sight of a Louis Vuitton suitcase and matching carry-on bag, my eyes narrow.

"What's that?"

"*Summer people.*" Cank shrugs, but one corner of his lips pulls up.

"Can't be."

It's not time yet. Not a single rental on this island opens before Memorial Day. Even the inn isn't ready for guests until next weekend. The only tourist coming to the island today canceled her chopper. And thank God for that. The last thing I need is a spoiled superstar hanging around.

"She arrived about a half hour ago on the trash boat."

I cock my brow. No way.

"You heard that right." Cank puffs out his chest. "The infamous Elizabeth Sweet just climbed off the trash boat and is now officially on our island."

"Fucking hell." With a huff, I pick up the first box and get started loading.

Elizabeth Sweet is Hollywood's pampered princess. My life will suck if the media or her crazed fans follow her the twelve miles off the coast to our island. I refuse to get ahead of myself and stress about that right now, though. There's no way the twenty-five-year-old starlet will last one week in this godforsaken place.

"Don't forget her bags." Cank smirks as I drop the last box onto the flatbed of the rusted truck I refuse to call mine.

My already overworked muscles lock.

"Island hospitality," Cank reminds me. "I promised her a personal drop-off."

I hate this place.

"You know, she's prettier in person."

"Not interested." I yank her suitcase off the dock and sling her carry-on over my shoulder. I toss them into the back seat on the passenger side, then haul myself into the driver's seat. "Come on, Bing."

My dog, who's lounging in the mostly dead grass, hops up and takes off down the dirt road toward the small store. Dog knows the drill as well as I do. And Doris, at the grocery, will be waiting with another treat for the spoiled boy. I shake my head as I put the truck in gear and move the half mile, rolling at the snail's pace the pitted single-lane dirt road allows.

"Sheriff."

The truck has barely come to a stop when I'm hit with two syllables that feel like a wildcat clawing the insides of my ears. Yeah, she's my late sister-in-law's cousin, so maybe I should have more patience, but I hate most people. Plus Flora's hair is too bright red and her voice is too nasal. Not to mention she doesn't respect personal space.

Fighting the sigh working its way up my chest, I step out of the truck and face Flora.

"It happened again." She points a long red nail at the roofline of the tiny white cape.

I don't need to look up to know there's a gray puff stuck up there.

"I'll get him." I hold in my huff of frustration. At this point, I'm so intimately acquainted with the damn rodent that I'm aware of its status as a him.

"You're my hero." She shoots me a crooked-tooth smile.

Fucking ridiculous. I'm not fighting a war or keeping a town safe. I'm no one's hero. I'm just the man who is going to once again yank a fat squirrel out of a rain gutter. I lean into my truck, flick open the center console, and remove the gloves that do little to protect my hands and arms from the feral beast. Then I stomp across the road to Flora's house.

"I'll hold the ladder, Sheriff," she offers, like she does every time.

I don't need her help, and her offer has nothing to do with being helpful anyway.

"Did you hear that Elizabeth Sweet arrived on the garbage boat?"

I grunt in Flora's direction and leave it at that. This won't be the last time someone in town brings it up.

"And *she didn't even have a coat.*"

Add that to what I can only imagine will be a long list of fun details I don't care about. Though I can only imagine I'll end up having to give the woman my coat so she doesn't die of hypothermia.

I spend the next five minutes ignoring her yammering as I wrestle with the damn squirrel who keeps trying to squeeze his entirely too large body into the freaking gutter.

The second he's free, he squirms out of my grasp and takes off with a running leap off the roof. For as thrilled as he is to escape, one would think he'd stop getting himself stuck like this. But I can almost guarantee I'll be back to rescue him again tomorrow.

"Thanks so much for your help. I wouldn't know what to do without you."

I grunt. Because what am I supposed to say? *My pleasure*? Fuck no, it's not a pleasure. *Happy to help*? Yeah, no. I'm definitely not.

"Want to come in for a drink? I picked up a six-pack of Balmy Days."

"Gotta get to Sutton." Without turning to see her pout, I stomp back to the truck.

I've got two boxes in my arms and am hardly through the door when Doris starts in on me. "Did you see she's here?"

I fight a sigh and drop the boxes on the counter.

"Not only did she come on the trash boat, but she didn't have a coat. And worse? She was in heels." Her eyes bulge. "Heels, Sheriff."

What the fuck am I supposed to say to that? Heels aren't a crime. Completely impractical? Of course. But nothing about Hollywood's golden girl will be practical.

"Only two more," I inform her as I step outside. Then I can haul ass away from the woman who never shuts up.

Next, I roll the five hundred feet to the inn, where Sutton is helping Mrs. K get ready for opening weekend.

If not for Sutton, I wouldn't be doing this shit.

I swallow back the pain that comes with thoughts of my brother and sister-in-law. Life isn't fair, that's for damn sure. I'm all Sutton has, and she deserves the life her parents wanted for her.

I might have left Monhegan at eighteen with no intention of looking back, but my brother loved it here. He got joy out of pulling squirrels out of the gutters and dealing with fucking goats. He loved the people. He loved the bullshitting and laughs.

I shake my head.

He was charming as fuck. I swear he got all the genes that make for a well-liked, social person, so by the time I came around, none were left.

With two more boxes in my arms, I stomp up the four steps to the large porch. The white rocking chairs have already been placed in front of the windows so the guests can enjoy the ocean view. The view I don't bother to take in. It does nothing for me.

"Sutton," I call. As I step through the door, my boots thunk against the old, knotted hardwood floor.

"Fisher!" My niece flies down the narrow staircase, and when she screeches to a halt in front of me, she bounces on her toes. "Is it true we get to deliver Elizabeth Sweet's bags?"

"Were you a big helper today?" I drop the boxes on the large table in the dining room where Mrs. K serves breakfast to her guests.

"Yes." Her blond braids bounce as she nods. "I made up twelve beds."

"She's always the best helper." Mrs. K pushes through the swinging door, wiping her hands on a long denim skirt that buttons up the front. She must have a whole closet full of them. I've known her all my life, and I swear I've never seen her in anything but the skirt, the lace-up Keds, and the long-sleeve V-neck.

"So do I get to go meet her?" Sutton tugs on my jacket.

"Yeah. We have to drop off her bag."

Mrs. K's eyes light up. "Did you hear—"

I lift a hand. "At least five times, and I didn't care the first time."

"Always the life of the party, Sheriff." Her blond hair doesn't move when she shakes her head, the Aqua Net doing its job.

"Come on." Sutton grasps my gray M-65 military field jacket with a tiny hand and tugs. "I want to see her. Everyone says she's prettier in person. Her hair is longer too."

I sigh. "Tell Wilder that if he and Lindsey want to come by later, he should bring beer but leave the words at home."

"I heard that." My best friend's deep voice echoes off the walls an instant before his feet hit the steps. "You love my voice. It makes your soul sing."

I roll my eyes. But the truth is, he's one of the few people on the island I can spend more than a few minutes with.

"Come *on*." Sutton yanks harder.

"Okay." With a deep breath in, I give Mrs. K a wave and follow my niece out the door.

"Bing," I call.

Ten seconds later, the dog appears. He hops into the back of the truck, and once we're buckled, we creep along the streets, headed for home.

The island is only four square miles, but we could walk home as quickly as it takes to drive along the narrow dirt paths we call roads. Three minutes later, our house on the far end of the island comes into view.

There are only two homes out on the point. Mine, and the one owned by Elizabeth Sweet's family. I've been taking care of the place since my brother passed, and he'd been doing it for years before that without once seeing the family, so I was shocked when Dan called and asked me to do a couple of things around the place before his daughter arrived.

I park in front of the large white-cedar-shingled house. The sun is just setting, and nothing about the dark house looks inviting. Even with the large wraparound porch and the massive second-story windows, the structure looks angry. Like it doesn't want a Hollywood princess here either.

"Hurry up!" Sutton hops out of the truck and takes off across the grass I cut last week.

I'm reaching for the luggage when a feminine scream pierces the air.

"Stay here, Sutton," I demand. Heart thudding, I take off toward the house. Just as I hit the porch, another scream sounds from inside, making the hair on the back of my neck stand up.

I throw the door open and find a tiny blonde in jeans and a tight shirt standing on the table, feet bare, with a broom in her hand.

"Get it off. Oh my god, it's in my hair." She steps back, her foot teetering on the edge.

I rush across the six feet, arms out, and catch her as her arms windmill and she falls backward.

She smacks into my chest, still thrashing like a wild woman, causing me to stumble.

"It's in my hair," she shouts again.

I have one heartbeat to decide whether to drop her or just go down with her. I curse myself for being a gentleman as I hit the ground with an *umph*.

All the while, her hands never stop flapping. We're flat on the floor, yet she's flailing, hitting herself and me in the process.

"What in the holy hell is the problem?" Deciding it's best to keep my hands to myself rather than try to stop her, I drop them to my sides, leaving the young superstar on top of me.

"There's a spider on me." She shudders, though the erratic movements finally slow.

I survey the silky blond strands, and sure enough, I spot the little guy. Gently, I pick it off her head, then fling it away.

"You touched it with your hands?" Huge blue eyes fixate on my fingers.

I shake my head. "They're everywhere. Better get used to them."

"I hate spiders," she whispers, her voice shaky.

No shock there. I smirk. "Ready to go home yet, Princess?"

Libby
Chapter 4

"READY TO GO HOME YET, PRINCESS?"

Heat rushes my cheeks and anger and embarrassment war with one another as I stare down at the giant of a man who broke into my house and then saved me from the spider.

I hate being called princess. But I hate spiders more.

I think.

Plump lips lift in a smirk of sorts. The expression is at odds with the man's cranky aura. It's almost like he's angered by my presence, yet he's in *my* house.

I press my palms flat against his chest and try to ignore the hard muscles that flex beneath my fingers as I push off him. Once I've extricated myself, I swipe at my legs. Maybe I can brush off the feel of his touch. God, I hope so.

"I am home." Miraculously, I refrain from tacking the word *asshole* on under my breath. I'm good at holding my tongue. I've been doing it for years.

With my luck, this guy is a reporter or would be happy to call one up. Everyone has a price, and I imagine as soon as the papers discover I'm here, he'll give them any tidbit I offer.

Brown eyes flecked with gold dance, probably at my expense.

"We'll see about that." His eyes remain trained on me as he gets to his feet.

It's not until he's standing beside me that I realize just how big he is. Wide shoulders, big arms folded across his chest, narrow hips, and thick thighs parted in a way that only magnifies his presence. He takes up twice as much space as I do, above me and to the side. He's like a cloud, hovering about and blocking out the rest of the room. If not for the scowl he wears as well as a cowboy wears a pair of Wranglers, I'd actually enjoy the view.

He's older than I am by at least a handful of years and nice enough to look at for anyone who likes that whole dark, broody thing.

I certainly don't. Not that I like the Hollywood look either.

An image of Brad, dressed in a tuxedo, jeering at me, flits through my mind. The thought is quickly followed by a shudder.

I think it's just men in general that I don't like.

If I've learned anything recently, it's that men can't be trusted. Especially men who call me princess.

I'm just about to tell him where he can stick it when my door flies open for the second time in as many minutes, and a little girl yells, "Fisher! What's taking so long?"

"I told you to stay in the car." His voice holds no malice, though, as he turns and shakes his head.

When he steps back, I get a better view of the pint-sized intruder. She's about half his height, with golden blond hair done in two braids. When her blue eyes land on me, they widen comically, and her mouth falls open in an O.

"Fisher." She brings a hand to the side of her mouth like she's trying to hide her loudly whispered words. "Did you know that Elizabeth Sweet is standing right in front of you?"

I snort. She's kind of adorable. "You can call me Libby."

I didn't think her eyes could get any bigger, but I swear they double again. They glitter with excitement too. "She said I can call her Libby." Her hand is still cupped and her voice is still a whisper-shout.

The guy—Fisher?—rolls his eyes. "Yeah, you don't need to repeat everything she says. I'm standing right here."

The girl gives him an unamused glare that tells me she holds all the control in their relationship. "You're so embarrassing."

"My dad's the same way," I tell her. "I'm guessing his name is Fisher, but what about yours?"

"You don't need to—" he starts.

"I'm Sutton," she says, cutting him off with another glare. "Fisher and I live next door. If you need anything at all, just come knock." She leans forward as if she's telling me a secret. "Doorbell doesn't work."

"Sutton, you can't just invite—"

Her once wide eyes are narrowed into thin slits now, the expression fierce enough to shut the guy up.

He lets out a heavy sigh. "The doorbell doesn't work."

I think it's supposed to be an invitation to stop by if I need something, yet it's obvious he's offering under duress. He clearly doesn't like to be bothered.

But if that's the case, then why did he come running into my house? I would have figured out the spider situation eventually. Or I would have burned the house to the ground.

Come to think of it...

"Where'd that spider go?" I scan the floor, my pulse picking up. Where did the eight-legged terror scurry off to? The last thing I need is for him to find me while I'm sleeping and crawl into my mouth and choke me in my sleep.

Images of the possibility have my body shuddering once more.

Sutton smiles. "Oh, there's lots of spiders around here. I'm sure we can find you another friend."

"Friend?" My voice is far too high, but I can't help it. Not when the creepy-crawly sensation of phantom spiders has hit.

Her brows pinch together, like maybe this guy has convinced the poor, unsuspecting child that spiders are friendly.

"And what do you mean plenty of spiders around here?"

Amusement dances in Fisher's eyes. "Like I was saying before."

"Y- you need to get rid of them," I sputter. "I can't—no, I *won't* stay here if there's going to be spiders crawling all over me."

"You could stay at our house," Sutton says, face lit up. "I haven't seen any spiders in our house in a long time."

Fisher glares at her. "Your nose is growing, sweet pea."

She rubs at it, bottom lip stuck out. "Is not."

He huffs. "I'll do a sweep. Take care of any spiders I find."

A smile rips across my face. "Really?"

With another sigh—it's gotta be his fifth since he barged in—he deflates. "Yes." He turns toward Sutton and points a finger. "But you stay right here. And for once, actually listen to me."

Sutton puts her hand behind her back and nods. "I promise."

I try not to laugh. That girl definitely had her fingers crossed back there.

He glances at me once more before shaking his head and disappearing down the hall.

"So what do you think of our island?" Sutton asks, toeing the floor with one tiny shoe.

I take in the house. It looks nothing like I remember. The magical space where I spent my last summer with my mother is drab. The white couch with the bright blue and teal throw pillows has gone a bit yellow. The dark shiplap floor lacks shine. The windows are cloudy. With any luck, it's from age, not spider webs, but I can't risk looking too closely. I should have agreed when my father suggested sending a cleaning crew out here first. But I was in a rush to get here, and now I've got to live with the consequences. The last thing I want to do is prove my dad right.

In general, the last thing I want to do is call my dad, period. Every time I do, I risk uttering the truth in one long-winded confession.

And if I give in and do that, then keeping all these secrets for the last few years will have been for nothing. I'll destroy the only family we have left. And worse, Dad could end up in jail. Then I'll really be alone.

Or—and maybe this is what I'm most concerned about—he won't believe me.

This is a no-win situation. Better I just keep my mouth shut and smile, like I always do.

I steel my spine, pull my shoulders back, and do just that. "It's charming."

Sutton's lips lift in a wide smile. "Fisher says people say things are charming rather than calling them old."

I snort.

"Or junk."

This time I let out a full laugh. "Well, he's not wrong."

She rocks back and forth on her pink and white Nike Court Boroughs. "Are you staying here the whole summer?"

I nod. "Yes." Maybe if I say it loud enough, I'll come to terms with that truth.

"Then you have to do the summer play with us. It's *Grease* this year. You would make the best Sandy!"

"You have a town play?"

How adorable. I haven't done theater in a very long time, but god, the idea of it sets my pulse racing. Working in television is nothing like live theater. It's hours and hours on set just to film a single scene. It's makeup touch-ups and constant fluffing of hair. Directors who yell because they like the sound of their own voice and costars who stand just a bit too close and then...

"Yup!" Sutton bounces on her toes, her excitement pulling me back from the dark past I'm running from. "So will you do it?"

"Do what?" Fisher booms as he saunters back into the living room.

I turn to him, giving him a hopeful smile. "You took care of all the spiders?"

Hands on hips, he assesses me, his expression fixed into one that probably should look like annoyance but is more like a smolder. "They don't call me the spider whisperer for nothing."

Sutton scratches her head. "I've never heard anyone call you that."

The man huffs and lumbers toward the door. "Come on. It's time for dinner."

"Have you got something to eat?" Sutton asks, her blue eyes hopeful.

I don't have to look at Fisher to feel his disapproving glare. I don't actually have anything to eat, but if I tell them that, he'll probably make some comment about how this is only further proof that I can't take care of myself. Then she'll strong-arm him into inviting me over. Which will lead to spending the night being glared at and judged. No thank you. I've spent enough time with disapproving men already. I've met my quota for the year. Hell, I've met the quota for a lifetime.

"Yup. And it's been a long day. I left California last night, and I still haven't slept or showered."

She scrunches her nose.

Yeah, I agree. I can practically feel the dirt collecting on my skin.

"Say good night, Sutton," Fisher growls.

"Good night, Sutton," she singsongs.

I hold back a giggle. "Thank you for getting rid of the spiders." I rub at my arms as I follow them to the door.

Fisher surveys me, his brown eyes narrowing on my bare arms like they offend him. "I'll drop off a jacket in the morning," he grumbles.

"Huh?"

"Your jacket. Heard you didn't have one."

I shrug. "I have one. The airport lost my luggage. It was in one of my bags. I'm hoping it turns up tomorrow, though."

He shakes his head. "Until then, you need a jacket."

I resist the urge to scoff. "It's not that cold."

Clearly exasperated by me, he sighs. Is that number six? Or

seven? Either way, I think I might like annoying him a bit more than I should. "You'll change your tune when the breeze comes in off the ocean in the morning." With that, he guides Sutton down the wooden steps of my cottage toward a pickup truck.

Hmm. Didn't think there were any vehicles on the island. Wonder if I can get one...

He backs out of my driveway, and about five seconds later, they pull in next door. Sutton hops out, blond braids flying, and runs into a house that looks almost identical to the one I'm staying in, though far more lived-in. The windows aren't as weathered, and the adorable navy blue shutters have a fresh coat of paint. Small blue flowers bloom in pretty window boxes that are painted pink and white, each a little different from the last. Hmm, he must have a wife to have such a pretty home.

Poor woman. I can't imagine dealing with a grump like him is easy.

I shut the door, making sure to twist the lock, then head up the stairs. After twenty-four hours of running, I'm finally here. Yes, maybe I endured the trip from hell—the broken plane, the sick passenger, a missed chopper, and a ride on the garbage boat—but I made it. My house is spider-free, and I can already feel the magic my mother spoke of settling around me.

A warm shower and a good night's sleep are all I need to rid myself of the residual stress of my travels.

I enter the bathroom, ignoring the musty smell, and peek behind the blue paisley curtain. With no spiders in sight, I let out a breath and reach in to turn on the water. While the water warms, I pull a set of pajamas from my suitcase.

Stripped down, I step into the tub and slide my head back into the spray. The ice-cold water that pulses down on my skull pulls a shriek from me, ramping up the tension in my body once more.

A cold shower, it is.

Libby
Chapter 5

MONHEGAN ISLAND IS twelve miles off the coast of Maine. Though from the view outside the kitchen window, it might as well be a million miles from civilization. All I can see here are rolling hills that lead to a daring cliff and the angry ocean. For the first time in my life, there's not a person in sight. No assistants or lackeys bugging me for my breakfast order or reminding me of what time I need to be on set.

My phone isn't buzzing with invites to restaurant openings, and my publicist isn't texting with lists of events I'm expected to attend.

I'm surrounded by silence and I'm okay with that.

Though I wouldn't mind a coffee right about now.

I lean against the pale blue counter in the kitchen and smile. God, I can feel Mom in here. She had nothing to do with the decorating—that was all her great-grandmother—but she loved this place so much.

There's a small wooden table pressed against the wall. If I close my eyes, I can picture her moving about this space while six-year-old me sat at one of the three chairs, eating a bowl of cereal. She always wore robes in bright colors. They would billow around her as she told me about what the day ahead would bring. A beach excursion, hiking the cliffs along the back of the island to watch for whales, a boat ride to the mainland for a lobster roll at lunch.

My mother made even simple afternoon strolls seem as exciting as a night at the symphony.

She made everything special.

With an exhale, I open my eyes. Instantly, I'm engulfed in the silence of the muted space. Even the teal walls are duller than I remember.

Everything seemed so much *more* in my memory.

The reality doesn't quite match up.

But that's a me thing. If my mother were here, she would remind me that it's all about perspective. No coffee pot? A reason to go into town and explore.

No hot water? Cold water is better for your skin.

No luggage? An excuse to go shopping.

Spiders? At least they'll keep the bugs away.

The grump next door? A challenge. She'd find a way to make the man smile.

I grin at that, head tipped back. Even long gone, she can still make me smile. She'd have liked Sutton too.

She liked everyone.

Scratch that. Almost everyone.

She wouldn't have liked Brad.

The mere thought of him sobers me. I really do need to turn on my phone.

I powered it down yesterday. Otherwise my publicist and father and everyone else in LA would be hounding me.

Renee is convinced she could fix this if I let her. My father doesn't understand why I won't fight back.

But Brad? Brad Fedder will destroy every last shred of goodwill I've earned in my lifetime if I don't stay quiet. And if that happens, the world will question why I stayed quiet for so long.

And not one of them would believe me. I can all but guarantee it.

That is why I ran.

That's why I'm here.

I push myself off the counter and head upstairs to change. My mother is right. The lack of coffee is an excellent reason to go explore. And an excellent excuse not to turn on my phone.

At least not yet.

I could really use that second suitcase this morning. My pink hoodie is too thin to protect from the cold wind—just like Fisher warned me about yesterday.

Arms crossed to hold in as much warmth as I can, I head down the dirty path I followed to get here yesterday. The island is tiny, and the paths are deeply traveled, making it nearly impossible to get lost. Within minutes, I make it down the hill. I pass several small homes and a sprinkling of businesses. There's no downtown, per se. It's more like a pathway with signs that direct visitors to more paths.

Grocery This Way.

Lobster Rolls Here.

Best Clam Chowder Down the Path!

Ice Cream Up the Hill.

A sign for a brewery piques my interest.

It's not a champagne bar on the ocean, but alcohol is alcohol, and I'm sure I'll need a glass or two after another day with no hot water.

I make a mental note of the brewery's location, then continue on.

Before I left the house, I gave in and turned my phone on, but only to call my father. It's still early in LA, just barely six a.m. but he's a workaholic, so like I knew he would be, he was up and showered and ready for the day.

I made him promise—again—to keep my whereabouts a secret and assured him that I'm fine. I swore the house was exactly as I remember—*a fib, for sure*—that the island has everything I need

*—clearly a lie—*and that I'm going to enjoy this much needed break. *A half-truth at best.*

This is a much-needed break I'm just not so sure I'll enjoy it.

Like my father, I'm a workaholic. Since childhood, I've been a working actress. By some stroke of luck, I landed a movie deal at just four. Outside the year my mother died, I've never slowed down.

The call to my dad was the only one I made. I didn't even look at the messages from my publicist or my agent.

And I definitely did not reply to Brad.

I take the turn that leads down to the ferry docks and spot a woman sitting on a rocking chair on the deck of the inn. The island is quiet, empty, though I'm sure once Memorial Day hits, the chairs on that deck will all be filled. The woman waves to me, and I wave back, already feeling a bit lighter.

Close-knit community. This is what I came for. Neighbors who say hello, a small grocery store where the people shopping all know one another and chat about what they're making for dinner, adorable coffee shops with specially made treats.

As the pier comes into view— along with a cluster of bags on the wooden planks—I hasten my steps. Could my luggage have already been delivered?

The water in the inlet where the ferry docks thrashes angrily, sending a chill through me. I'm glad I don't have to be out on the ocean today.

As I get closer, I inspect the bags, and when I don't spot my luggage, I shrug and head into the tiny store that sits beside the dock, hopeful that I'll find breakfast and caffeine.

The older woman behind the counter looks up, eyes bright, when the bell above the door announces my arrival.

"Cank," she hollers, "we have a visitor!"

Smiling, I glance at the menu written on a chalkboard above her head.

Coffee

Orange Juice

Egg

Seasonal Fruit

Muffins

Hm. What does *egg* mean? Can I just ask for it any way I want it? And what kind of fruit is in season?

"What can I get you?" the woman asks, her New England accent thick as she slides the pen from behind her ear.

"Um, I'll take a sugar-free venti caramel macchiato with two pumps of syrup, one pump of cream."

The woman blinks, pen held an inch from her pad. "We've got coffee." *Caffee.* Like taffy with a C.

Heat creeps into my cheeks. "I'll take whatever you have."

"Milk and sugar?" She grabs a white mug. I'm guessing they don't have to-go cups. "Real sugar." She gives me a toothy grin. "None of that unsweetened kind."

I laugh, praying she can't see how red my face is, and nod. "Sure, coffee with milk and sugar sounds great."

The door behind her swings open and the dock master from yesterday appears. Despite the chill in the air, he's only got a white T-shirt on beneath his overalls.

Just looking at him makes me shiver. Though I can't help but feel affection for the virtual stranger as well after he was kind enough to tell me where to leave my luggage and to point me in the direction of my house last night.

"Ms. Sweet. Good to see you."

I give him a genuine smile. "You as well."

"Did my wife offer you a muffin? You should take a few home. The grocery store doesn't open until this afternoon."

He snaps open a small paper bag and shoves three or four muffins into it.

"How's the house? Everything in working order?"

"Everything's great." I frown. "Well, except I have no hot water."

"Ah, the pilot must have gone out." He pushes the bag into my hands.

"The pilot?"

"Yup." He adjusts his floppy hat, drawing my attention, not for the first time, to the placement of the whale and the puffin. "You just have to light it. Want me to send Fisher over to—"

I'm shaking my head before he can finish the question. "I can handle it. Thanks, Cank."

His wife hands me my coffee and I take my bag of muffins. Then I settle on the stool and survey the ocean outside the window.

This is precisely why people come to this island. Nothing but rolling hills that lead to the ocean, a gorgeous lighthouse, and the birds to keep me company.

I take a sip of my coffee and hum, surprised by the rich flavor. Who needs a caramel macchiato anyway? Nothing is better than a warm cup of coffee. Except maybe a warm cup of coffee and a hot shower. That's next on my list. I saw matches in the kitchen this morning. Now I'll just have to figure out where the pilot is. It's probably connected to the big tank in the backyard. As soon as I finish breakfast, I'll head back to the house and light the pilot. Then, finally, I'll have that warm shower I've been itching for.

See? Today is already better than yesterday.

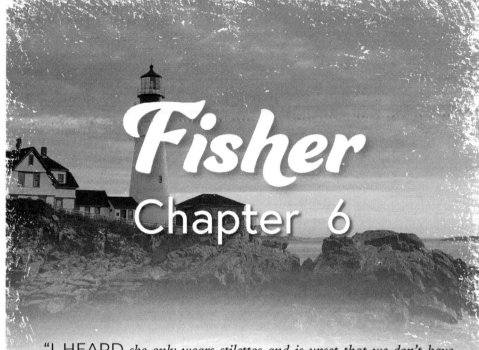

Fisher

Chapter 6

"I HEARD *she only wears stilettos and is upset that we don't have paved roads.*"

"*I heard she doesn't wear anything but tube tops and she's coming to the town meeting this morning to demand we set up outdoor heaters.*"

Neither of those rumors is true, yet I'm not the least bit surprised that the gossip mill is already running at full power with fake Elizabeth Sweet stories. Every person I encounter is obsessed with talking about her. Not me. I'd rather not think about her, let alone bring her up in conversation.

And I definitely don't want to think about the sweet floral scent that lingered on my coat and flannel for hours after I left her last night. I don't want to think about the way her eyes lit up when she smiled. Because I don't need another thing to think about, period. I have enough on my plate. Elizabeth Sweet is too young and too beautiful and will be nothing but a pain in my ass.

"I heard that Saturday is donut day at the bakery and that if I came in before you close up for the meeting, I could buy some," I say, trying to get the attention of the women gossiping behind the counter.

It's beyond idiotic that they'll close up the bakery at nine thirty so the two of them can go to a town meeting that's sole purpose is to waste everyone's time.

Flora and her mother turn my way.

"Fisher!" Flora says, her nasally voice making me wince. "I didn't hear you come in."

I fight a frown. Sutton wants donuts. So I have to be nice *ish*.

"Any chance I could get two double chocolates and two glazed?" I should smile, but I hate smiling. The best I can do is not to glare.

"Absolutely." She hurries to the glass case and drops the donuts into a bag one by one. "And your usual coffee?"

I give a clipped nod just as the door behind me opens.

"I feel for the poor girl," Cank says as he and his wife, Cheryl, walk in.

"And since she's all the way out on the point, she probably didn't think to walk to the inn for a shower."

My brows slam together. The point? They have to be talking about the Sweet place. Why would she have to walk to the inn for a shower? I made sure everything was in working order yesterday morning.

"Good thing she stopped by," Cheryl says.

Cank nods. "I told her the pilot was probably out. I'm sure she'll get it all fixed. Sent her home with a few muffins to tide her over until Doris opens up this afternoon."

Well, fuck me. There is no way the princess knows anything about a pilot light. At twenty-five, I'm not sure I even knew what a pilot light was, let alone how to light it. And I didn't grow up with a silver spoon in my mouth.

Also, not even Bing will eat Cheryl's muffins—they're hard as rocks. If she doesn't blow up the island, she'll definitely break a tooth.

Flora hands me my coffee and the bag of donuts, and I drop a twenty on the counter, then rush out without a goodbye.

I should have taken the truck. The knowledge that Libby might be heading into her basement has me picking up the pace. It'll be a matter of seconds before she comes across her first eight-legged creature. I'd be surprised if I couldn't hear her screams all the way over here. Got rid of all the spiders, my ass. We're in Maine. Spiders are as abundant as salt water and fog.

I jog up the hill, heading right at the fork and passing by Blue. Where else would he be this early? Everyone knows what the island needs is another watercolor of the harbor. Fifty million isn't nearly enough. At least he's fully clothed for the time being.

He lifts his brush to wave at me, and I give him a quick nod, kicking up dust as I rush down the dirt path.

I hurry past the brewery and tip my chin at Jamie. He waves too. Everyone on this island waves.

As I round the last bend, the Sweet house comes into view, along with Libby, who's clad in a pink sweat suit and is bending over and reaching beneath her massive propane tank.

My gut sinks. What the fuck is the woman doing now?

Talk about a good way to find spiders.

"Libby?"

She rolls back to her haunches and beams up at me. "Oh. Hi, Fisher."

As if she got the island memo, she waves. The movement draws my attention to the match pinched between her thumb and forefinger. *A match.* Near a massive ball of gas.

"What the fuck are you doing?" I glare at the matchstick, the tip of which is charred rather than red. She did not stick that under the tank, did she?

Shit.

She shrugs. "I wish I knew. Cank told me to light the pilot."

I blink at the match, then eye the tank. "Please tell me you didn't have that lit near the propane tank."

Head cocked, she studies me, her ponytail dropping over her shoulder. "Propane tank?" She purses her lips and scans the massive gas-filled tank that she apparently just tried to light on fire. "This isn't the water heater?"

"No," I snap. "It is not."

"Huh." She giggles, one shoulder lifted.

"What's so funny?" Jesus, she almost blew herself up, and she's *laughing*.

"Do you know what would have happened if the wind hadn't kept blowing out the matches?" Her laughter continues.

Annoyance bubbles in my veins. Oh yeah, I'm very aware.

"I thought the universe was messing with me, but it turns out mother nature was actually protecting me with each gust of wind."

Another hard burst of winds blows past us, and she shivers.

Huffing, I grasp her arms and pull her to her feet.

She shivers again. Last night I promised her a coat, but I've yet to stop by her house to check in. How could I when my niece woke up and instantly demanded donuts?

"Here." I begrudgingly set the paper bag on the ground and shuck off my coat.

As I hold it out, she shakes her head. "It's okay. I'm just waiting for my luggage to be delivered. I'm sure it'll be here any time now."

Does she really think United is going to shuttle her bag twelve miles out into the middle of the ocean?

"Just take it," I grumble.

She hesitates, her eyes searching mine, but when the wind hits her, she slides it on. "Thanks."

I grunt. Shit. The damn thing is never going to stop smelling like flowers and sunshine now.

"Fisher?" Sutton calls from the porch.

Bing lets out a sharp bark, then leaps over the railing and sprints over to Libby and jumps up on her.

Though I expect her to shriek and back away, she surprises the shit out of me by dropping to her knees and giggling as my dog covers her in kisses.

"Aren't you a good boy." She squirms, her giggles light and airy, and rubs his back.

"Hi, Libby." Sutton comes up beside me, her chin tucked into the collar of her coat and her shoulders hunched to fight off the cold.

"Bing, enough." I snap my fingers, and instantly, he settles.

"Bing?" Libby looks up at me, brows raised.

A lead ball forms in my gut and sinks. Fuck.

"That's the name of the dog from my show." She tilts her head and assesses me.

"Oh really? I don't watch it. He's Bing, like Chandler Bing from *Friends*."

She snorts, grinning at the dog like they're already buddies. "That's the line from the show."

I affect a completely indifferent shrug. "I wouldn't know."

"Fisher, your nose is growing." Sutton's whisper is loud enough to be considered a yell.

Shit. I actually forgot Sutton was standing here. This is bad. My niece complains that she can't make a move without me seeing, but Libby has been here for less than twenty-four hours, and I'm already taking my eye off the only person that matters.

Libby laughs again, the sound lighting up my nerve endings. Damn, why does she have to have such a pretty laugh?

We're hit by another gust of wind, and both Sutton and Libby shiver, although I'm the one without the fucking coat.

"Can we go in?"

"I need to get my water heater working so I can finally take a warm shower." She straightens and spins back to the propane tank. "I just need to figure out where the pilot light is."

Brow creased, Sutton looks up at me. "Isn't that in the basement?"

"Yup." I nod.

"Oh." Libby's shoulders drop.

For a second, I almost feel bad. That sensation evaporates quickly, though, when Sutton jumps in.

"Fisher will fix it. And while you wait, you can hang out with me. Or take a shower at our house."

My heart clenches tight at the hope in her tone. My niece loves this woman. Libby spent over a decade playing a girl who was raised by her older brother after their parents died in a car crash. Because of how closely the storyline mirrors Sutton's life, her obsession with Elizabeth Sweet is more intense than that of most girls her age. And every eight-year-old in the world loves her.

"I don't know about that," Libby says softly, her eyes cutting to me. It's obvious she's uncomfortable, and it's because of me.

"Please, Fisher?" Sutton pleads. "You don't mind, do you? You don't want her to be cold. It's only neighborly to offer."

"Fine." I have to force the single syllable out because I don't want Libby hanging out at my place. I don't want her in my shower. Fuck, just the thought of her naked under the spray does things I didn't think I was capable of anymore. It excites me. Thrills me. Spikes my blood pressure to a brutal degree.

But Sutton is smiling, and I'll do anything to make her happy.

"Yay!" She snags the small paper bag from me and holds a hand out to Libby. "You are going to love these donuts. The double chocolate ones are the best."

I fight a scoff. I don't believe for a second that the young superstar eats sugar or carbs.

"Ooh," Libby says, stunning the shit out of me. "I can't wait." She takes Sutton's hand, and when Bing gets into step beside her, she pats his head. "What a good boy."

Then they're off, leaving me in the cold. Just fucking great.

Once the girls are safely inside my house, where I'm hoping like hell Sutton can keep Libby out of trouble, I head the other way. Once again, I'm stomping down the stairs to her basement.

I was down here yesterday, and I could swear the pilot was lit, so I figure I'll wait a bit to make sure it doesn't go out again and that the tank heats.

With a sigh, I lean against the wall and pull out my phone. I'm replying to a text from Wilder when a new message comes in.

> May Job 3: I want it done by Monday. At the very latest.

This is what I should be doing. My actual job. What I do may fall into a gray area, but it ensures that Sutton has the life my brother and his wife wanted for her. And it guarantees that I'm around for her and the rest of these damn island people every day.

But fuck, does it make the days long. Checking off all my duties around the island during the day, then doing the real work after Sutton goes to bed.

> Me: Don't worry, it will be done.

Before I can slip the device back into my pocket, the damn thing buzzes again.

> Todd: The goat is back.

I sigh. I hate this island.

> Me: I'll be right there.

I stomp up the stairs and turn on the hot water. It's only been twenty minutes, but right away, the water turns lukewarm. Good enough. I'll swing by after I deal with the damn goat and check again.

With my hands shoved into my pockets and my head ducked against the cold, I hurry across the yard and into my house.

I'm instantly hit with the sound of the girls' laughter, and when I catch sight of them on the sofa, a weird twist pulls at my gut. Libby's hair is wet, and she's dressed in my T-shirt and sweats.

She leans in and whispers into Sutton's ear, and they fall into another fit of giggles. Without my permission, my lips tip up.

The second I realize what I'm doing, I lock my jaw and school my

38

expression. I might want Sutton to be happy, but that's as far as this could ever go.

"They go to the brewery at night. You should go too," Sutton suggests.

Irritation shoots down my spine. The idea of having Libby at the brewery with Wilder, Maggie, Eddy, and me is too much.

I scowl. "We don't invite summer people."

Libby's eyes dart to me, hurt flashing in them.

Regret washes over me, but I ignore the sensation. I can't have her getting too comfortable here. We all know she'll never last, and it's better for her if she stays far away from us.

Libby
Chapter 7

"DID you hear the princess asked for straws?"

"And what's her obsession with white bread? Girl must eat a loaf daily."

"I heard they killed her off that show because she's difficult."

"I heard it was because she had an affair with the producer."

Lips pressed together, I back out of the grocery store, hoping no one spotted me. I'm not embarrassed. I'm angry.

It isn't the small-mindedness of people here that bothers me. They're simply parroting what they read in magazines and on the internet. I saw the headlines at the checkout counter with my own eyes. It's the network I'm pissed at, because, apparently, they're just going to let this story fester.

I left too quietly. I should have stood up for myself.

Outside, I take a minute to focus on my surroundings. The view of the ocean, the birds flapping above me. I think they're seagulls, but what do I know? Lord knows I'm not going to ask. Everywhere I turn, I exasperate someone, and on this tiny island, that's a feat.

But I need bread. Cank's offer of muffins was sweet, considering I had little food at the time. Not that they could be categorized as food. Maybe they were dog biscuits? Or perhaps they really were supposed to be that hard. Either way, I threw one into the yard to see if it would actually break when it hit the ground. That's when the flock of birds swooped down. To avoid becoming their meal, I threw the rest of the muffins to them and darted into the house. They've been back every day since, looking for sustenance. And damn, can they eat. So I've been buying bread, tearing it into pieces, and sprinkling it in the yard. I'm not mean enough to feed them more muffins. Though maybe if I did, they'd leave me alone. Pretty sure those things have to be made of lead.

I was told that if I wanted any specialty items, I'd have to order from Doris by today. I brought over a list yesterday so I wasn't showing up at the last minute, but from the sounds of the discussion going on when I walked in, they didn't like my list anyway.

God, this is hard.

I push away from the store and begin my trek back to the house. It's too quiet here. I've met exactly five people since arriving, and two of them are Fisher and Sutton. It's clear that Doris doesn't like me, but Cank and his wife, at least, have been kind.

I glance down at my list again and frown.

Straws, diet ginger ale, and sherbet.

The list may seem odd, but as a little girl, when I'd have a bad day, my mother would let me sip from her diet ginger ale—she drank it to help with her nausea—and she'd give me a scoop of the colorful ice cream. She said there was nothing a little sugar couldn't fix.

At six, it was magic. I no longer believe in magic, but it can't hurt, and the comfort the tradition brings would go a long, long way right now.

"Get outta the road!" a man yells as he whizzes by me on a golf cart.

Oh, a golf cart would be fun.

I wonder if they make them in pink.

"Summer people," a woman grumbles from her porch.

I keep my focus fixed on the ground ahead of me. I'm not sure why they say it like it's a bad thing. Summer people keep this island going. If not for tourists who visit during the four months out of the year this island is worth visiting, the residents wouldn't be able to afford even these little shacks they have.

Also, there are no actual roads here, so screaming *get out of the road* is slightly comical. The dirt paths are far smaller than a two-lane road and have patches of grass sprouting up like those little chia plants on late-night infomercials.

Do Chia Pets still exist? That's the closest thing to a real pet I could keep alive. Does Amazon ship out here? Maybe I'll order one. That would really spruce up the house. Maybe with flowers. I wonder if Chia Pets with flowers are a thing.

I make a note to order one but make sure I don't inadvertently walk into the *road* as I do. I've just stepped onto my property when another voice calls out, though this is a welcome one.

"Libby! Libby! I've got the bestest news!"

I spin to find the sweetest next-door neighbor waving at me as she runs up the hill, her face lit up in the brightest smile.

"Oh yeah?" I heave in a deep breath, exhausted just watching her hoof it uphill.

Sutton grasps my hand and tugs. "Yup. But we've got to go quick."

"Go where?" I ask, laughing, though I let her lead me back down the hill.

"To the schoolhouse. Maggie, our teacher and the director of the play, said you can help."

Oh, lucky me.

No, seriously. Lucky me. Finally someone actually wants me around.

Sutton drags me to the most adorable red schoolhouse I've ever seen. It's the kind of building I imagined when I was a kid and my weird great-aunt would fold her hands together and say "Here's the church. Here's the steeple. Open the door and see all the people."

As we approach the tiny building adorned with a high steeple with an open-air peak, a little boy darts across the grass and grabs the rope dangling from up high, and suddenly, the bell is moving. When the sound finally reaches us, the gong is loud and beautiful.

"It's time!" Sutton screams.

Eyes wide, I take in the sight. Did that young kid really just pull on a rope to ring that bell?

I think he did.

Wonderstruck, I follow Sutton inside the building.

Inside, about a dozen people wander about, most of them children. Though they vary in ages from about five to sixteen or so. It's hard to tell how old the teenager is since I can't really see his face. His attention is focused solely on the woman at the front of the room.

That must be Maggie. She looks exactly as I would imagine a schoolteacher on a small island would. Long brown hair tied in a bow, rosy cheeks with a dusting of freckles, overalls that have seen better days, and the warmest smile I've ever been the recipient of.

"You must be Libby." With quick steps that could be considered a skip, she heads in my direction, and then she's holding out her arms and engulfing me in a hug.

Maybe it's because I've met nothing but resistance since I arrived —with the exception of Sutton and Cank and his wife, of course—or maybe it's because being here has made me miss my mom more than I have in years. Or maybe I'm just exhausted from having to fake it on the show for so long. Whatever the reason, experiencing such genuine kindness truly throws me, leaving emotion swirling tight in my chest.

When she pulls back with an even bigger grin, I know I'm exactly where I need to be. "Thank you so much for agreeing to help us this summer. It will be so nice having a real actress lead us."

I shake my head. "Oh, I don't need to lead. I'm just here to help. Whatever you need."

"What I need is a friend." She leans in close, eyes dancing. "The acting will be the cherry on top." Then, lips forming an O, she brings a hand to her mouth. "You should come to the brewery Saturday night. I can introduce you to everyone."

"Everyone!" Sutton rolls her eyes, then cups her mouth like she did the night I met her and whisper shouts, "She's got one friend."

With her hands on her hips, Maggie gives my new bestie a half-hearted look of disapproval. If she were Fisher, it'd be a scowl, but I don't think Maggie has the ability to make a disappointed face. "I've got Eddy and Fisher."

"Don't forget Wilder," the boy who rang the bell hollers.

Maggie's cheeks flush a bright red, the expression immediately piquing my interest. Who is Wilder? And why is the local town sweetheart blushing so fiercely?

"Who could ever?" she mutters. Then she brightens again. "So what do you say? Will you come with me Saturday?"

I nod eagerly. I can't help but think that Fisher isn't going to like this.

And for some reason, that makes me smile.

Fisher

Chapter 8

WILDER TIPS BACK on the high metal stool. Damn, I wish he'd fall on his ass in the grass. That would make my week. Especially since this time of year, the ground around this whiskey barrel table is pretty much mud. I'd love to see his pretty face splattered with dirt.

"Elephant in the room." Wilder smirks as he drops the code for *I'm about to point out something obvious, whether you want to hear it or not*. "As unbelievable as it sounds, you're in a worse mood than normal."

Scowling, I avert my gaze and lift my can of Balmy Days to my lips. I'm careful not to lock eyes with anyone else, either. Especially Flora, who's sitting two tables away. If I so much as look her way, she'll scamper right over to the table to chat. But I don't have any words left today. And I really don't like her.

That leaves me with no other choice but to focus on the wall of lobster traps that cuts off the brewery's makeshift outdoor dining room from the dirt road.

It's Memorial Day weekend, so the place is hopping. This beer is much-needed after dropping off a ridiculous amount of luggage at the inn and cottages that pepper the island. *Summer people* season has officially begun. For the next three months, our island will be crawling with fresh faces. Wilder loves it. Me? Not so much.

I make the effort. I come out to the brewery with my friends on Saturday nights and try to be social. I can't even use Sutton as an excuse, since Mrs. K insists on keeping her and her granddaughter Lindsey for weekly sleepovers. It's her way of helping me out. Giving me the break to be something other than a pseudo-dad for my niece. She means well, but people make my skin crawl.

I've never been popular with the islanders. Not even when I was growing up. I was always the weird kid. The one who was more into computers than playing kick ball. Besides Wilder, I rarely talked to anyone, and that hasn't changed.

"Seriously, what bug crawled up your ass? This seems worse than the normal *it's tourist season* funk."

Wasn't a bug, and it's not a funk. It's a giggling, pink-shirt wearing blond pain in my ass.

I knew Elizabeth Sweet would make my life hell. But I didn't realize exactly what a pro she would be at it until she moved in next door.

Not all of it is her fault. I have no idea why her pilot light goes out almost every day, but I've been over five times in the last week to relight it. Even if she is making me insane, I don't want her blowing herself up.

And she will not get over the idea that a magic ferry is going to show up with her luggage. I'm not even convinced she called the airline about it. She swears they know where she lives, so they know where to drop it off. It's ridiculous.

She insists on hanging her clothes to dry, and maybe I'd be impressed that she was conserving energy if the woman didn't have lace panties in every color under the sun. I swear I've never hated lace more than I do this week. I can't focus on anything because all I can think about is that perfect ass covered in the lace that is constantly blowing in the northeast breeze.

I shift on my stool at the image that's taunted me for at least the fiftieth time today. Fuck, what is wrong with me? I don't like her. If only my damn dick would get on board.

If all that isn't bad enough, Libby has gotten in the habit of feeding the damn birds. Every day she throws bread onto the rocks out in front of the house. I don't understand the need she has to turn our yard into a bird sanctuary. All I know is it's driving Bing insane. He whines at the door all day, and when I can't stand the noise anymore and finally let him out, he chases the gulls away, only to return covered in bird shit.

After one very large white glob of shit landed in my hair this afternoon, I'm pretty sure I developed a twitch.

Libby's laugh floats above the noise of the crowd, but I refuse to look over to the table where she is sitting with Maggie and Wilder's sister Eddy. Libby has invaded enough of my life. I'm not giving her my free time.

Not that she would want my time or attention anyway. What interest would Elizabeth Sweet have in someone like me?

"Fisher?" Wilder's voice brings me back to the moment. And the brewery. "I'm seriously worried about your teeth."

"My teeth?"

My best friend throws his head back and laughs. "Yeah, you're grinding them to dust."

The man thinks he's funnier than he is.

"Jeez, tough crowd." He tips his number seventeen mug at me.

I have a mug too, every islander does, and they're all numbered. I don't use mine; the whole thing is ridiculous. I want my beer in a bottle or a can just like I'd get it at any bar in Boston, not a ceramic thing that never gets run through the commercial dishwasher inside. But Wilder takes pride in the cup that proves he's a Monheganer.

Although I could have sworn he's number twenty-five.

"What happened to your mug?" I ask.

"Nothing." He shrugs. "Old man Wayne died over the winter."

47

I frown. Although common knowledge, I don't see how it relates to his beer mug.

"So I get his." He says it like it's obvious. "I made a deal with Rip —every time someone dies, I get their mug. I'm moving up in life, man."

With a shake of my head, I scoff.

"What? I'm shooting for the one spot."

"You're telling me your life goal is the Monhegan Brewery mug number one?"

He shrugs again. "We can't all be Boston hotshots."

The statement makes me want to cringe. Maybe I was a big city hotshot back in the day, but I haven't been that guy for years. I roll my shoulders in a vain attempt to rid myself of the constant unease I feel at the loss of the life I built for myself. "Right, but someone has to die for you to reach your goal."

He nods, his lips pressed into a serious frown. "Sixteen someones."

"Jesus."

"It's not like I'm waiting for you to die, Mr. Fifty-Five." He eyes my cup where it's still hanging on the wall and shudders, then turns back to me, his grin growing wide again. "So like I was saying, this is the start of the good times. New women and a summer full of weekend fun."

Unlike most of the islanders—who put up with the summer people for the income they bring us—Wilder loves the fresh blood. He lives for new faces and new people. Just like Hunter was, Wilder is a people person. The asshole should be the sheriff. I petitioned for it when I moved back, but no one listened to me. Even Wilder is insistent that it's my job. No one seems to mind that I have no qualifications or patience for it.

"Yay for new people," I mutter into my beer.

"I like that group." Wilder tips his mug to six women huddled together around the picnic table closest to the heater. "They're out for fun."

"Looks like a bachelorette party," I grumble. Too much giggling and screeching.

"Exactly." His lips kick up on one side. "And I happen to be the fun they're looking for."

"Better get over there, then, or those guys will beat you to it." I tip my bottle to the two men about our age across the space. One of whom is already pushing to his feet.

I watch him saunter away from his buddy, but instead of heading toward the women Wilder's checking out, this tool heads straight for Libby's table.

My grip on my beer can tightens, the aluminum crinkling. Of course he's going to her. Who in their right mind would go for anyone else if they had a shot at Libby? Not Elizabeth Sweet, America's Sweetheart, but Libby, the most gorgeous woman in any room.

I shake my head. What the fuck am I saying? She's making me crazy.

The makeup-free, ponytail-sporting woman looks nothing like Elizabeth Sweet, and everyone on the island—although more than happy to gossip amongst themselves about her—has been utterly silent to outsiders about Elizabeth Sweet's presence here.

So this guy isn't heading over to Maggie, Libby, and Eddy for an autograph.

"Where are you going?" Wilder asks before I even realize I'm standing.

"That guy's going to bother Eddy. You know how much she hates the summer men."

Wilder chuckles. "My sister can handle herself."

That is true. Growing up, Kennedy Knowles was the sweetest girl on the island. But after she wound up pregnant—by a mystery man she still won't name—Eddy toughened up.

"Unless the disappearing dad waltzes in, she doesn't need anyone's help." He narrows his eyes at me, then, bringing his mug to his lips, zeroes in on Libby. "Elephant in the room," he challenges as he sets the mug on the table with a fucking smirk that pisses me off. "You like her and you want to be the only one hitting on her."

I grit my teeth and consider sitting down again. Fuck him and the smarmy look he's giving me.

Wilder just laughs. "Better hurry up."

Libby
Chapter 9

"WE CAN'T FORGET to tell her about Blue," Maggie says. For the past hour, she and her friend Kennedy—a pretty blonde who's been nothing but kind to me, just like Maggie—have been dishing secrets about everyone on the island.

I can't help the smile that lights up my face. This sensation is so foreign to me. For years I attended the swankiest bars and the nicest parties, but I never had anyone to share a secret with. No girlfriends, no sisters. Just directors, castmates, and acting coaches. There were rarely even other kids on the set of the show.

It's clear from this small interaction alone that Maggie and Kennedy have a sisterly relationship. With less than seventy people on the island, I suppose there wasn't much choice. But it's clear their friendship is based on more than convenience.

"Oh god," Kennedy groans. "Please don't."

Maggie squeezes my arm, the warmth of her hand soaking into me. I relish the feel because I'm freezing again. This is supposed to be a summer island, yet I've been cold every single second I've been here.

When the ferries arrived yesterday, so did people. Tourists came in droves—at least by this island's standard. There are at least twenty people here at the brewery I've never seen before.

I press closer to the outdoor heater beside me and try to focus on what the girls are saying. Apparently Blue is Kennedy's grandfather, and...

"He paints naked people?" I ask, hoping I heard them wrong.

Kennedy covers her face. "No." She groans. "He sits out on his lawn in the nude and paints."

I snort. "Is he at least nice to look at?"

"Ew!" Kennedy yells.

Maggie cackles so uproariously she almost falls off her stool. "Not a day in his life," she says through her wheezing.

Kennedy shakes her head, though her eyes are still all smiley. "Being the only nurse on the island, I've seen just about everyone here naked, but I do draw the line at my grandfather."

"Even Fisher?" Dammit. The words slip out before I have time to think them through.

I shouldn't be thinking about him, let alone saying his name. But it's impossible to keep him out of my head with the way he's been glaring at me all night, as if my mere existence offends him.

The two women share another look.

Stomach sinking, I curl in on myself. "Sorry, he's the only person I know on the island."

Kennedy bites her lip. "I don't think anyone really *knows* Fisher."

Frowning, I consider asking what she means. Instead, I keep my mouth shut. Don't want to appear even more interested than I already sound.

While I've yet to see anyone of the female variety coming or going from his house, I did see some pictures of a younger Sutton with a beautiful woman around the living room. Maybe Fisher's wife doesn't stay on the island?

Again, I keep the question to myself. The last thing I'm going to do is gossip. Lord knows I hate when people do it about me.

I'm pulled from my thoughts when two men I hadn't even noticed before stop at our table, both wearing cocky smirks.

"Ugh, summer people," Kennedy grumbles under her breath.

My fingers curl around my beer can. I'm beginning to hate those two words.

Maggie beams at the strangers, seemingly unbothered by their status as summer people. "Hello. Are you enjoying your Balmy Days?"

The guy wearing a Revs baseball cap looks at his friend, brows pulled low in confusion.

Kennedy points to his can. "It's the name of the beer."

"Oh." Revs guy shrugs. "It's okay, I guess. The bar doesn't have many options."

Maggie's face falls. When we arrived, she introduced me to her parents, Rip and Annette, who own the brewery. They were genuinely welcoming, which is the opposite of how the vast majority of residents have been.

Chest tightening with sympathy for her and her parents, I step in. "It's the best menu I've seen in a while."

His friend chuckles, his eyes roving over me. "You drink a lot of beer, pretty girl?"

A low grumble sounds, the growl so fierce the items on the table rattle. "Does she look like she drinks a lot of beer?"

Heart stumbling, I look up and find Fisher, eyes narrowed to slits, standing a foot away from our visitors.

I'm not sure what he means by that, but the guys laugh, obviously finding his statement funny.

Rather than laugh along with them, Fisher continues to glare. He holds the look for an uncomfortably long time.

Finally catching on, the guys let their laughter die off.

The one without a hat clears his throat. "So, are you visiting?"

Fisher takes a single step closer. "Does she look like she lives on the island?"

While both guys smile and murmur about how no, I don't look

like I live on the island, Fisher turns his glare to me. He's judging me. He's always judging me. And while I'm not trying to fit in—my mom always said *why fit in when you can wear pink?*—his tone bothers me.

"So are you staying at the inn?" Revs hat says.

"She's not." This time Fisher steps between the men and me, blocking their view of us completely. Then, as if the men don't even exist, he turns his attention to Kennedy. "You taking Lindsey with you next week, Eddy?"

"Eddy?" I frown at my new friend.

"That's what everyone calls Kennedy," Maggie mumbles.

The blonde shrugs. "I'm waiting to see if I can get a sitter on the island. If not, she'll stay with Wilder."

Fisher nods like this all makes sense, but I'm left completely lost. Not that it matters. If his goal was to get rid of the guys, he's accomplished it. The two of them are already walking off.

"You staying for another beer?" Maggie asks Kennedy.

She glances down at her mug and then toward the gate, her shoulders drooping.

Maggie sighs. "The two of you are pathetic. You get a kid-free night, and neither of you are enjoying it."

Fisher's lip twitches like he's fighting a smile. "I don't know. I enjoyed getting rid of those summer people."

The laugh that bubbles out of Kennedy is airy. "Fine. One more." She hands her mug to Maggie.

Maggie eyes me in silent question.

I eye the mugs she's holding, then turn to Fisher, who's drinking from a can. "How come you don't have a mug?"

Maggie laughs. "Oh, he does."

"He just never uses it," Kennedy finishes.

Frowning, I assess him—the dark hair, the perma-scowl, the broody demeanor. "But why?"

He grunts.

Sighing, I turn to Maggie. I don't know why I bothered trying to get a real response from him. "What do the numbers stand for?"

She shrugs. "Just the number you get when it's assigned." She holds hers up so I can see the thirty-six stamped into the side. "Sixty-eight people live on the island. Obviously the kids don't have mugs yet. We all get them when we turn twenty-one."

"Sixty-nine people if you count me," I say with a smile.

"We don't," Fisher grumbles.

Maggie sighs. "Ignore him."

I do. He's grumpy and miserable, and I refuse to let him bring me down. "So how do I get one?"

"You don't," he grits out. "They're not for summer people."

"I'll talk to my dad," Maggie offers, giving me a sweet smile. "You're not really summer people since you're staying here the whole summer."

"That's literally the definition of summer people," Fisher says with a smirk.

Kennedy rests her forearms on the table and leans forward. "I don't think I've ever heard you speak so many words."

A loud laugh cuts through the dark, and instantly, Maggie's head snaps up.

From here, it looks as though the women from the bachelorette party are being wooed by the man who was sitting with Fisher before my annoying neighbor inserted himself into our conversation.

"Your brother is such a flirt," Maggie grumbles.

Chin lifted, Kennedy squints. Then she gives her head a shake. "On second thought, no more beer for me. I'm not in the mood." She looks at Fisher. "You ready to go yet?"

His brown eyes cut to mine, then drop to my beer. "You sticking around, Princess?"

Annoyance flares, heating me for an instant. "Yup."

He dips his chin at Kennedy. "Go on without me. I'll see you tomorrow."

She bites down on her lip, though a smile peeks through anyway. "Right. See you tomorrow." She hugs Maggie goodbye and then grins at me. "It was so nice to meet you, Libby. Hopefully I'll see you around more often."

With that, she's rushing out the gate like she can't get home fast enough.

Another laugh rings through the yard, and Maggie eyes the group of women. "I should go see if they need anything."

"Want me to come with you?"

"No. You stay here," she says, her tone teasing. "I'm sure Fisher" —she gives him a knowing look I don't understand—"can keep you entertained."

As she strides toward the loud group, the heat that sparked in my veins fizzles out, and I lean closer to the heater.

"Told you to wear a jacket," Fisher grumbles as he sets his can on the table.

I blow out a breath and turn my entire body toward the heater so I don't have to look at his judgmental face. "My luggage still hasn't arrived, but I ordered one."

The scents of sandalwood and pale ale surround me, and then I'm engulfed in warm, soft fabric. "Lift your arms." Fisher's words are low, his breath teasing my neck.

I curl in on myself as another shiver rolls down my back. "What are you doing?" I say, though the word comes out scratchy.

"I'm giving you my flannel. You're shivering, and I don't need you getting sick on top of all the other trouble you've been causing."

A bolt of anger zaps through me. God, the man is infuriating. Even as he does something nice, like giving me the literal shirt off his back to keep me warm, he has to throw in a barb.

For years I've been told—by man after man after man—that I'm difficult. Even my father, god love him, treats me like I'm a task to be checked off on his list. Just once I wish I didn't feel like an obligation or burden.

He squeezes my upper arms, then slides his hands down, sucking in a lungful of air as he does.

Is he...could he be...did he just *smell* me?

With both hands, I grasp the fabric and tighten it around me. The urge to tuck my nose beneath the collar is too strong to resist, and I find myself doing exactly what he just did, inhaling the scent of his shirt.

Soap, a hint of something smoky, and sandalwood.

Why does he have to smell so good? Why do we have to keep running into one another? I don't like him. He doesn't like me. And yet here we are...*again*.

"You don't have to entertain me. I'm pretty good at being on my own." I finally turn around and look up, certain I'll find him glaring again.

Instead, his brown eyes dance in the moonlight, stealing the breath from my lungs.

With a hissed curse, he looks away from me. "I'll go when you go."

"What?"

He turns back to me, and this time he doesn't hide the way he assesses me as he lifts his beer and takes a long pull.

"It's my job as sheriff to make sure everyone gets home safe. So I'll go when you go."

"Suit yourself," I mutter as I stand and head toward the bar for another drink. "But I'm not leaving anytime soon."

Just as I settle beside the bar, the two guys from earlier reappear. "So, you have a house on the island?" Revs Hat Guy says. He steps in so close I can smell the beer on his breath.

My body clams up at his proximity. I'm used to men taking a few too many liberties when it comes to my personal space, but honestly, in LA, I was typically too busy to get out much, so I've forgotten how relentless they can be.

I turn away, but when a hand settles on my waist, I go on high alert. I'm just about to turn around and tell this guy to get lost when that soap and sandalwood scent hits me. Then Fisher's mouth is at my ear and his chest is pressed to my back. "Ready to go home yet, Princess?"

Instinctively, my body relaxes. Relieved, I nod. "Yes, please."

Libby
Chapter 10

I WAKE to the sound of a dog barking, a big smile spreading across my face before I've even cracked my eyelids open. I always wanted a dog, but between my father's busy schedule and mine, we never did get one.

Bing—the dog from the show—was actually Brad's, and I'm pretty sure he could sense my disdain for his owner.

I sit up and swing my feet over the side of the bed. When they settle on the cool wooden planks, I let the sensation overtake me, refusing to give that man any more of my thoughts.

It's bad enough that my inbox is filled with his threats and that millions believe his lies. A man simply has to breathe to be believed. No sense in wasting my own breath with the truth.

From here, I can see Bing bounding through my yard, chasing away the gulls. Thank god. I really didn't feel like facing Doris so I could buy more bread.

From his porch, Fisher hollers, "Come on, boy. The donuts aren't going to get themselves."

My mouth waters at the memory of the donuts Sutton shared with me last week. That sounds like a perfect way to start my day. I'll take a shower, maybe even do one of the face masks I brought, then head into town for donuts.

Despite Fisher's general grumpiness last night, I had a good time at the brewery. He barely said two words to me on the way home, and the "good night" he forced out as he walked me to my door was more of a grunt, but I think we've turned a corner.

Does he want me here? No. But he did come to my rescue when I needed him. Maybe I'll even see if I can hang out with Sutton later so he can have some time to himself. He could probably benefit from a calming face mask more than me. Just the image of him wearing one of my blue or pink masks makes me giggle.

Smiling, I head for the shower. I'm not the least bit surprised when the water is cold again. He must be doing something wrong with the pilot. Despite what he thinks, I don't need his help. So I stomp down to the basement, ignoring the corners where spiders are sure to lurk, and do what I've seen Fisher do five times this week.

The knowledge that I solved the problem myself makes the warm shower I take a half hour later feel that much more luxurious.

From the outside, the bakery looks like an outhouse. The small white building is attached to a pizza shop, and inside, a woman with bright red hair helps the patrons standing in line.

I step into the queue, excitement filling me as I scan the selection of donut flavors written in bright chalk above the counter. From the note at the bottom of the sign, it looks like they change out the choices regularly.

I absolutely love that. More options to choose from.

I snap a picture of the list with my phone and on instinct navigate to Instagram. The second the app loads, my heart stutters.

Dammit. That's something I would do in the past. Hell, big-name brands have offered ridiculous amounts of money in exchange for social media posts. I've never taken any of them up on it, though. I only post about places and products I truly enjoy. Little boutiques with the best shoes, restaurants that source their own food. Places like this. Except posting about this spot would mean drawing attention to where I am, and the last thing I need is for Brad to find me.

As long as he can't find me, his threats are empty.

By the time I step up to the counter, my mouth is watering again. "Good morning, can I have a Fruit Loops donut and a coffee?" I pull out my wallet and dig out cash.

"We're all out."

I look up, eyes wide, only to be met with a frown, and not the sympathetic kind.

"Oh." My gaze goes to the blackboard. "What about the coconut cake one?"

"All out of that too."

Okay... "Hmm. Well, what flavors do you have?"

She shakes her head. "We're all out of everything. Sorry."

The way the woman smiles when she says sorry rankles me. Yeah, she's not sorry at all. With a deep breath in, I keep my cool and step to the side. I guess I have to find something else for breakfast.

The line has grown quite long behind me. Damn, a lot of people are going to be disappointed when she closes up early.

I'm still considering my options when the man who was behind me in line asks for a half dozen donuts and she rings him right up.

What the hell?

She serves two more customers before she notices me and has the audacity to smirk. I have to squeeze my fists to keep myself from giving her the finger.

Before I do something I'll regret, I stomp off. I'm so angry I'm not focused on where I'm going and almost walk straight into a golf cart. Bracing myself to be yelled at, I squeeze my eyes shut and click my shoes together. "There's no place like home. There's no place like home—"

"Libby?" a woman calls, startling me. "Are you okay?"

Eyes flying open, I find Kennedy looking at me like she's worried I might have had a mental breakdown.

She wouldn't be too far off.

I shake my head. "Not really."

She pats the empty seat beside her on the golf cart. "Why don't you join me for breakfast at the inn? Then you can tell me all about it."

I shake my head. "You don't want to be seen with me."

She reels back, brows pinched. "But why?"

"They probably won't serve you if you're seen with me."

"What do you mean?" Frowning, she scans the street behind me. "Have people been mean to you?"

With a shrug, I shuffle to her cart and sit beside her. "The grocery store won't deliver anything I order, and the donut woman wouldn't serve me."

She sighs, her body deflating. "Have you not had grocery delivery at all since you moved here?"

I fold my lips in, racking my brain for a polite way of explaining that I've been here for two weeks and have yet to receive a single order I've put in. I've been settling for what I can find in the grocery store, which isn't much after they deliver everyone else's food, and especially since the tourists arrived.

Before I can put it all into words that won't ruffle feathers, she takes off. "Hang on. We're going to get you fed, and tonight you'll join us at the inn for family dinner."

"Oh, I couldn't impose—"

She holds up her hand, her focus fixed on the road. "I'm deeply disappointed in the people of this island. This isn't how we treat our guests. I'm sorry you've been so mistreated, but that ends today. You're my guest, understood?"

Her words leave no room for objection, so I simply nod.

I can't remember the last time I was invited for a family dinner, and although I don't like being pitied, I won't lie and say the idea of it doesn't sound nice.

Fisher
Chapter 11

"COME ON, it's already six twenty-five." Sutton tugs on my arm, causing me to tap a couple of random keys.

I was so engrossed in my work that I didn't hear her come into my office.

With a sigh, I run a hand down my face and try to focus on the world around me. Damn, I was so freaking close. The white cursor blinks on the otherwise black screen. If I had another thirty minutes, I'd have done it. Walking away at this moment is physically painful.

"Please." Sutton's small voice has my jaw locking. I've been working for the last four hours, but I promised her that we'd go to Mrs. K's for dinner if she could entertain herself until it was time to leave.

Since my parents moved to Florida and my brother passed away, the Knowleses are the closest thing we have to family.

Shoulders sinking, Sutton blinks those big blue eyes at me. "We can skip it if you need to work."

It would not be the first time I've canceled because I need more time. Sometimes walking away isn't possible. But the hurt and disappointment rolling off my niece are extra palpable today. I can't crush her dinner plans. She's like her father—social, fun, and in desperate need of time outside this house. So I have to provide it for her.

"Nope, I'm ready." I hit the keys to kill my program, along with any chance of finishing this project quickly. If only I could shut off my head just as easily. This idea is going to fester until I can get back to my keyboard. "Let's go eat."

I might be shitty company, but the Knowleses are used to it.

"Yes!" She spins and takes off running down the narrow stair-case. "Come on, Bing."

His nails tap along the hardwood floor as he races to the front door.

I'm halfway down the stairs when the screen door slams shut, making me wince. "Sutton, you gotta stop letting the damn door slam."

She probably can't even hear me out in the yard. Grumbling, I slip my Timberlands on and grab the leather jacket I never wear now that I live on Gilligan's Island. Libby still has my coat, and although most days I'd just go without a jacket, there is a chill in the air tonight.

"Sutton," I call again as I step outside.

"Guess what!" Sutton calls as she drags Libby by the hand toward the porch.

Libby peers up at me, and the bright light from the full moon catches the deep blue of her eyes, making them sparkle.

Heart stuttering, I blink twice. Damn, she's pretty in the moon-light. Her hair is down, flowing just past her shoulders so it brushes the high pockets of the coat—my coat—she's actually wearing. It's several sizes too big, but the vision of her in it has me almost smiling.

Before the expression has a chance to form, I lock my jaw. I will not allow myself to be interested in this woman. I will be friendly and make sure she's okay until she leaves. That's it.

That's my mantra. My mission. But when she shoots one of the gorgeous smiles at my niece, my gut tightens. My body really needs to get on board with what my head already knows.

"Where are you going?" It better not be to dinner with one of the fuckers who followed her around at the brewery last night. Just the idea has my fist clenching at my sides.

Sutton cups one hand to the side of her mouth, and in a voice entirely too loud to whisper, says. "That's the secret. She's coming to Sunday dinner."

"Oh." A wave of relief mixed with apprehension surges through me. I'm not sure if I'm more or less annoyed by the idea that I'm the fucker she's eating with. My eyes lock on hers, and my stomach flips. Definitely less annoyed.

But now I have to spend the next two hours trying not to stare at her, forcing my hands not to reach for her.

The breeze blows, and like a hard punch to the gut, I'm hit with the sweet floral scent that follows Libby. A zing rips up my spine, and my instincts scream at me to step close, lean down, run my nose along her neck. Fuck, my every cell wants more of her. Giving in to this feeling growing in my chest would be so much easier than fighting it. If not for one thing: Libby will leave. This would be nothing for her but a summer fling. I can't fall for her just to lose her. I can't lose anyone else.

I hold tight to that thought and keep it at the forefront of my mind.

"Kennedy invited me," she says.

What? I blink. I've lost the entire conversation.

Thirty seconds ago, I was worried I wouldn't be able to get the code for the wormhole out of my brain. Now all I can think about is touching Libby. A woman who's too young for me. A woman who has her entire life ahead of her. Who, any day, will realize that life here is too dull for someone with her sparkle. She'll leave. And I'll still be here.

"Don't worry." Sutton pulls on Libby's jacket. "Fisher doesn't care. He hardly says anything at Sunday dinner. He just eats and grunts."

I wince. Comments like those make me question why my

brother and his wife appointed me Sutton's guardian if anything should happen to them. Who in their right mind leaves their daughter to the grumpy nerd who is better with computers than people?

"Come on, you can ride with us. It's way too far to walk." Sutton heads toward my truck, dragging Libby with her. "Bing," she calls as she climbs into the back.

The dog hops in beside her. He's probably just as excited to hang out at Mrs. K's as Sutton is, since the woman loves giving him the table scraps. Every Sunday is like Thanksgiving for him.

Libby stops beside the truck and gapes at the passenger seat. For a heartbeat I worry she'll refuse to ride with me. The woman never makes anything easy. Even last night at the brewery, she gave me trouble before eventually letting me walk her home. When she glances toward the dark road again and my heart plummets in response, there's no denying that I want her with us.

And not just because I've been forcefully tasked with keeping everyone on this damn island safe. No, some traitorous part of me wants to hear her laugh with Sutton or even earn a smile myself. Fuck. I shouldn't want that. But I can't seem to stop myself.

"There aren't any doors," she finally says.

I nod, more relieved than I should be to discover the issue behind her hesitation. "They just get in the way."

Brow creased in confusion, she tips her head up to look at me. "Of what?"

If only I could explain it to her. Truth is, I don't fucking know. I'm just repeating what Hunter always said about his truck.

"In you go." I grasp her arm lightly and usher her onto the seat before she can put up a fight. Because, for some unexplainable reason, I want her with me. I want her driving me nuts.

We're hardly around the bend when she says, "At least he's wearing clothes."

Blue is standing in the middle of his yard, staring up at the sky like it holds all the answers.

"Gramps would never eat dinner naked." Sutton pops up between our seats, her tone full of confidence.

A chuckle escapes me. I would *not* make that bet. If Mrs. K allowed it, Blue would absolutely show up to Sunday dinner in his birthday suit.

"Was that a laugh, Fisher?" Libby teases as I slowly pull to a stop.

"Nope, clearing my throat." I cough for good measure. "Blue," I call. "Let's go."

The tip of his more-salt-than-pepper beard brushes his flannel as he turns our way, and in true Blue fashion, the tall, lanky old man takes his time shuffling over.

"Love sliding in bare. Gives me the shivers."

Libby chokes on a scoff, and I shake my head.

Sutton leans forward again, cupping one side of her mouth, and not really whispers, "Gramps always says the weirdest things."

Thank fuck my eight-year-old doesn't understand most of Blue's inappropriate comments. Not yet, anyway. "Without doors, you mean." I glare at him through the mirror, only to find his blue eyes dancing with amusement. I don't know why I waste my breath.

"Gramps, do you know Libby?" my niece asks. At least one of us here has manners.

"I've seen the lovely Libby around. I'm Blue." He leans forward and holds out a hand.

A growl escapes me, and before I know what I'm doing, I say, "Two feet."

Blue raises his brows. Although Wilder has a girl a week during tourist season and has to warn Blue off all the time, I've never claimed anyone before.

Libby cocks her head, her blond hair slipping past the swell of her breast, garnering my attention. She ducks, following my gaze, then straightens and locks eyes with me for the space of a heartbeat. I swear the air crackles.

Swallowing thickly, I force myself to focus on the path and slowly ease off the brake.

Blue chuckles, but I ignore the asshole.

"Libby," Sutton chirps, thankfully breaking through the tension. "Did you see the casting for the play? I get to be Frenchie."

By the lightness of her tone, she's excited. Although why the hell Sutton wants to be French is beyond me. Maybe the idea is alluring because it's unlike anything she's used to on this island. Although I keep Sutton here because that's what Hunter and Marissa wanted, my niece's desire to see the world isn't lost on me.

"Oh my gosh. That's *so* cool." Libby spins in her seat, and the two girls gush about the summer play all the way to the inn.

I half listen, mostly grateful that they can prattle on so easily without my input. Sutton requires so many words every day. She has so much to say, and I'm typically the one stuck responding to most of them. I can easily reach my daily quota by breakfast. So this? Quietly listening to them chatter and not having to say a single word? I could get used to this.

When I peer into the rearview mirror as I round the inn, the man behind me catches my eye, his smirk far too knowing. Fuck.

Blue is climbing out before the wheels have come to a complete stop on the dirt patch behind the house. But I know better than to try to control the man who's lived on this island his whole life.

During the offseason, a peaceful silence hovers over the piece of land floating in the ocean, especially at night. And with so few lights, the entire night sky is visible.

But tonight, the inn is lit up. Almost every window shines with a yellow haze that even the blinds can't hide and the air buzzes with noise. It's nothing like Boston, but also nothing like the peace of a month ago.

"No, we don't go to the inn *inn*." Sutton yanks Libby's hand, pulling her toward the back of the large bed-and-breakfast where Blue has just disappeared. "We go to Mrs. K's house. Only family comes to Sunday dinner."

In this case, *family* means Sutton and me, Mr. and Mrs. Knowles, their kids Wilder and Eddy, and their granddaughter Lindsey. And, of course, Gramps, a.k.a. Blue, a.k.a. Mr. Knowles's almost ninety-year-old father. That's it. Yet tonight, Libby is here, having somehow wrangled an invitation.

As I follow her toward the house, unable to avoid noticing the way her blond hair shines in the moonlight when she gently bumps her shoulder against Sutton's, I don't feel like complaining.

I lock my jaw. I'm not dumb enough to believe the Hollywood princess will make it more than a few weeks on this island. But so far, Libby has surprised me. She's nothing like what I expected when her father called to let me know she was coming. She's got grit and personality. She's nowhere near the plastic Hollywood drama queen I expected.

Honestly she seems more like her character on the show than the girl plastered across the cover of every tabloid.

"Fisher, you comin'?" Sutton asks as she holds the back door to the Knowleses' home open.

With a nod, I quickly eat up the space between my truck and the door. The second I step inside, the scent of the salt air is replaced by the aroma of coffee and Murphy's Oil Soap.

"Did you hear she's tired of getting things rammed down her throat night after night?"

I fight the smirk, though I have no idea what prompted that response from Gramps.

"You did not just say that." Eddy groans. "Especially in front of Lindsey."

Wilder chuckles. "Like Lindsey gets it."

His mom steps up behind him and whacks him on the back of the head. "Do not encourage your grandfather."

"Ouch." He runs a hand through his hair, but his face quickly splits into a grin. "But he's life goals. I want to be just like him when I'm old."

"We're here," Sutton calls out.

Lindsey lets out the kind of ear-piercing shriek only a three-year-old can make. Jesus, it's going to be a long night.

Thirty minutes later, I'm proven right.

"Fisher, don't be slipping her the sausage at the table."

Eyes wide, Libby gapes at the plate of sausage and peppers I just passed to her, then blinks at Blue.

Eddy groans, Wilder laughs, and Mrs. K shakes her head. Mr. K has spent sixty years ignoring his father, so he's got it down to a science.

"Why? Don't you like sausage?" Sutton asks, blissfully ignorant to the innuendos constantly spilling out of Blue's mouth.

"No, I love it," Libby says quickly. Half a heartbeat later, her cheeks go pink. Maybe because she's worried about hurting Mrs. K's feelings, but more likely because of the double entendre.

Wilder waggles his brows at me. I glare back. I'm not going there. I absolutely can't picture Libby on her knees in front of me. Her big blue eyes shining up at me as her lips part—

Wilder barks a laugh so loud everyone around the table jumps.

Fucking hell.

Between Gramps and Wilder, this meal has gone off the rails.

We need a change of topic. "Talk about the dancing show," I practically growl at my niece.

"*Dancing with the Stars*?" She shoots up in her chair.

Typically I dread listening to her go on and on about the voting and her theories, but I'm desperate.

"Oh my gosh," Libby squeals. "I love Joey. I hope she wins."

"Me too," Sutton says. "She's going to crush it tonight."

"I really hope so." Libby shrugs. "You'll have to tell me how she does."

Eddy tilts her head, studying Libby. "Do you have plans tonight?"

My chest goes uncomfortably tight. I feel like I'm on a roller coaster with the way my adrenaline has spiked over the last hour and a half.

I grit my teeth and ignore the sensation. We'll be out of here by eight thirty, and since I've got a kid and a job to get back to, my night will be over. But I guess for a lot of people, the night only starts around that time. Especially people from Hollywood. I shake my head. I've been on this island too damn long.

"My cable and Wi-Fi aren't working."

"At all?" I ask.

Head lowered, she lets out a long sigh. "Nope."

How? Her place has a satellite dish. We all do. That's the only way we can watch anything out here. Dammit. I should have confirmed the dish was functioning correctly when I made sure the house was ready for her.

"You can watch with me," Sutton offers. "Right, Fisher?" She smiles up at me.

The idea of bringing Libby back to my house has my heart rate picking up. It's either the best idea or the worst. All I know is that now that the idea is in Sutton's head, I don't have the heart to refuse.

Across from me, Wilder spins his beer bottle on the table. "Fisher would love that."

"Why isn't your cable working?" Eddy asks.

Exactly. That's what I want to know.

Libby shrugs.

"It happens," Mrs. K assures. "It can be spotty here."

Accurate, but not for one house, and no one else has had any issues. If they did, I'd have heard about it. Unfortunately, I'm like the customer help line on the island.

"I'm sure Fisher can fix it." Mr. K points his fork my way. "He's a genius with computers."

Told ya.

And while it might be true, thirty minutes later, when I'm standing on her roof, looking at the satellite, it's clear my computer skills won't help me fix this problem.

I crouch and pick up the sliced wire, then peer across the yard to where Libby and Sutton sit together inside the large window in my living room, smiling while they watch the stupid dancing show. Gut tightening with unease, I survey the roof, then the yard.

"Who the hell would want to cut your internet access, Princess?"

Libby
Chapter 12

I CAN'T HELP but peer out the window of Fisher's house to look up at mine every minute or so. Fisher is *still* on the roof, staring at my satellite dish. He swore it would be an easy fix, but he's been up there an awfully long time. Crap. I hate burdening him with this. It's just one more reason for him to hate me. Another thing for him to fix. More proof that I'm nothing but a nuisance.

I promised myself that the new me wouldn't care what people thought. That I wouldn't seek the approval of others any longer. Yet I can't help but feel like it's an impossible expectation. Not only because it hurts to know the people on the island don't like me, but because I really want *Fisher* to like me.

Why? I haven't a clue. It's a waste of my energy. Every time Sutton drags me along, it's clear as day he can't wait to escape my company. And I'm sure the last thing he wanted was for me to show up to dinner with the people he clearly considers family.

"Oh my gosh," Sutton squeals beside me, bouncing on the couch cushion. "I think Joey is going to win."

Joey Berkshire has been the clear favorite since episode one. She's a socialite who I'm pretty sure has never held a job in her life. Must be nice. I've been working since I was four. I met her once and liked her instantly. She's kind, funny, and the life of the party.

The door swings open just as the host announces Joey and her partner are the winners. When the screen door clangs loudly against the frame, Sutton jumps off the couch and runs right into Fisher's legs. "They won, they won!"

It's hard not to melt a little when the grump's mouth tilts up and his eyes do this twinkly thing that, in reality, is probably caused by the way the mirror ball on the television sends speckles of light refracting off every surface.

Whatever the cause, he looks deceivingly happy. "Oh yeah?"

"Yes, and did you know that Libby knows her?"

Fisher looks up, eyes finding mine, and his lips straighten into a firm line. Right. No smiling for me. "Yeah, she mentioned it at dinner. Anyway, it's late, sweet pea. Say good night to Libby and go on up and brush your teeth."

Sutton sticks her lip out. "But Fish—"

He tilts his head and hits her with a look that immediately has her mouth snapping shut.

"Fine." With a glare at him, she darts away. She rushes toward me, landing in my lap with all the pizzazz of a goose learning how to fly. "Thanks for watching with me. Promise me you'll come to Sunday dinners from now on?"

Fisher grunts, still standing across the room. His arms are crossed over his chest and his feet are planted wide. "We don't invite people to other people's houses."

Not wanting her to get in any more trouble and certainly knowing my place, I squeeze her hand. "I had so much fun tonight. Thank you for letting me watch TV with you."

Without another second's hesitation, I stand and head for the door, giving the growling man a wide berth.

It's no use. Just as I pass him, he grabs me, his fingers circling my wrist in a way that sends heat flooding through me. I haven't enjoyed another's touch in a long time. Normally I flinch when I'm not expecting the contact, but for the first time in a long, long time, I don't startle or pull away on instinct. It's as if my body has determined that Fisher's touch is acceptable. No, it's more than that. It's wanted. God, it's *electric*.

Cheeks heating, I look up at him. Only he's not even looking at me. He's watching Sutton walk away. Only when she's gone does he say, "We need to talk."

I tug myself free of his hold, annoyed with the way my nerve endings light up at his touch. I'm not wanted here. This man wants nothing to do with me, yet my body hasn't gotten the message. "Don't worry, I won't show up next Sunday expecting you to take me to the Knowleses' for dinner. I get it. They're your people."

He frowns and his glare deepens, if that's even possible. "Sutton is my people. You can go wherever you're invited. And if they do invite you, you should ride with us. Don't walk around here in the dark."

I cough out a laugh. Is this his idea of hospitality? If it is, he sucks at it. "Okay, then." Lifting my chin, I head for the door.

"Wait," he says again.

Shoulders sagging, I stop, though I keep my focus fixed on my house, refusing to turn around again.

"The wire to your satellite dish was cut. You have any idea who would do that?"

Gripping my chest, I spin. "What?"

He holds out his phone. On the screen is an image of what appears to be two pieces of a wire that have clearly been torn apart. It doesn't make sense. Why would someone cut the wire on my roof?

"Maybe it was the birds?"

Fisher gives me a *you've got to be fucking kidding me* look. It's the expression he wears every time I open my mouth, so honestly, it's not a surprise. "And someone's been blowing out your pilot light."

I give him that scowl right back. "What are you talking about?"

"It's gone out five times, Libby."

Six, since I lit it without his help yesterday. Not that I'll tell him that.

"Someone is trying to scare you off this island. Any idea who it could be?"

Scoffing, I fling my arms out wide. "Take your pick. No one wants me here. Least of all you, right?"

His facial expression doesn't change. "You're not staying. I don't need to do anything to run you off."

I roll my eyes. God, this man knows how to twist a knife.

"I need you to be honest with me," he grits out. "What are you running from? Because whatever it is, it's come to this island, and I can't help you if you don't tell me who it is."

God, I wish I could muster even half the indifference Fisher has. More than that, I wish his words didn't cut me so deeply. I am running from something, and the man I'm hiding from is capable of far worse than cutting a cable line or forcing me to go without hot water. That's child's play. A prank. Nothing I'll lose sleep over, considering Brad has no idea where I am.

So long as these islanders keep their mouths shut, I'll be safe.

"There's nothing to tell. It's no secret that none of you want me here, but you'll have to do a hell of a lot more than force me to endure cold showers and refuse to serve me or order the groceries I request."

Fisher steps onto the porch, his brows drawing together. "Refuse to what? What are you talking about?"

I keep moving as I wave him off. "It's fine. I don't need cable. Thanks for allowing me into your home. I'll make sure to stay out of your way, and unless Sutton talks to me, I won't bother you."

"Libby, that wasn't—"

Without waiting for him to finish, I dash across the lawn and rush into my house. I shut the door without looking back and lean against it to catch my breath. I can't hope that he's standing at his door watching me. I can't wish that he'd chase after me.

No one chases after me. At least not in the way I want to be chased.

Once my heart rate has settled, I jog up the stairs to my room and text my father.

> Me: Hi Daddy, you haven't told anyone where I am, right?

My phone rings immediately, my father's name on the screen. Rather than answer, I send it to voicemail and text him again.

> Me: Sorry, I'm out with friends so I won't be able to hear you.

> Dad: Glad to hear you've made friends. Hope you're enjoying your summer so far. No, I haven't told anyone. Is someone bothering you? Brad?

Breathing out a sigh of relief, I hold the phone to my chest. Not Brad. Like I told Fisher, it's nothing. Well, not nothing, but not anything sinister. People don't want me here, and they're making it known. I can deal with pranks and grumps who think I'm trying to ruin their island. And I'm more determined than ever to change their minds. I grew up as Hollywood's darling. I know how to make people like me. No matter what it takes, I'll make sure every person on this island loves me before the end of this summer. Everyone but Fisher. I know a lost cause when I see one.

> Me: Nope. Just checking. Miss you, Daddy. Love you!

It is surprisingly difficult to avoid my next-door neighbor. Despite my certainty that I'm the last person Fisher wants to see, I can't go anywhere without seeing him. In the two days I've been avoiding him, I've already hidden in two bushes, beside one tree, and behind one oversized tourist who smelled like roasted walnuts and seaweed. It was not my first choice, but I held my breath and bore it.

I've just stumbled down the hill behind our houses, rather than taking the path into town, when I hear a hiss and then a spitting sound, then come face to face with a goat.

"Oh, hello, there." Hands up, I take a step backward, then another.

The animal bows its head, showing off his impressive horns. Yeah, I don't think that's a good sign.

"I'm Libby," I say as I continue to back away. "Everyone loves me. Well, okay, not everyone. But you should love me. I'm very lovable."

"I think you're lovable."

I jump, my heart lurching, and the goat bleats loudly.

"Oh, Betty," Maggie says as she walks up to the angry goat and pats him on the head. "Don't scare Libby, you old fool."

The thing merely grunts at her and then turns around and walks away.

Heart pounding from my near-death experience, all I can do is blink at Maggie. She's wearing another set of overalls—deep red this time, with a hole in the knee.

"How'd you stay so calm?"

She giggles. "She's harmless. We do need to let the sheriff know when she escapes. Though I reckon he's a bit busy right now."

Still a little out of sorts, I frown. "Huh?"

She smiles. "Because he's on your roof at the moment."

"Who is?"

"The sheriff?" She says it like it's a question.

"Is there a sheriff other than Fisher?"

She giggles again. "No, and Fisher's not really the sheriff."

Now I'm really confused. I close my eyes and shake my head,

hoping to clear away the fog of panic that hit me when the goat appeared. "He's not?"

"Well, he is, but he's not."

Yeah, still not making any sense.

"He's the acting sheriff. He took over for his brother. We just haven't gotten around to electing a new one yet."

I nod, though she lost me.

"So we should let him know about the goat." She points to a tall wooden box at the top of the hill.

"What's up there?"

"The police box."

I squint at the windowless white structure with *POLICE* painted on the side in bold black letters.

"Fisher fits in there?" The roof of the structure comes up to my chest. I can't imagine anyone bigger than Sutton fitting in there comfortably.

She giggles. "The police *call* box. It's how we contact him."

"Why don't we just use a cell phone?" I pull mine from my pocket and give it a shake. Not that I have Fisher's number.

"Because that's not how you get in touch with the sheriff," she says with a laugh. "But since he's on your roof, he won't get the message until later."

"Right." I do my best to keep my facial expression neutral. I'm so damn lost. "So why do we need to tell him about the goat?"

"Oh." She peers over her shoulder in the direction the goat wandered off. "Because Betty clearly escaped."

I nod. "Okay. Is there, like, a goat yoga class we need to return him—or her?—to?"

Maggie's face screws up like she's eaten a lemon. "Goat what?"

I shrug. "Goat yoga. It's a yoga class with the goats." I plant my hands on the ground and get into downward dog position, then throw one arm out. I have no idea how a goat would do yoga, but this is close enough.

79

Maggie snorts. "Oh no, the islanders don't even yoga. Our goats definitely don't."

I hop back up to my feet and wipe my hands, a zing of pleasure coursing through me. It's nice to smile with someone. "Well, then what do they do?"

Maggie tilts her head. "I haven't the faintest idea."

I burst into laughter, and after a second, she joins me.

"I'm not sure what's weirder: that your goats don't yoga or that any goats do," I say as tears blur my vision.

"Definitely that any goats do," Maggie hiccups. "So should we let Fisher know to watch out for the goat?"

"That's all you," I tell her, waving as I go. I'm avoiding Fisher. And, apparently, the goats.

Fisher

Chapter 13

"DAMMIT." With a grunt, I yank Betty's collar again. "I know you love the strawberries as much as Sutton does, but Todd is going to turn you into goat stew if you keep breaking into his greenhouse."

"Maaa," she bleats, stubbornly digging her hoofs into the dirt floor.

I don't know why Doris needed a white horned billy goat, or why she can't keep the damn thing in its pen—or why it's my job to deal with the damn thing—but apparently, these are all facts I'm supposed to accept.

"Grrwoof." Bing pushes his head against Betty's side, forcing her from the berries.

"Thanks, buddy." I can always count on my dog to help herd the goat.

Together we get her through the greenhouse door and out into the chilly June air. The days are getting warmer as we move into summer, but it's still only about fifty-five.

"Tell Doris she needs a higher fence, or we'll kick Betty off this rock." Todd points a crooked finger at me. "I'm taking this back to the town meeting. This island should be menace-free."

I nod, still leading the goat to the dirt road. Now that we're away from the fruit, I suppose she's the one leading me. I release her and follow as she trots happily back to the fenced area behind the general store, where tourists stop and put quarters into a machine to buy food for her. Summer is her season. People from all over love to feed her and watch her scale the bridged towers that Doris's husband renovates weekly.

"I mean it, sheriff," he calls after me. "I'm going to take matters into my own hands. I will get bear traps."

The threat is nothing new, but he's never followed through. He's cranky, but not cruel. He won't hurt the goat. He won't even force her out of the greenhouse. If he would, it would make my life a whole lot easier. Although I don't respond, Bing barks in answer, then takes off. He makes his way past the gray building with sky blue trim that serves as the town's art gallery and the much plainer souvenir shop next door, heading for the dock, probably to beg Cank for attention or treats.

"Look, it's Betty!" A tourist a bit younger than Sutton comes running my way with her parents behind her.

"Oh, I don't know if it's a good idea to touch her," the mother warns.

It's not. But before I can say that, the dark-haired girl gives the goat a hug.

"Baa," Betty protests, dancing away from the child and kicking up a cloud of dust as she goes. It's been dry this spring, leaving my boots constantly covered in a layer of fine dirt. If we don't get rain soon, I'll have to start worrying about fires.

"I need to get her back," I say as I pull the goat past the girl and her parents. "Enjoy your stay."

I'm coming up on the gray shingled house we use as the medical center when Lindsey appears.

"Betty." The three-year-old waves wildly from the porch.

Eddy peaks out the door and smirks. "Driving Todd to drink again?"

"We know the brewery needs the business. And that old man

needs the stick out of his butt." Doris frowns from the porch of the general store, arms crossed over her long, flowing red dress. Although she's probably had it since the seventies, it's finally back in fashion. "Come on, Betty."

At the sound of her owner's voice, the goat takes off, freeing herself from my hold, and follows Doris behind the building.

"She's in a mood. She's complained all morning about hating sherbet. Apparently it melts on everything and makes a mess." Rolling her eyes, Eddy tucks her long French braid over her shoulder. "Like ice cream doesn't."

This is one of those situations where I should probably ask her to explain what the hell she's talking about. Luckily I'm saved from responding when Bing shows up beside me.

"Puppy," Lindsey says. "I can ride him?"

"Sorry, sweetie. You're too big for that." Eddy bends down to pick Lindsey up, but before she can, the three-year-old shrugs her off and darts away.

"Rocks," she shouts, taking off toward the water, little pigtails bouncing, with Bing hot on her heels.

"Lindsey." Eddy sighs. "This girl is going to be the death of me." She flings a white box at me, then takes off. "Take that first-aid kit to Maggie for me," she calls over her shoulder.

"Sheriff? More like errand boy," I grumble.

"At least no one asks you for diet ginger ale." Doris stomps up the porch steps, huffing.

With a sigh, I say, "Keep Betty away from Todd's shit."

She grumbles and waves a dismissive hand.

Whatever. Happy not to be pulled into any more drama there, I head up the dirt road to the schoolhouse on top of the hill.

I pass a crowd of people hanging out at the Monhegan Fish House. All the tourists love Sherman's crab rolls, so I duck my head and pick up the pace, doing my best to not make eye contact. The last thing I need is more chitchat. I scoot past the red wooden announcement board and stride up the hill without incident. Just as I round the corner, a flash of pink catches my eye, and when I catch sight of the accompanying blond hair, I almost smile.

But what the hell is she doing half crouched on a boulder along the path? The woman makes my head spin. But my stupid heart picks up just a hair at the prospect of talking to her.

"Princess," I call.

She lifts her head, her eyes going wide, and sniffles. And is that— is she crying?

My heart lurches oddly at the thought, so I pick up my pace, jogging the last few feet to the rock.

"Go away." She lowers her head, averting her gaze, but she can't hide the red-rimmed eyes or the damp cheeks.

Dammit. I was right about the tears. Like hell I'll leave her.

"What's wrong?" I fist my free hand at my side, clenching so tightly it throbs. With a forced inhale, I stretch it out and rack my brain for a way to make her feel better. Being nice, being humorous, even being friendly, doesn't come all that naturally, so the effort is in vain.

"No need to growl." Her still misty eyes snap up, but now they're blazing.

Good. I can handle mad, but the forlorn expression won't do.

"Growling is the only way I know how to communicate."

Like I hoped, her lips lift a fraction.

My stomach jumps at the idea that I could make her happy. God, I'm a sappy idiot. "Get used to it."

She rolls her eyes and huffs. Hands planted on the rock, she drags her focus to the ground between us. Instantly, she shoots up to standing and teeters on the rock.

On instinct, I dart forward and grasp her hip.

"It's going to get on you," she says, though she clutches my arm to steady herself, her nails biting into my skin.

Get on me? What the hell is going to get on me?

Frowning, I follow her wide-eyed stare to the dirt by my feet. "Oh. A fish spider."

It's relatively small—only about twice as big as my thumb. I shift closer and set the first-aid kit on the rock. Then I wrap an arm around her waist, settling my hand along the hem of her high-waisted black leggings. She's got an irrational fear of the eight-legged creatures, and the last thing I need is for her to fall off the rock the way she tumbled off her dining room table the day we met.

Instead of shrugging out of my hold like I expect, she relaxes against me. As her sweet scent fills my nose, my body buzzes. Every nerve ending keys up at her proximity. I swallow, trying to fight the sensation. Fuck, I hate the way I lose control when I'm around her.

"Is it going to hiss again? Because when I was trying to poke it away with the stick, it *hissed* at me."

The insane image of Libby poking at the spider with a giant stick flashes through my head. No wonder the little guy hissed.

Chuckling, I shake my head. "That was probably the issue."

The silky strands of her hair brush against my cheek as she turns and locks those blue eyes on me. I have to fight the shiver working its way down my spine. Jesus, I swear this woman possesses some kind of magic that makes my body react. As I tuck the hair behind her ear, my finger brushes her soft cheek, and she still doesn't pull away.

"No one likes to be poked by a stick, especially spiders. Next time try being sweet. Maybe if you smile pretty, it'll move for ya."

The words are out and her eyes are wide before I realize how flirty that sounds. I don't even know what to make of it. I don't flirt.

She shudders. "I hate spiders."

"Ready to go home yet, Princess?"

For the first time, I hope she snaps back with a quick no.

She straightens her shoulders, taking the bait and pulling herself together. "Neither spiders nor mean grocers will get me to leave. I *am* home."

My lips twitch, coming dangerously close to tipping into a smile. That is until her words sink in. "Mean grocers?"

Yeah, Doris can be cranky, but she isn't usually outright mean.

Eyes narrowing, she lifts her chin.

Fuck, I love the defiance in her expression.

"Apparently the groceries I request are either ridiculous or items she can't get."

Items she can't get? What the hell? Doris can order pretty much anything that the Hannaford mainland stores carry. Spider issue aside, Libby isn't the high-maintenance Hollywood prima donna that the tabloids make her out to be, so I can't imagine that her requests are outrageous.

"Anyway." She huffs. "I'll figure it out." She glances back to the ground where the spider about the size of a silver dollar is still milling about, her body racked with another shiver. "Probably from this rock. Because I'm never getting down."

"Never?" I release her slowly, and once she's steady, I take a step back so I can look at her.

She eyes the spider again, lip caught between her teeth. "Never," she confirms. "Please let Maggie and Sutton know that a spider is holding me hostage."

I shake my head. Nope. Sutton would never let Libby skip play practice. If I show up and admit to leaving Libby halfway to the school, my niece will hit me with that awful side-eye. So, begrudgingly, I spin, offering her my back. "Okay, hop on, Little Miss Drama Queen."

"On?" she asks, her voice quiet.

"Yes. I'll give you a ride." I back up another step, arms out.

She doesn't, in fact, hop on. And she's silent for so long I'm certain she'll choose death by spider over having to touch me. But just as I'm sighing in disappointment, she slips her hands over my shoulders. Hesitantly, she leans her chest against me, and when her full tits press into my back, I can't stop the way my breath catches. God, the feel of her against me is better than I remember. Warm and soft and so damn sweet. When she loops her legs around my waist, it feels like I swallowed my own tongue.

It isn't until she clears her throat that my brain finally engages and I grasp her thighs to steady her. Fuck. The warmth of her seeping through her leggings is enough to unravel me, and when her breath dances across my neck, my knees wobble, and I'm certain she can feel my heart hammering.

I don't want to like Libby. I don't want to want her. But in this second, with her wrapped around me, it feels like the two of us are exactly where we should be.

"You sure you can make it up the hill like this?" she asks, probably because I haven't moved in at least ten seconds.

I clear my throat. "Of course I can." Adding a little extra grumble, I turn and head up the steepest part of the hill to the school. Despite the pitch, it's an easy climb. The woman is so small I could carry her for miles. I could carry her forever. And fuck if I don't want to.

I clench my jaw. I can't think like that. Even if Libby survives an entire Monhegan summer, she's leaving as soon as fall rolls around. Summer people don't stay into the fall. I can't forget that.

"I heard you fixed my satellite. Thank you."

Yeah, I rewired the dish, but the cut wire and her lame explanation don't sit well with me. Not when I factor in the issue with her pilot light.

I could lie and say the only reason I care is because my niece spends as much time with Libby as she can, and if someone is messing with Libby, Sutton could get caught up in it, but it's so much more than that. The idea of someone hurting this woman I can't get out of my head feels like a sharp knife to my gut.

I can't picture anyone here trying to scare her off like that. Yeah, they might grumble that she's summer people, but we all know those summer people keep this island going.

"Did you think any more about who might have it out for you?"

"Yeah." She adjusts her arms around my neck, her fingers ghosting over my chest and sending a ripple of need through me. Fuck. Does she have any idea what she's doing to me? Probably. She's probably relishing the ability to torture me. "Doris from the store."

"Not likely." I shift her slightly, and when her fingers halt their movement, I'm both relieved and disappointed.

With a deep sigh, she sinks against me. "She's been nothing but mean since I arrived. Yeah, she'll happily take my money for anything on the shelves, but she refuses to put in my order with everyone else's."

I choke back a growl. I need to have a conversation with Doris. That doesn't make any sense.

"The woman is terrified of heights. She won't even use a step stool at the store. There is no way she'd climb on your roof."

"Then I don't know." Libby shifts, rubbing her body against mine, and I fight the groan trying to work its way up my throat. Carrying her was such a mistake.

The worst part? She doesn't seem even the least bit affected by me.

Fisher, you're a fucking idiot. Why would she be? She's gorgeous and so damn sweet. She could do so much better than the island grump.

Before I can spiral into a storm of self-pity, she rests her palms against my chest, her hands trembling. Almost like she's afraid...

"How about you tell me what happened to make you leave LA?" I suggest, needing to know now more than ever.

When her only response is a quick inhale, I go on, trying to make the question easier.

"Is there anyone back in California who might be upset with you?"

"I'm not talking about it with you," she hisses, her body tensing.

I tense too. Because shit, that was the opposite of denying a problem. It was damn near confirmation that there is an issue, and I know myself well enough to know I will not be able to let it go.

She releases me and squirms out of my hold. When I spin to look at her, her arms are crossed and she's glaring past me, unwilling to meet my eye.

"Why is that such an upsetting question?" She's clearly deflecting. She absolutely has something to hide. "I'm just trying to help you."

"I don't need help." Her voice cracks, belying her statement, and her throat bobs as she swallows. "I'm not anyone's business. And with the way gossip works here, if I tell you, then the entire island knows. And then the tabloids do. So I'll pass."

My heart splits wide open. Damn. The loneliness in that statement is one I relate to deeply. Maybe not the part about the tabloids, but I understand island gossip.

Growing up, I was the weird kid, and people were always whispering about me.

"What do you think he does in that room with those computers?"

"I heard the mainland police were out because he broke into something."

"Poor boy can't make friends."

"I think the screens are messing with his brain. All he does is grunt."

"I hope he doesn't come over here. He's so weird."

Since moving back, I've kept my night work quiet. Only a select few have ever even seen my office. And no one knows what I do.

"You can trust me, Libby." The words are like sandpaper, painful to get out.

Finally she looks at me, a war raging behind her blue irises. She opens her mouth and inhales, and I take a step closer, eager to be the holder of her secrets.

But rather than speak, she shakes her head. "Thanks for the ride."

She spins and darts for the schoolhouse. The building where my niece is currently hanging out with her friends. And I have no idea if that is something I should worry about or not. I made a promise to my brother to always take care of his little girl, and I have to do that.

Fuck. I feel guilty about what I have to do, but not enough to even hesitate.

I head back down the hill, eating up the distance in quick strides. After a quick stop at the grocery store to chat with Doris, I go straight home and don't stop until I'm sitting in front of my computer. Normally hacking into an email account is a mindless task. One small item to check off a list. I don't think about whose inbox I'm accessing or care what they think. But knowing it's Libby's, knowing that she will care, makes it a painful process. For a moment I question if I'm making a mistake, but the first email changes my mind quickly.

As I scan its contents, my jaw locks and anger pulses up my throat. All my plans for the day shift. I've gotta borrow a boat. It's not the only thing I'm taking from someone today, but it is the only thing I plan to return when I'm done.

Libby

Chapter 14

Hollywood Star Brad Fedder donates one million dollars to women's shelter in Los Angeles.

MY JAW DROPS as I read the alert that popped up on my phone. I'd rather not ever see that man's name again, but if I have to, then I suppose I prefer this over anything else. God, now what is he trying to cover up? It must be bad to warrant such a big donation. There's no way he did this willingly. The man's only friends are the figures in his bank account, and he hates women.

Or maybe he just hates me.

Either way, he certainly doesn't respect women. That was clear every time he touched me despite my obvious disdain for him and the many, many times I begged him to stop.

I focus on breathing, willing the anxiety that clutches my throat and threatens to swallow me whole to abate. It's the way my body reacts every time I think of that man and his touch.

Instead, I focus on how good yesterday afternoon was. Despite the run-in with the spider and Fisher, practice was everything I needed.

Community theater is nothing like being on a television show.

Every moment I spent with the group yesterday reminded me of why I fell in love with the stage. The instant gratification is a high I haven't felt in forever. There's no waiting for some critic—or thousands on the internet—to react to my work. The dopamine hit that comes when a scene goes right is instantaneous.

While I'm only helping with the production, the way the kids listen to my suggestions is far more satisfying than any part of acting has been in a long while.

A round of applause from the kids or an overjoyed smile from Maggie are all it takes to make my day. Maybe it's pathetic that such minimal affection has this kind of effect on me. Hell, just thinking about practice makes warmth bloom in my chest. Yeah, maybe it's sad that I'm so starved for kindness, but I won't worry too much about it. I'm happy. That's truly all that matters.

Though I'd be a tad bit happier if I had some of the items from the grocery order Doris still won't fill.

God, that woman makes me angry.

But I refuse to be labeled as difficult.

I refuse to be what others say I am in general.

So I sip my Diet Pepsi, which apparently Doris has no trouble getting, and enjoy the sound of the ocean and the way the sun warms my skin. June hasn't just brought more tourists. Warmer afternoons and a balmy breeze are also welcome changes on the island.

I've just let out the loudest of sighs, content in a way I've been striving for since I came up with the idea to run off to this island, when the lightest of giggles carries over the summer breeze. "Libby! Libby!"

I lift a hand to block the sun and spot Sutton rushing toward me, her hair back in braids that bounce with as much enthusiasm as she does.

Behind her, Fisher follows, his movements much more subdued.

Dammit, he's not making it easy to avoid him.

After the way my stomach did that little swoopy thing yesterday when he carried me to practice, the last thing I need is another run-in with the man.

"Hi, pretty girl. What's all the excitement for?"

I keep my eyes on Sutton despite the intensity of Fisher's gaze.

"Fisher and I are here to take you for a picnic."

Fisher and picnic do not belong together in a sentence. Eye twitching, I sit up. "A picnic?"

Blue eyes brighten as she swipes at a stray hair with the back of her hand. "Yeah. It's a tradition. Wednesday nights in the park."

"There's a park?" This time I can't help but look at Fisher. No one has mentioned a park.

He grins. The man fucking grins, and my heart somersaults down the path and lands with a *kathwump* at his feet.

"Sure is." He holds up the picnic basket as if trying to prove to me that he hasn't been possessed by aliens who've come to earth to kill me with the unsuspecting promise of a smile. It only makes me more suspicious. "Even got some of your favorite things."

"He did. He got your sodas and straws and strawberries and the —" She tilts her head back, peering up at Fisher, and snaps her fingers. "What's the nut called again?"

"Pine nuts," he says.

Sutton raises a finger in excitement. "Yup. Pine nuts for your salad. We even looked up the recipe for your favorite salad." She holds her hand up to her mouth, my favorite of her little quirks, and whispers loudly, "Did you know there's a whole article on what Elizabeth Sweet eats for lunch?"

A laugh bubbles out of me, and I finally haul myself out of my chair. "Yes." I brush off my leggings, then straighten. "People on the mainland are a bit ridiculous."

Head tilted, she purses her lips. "But there's a lot more to do there too."

"We've got goats," Fisher says, his lips twitching. When he lifts his gaze to mine, like we're sharing some sort of secret, I swallow my tongue.

I only now notice that his typically messy hair is swept to the side like he took time to get ready. And I think he may have even trimmed his beard. His brown eyes are brighter than I've ever seen them, like he's truly happy. Why is he happy? And why do I feel like I'd do anything to keep him this way?

"So what do you say, Princess? Come with us to the picnic?"

I have to look away from him. Those words combined with the earnest hopefulness in his expression are screwing with my mind. "Is this a tourist thing?"

"Nah." He adjusts his hold on the basket. "It's an islander thing, but tourists tend to discover it."

"So summer people are invited?" I swallow past the lump in my throat. I'm tired of feeling unwelcome, so while I appreciate that Sutton and Maggie do their best to include me in activities reserved for islanders, I don't particularly feel like getting the stink-eye from Doris or being run off by the woman from the bakery. Especially when I'm feeling better than I have in a long, long time. Why ruin the vibes?

Fisher's eyes flash with an emotion that, if I weren't so jaded, I'd think was empathy. "You're invited, Libby. Come with us to the picnic. Please? Like Sutton said, we've got your favorite salad, diet ginger ale, *and* straws. And if you're a really good girl, there's a carton of sherbet in the freezer when we get home."

The husky quality of his voice makes it impossible not to imagine him saying those two words—*good girl*—in a completely different way. When he's wearing significantly less. When I can feel the burn of that scruff between my thighs.

Somehow I know that Fisher is the type of man who would praise me for coming. He'd work hard to get me there, and then he'd be the one thanking me.

A fierce shiver works its way down my spine, sending goose bumps erupting along my arms.

"And make sure you bring a jacket," Sutton adds, eyeing me pointedly as I rub at the goose bumps erupting along my arms. "If you're cold now, it'll just get worse when the sun goes down, right Fisher?"

He rolls his tongue against his bottom lip in the cockiest way, his eyes dancing. The man knows precisely why I'm shivering, and it has nothing to do with the weather.

Fifteen minutes later, Fisher comes to a stop on the side of the road in front of the park—and by park, I mean the open space beside the pier between the inn and the water. It's the perfect spot for such an event, especially if tourists come. The rolling hill off the rickety white deck of the inn is covered in blankets and picnic baskets.

There's even a guitarist sitting on a stool near the building, strumming tunes. I haven't seen him around, but I'm not sure I've met all sixty-eight people on the island yet. I'm just about to ask Fisher about him when Bing barks and takes off toward a loud whistle.

"Yoohoo! Over here!"

Fisher bumps me with the picnic basket, herding us in the opposite direction. "Just ignore him. Bing will find us eventually."

Wilder jogs up to us, gasping for air when he stops. It's an exaggerated display, but I'm smiling, nonetheless. Especially when I see the T-shirt peeking out from under his flannel. It reads: *When God made me, he grinned and said "this will be fun."*

"I won't take that personally," he mumbles to Fisher. "I've got a spot set up over here." With a hand to my back, he steers me toward his blanket.

"We've got our own," Fisher grumbles.

"Oh, Lindsey's here!" Squealing, Sutton takes off.

Fisher deflates, like he knows there's no chance we aren't joining them and he's not thrilled about it.

I don't mind in the least. Being surrounded by people means it'll be easier to avoid looking at the man whose eyes keep boring into me, who's speaking to me in a gentle tone that's as strange coming from him as it would be coming from Betty the goat.

Since the piggyback ride yesterday, it seems as though the man has gone from despising my existence to wanting me around. And I don't know what to do with that. Every time I look at him, I catch him watching me, and the affection in his eyes makes my cheeks heat.

Is this change in his behavior because he feels bad for me? God, I hope not. The idea that he's only being kind because he pities me is far worse than dealing with his annoyed scowls.

"Where's Kennedy?" I ask Wilder.

"She's working off island for the week. She helps out at the clinics on the other islands throughout the summer."

"Hmm." I've never thought about the other islands off the coast. Are they like this one? They couldn't possibly be smaller than Monhegan.

"How's island life?" He drops onto his knees and pats the space beside him. He's like a giant golden retriever. Always smiling, always looking to play. He couldn't be more different from the grump who's currently scowling at him.

As I ease onto the blanket and pull my legs in, Fisher's scowl deepens and he whips out his own blanket, practically setting it on top of Wilder's. He lets out a heavy sigh and shuffles closer. But before he can sit, Bing reappears, taking the spot on the other side of me.

Biting back a smile, I focus my attention on Wilder. "Not too bad. I'm loving the weather now that it's finally getting warmer. Is there a place to go swimming when it gets hot?"

With a frown, Wilder leans forward, peering at his friend. "Fisher hasn't shown you the beach?"

I shake my head. "Oh, no. He doesn't have—"

Wilder winks. "Don't worry, I'll take you to all the good spots."

Fisher grunts and eyes his dog as he settles on the other side of him.

I open my mouth, ready to tease him about it, but snap it shut again when my phone dings. With a muttered *excuse me*, I dig it out of my pocket and look away from both guys and the dog sandwiching me.

> Brad: What the fuck kind of games are you playing? If the money isn't back in my account by morning, you'll regret it.

I frown at the text. What money? I haven't taken any—

The words from the headline materialize in my mind, and I snort. Of course the asshole didn't make that donation. But why does he think I had anything to do with it? The humor dies quickly when I realize that this will just be another thing I have to deal with, and it doesn't even involve me. Though I'd like to kiss whoever did transfer the money to that charity. What sweet karma that is.

"Everything all right?" Fisher asks, peering over Bing.

I press the button on the side of the phone so that the screen goes black and smile. "Everything's perfect. Oh, people are dancing. Want to dance?"

While I do like dancing, the words were the first to come to mind in my effort to distract Fisher from what he may or may not have seen on my phone screen. He's already more interested in my problems than I'd like. The last thing I want is for him to discover what I've been hiding.

"Fisher doesn't dance." Sutton drops to the blanket with a harumph.

Lindsey jumps into her lap, her head tilted and the sweetest smile on her face, and says, "I dance."

Wilder pushes to his feet and offers me a hand. "So do I. Come on, Libby. Let me show you the best thing about this island."

With a snort, I accept his outstretched hand. "The grass?"

He winks as he pulls me close. "No, my moves."

He spins me out and pulls me back in. Then he guides me to a small area in the middle of the park where a few couples are dancing. When the music shifts to a slower ballad, he tugs me close and sways to the music. "Don't look now, but we've got an audience." Despite his command, he spins so I can't miss the way Fisher watches us.

For a moment, lightness fills my chest, but as Lindsey chatters beside us and Sutton laughs in response, I shake it off.

"Yeah, Fisher never takes his eyes off Sutton."

Wilder chuckles, eyes locked on me. "You still don't get it, do you?"

"Get what?"

Brow arched, he looks down at me. "Fisher likes you."

I scoff. "He definitely does not like me."

The smile that splits his lips is wicked. I can see exactly why the tourists enjoy him. I bet he's a lot of fun. "Oh, he likes you, all right."

Flustered, I look away, but doing so puts Fisher right in my line of sight. His stare has turned to a glare, and he doesn't even try to hide it, nor does he look away. Does he like me? Or is he just annoyed with me?

"I'm not dating this summer."

Wilder smirks. "Neither am I, but see that girl over there?" He spins so I'm looking at a group of three women huddled together. One of them, a blonde, is staring daggers at me. "She's not getting the message, so I'm going to pull you a little closer." He tugs me tight against his chest, making it impossible not to feel every ridge and peak of his muscular body. Because he warned me that he'd be touching me, I don't pull away, and because I know this is all for show, I relax into his embrace.

Two beats later, his chest rumbles with laughter.

I pull back and peer up at him, only to be yanked away from his hold by a hand on my waist.

"Time to eat," Fisher grumbles.

My heart stumbles as his scent washes over me. "I don't want to eat. I want to dance."

"Woman says she wants to dance," Wilder teases, grasping my hand in an attempt to spin me away.

Fisher holds tight to my hips. "Fine, then you're dancing with me," he murmurs in my ear. His words, and the teasing breath that escapes when he says them, cause another chill to slide down my arms.

To hide the effect he has on me, I grin and spin in his direction, looping my arms around his neck. "If you wanted to dance so badly, you could have just asked." Behind him, a handful of women are watching, including the one from the bakery, and she doesn't look happy. "Or you could have asked one of them."

Without turning to see who I'm talking about, he tucks an errant hair behind my ear and pulls me close.

As if on cue, the guitarist begins the opening to "Crash" by the Dave Matthews Band.

"I didn't want to dance with them."

I don't argue with him. I don't even question his motives. I just rest my head against his chest and smile, enjoying the feel of his body pressed to mine a little more than I should.

Fisher

Chapter 15

MY VISION BLURS as I stare at the cursor blinking inside the black box on the screen. My fingers should be moving over the keyboard. I should be creating the code I need to slip through the bank's firewall. Instead, I'm humming the tune to that damn Dave Matthews song again. The lyrics—hell, the damn moment—have been on repeat since Libby rested her head on my chest.

The warmth of her body against mine in the cool night. The satin of her skin beneath the pad of my thumb. The way she shivered—and not because of the cold or a spider.

What would it have felt like if I had slipped my hand beneath her thin shirt? Pressed my palm to her bare skin. Tucked her closer. Her hair tickling my neck, her heart pounding against mine. She'd look up at me, and I'd lean down, closing the space.

I blink. Jesus. I should be working. Instead, I'm turning myself on thinking about a fucking dance.

I yank my headphones off and slump back in my chair. Focus is my superpower. Slipping into the world of code, where everything is black and white and controllable, that's what I live for.

Yet right now, I can't do anything but imagine what it would be like to kiss her. To press my lips to hers and finally taste her. Swallow her moan and make her crave me the way I crave her.

Head dropped back, I groan. The move gets Bing's attention. He perks up, eyes on me.

"I know. Looks like I'm not getting anything done tonight." I straighten and switch one of my monitors over from PowerShell to the cameras set up around my house. Do I feel guilty about changing the angle of the camera by my front door to point at Libby's? Not in the least. Brad Fedder is harassing her, and I have no idea how far the famous actor will go. A quick phone ping tells me his Apple ID is still in LA, but that doesn't mean he didn't pay someone to harass Libby. If not for the respect I have for her privacy, I would have gone through every email between them in search of clues about what the fucker did to her on the set of their show.

When the white house next door appears on screen, I scowl.

When I made the donation to the charity from his account, I hadn't even considered that he'd suspect Libby. Not a single string leads back to her or me. Or this island. A person with the skill set to track me would think I was overseas. From the look of things, the guy is just being an ass. Even so, I want to make sure nothing happens to her.

It's after eleven, but there are a couple of lights on inside. I've just zoomed in on her blurry figure standing in the kitchen when she jerks back. Through my open window, her scream is audible half a second later.

My heart stops for one beat. Then I'm on my feet.

I stand, sending my chair clattering to the floor, and fly out of the room.

"Stay with Sutton." I eye Bing as I point to my niece's door.

Once he's lying in her doorway, focus fixed on me, I step into my boots and take off at a sprint. As I race through the grass separating our lawns, my heart pounds in my ears.

I tell myself it could be another spider. Or a shadow. But my gut is screaming that's not the case.

"Libby!" I bellow as I throw open the front door. Fuck. Please let her be okay.

Hands to her chest, she spins to face me. She blinks several times, her full lips parted in shock, either because of the original scare or because of my sudden appearance. Regardless, she's here and breathing.

"Are you okay?" Though my nerves settle slightly, I'm still shaking as I eat up the distance from the door to her kitchen, inspecting her for injury. She's wearing an oversized white crewneck, and she's barefoot. The tiniest shorts I've ever seen highlight her toned legs.

I have to fight a groan. Because she doesn't just look fine, she looks fucking gorgeous. "You screamed."

With another blink, she points to the shattered window that faces my house.

"You broke the window?" Jesus, I thought she'd been attacked.

"I didn't," she growls. "It shattered out of the blue. One minute, it was fine. The house was quiet. And the next, glass was flying."

Huffing, I take a step closer to the damage. If not for the tightness in her features, I'd be sure she's fucking with me. Windows don't just shatter.

"It scared me," she whispers.

Heart aching in the strangest way, I cup the back of her neck and pull her against me. She comes without argument, instantly burrowing into my chest and sighing. The move causes that ache to morph into a deeper pang. I shouldn't love that she scares easily, but I can't deny that I treasure once again getting to hold this woman in my arms.

I drop my head and press my lips to her crown. "It's okay, Princess. I'll figure out what happened."

She clears her throat and pulls back, shoulders tightening. Damn, she looks cute putting on a brave face. "It just broke. Maybe one of the million birds that won't leave me alone flew into it."

I cock my head to the side. "You feed the birds every day."

She throws her hands up with a huff. "I know, and yet instead of leaving when they're satisfied, they keep begging for more."

My eye twitches. Is she fucking with me?

By the way she frowns and shrugs helplessly, I don't think so.

Crossing my arms, I rock back on my heels. "I don't think you understand birds."

"That's definitely true." With a nod, she steps around me toward the window.

I catch her arm. "What are you doing?" God dammit. She's barefoot and she's trying to get *closer* to the broken glass? Does she have any sense of self-preservation at all?

Brow furrowed, she lifts her chin. "I'm going to check out what happened and clean it up."

"No you're not." I loop an arm around her stomach and pick her up, then back away.

"Why are you always carrying me?" she huffs.

"Because someone needs to take care of you." And I'll be damned if it's anyone but me.

She glares. "I'm perfectly capable of cleaning up a mess, and I'm perfectly capable of taking care of myself." She stomps over to the closet, her hips swaying in the teeny-tiny pink shorts that are going to haunt me for days.

I turn away and mentally recite lines of code to keep my body from reacting. As I step closer to the window, glass cracks under my boots. A bird didn't do this. Half the window is lying in shards on the floor. Hands on my hips, I study the jagged pieces still attached to the frame, then scour the floor.

My heart lurches when I see it.

Fuck.

Crouching, I pick up the softball-size rock. This is exactly what I was afraid of. "Didn't break itself, Princess." I stand to my full height and heft the weapon used to shatter the window.

Across the room, her eyes drift closed. Her lip trembles and she curls in on herself, but only for an instant. She swallows audibly and pulls her shoulders back, and when she opens her eyes, they're clear of any inkling of fear.

"Kids and their pranks." Despite her bravado, her voice cracks on the word *pranks*.

I move across the room, dropping the rock on her blue Formica countertop as I go. Every part of me wants to offer her another hug. Give her some sense of safety.

But she steps back as I approach, making it clear she doesn't want me to touch her. Message received. I will, however, do everything I can to make sure she feels safe.

I take the broom from her and turn to get started on the mess. She doesn't say anything, but her attention on me is palpable as I sweep up the glass. Once I've dumped it into the trash, I zero in on her. "Get your shit."

"What?" she crosses her arms.

"I'm not leaving you here, and Sutton's alone next door. Get your shit. You're coming to my house."

She opens her mouth to argue, but I cut her off.

"I will carry you out of here if I need to, but I will not leave you here alone when someone is clearly fucking with you. If you want anything for the night, get it," I growl.

"You're so bossy," she snaps as she spins around and stomps off. In less than a minute, she's back, wearing flip-flops, with her phone in her hand.

When we're out in the cool night air, I pull the front door shut behind me and engage the cheap lock. Looks like I'll need to borrow Cank's boat again so I can install deadbolts on all her doors. Not to mention get a few more cameras.

"Why are you up?"

Her voice is quiet, but in the dark silence, it startles me. Maybe I should hedge around the question, but after tonight, after what I did to her costar, I have a feeling I'll need to give her some truths I don't share with anyone.

"I'm breaking into a bank."

With an adorable snort, she shakes her head. "Sure you are. Very sheriffy of you."

Exactly. I have no law enforcement qualifications. I didn't even think to put on a pair of gloves before I picked up that rock. I'm such a dumbass. The only thing I know is code.

Unsure of how to respond, I guide her across the yard silently.

As we step into my house, I nod at the stairs. "You can stay in my room."

Her blue eyes narrow, and she takes a half a step away.

I bite back a chuckle. "I'll be on the couch."

"Your house only has two bedrooms?" She scans the main living area. She's been in here before. She knows this house and hers have the same footprint.

"My office," I mutter as I herd her toward the stairs.

"Is there a Mrs. Fisher I should be worried about?"

My muscles go taut, and though I shouldn't be upset that she'd think so little of me, there's no denying the anger that ripples through my body. I pull in a breath through my nose and turn back to her. "Do you think I'm the type of man who would dance with a woman, then offer her my bed if I was *married*?"

Jesus. I may not possess the social skills most people do, but I'm not oblivious to what's appropriate and what's not, and I'm not an asshole.

Lips pressed together, she focuses on a picture of Sutton and Marissa on the mantel.

That's when it all clicks.

"That's my sister-in-law." I scratch at the back of my neck, willing the unease creeping through me to abate. "She and my brother died a few years ago."

Libby's breath hitches, but rather than respond, she silently surveys the room.

"So," I say, eager to move on, "this way?"

At the top of the stairs, she turns toward my open office door. My gut sinks. Shit. Will she be upset about the camera I have pointed at her house?

A relieved breath escapes me when I peek into the room behind her and discover the screen protectors have kicked on. All she can see is the white ball bouncing around the black screen, and without my fingerprint, the computer can't be unlocked.

That little scare should encourage me to mention the cameras I plan to install, but it's late, and after the stress of the last thirty minutes, I figure it can wait until morning.

Bing slinks down the hall, and after a quick pat to his back, I tiptoe to Sutton's room. Everything settles inside me when I find her curled up and sleeping soundly under her pink quilt.

"That's a lot of screens," Libby says as I step back into my office.

Again, I decide not to lie. "When working through multiple firewalls, it's easier to have multiple portals open."

She licks her lips, her attention darting away from me. "What do you do exactly?"

I shrug. "Fuck with people and make their days miserable."

Her lips part, but before she can respond, a yawn cuts her off.

"Come on, Princess. Let's get you into bed." I lead her to my bedroom and pull back the comforter.

She's frozen in the doorway, her eyes bouncing from the watercolors on the walls, to the thick blue plaid bedding, to the matching drapes. That's all there is to see here. The space looks exactly like it did when it was a guest room. The only difference is the closet and dressers are now full of my clothes.

"There's an extra blanket on the rack." I tip my head to the navy quilt.

Bing jumps up onto the bed, ready to make himself at home.

"Down."

"No," Libby says, taking a hesitant step forward. "He can stay."

"Be aware," I warn, "he's a bed hog."

She giggles. "I don't mind." She plops onto the mattress next to my dog, who buries his nose in her abdomen.

Fuck. How pathetic is it to be jealous of a damn dog?

I turn, hands in my pockets, and shuffle toward the door.

"*Fisher.*"

Pulling up short, I spin and meet her eyes. They're sparkling, but not in the dreamy, wondrous way I've seen so many times since she arrived. No, this is an overwhelmed sparkle. Her wide eyes are wet like she might cry if I don't leave the room.

She swallows audibly, hands buried in Bing's fur. "Thank you."

Her voice is so soft and she looks so lost. Fuck. If I don't get out of the room now, I'll be in trouble. So I simply nod and head for my office.

Once I'm situated behind my desk again, I get back to work quickly, this time leaving my headphones on the table rather than covering my ears. Just in case she needs me. I expect my focus to still be shit, but oddly enough, knowing Libby is just down the hall settles me.

In less than two hours, my job is done. I push to my feet, stretching. The move rouses Bing, who watches me from his spot on the floor. I hadn't even heard him come in.

Before heading down to the couch, I stop at my open bedroom door.

Libby's blond hair is bright against my dark pillow. She's on her side, facing the door, with her hands tucked under her cheek. Before I can stop myself, I'm at her side, pressing my lips to her forehead.

"Sleep well, Princess." I straighten and back away. And damn if leaving the room might be the hardest thing I've done in a long time.

Libby

Chapter 16

THE HEAVY WEIGHT settled against me eases me from unconsciousness. Eyes closed, I turn my head and inhale the warm male scent. It's clean, with a hint of something spicy. *Fisher.* I'm cocooned in him.

I blink, forcing my eyes open, surprisingly content with his presence beside me in bed. Vision blurry, I reach out. When I'm met with nothing but empty sheets, I push myself up. Quickly, I discover that my movement is restricted by the giant dog sprawled across my legs. Bing lifts his head and wags his tail, his mouth falling open in the canine equivalent of a smile.

It's not Fisher keeping me warm, just his dog.

The disappointment that surges is ridiculous. I love dogs. I don't love Fisher. I should be happy he didn't sneak into his own bed last night. *That* would have been a red flag. Besides, Fisher doesn't even like me. He might tolerate me—and that's an upgrade from the disdain he showed me until a day or two ago. He may feel this need to protect me—and, strangely enough, I like it—but he doesn't like *me.*

Or maybe he does.

The man is confusing. He barely talks, and when he does, it's to complain. But he keeps showing up.

At the realization that I was hoping it was Fisher beside me, a pit settles in my stomach. I try to ignore it by stroking Bing's fur. "Hey, buddy. Thanks for letting me sleep here last night."

He army crawls up my body, and when we're face to face, he greets me with sloppy doggy kisses.

Laughter bubbles out of me. I wish I could have a dog. With the hours on set, it's never been possible. Though I have all the time in the world now. While my agent continues to leave messages about cleaning up my image, I've yet to hear a word about potential projects. It seems I'm no longer Hollywood's darling. My, how quickly the community I've been part of my whole life has turned on me.

"You wouldn't turn on me, would you?"

Bing licks my outstretched hand and lays his head on my chest, his dark eyes fixed on me. No, I don't suppose this dog would even know how to turn on someone. He's too loving. Too sweet.

Just like I used to be.

Trusting. Loyal. Naive.

For years I kept my mouth shut and dealt with the unwanted advances, all because I was too afraid to rock the boat.

The job of every person on that set depended upon me. Outside of my dad and Brad's parents, the only family I ever had worked on set.

And I was right. The moment I said something, the moment I had the audacity to say no, I was fired.

I sink back into the mattress and inhale Fisher's scent. He wouldn't have kept his mouth shut. He'd never have allowed another person to dictate his life.

Then again, when a man acts like a grump, he's considered broody and desirable. Someone to win over. If a woman tried it? She'd be labeled a bitch.

I suppose I should get up. Even if the idea of seeing Fisher this morning has me all sorts of twisted.

He's convinced I'm not safe. That someone is trying to scare me.

It could be Brad, though I don't understand why he won't leave me alone. If he's behind the rock through my window and the other strange happenings, how did he find out where I am? And wouldn't he prefer I stay off the grid like this? The longer I'm gone, the easier his lies are to weave. Sadly, I can't get myself to care. Not enough to go back and fight, anyway.

I'm in no rush to go anywhere. I'm set for life financially, so the next time I work, it will be on a project I truly care about. One I'm passionate about. For so long, I've done what I'm told. I don't even know what I'd choose for myself anymore.

While I came here to escape, to run away from my life, what I've discovered isn't a hiding place, but a place where I can start over. Here, I have the time and the privacy to figure out who I am when I'm not pretending to be someone else.

Who the hell is Elizabeth Sweet?

Who do I even want to be?

I shift, figuring I should probably get up rather than having deep, existential thoughts while lying in someone else's bed. Instantly, Bing jumps off me and bounces to the floor, running in circles, clearly excited to start the day.

He probably needs to go out.

I slip out from beneath the covers and run my fingers through my hair. It's pointless, really. Fisher probably won't even notice how I look, let alone care that my hair isn't brushed.

Silently, I creep to the door and peek out into the hall. From here, the faint sound of cartoons floats through the air. I follow the noise downstairs to the living room, where Sutton is curled up beneath a blanket, watching television.

Does she already know I'm here? Shoot. I don't have the first clue how to explain my presence. I glance toward the back of the house, willing Fisher to appear and give her an explanation, but the kitchen is quiet. Where is he?

"You looking for Fisher?" Sutton asks in a sleepy, unsurprised voice. Normally when the girl greets me, she's all smiles and squeals.

"Yup." I point to the stairs. "He let me stay here last night because my house was—" I snap my mouth shut. I don't need to terrify her by telling her that someone may have tried to break into my house. "I, uh, I saw another spider."

She gives me an indulgent smile. "You really don't like spiders, huh?"

"I really don't."

She curls up into a tighter ball. "Come sit. Fisher went to get donuts."

I pad across the room and sit beside her. "You didn't want to go pick out your own donuts?"

She shakes her head and her little button nose scrunches. "I don't like how Flora talks to Fisher. Her voice gets high-pitched like this. *Fisher*—" Her voice takes on a sultry tone that has a shudder rolling down my spine. "It gives me the heebie-jeebies," she finishes.

"Does he like her?" I don't know how I feel about that. Any connection between Fisher and the donut woman—*Flora, apparently* —is none of my business. But that doesn't stop my stomach from rising up into my throat when I imagine Fisher smiling at her the same way he did at me when we were dancing.

Sutton scrunches her nose again. "I don't *think* so. He should like you. I like you. And then you could sleep over *all* the time."

I cough out a laugh. "That's not how it works."

"But it could. Sounds like you've got a spider problem at your house. We don't have a spider problem here." She crosses her fingers, apparently not realizing I can see her hands. Or maybe assuming I wasn't once a little girl who did the same thing when I told a fib.

My stomach sinks at the implication. If she's fibbing, that means they do have a spider problem. Shoulders tense, I turn, scanning my surroundings to make sure there aren't any creepy-crawlies nearby.

"Then we could have donuts together all the time and I would never have to have dinner at Flora's house and we'd be like a real family."

Any concern I had about bugs flies out the window at her words. "Sutton—"

She shakes her head, cutting me off. "It would be so much fun, Libby. Please."

"You only have two bedrooms, and I don't think Fisher wants to sleep on the couch every night. But I'm right next door, and I'm always happy to hang with you."

She frowns. "We have a third bedroom."

Lips pursed, I tilt my head and sneak a peek up the stairs. "You do?" Then why did Fisher put me in his room? Why did he give me his bed, then sleep on the couch?

Sutton looks away, her shoulders sagging. "Yeah, but he never opens the door to it."

"Huh?"

Tiny fingers pick at the fabric of her blanket as she keeps her focus downcast. "My parents' room. He won't even open the door, but everything inside is exactly like they left it."

Oh, Fisher. My heart cracks for both of them. For the man trying his best to raise a heartbroken little girl, all the while probably struggling with his own loss. Grief is so damn difficult. There's no right way to handle it. Reality ebbs and flows, mingling with doses of the past. The tiniest flicker of a memory can derail an entire day. One moment you're laughing, and the next, it's impossible to breathe. A joke can lift your spirits, only to be undercut by a few simple notes from *their* song as a car with its windows down rolls by.

That's how grief feels now, at least for me. As a child, I was desperate to hold on to every memory I had. I hoarded every item my mother had ever touched, hoping that holding it would bring even the most fleeting comfort.

I inch closer to Sutton, and as if she knows I need it, she rolls out from under her blanket and snuggles up against me. "But you go in there? Because it makes you feel closer to them?"

"I don't remember them. Not really." She takes a heavy breath for such a small person. "Maybe small things, like how Dad smelled like the ocean. And Mom's laugh. But that's it."

God, do I wish I could remember my mother's laugh. So many years later, I think it's more of an impression of a memory than the real thing.

Sutton's blue eyes shine as she studies me. "Is that bad?"

I strum my fingers through her silky blond strands. "No, pretty girl." My voice cracks. "That's just what happens. Time goes on and memories fade. I hardly remember my mom. That's why I'm here this summer, even if no one wants me here. I stay because this island holds my last memories of her."

Frowning, she grasps my wrist. "*I'm* glad that you're here. I don't know anyone else who's lost their parents. It's nice to have someone to talk to about it."

God. My heart squeezes, and I have to inhale through my mouth to keep from crying.

I rest my head against hers and close my eyes. "I'm always here to talk, pretty girl."

I may not have the answers, but like Fisher, I want to be here for her. Even that feels selfish, though, because just this simple talk means more to me than she could ever know.

Fisher
Chapter 17

"WELL, look what the cat dragged in." Flora leans forward, resting her elbows on the butcher-block counter.

If I bother to look away from the donuts in the glass case, I'm sure I'll be met with an eyeful of cleavage. But I have no interest. Wish she would take a freaking hint.

"I put two double chocolate donuts aside in case you came."

They're Sutton's favorites, and the spot in the case where they usually sit is empty, so despite how much I don't want to be, I'm grateful for the annoying woman.

"Wasn't sure you'd be in," she continues in that high-pitched nasally voice that makes me wish I'd brought my noise-canceling headphones.

"Always here on Ruckus donut days," I grumble.

Sutton wouldn't let me miss it. Her big blue eyes would go dull, just like they did the day of the funeral. And that helpless sensation would wash over me. My job is to make her happy, to make sure she lives her best life. If that means I drag my ass to this shop and deal with Flora, then so be it. Every Thursday and Sunday.

"Hey, Sheriff." Cank steps through the door, pulling his hat from his head. He tucks it into the pocket of his overalls and pulls out a dog treat. "Where's my boy?"

"Home." I didn't love leaving the girls, but I adjusted my camera settings and turned on notifications, so my phone will alert me if anyone even steps onto my grass. Bing is the extra level of protection, so I left him behind.

"Saw you dancing with Libby last night." Cank waggles his brows as he holds Bing's treat out to me.

I keep my expression flat. The last thing I need is the gossip mill working overtime.

"Now that the island knows you dance, I'm sure your card will be full every Saturday." Flora taps my arm with a bag. "You'll have to save me a dance next week."

I frown. "Doubt I'll dance again." I take the bag but set it on the counter between us. "I need a few extras today." I try not to scowl. "Please."

"Got some company, huh?" Cank chuckles as he pats my shoulder. "I bet someone will be a happy man this summer."

I heave out a sigh and consider faking an emergency to get the fuck out of here.

Flora crosses her arms, one brow arched, waiting. Right, the donuts. I'm not sure if Libby likes chocolate, so I figured I'd get a variety. I should have looked on that stupid site Sutton found that listed all of Libby's favorite things. I can't very well ask Flora to wait while I look it up on my phone. Not without making this encounter even more uncomfortable.

So with a deep inhale, I point at the case.

"Can I have one espresso cream, one Berkshire maple, one tiramisu, and one strawberry shortcake?"

"Oh, you're having Wilder over." Flora beams as she eases a donut into the bakery box she's pulled out for my ridiculously large order. "That man can eat his weight in donuts. Give him my love."

With a grunt, I take the box. I have no idea why she thinks Wilder is coming, nor am I giving him anyone's love.

"By the way, Sheriff." Cank shifts, his boots scuffing the old wooden floors. "There are a few packages over on the Boothbay dock waiting for pickup. Apparently, Ms. Sweet ordered some stuff from Amazon."

I sigh. Libby hasn't mentioned ordering anything, but if I know her, she probably assumes the magic ferries that have yet to show up with her luggage will also deliver the packages.

"I'll take care of it." I tap my card against the reader, and the second *approved* flashes on the screen, I stomp out.

Keeping my eyes down and a scowl on my face, I hurry down the street. If I look cranky enough, there's a good chance no one will stop me. It's summer vacation, and with Sutton out of school, I don't even have enough words for her, let alone anyone else.

Maybe I'll have her FaceTime with my parents this afternoon. My mother loves chatting with her. I sometimes wonder why my brother didn't leave his perfect little sweet pea with them. But they had been down in Florida at a fifty-five plus community for two years when he passed. Even if Hunter had been open to Sutton growing up in Florida, they would have had to move. Instead, they come up for a couple weeks every year.

Bing perks up from where he's lounging on the porch. His presence outside means Libby's awake. He rushes down the steps and circles my legs as I trek through the half-dead grass. The lack of rain this summer isn't doing the lawn any favors.

"Yea, I have your treat." I've barely got it out of my pocket before he snatches it out of my hand. "You act like you haven't eaten in a year." My hand is on the screen door handle when Sutton's voice filters out.

"No. He won't even open the door, but everything inside is exactly like they left it."

I wince. She has to be talking about her parents' room. I shut the door the day I moved in and haven't opened it a single time since. Sutton knows she's free to go in, free to use the room. But I'm living enough of my brother's life. I can't take over his room too.

116

"Do you go in there because it makes you feel closer to them?" Libby's voice is gentle, careful.

"I don't remember them. Not really." Sutton pauses. "Maybe small things, like how Dad smelled like the ocean. And Mom's laugh. But that's it." When she falls silent again, I lean closer to the door, my chest aching. "Is that bad?"

Silently, I watch them. They're curled up together, and Libby is running her fingers lightly through Sutton's blond hair.

"No, pretty girl," she almost whispers. "That's just what happens. Time goes on and memories fade. I hardly remember my mom. That's why I'm here this summer, even if no one wants me here. I stay because this island holds my last memories of her."

"*I'm* glad you're here. I don't know anyone else who's lost their parents. It's nice to have someone to talk to about it."

"I'm always here to talk pretty girl." Libby rests her head against the top of my niece's.

Guilt rises in my throat. I wasn't thrilled when I found out she'd be here for the summer, and I was anything but welcoming when she got here. She's being threatened by a costar and tormented by someone trying to scare her off the island, and all she wants is to spend time in the place that holds memories of her mother. On top of all that, she's made time for Sutton without complaint.

Damn, I'm a jerk. That changes now. Libby won't stay past September, but while she's here, I will make sure she knows she's wanted every day. And not just by Sutton and me.

I've already spoken with Doris who, moving forward, will order anything Libby wants without so much as a frown, and if she can't get something, she'll come to me. I'll pick up Libby's packages, and I'll make sure the dock hand in Boothbay has my cell so I'm alerted if she orders more. And I will have a sit-down with anyone who doesn't actively work to make Libby smile.

I clear my throat, then step through the door. "Donuts have arrived."

Sutton pops up and tosses her arms in the air. "Yes!" She dances in a circle. "You got double chocolate, right?"

"Two of them. And I got one of everything else so you two can have a donut party." I force a cheerful tone, though by the way they both freeze and stare at me, I fear I've missed the mark.

"What's wrong with you?" Sutton frowns.

"Huh?"

"I don't know." She purses her lips. "You sound like you sucked air from a balloon or something."

I scoff, heat creeping up my neck. "No, I don't."

"Not anymore. It was just that weird voice before. Don't do that again." She skips over, takes the box from my hands, and wanders to the table. "Come on, Libby. Which one do you want?"

The woman I can't stop thinking about pushes to her feet and pads over to Sutton. "I don't know if I want Flirty Donuts."

The fuck?

"They're Ruckus Donuts. Everyone loves them."

"I think she means because Flora is always being..." With her hands tucked under her chin, my niece bats her eyes and makes a kissy face.

"According to Sutton, the donut lady is always flirting with you." Libby averts her gaze, her lips pulling down, almost like she's pouting. *Like she's jealous.*

My chest swells at the idea, and the corners of my lips turn up. I don't get to enjoy the feeling long, though, before Sutton whirls on me.

"Don't even try to deny it." She wags a finger my way, then cups her mouth and stage whispers, "And he doesn't even stop it."

Lips pursed, Libby crosses her arms over her chest.

What the hell? I came in trying to be nice, and now I'm in the hot seat. I don't even like the freaking woman. She makes my skin crawl. I can't say that now, though, because Sutton, a.k.a. the worst secret keeper in the world, will tell the entire town.

"That's not true. I've tried to stop her. But there are only four of us within flirting age for her on this island. I'm sure she flirts with Wilder too."

Sutton rolls her eyes, making her look sixteen rather than eight. "Everyone flirts with Wilder. He's everyone's favorite."

Libby chuckles, and when I scowl at her, she puts both hands up. "I don't flirt with your bestie."

That wasn't what I meant. Whatever.

"Eat the damn donuts." I point at the table and huff. I try to be nice, and they gang up on me.

Libby drops into the seat next to Sutton and picks up the Berkshire maple pastry.

"That's your friend's donut," Sutton says as she picks up a double chocolate for herself. "Joey Berkshire. They send the donut people their maple syrup. Everyone loves those."

"Everything the Berkshires make is amazing." Libby takes a bite, and the moan that leaves her lips sends blood rushing to my dick.

Fuck, I'd love to hear that sound when I have her spread out in front of me.

"This is heaven." She licks her lip. Jesus, I swear I can feel it. Like she's running her tongue along my skin.

I shake myself out of my haze. "I thought you weren't going to eat my donuts."

"Is that a smile, Fisher?" Libby taunts, her eyes sparkling. "Should I take another bite and see if you can do it again?" She brings the doughy goodness to her mouth again. "Do you like watching me eat?"

With a grumble, I spin and head for the door. The girls giggle behind me, but as I step outside, I can't help but smile.

Libby

Chapter 18

I IMAGINE BEING HERE on Monhegan Island is the closest I'll ever get to being able to tap my red shoes and wish I wasn't famous. The number of times through the years I've wished for privacy is immeasurable—whether I wanted to go shopping on my own on a whim or out on a date without having to shield myself from camera flashes. Celebrity status, unfortunately, means giving up just about all semblance of privacy. But here, even going to the grocery store on my own—despite Doris's now indifferent attitude —is like a breath of fresh air.

It's been a month since I arrived, and finally, I'm feeling settled and enjoying the freedom. I'd be lying if I denied that part of my happiness can be attributed to the smiles I keep catching on Fisher's lips.

When he drops off a donut at my house in the morning, swearing they bought too many, I get glimpses of smiles when he walks away. And when he pulls off the road in town when he sees me walking and insists I hop in, I swear his lips tip up as I round the hood. Though by the time I climb in, he's wiped the expression away. It's like he waits until he thinks I'm not looking to enjoy the moment.

I've found myself viewing every interaction differently. Wondering what will bring about another smile.

It's exactly how I thought my mother would have handled Fisher. That thought makes my heart float in my chest. Maybe the island really is helping bring her closer to me. Reminding me of who I want to be.

There's still plenty of the old Libby left. I can't imagine not being giddy when I open the door and find a package waiting. To my utter surprise, Amazon delivers all the way out here, twelve miles from shore.

The peach nail polish I ordered three days ago is currently being used as a prop in the play. "Should I actually paint Marty's nails?" Sutton asks from the stage.

She's playing the role of Frenchie, as well as Putzie and Mrs. Murdock. When I asked why we were doing a play with more characters than the number of residents on the island, Maggie looked at me like I'd lost my marbles. "Don't worry, the townspeople will be in the chorus."

"But who will watch the play?"

She smiled her adorable smile, like she found my confusion endearing. "It's called a participatory performance."

I googled the term later that night.

Now, Maggie glances at me for input.

I nod. "Not a bad idea. And the color totally goes with your skin tone."

Rowan, who is playing the role of Marty, sighs heavily. "Why do I have to be a *girl?*"

From beside me, Maggie hollers back, "Fix that attitude. You're supposed to be excited about the dance. She's doing your hair and your make-up, and you get to wear a dress!"

"Oh goodie," he grumbles.

As they run the scene again, Maggie looks at me, lips pursed. "You agree, right? They need to be more energized."

"You're asking the wrong person. While I used to love dressing up and doing my makeup, I'm perfectly content to slap on a layer of sunscreen and a pair of shorts and a tee before I leave the house."

"Guess that's good since you can't really get any of the stuff you're used to off-island," Maggie says, her attention set on the kids. "I wish we had the good stuff. Or that I even knew how to use it."

I shift in my seat and study her, confused by more than one part of that statement. "First, I can help you with your makeup. Show you some tricks. You don't need expensive products if you know what you're doing."

Maggie's green eyes lighten. "Really? You'd be willing to help me?"

"Of course. I'll order what we need from amazon. It will be here in like two days."

Maggie snorts. "What?"

"Amazon," I say with a frown. Are there seriously people in this country who don't have Prime packages delivered almost daily? "Ya know, the website that can deliver just about anything to your door?"

Maggie tilts her head, assessing me, then gives it a shake. "I don't want you to waste your time. It's not like I'll ever have anywhere to go."

"What about a date?" I suggest. "I always like getting pretty for a date."

Maggie's cheeks pink, and she looks away. "Oh, I've never been on one of those."

Never been on a date? Wow. I knew Maggie was innocent, but she's got to be in her mid-twenties like me. "Not even with Wilder?"

The pink turns into a crimson flush, and her expression oscillates between *are you fucking kidding me?* to *holy shit how'd you know?*

And I do know. Her little crush on her best friend's brother may be a secret, but I can see the way she looks at him.

Though I can't imagine watching him with a different tourist every weekend is any fun. I'm at a loss for what to say, feeling like I probably just put my foot in my mouth, when Sutton squeals. "Fisher!"

The name alone should not send a frisson of excitement straight to my toes, but my heart takes off, nevertheless.

He stands in the doorway, the sun a halo of light behind him, exaggerating his rugged features. He grunts by way of greeting and dips his chin.

"You coming to watch, or are you here to practice your part in the chorus?" I ask, my voice echoing loudly across the space.

Fisher steps inside, his shadow shifting into color. "Chorus?"

Maggie giggles. "Oh, Fisher doesn't sing."

Sutton bounces off the stage and skips past us. "Is it time yet?" she asks as she approaches him. "Do you have it?"

"Have what?" I ask, my feet forcing me their way, like there's a magnet attached to the two of them, pulling me in. The magical pull they possess also causes my lips to tip up in a smile that spans my face. A current flows through my blood, making every step I take feel like I'm walking on a cloud.

As I get closer, the blurred lines of Fisher's features turn vibrant. He's wearing jeans and one of his standard shirts, the kind that shows off his biceps when his arms are crossed.

His lips twitch in one of those smiles that makes me melt. "Your golf cart," he says, the three-word sentence probably the longest he's spoken all day.

"You got a golf cart?" Maggie asks, sidling up beside me.

My chest constricts. "I know summer people normally don't—"

Sutton grabs my hand and yanks. "It's pink! I saw it this morning. Can I drive it?"

"Sure," I say, just as Fisher growls, "Absolutely not."

Sutton snaps her head back, her gaze ping-ponging between the two of us.

"Why not?" I take a step closer to the growly man. At least he's consistent. Smiling one minute, then barely tolerating me the next.

He puts his hands on his hips, his eyes narrowing. "Do *you* even know how to drive it?"

As I position myself another step closer, the air around us charges. If I reached out right now, I could press my palm to his chest. If I tipped my head just a bit higher, his breath would fan against my lips. "I know how to drive."

He lifts a brow, angling his chin so we're nose to nose. "A golf cart?" The words skirt against my mouth. Without my permission, my tongue slides across my bottom lip, desperate for a taste of his arrogance.

"Are you gonna kiss?" The question comes from the stage. From Rowan, to be exact.

Breath catching, I step back, only now noticing that we've garnered an audience.

It looks like even in Monhegan, privacy is hard to come by.

"Of course not." With another of his signature grunts, Fisher storms out of the theater.

I stand there speechless, too shocked to be upset about the rejection.

Before I can sort out my emotions, his disembodied voice echoes through the theater. "Well, you coming?"

Sutton bounces on her toes. "Bet you he lets us drive it home."

Lets us. Internally, I scoff. He's not the boss of me.

She darts for the door, and I follow with Maggie at my side.

"We done with practice?" I cringe as I turn to my new friend. I don't want to shirk my responsibilities, but—

"Oh yeah. Fisher teaching you how to drive the—*pink golf cart?*" Her voice pitches higher as my gorgeous new ride comes into view. "I wouldn't miss this for the world."

The second I saw it online, I knew I had to have it. I wasn't sure it would make it all the way to the island, and I definitely didn't expect it to come so quickly. It seems all my packages are being delivered within a couple of days. That's a big change from the days before tourists started showing up.

Fisher stands beside it, the keys in his hand, his lip quirked in what constitutes a cocky smirk for him. "Let me see you turn it on." He nods at it.

With a haughty *ha*, I snatch the key from his hand. "Just you wait and see how good I am at this." I hop in and stick the key in the hole. "Step back."

The smile that splits Fisher's face is so big, a dimple I never knew he had pops. Damn. I'm tempted to take a picture. "You sure about that?"

With a roll of my eyes, I step on the gas, and the golf cart whizzes —*absolutely nowhere*. It doesn't even jolt forward. I push down harder, but it doesn't budge. "What the—"

"Want me to show you how it's done?" he rumbles in a quiet tone as he steps up beside me and hovers close.

I appreciate the low volume, since we have an audience, but with his chest pressed to my upper arm, the low notes vibrate through my sternum and send sparks of electricity to my core, making it hard to see straight.

"Sure, fine," I say, my voice reedy and my throat tight.

He talks me through how to go forward and how to reverse, pointing out the lever by my legs that has to be engaged to move.

"Do you want to drive home?" he asks me.

Once again I find myself dizzy from not only his proximity but his words.

Home.

He asked me if I want to drive home. As if this place is my home.

I shake my head. "Maybe you can show me again."

"Hop on, Sutton," Fisher calls, completely oblivious to the way he affects me.

We're stopped a total of ten times as we make our way through town. Everyone has a comment about my pink golf cart—which they assume is Fisher's. Over and over, they tease him, and each time he grunts rather than deny it, I feel a little more like myself.

When we pass the docks, Cank waves us down. "I see you been getting all your packages okay." He gives the top of the cart a slap.

"Yes. I'm impressed that Amazon delivers right to my door all the way out here. You must appreciate not having to deal with all my packages now that summer is here."

Cank tilts his head, his brows dipping low, but he doesn't respond.

Fisher doesn't join in on the conversation either, and after an awkward moment of silence, I clear my throat.

"Will I see you tonight at the lobster bake?"

He laughs. "Wouldn't miss it."

Fisher hits the lever to reverse and pulls away from the dock, then makes the final turn toward our shared road. "You're going to the lobster bake tonight?"

"Yeah, the guys at the dock told me I should come. Apparently there'll be dancing again and you know how I love to dance."

He pulls into my driveway, and the second he comes to a stop, Sutton jumps off and shouts that she's got to pee as she darts across the yard. Thirty seconds later, the screen door slams.

I laugh. "She's a handful."

Without a word, Fisher steps off the cart then turns, like he's waiting for me to follow. I slide into the driver's seat and glance up at him.

"Be ready at six thirty."

I blink. "For what?"

He bows his head and sighs like I've exhausted him. "The lobster bake."

"You're going?"

"Yes. I'll drive you."

I grin as I shift into reverse. "No need. I've got the golf cart. I can drive myself."

He grunts. "Which is why I'm picking you up. You don't know how to drive this yet."

"Does the sheriff give out golf cart licenses too?" I tease.

With a shake of his head, he turns so he's facing the house, but I can see the smile pulling at his lips again. "Be ready at six thirty."

With another laugh, I press on the gas, jolting backward, then slam on the brakes.

He spins around again, those damn lips twitching. "You ready to go home yet, Princess?" The words come out smooth this time, the fire in his eyes telling me has no interest in me leaving.

I laugh as I press on the gas, jerking backward again. "Nope. Not yet!"

Fisher

Chapter 19

THE RINGING in my ears startles the shit out of me. I jerk back, heart hammering, and yank my headphones off. On instinct, I search the monitor set to watch Libby's house. But it's not showing a motion notification. No one is there.

It's just the alarm I set to ensure I'm not late.

I rub a hand down my face, shaking off the shock. Maybe if I hadn't set the alarm's volume to the highest setting, I wouldn't be drowning in adrenaline, but then it could have easily become background noise, and I'm an expert at tuning that shit out. And the last thing I want is to be late for the girls.

An hour and a half ago, when Libby came by asking if Sutton wanted to get ready for the lobster bake with her, I welcomed the plan. Alone, I've had more time to work. And this way I won't have to deal with hacking Langfield Corp's email later tonight.

I didn't know much about Langfield Corp before agreeing to this job, but I learned quickly that everything the Boston billionaires who own the company have is the best. Including their cyber security. Their firewall is intriguing. It's different in so many ways from the systems most massive corporations use. That alone means that what should have taken me thirty or forty minutes took the entire hour and a half. Mostly because I spent too much time fascinated by how the Langfields' system operates and exploring ways to work around it.

A smile threatens as I hit the last few strokes that prove that as high-end as the firewall is, it's no match for me.

Not that anyone at Langfield Corp will know who the ghost that left them the parting gift is.

I rub my hands together just as my second alarm blares through the headphones sitting on the desk. I grab my phone and silence it, then shoot off a single text.

Me: I win.

Now that I've finished, I have to get the girls to a lobster bake.

Quickly, I toss on a clean white T-shirt and run my hands through my hair, then stride across the yard. I'm climbing the porch steps when the door opens.

"Thought it was six thirty sharp," Libby teases from the threshold.

I can't form an answer because, holy shit, one look at the gorgeous woman in front of me, and all the circuits in my brain short out.

Between the short pink sundress that clings to her perky tits, the long, wavy blond hair, and huge blue eyes sparkling at me, I can't decide where to focus. Everything about her is perfect.

"Did I take your breath away, growly bear?"

With a huff of a laugh, I climb the three steps and stop in front of her. A breeze rushes past us, bringing with it a hint of cold, and she shivers, her body breaking out in goose bumps.

On instinct, I brush a lock of hair from her face so I can see her pretty eyes. "Growly bear?" I cock a brow and lean in. Instantly, I'm hit with a whiff of her sweet scent. My stomach tightens and a desire to wrap an arm around her, to tuck her against me, almost takes over.

She shrugs, but I swear she shifts impossibly closer. "Yeah, that's not it. But I'll find a nickname for you eventually."

I search her face, drinking in every detail. Although I'm not willing to admit it, I love that idea. "Careful, Princess. A nickname might have the town folk thinking you like me."

"Never." She gives me a shove so pathetic I don't budge.

Instead, I grab her hip and hold her to me.

Her breath catches, and her body tenses almost imperceptibly.

Every time we're close, she hesitates, stiffens. I'm not sure if it's just my touch she doesn't like or if it's everyone's.

So, gut tightening, I let go, but I don't step back. "So did you dress up for the guys at the dock?"

Teeth sinking into her bottom lip, she peers up at me through dark lashes. "What if I told you it was for you?"

My throat goes tight. "Is it?" Shit, I'd love it if that was the case.

She bats her eyes at me and shifts back an inch or two. "No, it was for me."

I don't hate that answer as much as I thought I would. Not when it comes with a satisfied smile. One that makes me think that maybe this is the first time the girl who spent her life on camera has been given the opportunity to dress up for herself and no one else.

I love that for her. But I also love the way she pouts when I tease her. Although Cank swears a good woman will settle a man, Libby makes me feel anything but settled. No, she makes me feel keyed up. Turned up. Absolutely out of sorts. Settled? Not even close.

"Looks like you're dressed up for a date," I point out.

And here comes the cute little purse of her lips and that narrowing of her eyes. "I'm not dating."

I rock back on my heels and fight a smirk. She's protesting a bit too much, so I push her. "Good, because this isn't a date."

The frown that settles across her pretty face only makes me smile. Because that means she might want it to be. "It certainly *feels* like a date since you insisted on picking me up and refuse to allow me to drive my new golf cart."

Behind her, the door flies open and Sutton appears, looking adorable in her favorite sundress. I'm not sure the last time I saw her so fancied up. Maybe Ivy and Star's wedding last summer.

"Why do you always stand on top of each other?" she huffs.

Libby immediately steps back. Fuck. My entire system feels the loss of her presence instantly.

Now that there's room for her between us, Sutton spins in a circle, showing off her dress and curled hair. Normally we pull it up. I know nothing about blow drying or curling wands or whatever the fuck they're called. The kid's lucky I can braid.

Tonight, though, she's glowing. It kills me that her mom isn't here for these moments.

For the millionth time, I wonder what the heck my brother was thinking leaving his daughter to *me*.

"Doesn't she look pretty?" Libby cocks an expectant brow.

"Yes," I jump in. "Absolutely beautiful, sweet pea."

"Look, even my nails are pink." Beaming, she holds out her little hand, showing me the bubble-gum pink nails that match Libby's dress. "Just like the golf cart."

Yeah, that too.

"Nice."

With a twirl, she darts to Libby's side. "Can we take the golf cart?"

"No," I say at the same time Libby says, "Sure, we'll take Putt-Putt."

"Putt-Putt?" Sutton tilts her head, brow furrowed.

"I've decided that's her name."

My niece nods easily, as if it makes any sense that the damn thing should have a name.

"No matter what we call it, we're not taking it."

She whirls on me, hands on her hips, blond hair flying. "Why not?"

I scowl. "I'm not driving that pink-mobile."

"You did earlier," she points out.

"That was different. Libby needed a lesson."

That response is met with matching eye rolls.

Instead of replying, Libby just heads inside calling "I'll get the keys" over her shoulder.

"I said no," I bark through the screen door.

"I'll move the blanket and stuff from the truck." Sutton hops off the porch and darts for her dad's truck.

"But I said no," I call again.

Ten minutes later, I pull up to the stretch of grass the town calls a park and drop the girls off.

"You go park Putt-Putt. We'll find the perfect spot." Sutton hops off the back seat. With a sweet smile, Libby grabs the blanket and cooler I packed.

"Fine." Feeling ridiculous in the pink ride all alone, I ease down toward the dock. I've just climbed off the cart when my best friend steps up next to me.

"Elephant in the room," he chirps.

I scowl and sidestep the asshole.

He shuffles to one side, cutting me off. "I like the pink sparkles. It might clash with the whole grrr"—he gives me an exaggerated scowl —"you got going on, but it fits the rest of the family's vibe."

"Libby's not family," I grit out as I lean to one side, searching for the girls. When I find them smiling and laughing and spreading the blanket out next to Maggie and Eddy, I turn back to Wilder.

He's wearing an obnoxious smirk. "Yet here you are at another town event. Two weeks in a row. Must be some kind of record for you."

"I saved you a spot on my blanket, baby." The blonde from the bar a few weeks ago calls out. She blows Wilder a kiss and points a long nail at a red and white plaid blanket a few yards away.

He winces.

"Elephant in the room." I love it when it's my turn. "Your girl just keeps on staying."

I can't help but fuck with him. The woman came for a bachelorette weekend, and after she met Wilder, she extended her stay. She's been here for two weeks now. And everyone on the island knows it's because she has her heart set on my best friend.

"She's not my girl." The grumble is so unlike Wilder.

Movement behind him catches my eye, and irritation works its way up my spine. There's a group of guys heading toward Libby, Maggie, and Eddy. And fuck if that isn't my cue to leave.

"You can't say that about Libby, though," Wilder calls as I stride toward my girls.

And, oddly enough, this time I don't want to deny it.

Libby

Chapter 20

"OH MY FIRST TOWN MEETING. I'm so excited." I settle in my seat beside Maggie, my knees bouncing.

The stage curtains are shut to hide the set we've been working on. Like it matters. Half the people in this room have helped with it. By the night of the show, it won't be a surprise. Though I guess that's just how it's done on Monhegan. I'm beginning to realize that's the answer to a lot of things about this island. And if you question why, they look at you with expressions that scream *why not?*

Maybe there's something to that sentiment. *Why not?*

Just because it's done differently elsewhere doesn't mean it's wrong here. And I'm learning more and more every day just how much *different* works for me. This summer has been so much better than I could have even hoped for, and the people are more than half the reason.

Even when they're growly, like Fisher is 90 percent of the time. His gruff attitude just makes me giggle now.

And boy did he growl a lot at the lobster bake.

Every time someone came over and interrupted us, he'd let out this heavy sigh, as if interacting with other humans was exhausting.

Though he found his second wind when the music started. The

man seriously had me dancing nearly half the night. Every time someone suggested he take a break and asked to dance with me— mainly Wilder—Fisher's eyes narrowed, and I swear little darts shot straight out of his pupils.

He must really like dancing.

I didn't mind in the least. It may seem counterintuitive, but the more time I spend in Fisher's arms, the more relaxed I feel. Perhaps it's the way he smells. I've read a thing or two about how one person's pheromones can be attracted to another person's. It's science.

That, or I just really like him.

Doesn't matter either way. I'm not dating. Even if I were, there's no way I should get involved with someone who is raising a child. My life is a mess. The last thing I want is to drag an innocent child into it. I'm no good for either of them—or anyone else, for that matter—until I figure out who I am and what I want to do with my life.

This summer is about finding me. Discovering what brings me joy. I think I'm doing a pretty decent job of it so far. Take this moment, for instance. As I sit, surrounded by familiar faces with loud voices echoing off the ceiling, I feel nothing but joyful.

"Scoot down," a deep voice grumbles from my side.

I peer up, and when I meet Fisher's eye, my stomach does that weird flip. The tone of his voice is always at odds with the way his brown eyes brighten when they land on me. Like we're in on some secret. A secret that involves a hidden sweet side of him.

Before I can think too much further into it, Wilder appears at his side, wearing a T-shirt that says *I'm a f*cking delight.*

"Can I sit on the inside?" He cranes his neck one way, then the other, then his shoulders droop in relief. "Never mind. I think I'm in the clear."

He eases into the seat next to Fisher, and with a grunt of annoyance, Fisher leans away from him. The move causes our thighs to brush and a thread of electricity to course through me. Those brown eyes find mine again, silently confirming that our proximity is okay.

Without my permission, my lips kick up on one side.

Maggie leans across me and hisses, "What are you two doing here?"

I frown at my friend. "Doesn't he have to be here since he's the sheriff?"

Fisher's expression remains blank. Maggie, on the other hand, is smirking now.

"No. Neither Wilder nor Fisher ever come to the town meeting. They always complain that because they're on Saturdays, they're nothing but a nuisance."

"They are," he grumbles, the low sound vibrating through me and making me shiver.

She beams, chin lifted, like he's just proven her point. I've never seen the quiet woman so amused. "So like I said, *why* are you here?"

Fisher completely ignores the question, facing forward.

Wilder shifts our way and whispers, "I'm avoiding the level-five clinger."

Fisher sighs. "It's about time you stop hooking up with random tourists, don't you think?"

I fold my lips in, fighting a laugh. Maybe that's why Wilder kept asking me to dance at the lobster bake. The woman he was with did seem a bit clingy.

"There's no one else here," Wilder says as he leans back and folds his arms across his chest.

Breath held, I peer over at Maggie. Before I can get a look at her expression, the baker who despises me settles in the row ahead of us.

"Hi boys," she says in that high pitched voice that Sutton hates. I can understand the sentiment, especially when she winks at Fisher. "Are you going to the brewery tonight?"

His jaw ticks, and with a glance at me, he leans back, drapes his arm along the back of my seat, and spreads his thighs wider. "We'll see."

Flora's nose flares in annoyance as she eyes the way he's touching me. I can barely focus though because once again I'm surrounded by Fisher. His warmth, his scent, his almost possessive attitude. With a huff she spines around and Maggie leans across me again, talking to Wilder. "There's always Flora."

Wilder shakes his head, lips kicked up in his usual smirk. "I'm not the one she likes," he mouths.

Fisher breathes like a wild bull, nostrils flaring. It's far more endearing than it should be.

"Okay, everyone. Quiet down. We've got a lot to get through this morning." A man I haven't met bangs a gavel against the plastic table he's sitting behind at the front of the room.

From the back of the room, a man yells, "Yeah, we need to discuss this proposed ban."

"Sit down, Blue," Doris hollers.

"Naked painting," he grumbles as he shuffles closer to the stage and finds a seat. "Who writes a law banning naked painting? Heathens, that's who. You're all anarchists, I tell ya."

"I don't think that's the term you're looking for," Wilder's poor mother mutters, cheeks flushing.

Gosh, I love this town.

An hour and a half later, my head is spinning. All the volleying back and forth to catch the firework display that was my first town meeting has given me a crick in the neck. It was complete chaos from beginning to end. Shockingly, outside of Doris, no one voted for the proposal to ban the naked painting. Not even Mrs. K.

"All her stuff is in here?" Mrs. K asks Fisher as I step outside, relishing the warmth of the sun.

Fisher made a beeline for the exit the second the meeting was over, followed by half a dozen people looking for his help with one task or another. I stuck around with Maggie, who stopped everyone she could, asking for their help with the play. She's a little genius. Those innocent doe eyes and the overalls that make her look like a grown-up Pollyanna are impossible to say no to. Today her overalls are the same shade as my pink golf cart, I'm kind of obsessed—with her and the overalls. No one can say no to her, and she knows it.

Fisher pulls a pink overnight bag out of the back of the truck and hands it to Mrs. K.

"Yup. I'll be by first thing in the morning to pick her up. And my phone is on. Call if you need me."

As I approach, Mrs. K's face lights up. With a squeeze to Fisher's arm, she backs away. "Have a good night. Sutton will be fine. We'll see you tomorrow. *After breakfast.*" She tacks on the last two words like it's an order.

"Where's Sutton going?" I ask as Mrs. K heads off with Wilder and Blue.

"She's sleeping at Mrs. K's. She forces Eddy and me to leave the girls with her and go out and 'have fun.'" The last two words are accompanied by air quotes and a sneer.

I can't totally blame him for being resentful about a night without Sutton. What will I do with myself if she's not around this afternoon? She's normally the one who drags me along to all the activities she and Fisher participate in. Now I'll have to figure out something on my own.

"Well, enjoy your free time." I force a smile and head toward my golf cart. I've gotten better at driving it. Mostly. As long as I avoid hills. Though that can be a challenge when the island is one big hill. Regardless, I do my best to keep my speed low and tap the brakes when I get going a little too quickly. It does result in a bumpy ride, but when I'm alone, and don't have to worry about Fisher's grumbling, it feels like my very own roller coaster.

"Wait," Fisher calls, striding toward me with a diet ginger ale in one hand. He shoves it in my direction, pink straw and all. "I'll pick you up at six thirty."

I stare down at the heart-shaped straw in confusion. "Why?"

"So we can walk to the brewery together."

My breath catches in my throat. He wants to go to the brewery... *with me?*

And this time Sutton isn't the one dragging him out of the house.

His irises darken as he watches me, waiting for a response. What the hell is happening right now? When his focus snags on my mouth, a shiver rolls across my skin, and I can't help but imagine him dragging his lips against mine.

"Okay?" he asks, his brows folding in on themselves.

I shake the ridiculous thoughts from my head and inhale deeply. "Yeah, okay. See you then."

Fisher eyes me for another second, then turns and strides away without another word.

"Strange man," I whisper to my soda. Why does diet ginger ale taste so much better through a pretty straw?

Must be another one of those science things.

"So the brewery with Fisher, huh?" Maggie's voice startles me.

Dammit. I've literally been lost in space since Fisher walked away, and from the look of things, he's long gone.

"Huh?"

Maggie's smile is wide. "You're going on a date."

I scoff. "Oh, no. That's not—" I shake my head even as my heart skips at the mere thought that maybe Fisher did just ask me on a date.

Maggie's green eyes glitter with excitement. "That was so him asking you on a date."

"He barely said a word." I clamp my lips around the straw to keep myself from saying anything more. Like how I hope she's right. Or before I ask questions about whether he's ever dated anyone on the island. I squeeze my lips tighter to keep myself from inviting her to help me get ready because I really want to look good if this is a date.

Maggie laughs, the warmth in her tone easing my nerves a fraction. "He says more to you than he says to anyone. Believe me, that was Fisher asking you on a date."

I sip my soda and point to my cart. "Want a ride to the theater?"

With a giggle, she points past me. Right. We're at the theater. "Let's get some work done before your date," she sings as she skips toward the building.

"It's not a date!" I call after her, but like a glutton for punishment, I follow her back inside.

Several hours later, I step out of the theater, speckled in a rainbow of paint colors. I smile when I see my pink golf cart sitting in the shade of a tree. That is not where I left it. Fisher must have swung back this way and noticed it sitting out in the hot sun.

A girl could get used to this kind of treatment. *She shouldn't*, but she could.

Humming softly, I hop on and head back to the house.

I'm still not sure what I think about this whole date situation. It could be nice dating a man like Fisher. Maggie may have never been on a date, but I'd take that over "dating" other celebrities for the publicity only. Those are the only kind I've ever been on. I've never had time for a real boyfriend. Hell, I've never had time for friends. Just transactional relationships where I was seen out and about with the "right" people.

For all my bravado, I don't think I've ever dressed up just for the thrill of seeing how a man will react when he sees me for the first time.

But the way Fisher reacted before the lobster bake? I could get used to that. That was—I sigh, slumping in the pink seat—butterfly-inducing. Only the butterflies sucked on helium before they took flight in my stomach.

Everyone I pass gives me plenty of room, waving, then darting to one side of the road or the other. It's a huge change from only a few weeks ago, when everyone greeted me with grumbles. I think they're really starting to like me. Or at least tolerate me.

My butt leaves the seat as the cart jostles its way around the turn near Wilder's house. His yard slopes pretty sharply, so I press on the brake to slow myself down. I should order a Bluetooth speaker for Putt-Putt. Put music to the way the whole cart jolts every time I round this corner.

When the cart doesn't slow, I push harder on the brake. Only to find Putt-Putt speeding up.

Shit. I try again, stomping on the brake this time. But no matter what I do, the cart doesn't stop its forward momentum.

It's okay. I'll be fine. I'll just take my foot off the gas, and eventually it will run out of juice and come to a stop.

Except the cart picks up speed, careening down the hill, the steering wheel wobbling out of control. I'm feet away from the tree I swear just popped up in the middle of the path when I realize there's no way to avoid it. Dammit, Fisher is going to be so mad.

Fisher

Chapter 21

I SMOOTH the olive green shirt down one more time. Part of me hopes Libby likes it. The other part of me itches to punch myself for being a dumbass. I don't think I've ever in my life stood in front of the mirror and worried about how I look.

"The shirt isn't magic," I growl at my reflection, even as I tip my head to get a better look at my hair.

This is a normal Saturday night. I've been spending my Saturday nights at the brewery for the last three years, and not once have I put gel in my hair beforehand.

Why tonight?

Probably because Libby is used to fancy Hollywood faces and places. The kind of thrill that makes a person excited about tomorrow. Nothing on this damn island possesses that type of thrill. Nothing but her. The thrill that hits me when I see her has yet to dull. In fact, it's only become more intense. And not because she's Elizabeth Sweet. It's Libby, the shy, unsure, slow to smile woman, who makes me smile.

Not that the Libby I can't stop thinking about would want to date me either. It's ridiculous. I'm almost ten years older than her, and I have none of the light she possesses. I'm the opposite of that light. I'm the shadow threatening to dull her brightness.

I stomp into the bathroom, huffing as I go. Water running, I wet my hands and wipe at my hair, attempting a less formal look.

Tonight *isn't* a date. There is no need to dress up or worry about how she'll think I look. I need to get that through my head.

My eyes drift back to my reflection, and I wince at my stupid hair.

Fuck. It looks ridiculous.

Out of desperation, I pull on my Boston Revs baseball cap.

There. Now I look casual. From the neck up. Sighing, I unbutton my shirt. I yank it off and toss it to the floor, leaving myself in a white T-shirt and jeans, which is exactly how I started a half hour ago. It doesn't help. The knots in my stomach only tighten. This is exactly why I don't date.

I shake my head.

We're just friends. This is not a date. It's no different from hanging out with Wilder. Or Maggie. Though I don't kiss Maggie. Or Wilder. Not that I'm gonna kiss Libby either. But fucking hell, I'd like to. And I'm starting to believe maybe she'd like me to as well. Just that idea has my heart rate picking up like I'm a thirteen-year-old.

I scoff.

More like an eighteen-year-old.

Until I left this island, not a single girl had ever looked my way. Here on Monhegan, I was the weird kid. The boy who could help with a satellite dish or a new computer or phone. Not the kid people wanted to hang out with. Especially the girls. Stepping onto the grounds of Harvard was like being transported to a different world entirely. There, girls suddenly noticed me.

Because in Cambridge and Boston, I'm one of many. Here, I stand out too much.

I stomp down the stairs.

My cameras haven't notified me of Libby's return home yet, so she clearly isn't stressing about what she should wear or how she should style her hair.

143

I've got another twenty minutes to kill before I'm supposed to pick her up. Fuck. This afternoon has been the longest of my life. I stand in front of the window, watching her house, wishing I could speed up time. It's like watching paint dry. There isn't a light on in the entire place. I catch my reflection in the window and second-guess the hat.

Maybe she hates Boston baseball. The team has beaten the LA Dodgers more than a few times.

I toss my cap onto the counter and pull a water bottle from the fridge.

With a long sip and then three slow, calming breaths, I will myself to calm down. The effort is in vain.

Where is she? My stomach churns again at the idea of seeing her. Of making her smile. Of the possibility of eliciting one of those shivers that overtake her when I brush against her.

If I brushed my lips along her neck, would that shiver intensify? Would her breath catch? I can practically feel her pulse flutter with the same desire that pounds through me.

I blink.

Stop it. This is a *friend* thing. Imagining anything more will only lead to disappointment. And I've had enough disappointment to last a lifetime.

I set the water bottle on the counter and roll my shoulders. With another steady exhale, I run my hands through my hair.

Jesus, now it's probably sticking up all over the place. I swipe the hat off the counter and toss it on my head again.

Before I have a chance to overthink the hat for a third time, my phone buzzes in my pocket.

Whoever it is better not need anything. Tonight the only person getting my attention is Libby. Unless it's Sutton. I pull the device out, making sure it's not Mrs. K.

Wilder's name flashes on the screen, and for one second, I think about ignoring his call. Though a conversation with him might help pass the time. Plus, someone needs to tell him that he's got to man up and deal with the clingy tourist himself. Because he's not going to try to hang all over Libby like he did at the lobster bake. Fucker.

I hit the Accept button. "What?"

He chuckles. "Manners, Fisher. Manners."

Annoyance instantly pulses in my veins. "Are you calling to waste my time?"

"No. I have a little situation here in my front yard."

I sigh, shoulders deflating. Just what I need.

"There's no reason to panic—"

That's an odd statement. When has he ever known me to panic?

"But Libby crashed into my tree."

My heart stammers and then takes off to a gallop in my chest. "What?" I choke out. "Is she hurt?"

Without waiting for his answer, I shove my feet into my boots and race out the door, laces flapping. Bing keeps pace. Even he knows something is wrong. Normally he leaps and whimpers and barks his way through town. Instead, he passes me, running at full speed down the hill.

"She's awake and Eddy's here and—"

"I'll be right there." I end the call and tuck the phone into my pocket. My hat flies off my head, dropping to the dirt path, but I don't waste time collecting it.

Two turns later, the cotton candy pink golf cart comes into view, and my stomach drops. Its front bumper is butted up against a large pine tree. Dammit. Libby better be okay.

When I come even with the back tires, I finally see her on the ground with Eddy and Bing hovering over her.

"Are you okay?" My hands shake and my heart pounds, and even as I inspect her, noting that she's awake and, though she looks a little disheveled, she seems mostly unharmed. "Get back," I command Bing as I step in front of him and squat.

"Fisher?" Libby blinks at me. "What happened to your hair?"

I'm sure my hair looks like utter shit, but I couldn't a give a flying fuck about it anymore. Still, if she's giving me shit, that's a good sign.

Relief washes over me, relaxing my shoulders and almost causing a laugh to slip from my lips.

Eddy narrows her eyes at me, then turns the expression on her brother.

"Why did you call him?"

Wilder, who I only now realize is standing above us, rocks back on his heels and grins. "I want to file a damage report."

The gravel crunches under me as I push to my feet and clench my hands into fists at my sides. "Libby could be hurt, and you're worried about the fucking tree?" I snarl.

"Nah." Wilder chuckles. "I called you because you have a crush on her and I knew you'd want to be here."

Though the anger drains from me, it's quickly replaced by the heat of embarrassment creeping up the back of my neck. "I'm not twelve. I don't have crushes," I mutter, crouching to focus on Libby.

The fact that she's not freaking out about spiders has me worried. She's been sitting on the ground since I got here and hasn't once mentioned them.

"Is she okay?" Although my eyes don't leave Libby's, the question is meant for Eddy.

"She hit her head, but as I was explaining before you came barreling in here like a freight train, since she didn't lose consciousness and she doesn't seem confused, I don't think she has a concussion. She'll be okay. But she shouldn't be alone tonight."

"I won't leave her side." The words fly easily from my lips.

I drop to my ass and tie my boots tight so I can carry her home. Nothing in the world could pull me away from her.

Libby
Chapter 22

MY CHEEKS HEAT with mortification as I frown down at the ground. "I'm fine." I inhale deeply and let the breath out nice and slow, willing my heart to stop pounding. It's not the accident that has me out of sorts. It's Fisher.

"I'm not twelve. I don't have crushes." His words whoosh around in my brain, like a fire extinguisher meant to drown out all the silly little thoughts I've had about him. I should have known that I'm nothing more than a job to him. A nuisance. An obligation.

I press my fingers into the dirt and push myself up. When I sway to the left, Fisher hops up and sweeps me off my feet. "Still fine?" he rumbles in that cocky, self-assured tone.

I blow out a breath through my nose, averting my gaze. "Let me go."

Rather than loosening his hold, he grips me tighter. "You heard Eddy. You can't be left alone."

Eddy frowns apologetically. "He's right, Libby. I'm sorry. I'd offer to come over and keep you company, but I promised Lindsey I'd stay home with her tonight since I'll be off-island for the next week."

Not wanting her to feel obligated, I put on my best mask and smile. "Of course. Thank you for coming." It's ridiculous trying to have an adult conversation while Fisher holds me like I'm a freaking baby, but I can't exactly overpower the brute, so I'm stuck for the moment.

"Keep her awake for at least a few hours," she tells him. "If she shows any signs of confusion, call me immediately, and I'll come over. But I really do think she's okay." She frowns at my golf cart, which is definitely not okay. "And no driving for the next twenty-four hours."

I sigh. "I think my driving days are over, at least for now."

Fisher grunts in Wilder's direction. "Can you have Ryder come take a look at the golf cart?"

His best friend grins. "I already called him. He'll have that thing as good as new for you, Libby. Don't worry."

I highly doubt it, but I don't want to sound ungrateful, so I force another one of my practiced smiles. "Thank you."

Apparently done with the conversation, Fisher turns and strides away.

"You didn't even say goodbye," I mutter.

He glances down at me like he doesn't understand. He probably doesn't. The man confuses the hell out of me.

"Go ahead." I slump in his arms. "You can say it."

Lips dipping down at the corners, he side-eyes me. "Say what?"

"I told you so." I sigh. "I had no business driving the golf cart if I didn't know how to operate it."

He grunts. "I taught you how to drive it, and I've watched you drive it plenty. Accidents happen."

My stomach does that swoopy thing again. What does he mean he watched me drive it plenty? Like he followed me around? My heart pinches. That's kind of sweet, even if it is a little stalker-y.

As we continue down the path in silence, I get lost in my head trying to figure this man out. When the brewery comes into view, disappointment rears its ugly head. "I want to go to the brewery."

"No."

"Maggie said I'd get a mug," I pout. I really wanted a mug.

His lips twitch like he finds me slightly amusing. "I'll get you a mug, but not tonight."

There's already a line of people outside the brewery waiting for tables. Dammit. Just what I need. An audience. I bury my face in his chest to hide, and only when I inhale do I realize what a terrible idea it was. Fisher smells delicious. Like he put cologne on. I'm not sure I've ever smelled his cologne.

"Did you just sniff me?" He sounds amused, but I can't see his expression because I refuse to remove my face from his chest.

"Everyone is staring," I mumble, my lips brushing against the fabric of his T-shirt.

He chuckles, the vibrations working their way through his chest and all the way into my heart. "So? Thought you liked attention, Princess."

"Not if they take pictures and sell them."

"No one does that here." His words come out gruff, like the sheer idea of it angers him.

"Maybe not to you, but someone in town could. Or a tourist. They'd make a lot of money off a single image, and then everyone would know I'm here." Annoyance mixes with my blood and spreads to every part of my body. Pranks are one thing. An angry Brad discovering my whereabouts has far more concerning implications.

As if he can sense my panic, Fisher lowers his head, his breath warm when he says, "I'll arrest them." He punctuates the statement with a kiss to the top of my head. I think. It happens so quick that I can't be sure.

I lift my chin and look up at him, as if his expression will give him away. I'm met with his typical stoicism. It's infuriating how easily he can look so devoid of emotion. "You're not a real sheriff," I remind him.

His eyes glitter with amusement, though once again, they're the only thing that gives him away. The rest of his face is as impassive as it gets. "No one here seems to believe that."

"Do you even have handcuffs?"

His pupils blow out, nearly eclipsing his dark irises for half a second. Or maybe I imagined it. I can't tell. I'm too blinded by the smile that lances his face. "Yes, I do."

"Oh," I mutter, at a loss for how to respond and too entranced by the way he's watching me to think coherently.

"Yeah, oh." He looks away, that damn smile turning to a smirk, like he's pleased with himself.

Is he pleased with himself? Is he—could he be—oh god, I think he's flirting with me.

"Maybe I really do have a concussion, because I swear you're smiling, Sheriff."

He flexes his lips like he's trying to remove the expression, but it remains in place the rest of the way home.

When we reach the fork in the road that divides our houses, he doesn't even slow. "Where are you going?"

"You'll stay at my place."

"Why can't we stay at mine?" I'm being difficult for the sake of being difficult. I know that. But I want to shower, and my bed is calling my name.

"Because there's actual food at my house, and from the sounds of your stomach, you're hungry."

I smack his shoulder lightly. "Rude. You're supposed to pretend you didn't hear that."

He chuckles. "Impossible, Princess. I notice everything when it comes to you." His brown eyes widen, then he shakes his head, like he didn't mean to say that. "I mean—"

"Don't take it back now, Sheriff." I nod to the ground. "I'll come to your house, but can I please shower at mine? I promise I'll be over shortly."

To my surprise, he eases me to the ground without argument. I work to steady my balance. Not because I feel dizzy this time, but because the move is so unexpected. The man's yo-yo game must be strong. "All right, then." I turn and head to my place. "I'll be over soon."

When I turn to wave over my shoulder, he barrels into me, grasping my arms to keep me from tumbling. "Jesus."

"What are you doing?"

The grunt he lets out puts me at ease. This is the Fisher I've come to know. "Letting you shower like I said."

Hand on my hip, I huff. "Then *why* are you following me?"

"Did you not hear Eddy?" He thumbs over his shoulder. "I need to watch you."

My mouth falls open. "Fisher—oh my god, I don't know your last name."

"Jones," he says, that smirk twitching at his lips again.

I give him a patronizing smile. "Fisher Jones, you are *not* watching me shower."

He rolls his eyes and gives me an equally imperious look. "Obviously."

I drop my hand to my side and a sensation akin to disappointment washes through me. "Then why are you following me?" My voice has less spunk to it now.

He sidesteps me and strides for my house. "I'll stay outside the bathroom. Just holler if you get dizzy."

Knowing there is no way he's going to budge on this—stubborn ass—I stomp up the steps and hold the door for him. Inside, I insist he wait downstairs, but he follows me up the steps, only stopping when we hit my bedroom door.

I survey the room, looking at it through his eyes. It's simple. I've added a pale pink comforter and two pillows since I arrived. One pillow is pink and in teal it says *Just Keep Swimming*. The other is teal with pink writing and says *If it makes you happy...* They're perfect for me, the New Libby. At least for now, while I figure out *what* makes me happy, I'll just keep swimming.

The lamp on my bedside table is teal. The table on the other side of the mattress is bare. I didn't bother buying a second lamp. When it's only me in the bed, what's the point?

As I mull that over, it hits me. That would make me happy: the *need* for a second lamp.

I must have hit my head harder than I realized.

With a sigh, I push away the thought of a matching set of lamps for the nonexistent partner in my life and go in search of clothing. I pull sweats and a T-shirt from the dresser, opting for comfort since, apparently, I'll be up most of the night.

Fisher's still looming in the doorway, and as I try to exit, he doesn't budge, so I'm forced to squeeze past him. Fine, if he wants to be that way, I can play this game too.

With my head tipped up so I can watch his every expression, I slide right up against him, my breasts smashing against his chest as I do. He stops breathing and his jaw clicks as he mashes his teeth together. His exhale is harsh, his nostrils flaring. Maybe I'm moving more slowly than I would have if he'd been a gentleman and shuffled out of the way, but if he's going to mess with me, then he'll have to suffer the consequences. Inch by inch, I roll myself across him, relishing the way his Adam's apple bobs and his pupils dilate.

The man wants me. And screwing with him like this is the perfect distraction to the shit show that is my life.

When I finally make it to the bathroom door, I lean out into the hall and waggle my fingers. "See you in a few."

A half hour later, I'm dressed and sitting at Fisher's kitchen table while he minces garlic. Watching his arm bounce as he makes each slice is almost relaxing. When he turns and drops the garlic into the pan, making it sizzle to life, I can't help but ogle his ass.

He gives the garlic a quick stir, then spins and eyes me. "You're falling asleep."

I blink slowly and yawn. "I'm just sitting here."

"Stay awake," he says gruffly. I almost wonder if he says things so simply because he just expects people to listen. Like he could will my body into doing his bidding. Though only for an instant, because the thought quickly has my mind veering to images of other ways he could speak to my body. Now there's no way I could fall asleep. Though in my attempt to hide the flush that's rising up my chest, I lay my head against my shoulder.

A second later, I'm startled upright again when he barks, "You need to stay awake. Talk to me."

I let out an exasperated sigh. "About what?"

"Tell me something."

"Why don't you tell me something?" I fight back.

"Fine. A question for a question." He looks over his shoulder at me, one brow arched like he's waiting for me to agree.

I offer him a simple nod, eager for him to focus on what he's making before he notices how flushed I am.

Humming to myself, I inspect the room. "Why do you hate living here?"

Those eyes of his are on me again. "Why do you think I hate living here?"

I jut my chin. "Is that your question?"

"No."

"So then answer mine."

Finally, he turns again, his back rising, then slowly falling like he's letting out a slow breath as he browns the steak.

"Don't sugarcoat it," I remind him.

Between one breath and the next, the air shifts, and suddenly he's spewing words, though he's still not facing me.

"This wasn't supposed to be my life. I never planned to come back here. Before my brother"—his body stiffens—"Before the accident, I lived in Boston." He half turns and stares me down. "Don't get me wrong. I love Sutton more than anything. *That's* why I'm here. Because she needs me. But I never planned to be a father. Or a winter lobsterman or a pretend sheriff." His shoulders fall. "I don't like people. And they're everywhere here."

"There are only sixty-nine of us," I say softly.

"And sixty-seven of them are all up in my business," he grumbles.

I sit up straighter. "Hey, you made me sit here. I wanted to stay home."

"Didn't include you, Princess. You have to know by now that you're different." With a frown, he stares at me for a beat too long. "I seem to always want you around."

The admission makes my stomach flip. Those butterflies I'd thought had been extinguished are now back to flapping wildly, and the room seems to have taken on a hazy pink hue.

I'm either entirely too affected by Fisher's simple words or these are signs of a concussion. I don't want to stop this conversation, though, so I don't mention my symptoms.

Instead, I tilt my head and examine him more closely. What is it about him that's so intriguing? "So why not take Sutton back to Boston?"

"Isn't it my turn to ask a question?"

Lips twisting, I consider telling him no. But he'll only argue, so I give a simple shrug.

He folds his arms across his chest and lifts both brows, dark eyes intent on me. "Why are you really here? And don't sugarcoat it."

Fisher
Chapter 23

HER WHOLE BODY TENSES UP. Yeah, I know the jerk-wad of an ex costar is threatening her and that she's here hiding out, but I don't know what he's trying to force her to keep her mouth shut about. Every morning I wake with the desire to hack into her email again and search for clues about what he's done. To break into her text messages, or his. Like my craving for that first cup of coffee, the need for answers percolates in my system.

How easy it would be. With a few keystrokes, I'd have exactly what I want. But this other nagging pull overshadows my curiosity. More than I want the answers, I want her to *trust me with them*.

I've never experienced the sensation before. This desire for a bond with another person. It sits on my chest like a big, fat lump, reminding me to stay the fuck away from her personal communication. Trust can't be earned through hacking. That's for damn sure. She has to open up on her own. With any luck, the insight I gave her into why I feel more like a prisoner than a resident of this island will help.

Her eyes dart around like she's working on a plan to get herself out of the conversation. If I were better at this, I could probably ease the answer out of her, but communication has never been my strong suit. Trying to exude patience and nonchalance that I don't feel, I turn back to the steaks, though I continue to monitor her reflection in the door of the microwave.

Finally, she slumps and bows her head. "What do you mean why am I here? You made me sit here."

Frustration flares through me as I turn off the stove and slide the pan to the other side. "Don't get smart on me now, Princess." Arms crossed, I lean against the countertop and watch her.

Picking at an invisible dot on the perfectly clean table she sighs. "It's obvious that you read the papers, so this seems like a waste of a question."

"Do you really think I look like the kind of guy who reads the tabloids?"

Her emails? Maybe. But the tabloids hold no appeal. And nothing about the clips of information I've caught here and there through Sutton depicts the real Libby. They might talk about Elizabeth Sweet, the actress persona she dons when necessary, but they couldn't be more wrong about the girl who captivates my attention.

She huffs out a hard breath, causing her blond hair to ruffle away from her face. "Everyone reads something. All the information is there if you look for it."

I bite back another growl of aggravation and drop into the chair beside her. "I want to hear it from you."

Her baby blues widen at the intensity in my voice.

Uninterested in taking the words back, I grasp her small, cold hand. I create a connection. A physical tie to each other.

Her eyes lock there, flaring a little when I lace my fingers with hers. "For my entire life, the whole world has felt as if they know me." She swallows thickly and licks her lips. "Everyone has an opinion about who I should be. I needed to escape so I could figure out who I really am."

That might not have been the exact answer I was fishing for, but damn is it a good one.

She lifts her head and holds my gaze, and the entire room shrinks. It's only the two of us, nothing else.

I see it. Dressing for herself, learning to drive the golf cart and light the pilot. Wanting sherbet instead of ice cream. These are all ways she's been trying to find herself. Discovering the Libby I adore.

I squeeze her hand.

Her eyes glitter with unshed tears. "You're running from your life. And I'm running to find mine."

I rub my lips together and consider her words. "I'm not running from my life." Hell, most of the time I feel like I'm clinging to a past I should have let go of long ago. Only in the last few weeks have I felt like a single thing on this island is for me. I swallow hard at that thought. In the short time I've known her, this woman has changed me.

Lips pursed, she tilts her head. "Really? Because you seem like you're living your brother's life."

Not a single cell in my body can work up any type of disagreement. I am living his life.

"So why don't you go into their room?"

My chest aches at just the idea of it. I hate talking about Hunter. I hate talking in general. But talking about Hunter, missing him, remembering that I'm a shitty replacement for the original, is more painful than I can bear.

Libby gives my hand an encouraging squeeze.

"I can't get rid of their stuff. I just can't." My voice almost cracks on the last word. I clear my throat and swallow past the combination of loss and inadequacy. "I've already taken over the rest of his life, as you so aptly pointed out." I force a lighter tone to keep her from harping on that point. "So, what's your plan after the summer?"

Brows lowering, she deflates. "Why does everyone assume that I'm leaving?"

Because nothing on this island sparkles the way she does. And something that shines as bright as she does should not be stuck in the dusty salt air of Monhegan. "'Cause you'd lose your mind here, Princess. I promise."

With a sigh, she slips her hand from mine and rubs her temples.

"Head hurting?" I ask.

She nods, though she doesn't look at me.

An ember of worry ignites in my chest. "Badly?"

"No, just a dull ache. Kennedy said it might." Her posture sags further, her eyes getting heavy.

Knowing I need to keep her up, I stand. "No sleeping yet. Let's eat. Then we can watch a show so you can relax."

She puts up no fight, eating her entire steak and her favorite salad before she insists on watching *Friends*. And when she drops next to me on the sofa, I wrap my arm around her and tuck her into my side. As she rests her head against my shoulder, a peace I don't think I've ever felt settles over me. Watching stupid crap on the television has never appealed to me, but I wouldn't move for anything right now. The show might be dumb, but the company is perfect.

"I don't get what everyone loves about these people," I grumble halfway through the third or fourth episode. It's impossible to keep track of this nonsense.

"They're the friends I always wanted but never had. Most friendships in LA are transactional. Business. No one really cares about anyone but themselves." She yawns, her words slowing. "You and Maggie feel like my first real friends."

The words explode like fireworks in my chest.

I tighten my hold on her and swallow past the emotion clogging my throat. Minutes later, her body is limp and her breathing evens out. When I'm sure she's truly asleep, I carry her up to my bed and tuck her in.

Just as I lean down and press my lips against her forehead, she whispers, "Please stay."

Crawling into bed with her is simultaneously the worst and the best idea. But now that she's asked, I can't turn her down. So I flip off the bedside lamp and pad to the other side of the mattress, where I lie on top of the blankets. As the mattress dips with my weight, she shifts and rests her head on my chest.

"Night, Fisher," she mumbles.

For a long time, I lie awake, watching the way her long lashes flutter in the dim light of the moon. I brush a strand of blond hair off her cheek, my thumb sweeping across her silky skin. I could watch her forever.

I swallow hard. I promised myself I wouldn't fall for the woman who will leave me in a matter of weeks. But at this moment, I know it's already too late.

Libby

Chapter 24

I CAN'T BELIEVE this happened again. I can't believe I'm waking up in Fisher's bed again, inhaling this intoxicating aroma, reaching out for him, only to realize that he's not here.

Of course he's not here. Why would he stay in bed with me? After I made a fool of myself by asking him to stay, he probably waited around long enough for me to fall asleep before he snuck out. Hopefully he crashed in Sutton's empty room rather than on the couch this time.

It should be a relief. How awkward would it have been to wake up side by side? With my luck, I probably would have been sprawled over him. I never sleep on one side. I also never share a bed, so I have no reason to stay still.

Or could I have subconsciously known to keep to my space? That's probably something I should find out before I start dating.

My stomach sinks. *Before I start dating? God, Libby. A man is nice to you for one night, and you're already fantasizing about the future?*

Before my mind can conjure any more delusions, I fling myself out of bed. It's the comfort of his sheets that's throwing me. That's what I tell myself to avoid the disappointment threatening to crush me after waking up alone.

160

It's nearly eight a.m. and my headache is gone. I'll just head home, have a nice warm bath—assuming the pilot is lit—and come up with ways to avoid Fisher until these feelings subside.

It won't take long. He'll growl at me soon enough, and that'll be all I need to forget how kind he was as he held me on the couch last night. Or how good it felt when his thumb brushed the side of my arm, back and forth, back and forth, so gently it lulled me to sleep despite how I tried to fight it. Secretly, I wanted that moment to last for eternity. I'm not sure I've felt that comfortable, that at ease, in someone's arms since my mother.

I drop my head into my hands, a rush of heat spreading through my body.

Go, Libby. Get out of here before you search the man out and demand he touch you again.

I tiptoe to the door and slowly slip my hand over the knob like I'm worried it'll be hot to the touch. Nerves skittering through me, I twist it just so, then press my ear to the door and listen for footsteps. When I'm sure the hallway is empty—hopefully of humans as well as those pesky eight-legged creatures that won't leave me alone—I pull the door open slowly. Head stuck out, I scan the hall and the stairs. Then I widen the opening until I can see Sutton's door.

It's closed. Suspicions seemingly confirmed, I tiptoe down the steps. When I hit a creaky board, I nearly jump out of my skin. Frozen mid-step, heart pounding, I listen for noises that signal I'm not alone. I only lower my foot to the next step when I'm sure that no one is coming. Unwilling to risk being caught, I rush the last few steps and bound onto the porch. I don't even slow when the door slams behind me. I'm free.

Ten minutes later, the teapot whistles. It's followed quickly by loud knocking. The pounding sounds angrier than the steaming pot, so I holler that it's open and head for the door. Maybe the screeching coming from the kitchen will annoy him enough to send him running.

Fisher stomps toward me, his every step shaking the house.

"Why'd you leave?" He doesn't stop until he's right up in my face, hands pressed to my cheeks like he's inspecting my every expression, trying to pluck the truth from my brain.

He's fully dressed, a pair of jeans highlighting those thick thighs of his, a slightly wrinkled Boston Revs T-shirt covering his chest. The sight of him ready for the day angers me more. So does how much his touch soothes me. Is it possible to be angered and soothed all at the same time? If so, that is precisely what's going on. Clearly, all the belly-flopping confusion I put myself through ten minutes ago was for nothing. The way those brown eyes of his soften as he inspects me drags me right back into that warm bed of his. There can't be more than a couple of inches between his lips and mine, and yet it might as well be a mile with how my mind questions his every move.

The tea kettle continues to scream in anger, the sound giving me the wherewithal to pull back. I need air that isn't his. "I'm fine. No headache. You're off the hook, Sheriff."

I stalk back to the kitchen, filled with as much pressure as the kettle is. I'm on the precipice of bursting as I turn off the stove.

Before I can remove the kettle from the burner, Fisher's chest is pressed to my back. He puts pressure on my arm until I lower it, then he moves it for me, his warm breath ruffling my hair. "You can't keep running, Princess. It's not safe." He lowers his forehead to my crown and inhales deeply.

It's like being tossed beneath the rough waves off the town dock. His actions lull me into believing I'm safe with him, but his words are the jolt to my system that comes with the icy cold waters.

With a hum of annoyance, I push him back. "You can't keep using scare tactics to force me to listen to you. Spiders, broken windows, potential concussions. Give me a break, Fisher. I'm not Sutton. You aren't obligated to me."

Scowl deepening the grooves on his forehead, he scoffs. "Someone cut your fucking brake line. You aren't safe. Someone is trying to *hurt* you."

He takes a step closer, but I sidestep him and wrap my arms

around myself. My body is screaming that this can't be happening again. I shake my head. "Tell me exactly what happened."

Fisher grips his hair with both hands and tugs. "Wilder called while you were sleeping this morning. The mechanic came out to pick up the golf cart. Right away, he discovered that the lines had been cut."

Dread washes over me. I swallow it down and lift my chin. "Maybe it was the squirrels," I whisper.

Fisher shakes his head. "I saw it with my own eyes. That's why I wasn't in bed when you woke up. I—" He shakes his head.

My heart trips over itself. That means he was in bed before that. *He stayed.* "Someone is trying to hurt you, Libby. It's not safe." He drops his hands to his sides, his fists pulsing. His chest shudders as he takes a single step closer and says, almost desperately, "I can't lose someone else."

Speechless and paralyzed by the way his entire being vibrates with worry, all I can do is gape at him. This hard man is trying so earnestly to be soft. For me.

He takes another step forward, the movement jerky and his expression hardening again. "I'm serious. Move, or I'll toss you over my shoulder and drag you back home."

My lips twitch. "Well, I know that's a serious threat, since you keep carrying me around."

As if his patience is a tattered thread, he growls. "Princess, don't test me."

Now that I've seen beneath the rough exterior, I can't get enough of it. I want to worm my way beneath his ribcage and live there. There's a peace within him that I can't help but tug at. "Only if you admit why you want me to stay there. And don't sugarcoat it, Sheriff, we both know you don't do crushes."

"Crushes? You think I have a crush on you?" He licks his lips and his jaw ticks. "Twelve year olds have crushes, they want to hold hands and go to the movies. I don't want to just hold your hand. I want my hand wrapped around your throat while I devour you. The thought of anything happening to you makes me physically ill and the need to touch you whenever you're in the vicinity has my knuckles white from fisting them at my sides. So no, this isn't a fucking crush."

My heart races in my chest and I just blink.

Nostrils flaring, eyes narrowing, he takes the final step toward me. "Fucking hell, woman. Come here." He cuffs my neck and pulls me all the way to his mouth. And finally, freaking finally, Fisher kisses me.

I've been kissed before. Obviously I've been kissed before. But being kissed by Fisher is like a baptism. I'm renewed. Free. My mind will never again conjure the sensation of another person's lips against mine.

This isn't just a kiss. It's a reckoning. First he's gruff, channeling all his anger and concern into the way he holds me, plundering until I'm nothing but a puddle left for him to drink up. Our tongues tangle, our moans mingle, and there's a chance the slight pressure he's exerting on my neck may make me pass out. But like he knows just how much to give me, just how much I can truly take, he eases his hold and pulls back, offering me the tiniest reprieve from the onslaught.

Those kind brown eyes of his bounce like he's once again determining whether I'm with him, and when I whimper and tilt my head up like an offering, he dives back in. This time he's softer, and that hand on my neck drops to my pounding heart.

I clutch the front of his shirt, needing to keep him close. And when he tries to pull back again, I bite down on his lip.

"Please," I beg, the word a shattered piece of me.

He cups my cheek, and I turn my head into his hand, kissing his palm. "Please, Fisher."

"For you, the answer is always yes."

Chin lifted, I drink him in, getting lost in the dark pools he's got fixed on me. "You don't even know what I want."

His lips twitch, and then his smile unfurls. "Doesn't matter. The answer is always going to be yes."

An easiness rolls through me, allowing me to relax against him, tempering every worry I've had for the last year. Letting go of all my reservations, I choose to trust in this moment. In this man I'm beginning to think might understand me better than I understand myself. The man who knows what I need before I need it. I've been running for so long, holding everything in, hiding behind the walls I've erected to protect myself. And here Fisher is, showing up, day after day, tearing them down.

"Okay," I whisper.

Fisher arches a questioning brow. "Okay?"

"Okay, I'll come home with you."

Fisher

Chapter 25

"GET YOUR SHIT."

The tight fist that's been locked around my heart since Sutton and I walked into the house to find Libby gone has finally released. She'll come home with me, and she'll be safe.

She purses her lips like she's going to argue, but before she can, I angle in for a kiss again. I don't want to fight. I'd much rather she melt into me and let me make her feel good. The desire to claim her, to hear her cry my name as I sink inside her, is out of control. But she needs to be ready. She still hesitates when I touch her, so she's not there yet. But with any luck, she will be. I need her to want me with the same desperation that I crave her.

The moment I run my tongue along the seam of her lips, she parts and lets me in. Her mouth is warm and willing, causing my quick distraction to turn into something more. Unable to resist, I pull her in until the swell of her breast is pressed against my chest. I live in this moment, where Libby feels like mine, tuning everything else out. The sigh that slips out of her mouth settles deep in my bones. Damn, I could kiss this woman from now until the end of time. When I pull back and see the desire swimming in her endless blue eyes, I almost give in, but then I remember Sutton.

Home alone.

And someone is trying to hurt Libby.

"Get. Your. Shit," I repeat. "Get everything you'll need to stay."

She blinks at me, still stunned. "For how long?"

Forever is on the tip of my tongue, but I catch myself before I scare her. "Until we figure out who is fucking with you."

Uncertainty flashes in her eyes, like maybe she would have preferred if I'd said forever. But without a word, she nods and rushes to her room.

While I wait, I peer out the window, checking the area around the houses. It looks like it's just us. Bing is still splayed out on my front porch where I left him when I stormed over, and the camera will notify me of motion. But until both girls are under my roof, I won't feel settled.

I'll have to explain Libby's continued presence to Sutton, but I don't know how to do that, because I want Libby in my bed tonight. With me. For reasons that I can't admit to my eight-year-old.

The last thing I wanted was to leave Libby this morning. Waking up with her in my arms was like waking up from a dream, only to find I'm now living it. The way her body curled into mine, my arm wrapped around her, my palm flat on her soft skin, was addicting. However, when Wilder called at six thirty, I knew there was an issue.

His winter lobstering days make him an *early bird gets the worm* kind of guy, but he knows I'm rarely up before seven.

So the second his name flashed on my phone's screen, my heart took off and fear swamped me. Sutton was my first thought, though the news that Libby's brake lines were cut wasn't a whole lot less stressful.

And knowing someone is trying to hurt her, not just scare her, makes me desperate to keep both my girls close.

So after a quick trip to question Ryder about the golf cart, I picked up Sutton from Mrs. K's house. On the way back, I told her about the accident—though I may have played it down to keep from worrying her—so she'd understand why Libby was at our house again.

I rub my hand over my face and squeeze my eyes shut to block out the memory of the moment I discovered Libby was once again gone.

"Ready." Her voice chases away the pain and lights my body up with anticipation, with this deep desire to keep her close, to touch her.

She appears with a bag in one hand and another slung over her shoulder, along with her phone and her computer. Though she puts up a fight, eventually, she lets me carry her bags.

"Libby!" Sutton launches herself at the woman who is quickly becoming her favorite person. "Fisher said Putt-Putt broke and crashed, and that you hit your head—" She zeroes in on the bags in my hands, confusion creasing her forehead.

"She found a nest of spiders at her house this morning, so she's staying here until we get them all out."

Sutton's blue eyes narrow like she's working through something. When I'm certain she's going to tell me my nose is growing, she only shrugs. "Makes sense." She takes the smaller bag from me and turns to Libby, head tipped back. "Can you stay in my bed this time?"

"No," I bark. Unless Libby says otherwise, the woman is sleeping next to me.

Libby raises a brow, her lips kicking up on one side.

"It's too small," I add quickly.

Sutton crosses her arm and gives me a look I can only imagine I'll see a lot more of when she's a teenager, and shit, is it terrifying. "It's the same size as yours."

"But you have more pillows. Plus"—I tip my chin to my dog who has now settled in the corner on the big pillow he uses for naps— "Bing sleeps with you."

Sutton scoffs. "Only when you tell him to."

"And I plan to tell him to tonight."

"Fine." Sutton draws the word out, as if I exhaust her.

Libby pulls her lips in on themselves like she's fighting a smile, and as Sutton disappears, she leans close to me. "Subtle, Sheriff."

"Don't give me shit." I stomp up the stairs, fighting a smile as the sweet sound of her laugh follows me.

The pink designer luggage might not exactly match the simple navy plaid comforter and curtains, but the tension eases out of my neck and my shoulders relax a fraction at the sight of her stuff in my room. It feels like Libby is finally where she's supposed to be.

Maybe it doesn't make sense—the Hollywood star belonging in a small white house on an island in the middle of nowhere Maine—but I no longer care about what does and doesn't make sense. Because I'm almost smiling as I stomp back down the stairs.

"Oh, guess what?" Sutton says.

The girls are settled at the bar that separates the kitchen from the living area, breaking into the scones Sutton and I brought home from the inn.

Libby pauses with a pastry halfway to her mouth. "Mrs. K agreed to make the stew you wanted for dinner?"

I groan. There is no way they'll be okay skipping Sunday dinner at the Knowleses' tonight. Dammit. I sigh at the loss of the quiet evening at home I was envisioning. One filled with the girls' laughter and stolen kisses when Sutton isn't paying attention.

"No, she's making roast." Frowning, Sutton waves a hand. "But that's okay, because as of *this* morning"—she leans forward and stage whispers—"the water is officially fifty-eight degrees."

"Oh no." I jump into the conversation.

"Come *on*." Her face falls, her expression morphing into the pout she's been using against me since she was five. "You said once I was eight, I could *try*."

Jaw locked, I take a deep breath in through my nose. I hate the Monhegan Goodbye. This fucking island. "I said you could do it one time, and only when Wilder is doing it. Not by yourself, and he's taking his boat to the mainland today." Because I strong-armed him into going to get the parts to fix Putt-Putt.

Jesus, she's even got me using the ridiculous moniker now.

"Not fair," Sutton whines.

"What are you talking about?" Libby's head swivels back and forth between us.

"It's a fun tradition." She side-eyes me, then cups her mouth and whispers. "Fisher thinks it's dumb." She pops up straighter in her seat, one brow arched, like she's daring me to deny it. "It's so cool, though. It's called the Monhegan Goodbye. When the last ferry of the day pulls away from the island, the islanders jump off the dock into the water and wave to the boat."

"Oh." Libby lights up.

Knowing exactly where this is heading, I step closer. "No." When both girls look at me, I stare Libby down. "I'm serious. You have a concussion. You're not doing a ten-foot leap into ice-cold ocean water." I eye Sutton next. "And you are not doing it without an adult."

Sutton bats her eyes. "You could do it with me."

"Pigs will fly before I jump into that ice bath."

Sutton's shoulders slump, and even Libby's face falls.

"But..." I sigh. "Since we have dinner at Mrs. K's tonight, we can swing by and watch the others jump."

"Doesn't it look fun?" Sutton asks Libby for the tenth time as we trudge back up the hill.

Blue and a few other islanders came out tonight to perform the first of many of the summer's Monhegan Goodbyes.

Libby nods, her eyes sparkling. "And there is this energy in the air. It's like this exciting tingle."

My focus lowers to Libby's bare legs. That's exactly how I felt when she walked down the stairs dressed like that earlier. Like the air was suddenly charged, and when she came into sight, the current zapped through my entire body. The way she strutted down the steps, her legs on full display in the short white dress, her hips calling to me, nearly knocked me on my ass.

Thank fuck Sutton was still upstairs, because there was no stopping the urge to touch her. Of its own volition, my body practically floated across the room. Like a compass finds its true north, she drew me to her. To feel her, to touch her. To kiss her lips and fall under her spell. I was a glutton for punishment, letting her tease me. Hell, she's been teasing me since the moment she arrived. Her presence alone is the most exquisite torture. I claimed her mouth, and she wrapped her arms around me and pulled me close. There was no resisting the need to run my hands up and down her bare thighs. I teased the hem of her dress, taunting her, tempting myself.

The whimper that slipped through her lips had my dick begging to be released from my damn jeans.

Libby shivers, the vibration pulling me from my reverie. I glance over and find her watching me with the intensity I feel after reliving our moment together earlier. Like she's thinking about the way I skated a thumb across her panties the instant before Sutton flew down the stairs, interrupting us.

"Blue gets to jump every single time."

I blink, putting the past away, determined to remain focused on the conversation with Sutton. The ferry. The idiots jumping into the water and waving to the summer people heading back to the mainland while the rest of us are forever on vacation.

"He says he hasn't missed a single Monhegan Goodbye since he was six years old." Sutton sends me a pointed look. "I wouldn't know what that's like."

"Once Eddy gives me the-all clear, I'll jump with you," Libby promises.

"Yes!" Sutton spins in a circle, and I groan.

"Don't be such a grouchy bear." Libby bumps her shoulder into my upper arm.

I snag her hand and lace our fingers, only to realize that Sutton has zeroed in on our connection. Fuck.

Her lips tip up into an almost smile before falling flat again. Then, without looking at either of us, she takes off running, her pigtails flopping around her head. "Come on, Bing. I'll race you to Mrs. K's."

Libby clears her throat, drawing my attention. "It's okay to loosen the reins a little, even when it feels scary."

My body tightens in response to the comment. Sutton is already limited in so many ways. She's never seen a busy city street. She'll never play soccer with a group of kids her age. She won't drive off on her own the morning of her sixteenth birthday. She won't graduate from high school with a whole class of kids. She misses out on enough. I do not need to hold her back more because I'm afraid to lose her.

I swallow. "I know."

Libby squeezes my hand and gives me a small smile.

"Come on." Shoulders relaxing, I put my hand on the small of her back and guide her up the steps of Mrs. K's porch. "Let's get this over with."

"I love Sunday dinner. I don't know why you always act like it's going to be such a chore." She giggles, the sound floating away on the breeze.

"Because it's always a shit show."

And a shit show it is. The main event begins the second we're all settled at the table.

"Look what I picked up from the Amazon," Blue announces.

"Ordered from Amazon," Eddy corrects.

Without acknowledging his granddaughter, Blue places the two dark green trays on the table.

Eddy's eyes go wide. Libby gasps. Mrs. K groans. Wilder, naturally, laughs.

"Do not put those on my table." Mrs. K points at the already frozen ice trays.

"What? I thought pine tree–shaped ice would be perfect. Fitting for Maine." Blue's eyes dance with mischief. He knows damn well that the water has been frozen in the shape of anal plugs, *not* trees.

"I want a Christmas tree ice." Lindsey claps.

"Me too," Sutton chimes in.

Mrs. K and Eddy both watch in horror as Blue drops the "trees" into the girls' cups before moving on.

With the largest piece hovering over Libby's glass, he smirks at me. "It's a bit of a tight fit here. Fisher might need to work it in better."

I shake my head, biting back a laugh. Libby is doing her best not to smile. Under the table, I pat her thigh. She shifts, but instead of pulling away, she crosses her legs, trapping my hand between them.

All I'd have to do is shift my pinkie just a little...

"Th-thanks," Libby stutters as my finger brushes the lace of her panties. Instead of pushing my hand away, she flexes her thigh muscles, holding me in place.

My dick jumps in my pants. Fuck, this is going to be a long-ass dinner.

Fisher

Chapter 26

TWO HOURS FELT LIKE FIFTY. Dinner dragged on. The walk home was never-ending. I swear it's never taken so long to get Sutton ready for bed. Time crawled all night long, all because I've been counting down the minutes until I can have time alone with the gorgeous blonde who's taken up residence in my home.

After the quickest shower in history, I threw on a pair of gray sweats and followed the sound of Libby's voice. I found her in Sutton's room, reading *Charlotte's Web*.

She doesn't just read the words the way I do. No, she acts out the story. The voice of Charlotte the spider is so different from Wilbur the pig. The expression she puts into each word is impressive.

The girls are snuggled together in Sutton's bed. Sutton's under the pink quilt. Libby, in those tiny-ass shorts, sits with her legs curled under her on top of the covers. A strange battle rages inside me. Utter relaxation—a sense of peace, knowing my girls are content —mixed with a surge of desire at the sight of Libby.

I want to leave her here so she can giggle with Sutton and make her smile forever, and yet I want to wrap her in my arms, hold her close, and refuse to share her. Is this what it's like for parents? Loving their child while craving their partner? Peace and desire existing on different planes, though bearing the same weight?

"That's it?" Sutton whines as Libby closes the book. "One more, please? He'll never know."

Chuckling, I step into the room. "Oh, yes he will."

"Darn it." Sutton slumps into the zillion pillows on her bed. Pink hearts and white squares and even a tiara-shaped pillow. She always needs one more. Must be a girl thing.

"We can read the next one tomorrow." Libby straightens the bookmark and sets *Charlotte's Web* next to the moon lamp.

I click on the LED light and drop a kiss to the top of Sutton's head. "Sleep well, sweet pea."

After she's doled out hugs, I shut off the light and close her door.

I've been thinking of nothing but this moment for hours, but now, as we move into my room, an awkwardness hangs in the air.

Libby stops in the middle of the space, shifting on her feet, her attention downcast. "Is this a mistake?"

The breath leaves my body in a hard whoosh. "Mistake?"

She lifts her shoulders slightly and lets them fall. "You and Sutton have this perfect little life here, and my life..." She nibbles her lip, her eyes still averted.

I keep my mouth shut, wanting—no, *needing*—to hear her worries.

Eventually, she clears her throat and continues. "My life is not perfect. It's a big mess." She forces her chin up and meets my gaze, her blue eyes swimming with uncertainty. "So I'm worried that this" —she points to herself, then me—"will be a mistake for you."

"Libby." I step in close and rub my hands up and down her arms.

She leans in, her forehead resting against my bare chest, her warmth soaking into me, and trails her fingers along my abs.

The sensation is distracting as hell. I swallow and will myself to focus on the topic rather than the desire her touch inspires. Talking isn't my forte, but she needs to hear this. "The only time I feel like any part of my life is actually my own is when you're

175

standing next to me. So no, nothing about you could ever be a mistake." I press my lips to the crown of her head and tuck her close. She's nervous and I understand that. If she needs more time, I'll hold her for as long as it takes to make her comfortable. We don't have to go any farther than this. "You may be sleeping in my bed tonight, but that doesn't mean we have to do anything. I need you to know that."

Her body goes tense against me.

Worried I've upset her, I lighten the moment with a tease. "Besides, Sutton's down the hall, and I doubt you could be quiet."

Her head snaps back, the worry in her eyes replaced with the brightest sparkle. "You think you can make me scream?"

"Oh, Princess." I chuckle. "I *know* that when I finally have you spread out in my bed, when I'm inside you—tongue or cock, take your pick—you will be screaming my name."

She steps out of my embrace, and for a split second, I worry I've crossed a line.

The concern evaporates, though, when she grasps the hem of her T-shirt and slowly, torturously, pulls the garment over her head. With her flawless pale skin and pretty pink nipples on display, my heart kicks up. As I drink her in, the buds harden. They're begging for attention from my fingers, my mouth. It takes a ridiculous amount of willpower to force my eyes up to her face, but before I touch her, I need confirmation that this is okay.

"Want to bet?" She smirks. "Because I think you're going to be the one moaning my name."

That's all the okay I need. With a step closer, I run my finger along the waist of the tiny shorts, the pad of my thumb brushing her skin, and she shudders.

I cock a brow. "Don't get shy on me now, Princess."

In fucking slow motion, she slips her thumbs beneath the pink fabric, and as she lowers her shorts, exposing just a sliver of pale skin at the curve of her hip, my breath stalls. When she slips them over her ass, anticipation surges in my blood, and when I get my first glimpse of the apex of her thighs, the pussy I'm desperate to touch, to taste, my vision goes hazy.

"Are you going to touch me or stare at me?" she taunts as she steps out of her shorts.

Sassy and gorgeous. My kryptonite. "Just getting my fill." I force my attention back to her face. "We are not rushing this." To make my point, I zero in on her lips, then linger on her neck and her collarbone. As I work my way lower, I silently show her each place I plan to toy with. When my gaze lands on the swell of her tits. I step closer and ghost a hand over her shoulder, being sure not to touch her. She arches toward me, silently begging, her breathing picking up. I inch closer, move my hand so it's millimeters from her breast, still not touching but relishing the heat radiating from her body.

"Please, Fisher," she breathes.

I freeze, my focus snapping up again. "Please, what?"

"Touch. Me." She grasps my hand and guides it to her warm skin.

The second we make contact and the weight of her breast settles in my palm, we let out matching groans.

Head tipped back, she sighs. "I want you."

"I've wanted you since the second you landed in my arms." I might have spent weeks fighting it, but there's no denying I've been under her spell since our very first meeting. Thumbs brushing back and forth across the soft skin I want to spend the night touching, I swallow thickly. "But..."

Small towns suck and this admission does too.

She tenses, her expression shuttering a fraction, like she's bracing herself to be disappointed.

"I don't have any condoms." I should have picked some up the last time I was in Boothbay, but I was still fighting this then.

And fuck if I'll let anything that happens between Libby and me become fodder for Doris at the store.

She nods. "I'm on birth control. And I was tested right after I left the show."

My hackles rise in response to that statement, but I refuse to wreck this moment by getting into her history. She's mine now and that's all that matters.

Lightly, I graze her nipple with my thumb. "It's been two years for me."

Her eyes go wide with surprise.

I fight a grin. "I don't like people. Remember?"

She stretches up on her toes so our mouths are barely an inch apart. So close that her words vibrate against me. "You like me."

"You're different." I angle close enough to feel her breath on my lips.

"So make me scream, Fisher. I dare you."

Challenge accepted. Blood pumping, I capture her mouth. When she kisses me back with those full, soft, perfect lips, my cock aches. Groaning, I release her breast and pull her in so that her tits rub against my bare chest.

She shivers, her back arching.

Damn.

Without breaking our connection, I guide her back, then lower her onto the mattress. Only when she's splayed out beneath me do I release her so I can drink her in.

With one finger, I trace a line down her neck to the swell of her breast, reveling in the way goose bumps erupt in my wake.

"Fisher," she whispers, back bowing, greedy for more.

The sound goes straight to my cock. Painfully hard already, it strains against the gray sweats, begging to be free.

"Don't worry, Princess. I'll take care of you." I drop my mouth to her nipple, teasing her until she arches off the bed, rolling her hips against mine.

"I need you too—"

I slip a hand between her thighs, cutting off her demands, and slide my fingers through the damp heat of her pussy.

"Damn, you're so wet for me." I groan into her neck. "You want me to make you come with my fingers first?" I slip a digit inside her and curl it against her inner wall. "Or my tongue?"

"I don't...either...both." The words are broken as I toy with her.

I kiss my way down her body. Her scent fills my nose, spurring me on. "Both, it is."

With one last kiss to her hip, I trail my lips over her silky skin and use my shoulder to separate her thighs.

"So fucking perfect." I drag my nose against her flesh.

"Please, Fisher." She clutches at the sheets on either side of her, her pale skin in sharp contrast to my dark sheets.

Obediently, I lick her from opening to clit. "Yes."

Her taste explodes on my tongue. Fuck. One dose, and I'm addicted. I lap at her until she's moaning and thrusting against my face. I slip my finger inside her and curl at the same time my tongue circles her clit.

"Fisher," she moans as she rocks hard against me. "More. I'm so close."

Again and again, I lick and suck and nip, and when her pussy quivers, I double my efforts until she pulses around my fingers. As she comes down from her orgasm, I run my tongue over her, taking every drop of her pleasure.

As she sags against the bed, she grasps my shoulders and tugs. I peer up her body, over the smooth hills of her breasts.

Her eyes are dark with desire, her chest heaving with exertion.

"I want you," she says.

With my focus still fixed on her face, I push to my feet and slide my sweats down.

When my cock juts up like it's reaching for her, her tongue snakes out along her lower lip. I give myself a firm tug, and her eyes go wide. My heart beats hard as I drop down to hover over her. "Tell me you're mine, Princess." I line myself up, but hold still, teasing myself as much as her. I'm desperate to sink inside her, but I need to hear this first.

"Yes, Fisher." Her eyes meet mine. "I'm yours."

Slowly, I slide home, fighting the shivers that course up my spine with each inch I claim.

"Damn right this pussy is mine. It's begging for my cock." Her breath stutters and her core tightens around me. "You like that, baby? You ready for me to make you scream?"

"Yes," she whimpers, head thrashing.

Teeth gritted, I roll my hips. Fuck. Nothing has ever felt this good. She is my perfect fit. My heart takes off, pounding in my ears as I fuck into her over and over. Knowing I won't last long, I shift and lock her arms over her head, changing the angle until she's moaning and trembling.

When the tingles start at the base of my spine, I pull out all the stops to ensure she comes first. Knowing that my dirty girl loves words, I bring my lips to the shell of her ear. "Come for me, Princess. Strangle my cock with your pleasure. Milk me until I fill you with my cum." I swivel my hips.

"Shit," she whimpers. "Again," she begs.

Gladly. I thrust and then swirl. Thrust and swirl. Until, finally, her back arches and her hot pussy grips me rhythmically.

"Fisher."

I drop my mouth to hers and swallow her scream as my own release steals the breath from my lungs.

"Fuck," I mumble against her lips as I paint her insides with hot jets of cum. Filling her. Marking her.

Legs trembling, I collapse beside her, then yank her body over mine. Her hair splays out over my chest as we pant and gasp for air, our hearts beating wildly against each other.

As she curls into me, a sensation far deeper than pleasure spreads through me. In this moment, I know that no matter where she goes, I'll never get over Libby Sweet.

Libby

Chapter 27

IN A TWIST that will surprise absolutely no one, I woke up in Fisher's bed alone. Again.

Though there's a niggle of disappointment deep in my chest, I can't be angry about it. I have no idea what Sutton and Fisher's routine looks like. Maybe she likes to snuggle in the morning. Maybe he likes to go for a run.

Would I like to be snuggled?

Yes. More than I can explain.

I learn something new about myself every day, and apparently one of those things is that I like to snuggle.

I sit with that for a moment, soaking in the implication. And I can't deny that I like how sore my body is after last night. And how soft his sheets are. And how they smell like him.

Boy, am I obsessed.

This is bad.

Or maybe it's good?

As I replay last night, the way he kissed me, the way he tasted, how it felt the moment he sank inside me—like being torn apart, but in a good way.

Every time he touched me somewhere new, it felt like another beginning. Each graze of his fingers or his mouth or his cock wiped away the memories of unwanted touches. My body, which used to flinch when a man so much as came near, wakes up for Fisher.

The chill that used to engulf me has been replaced by a rush of warmth. The same way the summer sun warms the frost that encases this island in the late spring.

As butterflies flap wildly in my chest, I let out a silent shriek and kick my feet, making the sheets go flying. When I arrived on that trash boat, I never could have imagined feeling this way. I had no intention of falling for someone. But that's exactly what I'm doing.

Rather than sneak out of his room like in the past, I pull a sweatshirt over my pajama top and step into the hall with my head held high.

I find Sutton downstairs on the couch beneath a blanket, eyes trained on the television.

"Morning, pretty girl," I say, holding tight to the confidence I felt when I was still in bed. If I don't act like this is weird, hopefully she won't feel like it is.

Because it is.

I'm not the girl who dates the guy with a kid.

I'm not the girl who has time to date, let alone time to be an important person in a child's life.

Scratch that. Elizabeth Sweet is not that kind of girl.

More and more, I'm finding that Libby actually is.

Sutton lights up the moment she sees me. "Morning, Libby!"

"Where'd your da—" I snap my mouth shut before I blurt out the word *dad*. Maybe I'm not so good at this after all. "Fisher. Where's Fisher?"

Seemingly unbothered by my near slip, she turns back to the television. "He's outside somewhere."

Maybe he's a runner. Though he doesn't seem like a runner. But if he was, what would he wear? The man wears Timberlands and jeans every day. He's got nice thighs, though. He'd look amazing in a pair of gym shorts.

Good god. I wipe the drool from the corner of my mouth and head toward the door. I shouldn't be getting all hot and bothered while hanging out with Sutton.

Barefoot, I step onto the porch, and when I spot Bing, who is playing guard dog by rolling around in the grass, I can't help but smile. As the door creaks shut, his whole body spasms, and then he's on his feet and charging toward me. I drop to my knees and let him lick my face. Once he's covered every inch with slobber, I bury my head in his soft fur and hug him.

"Good morning, buddy. Yes, you are such a good boy. Yes you are," I coo ridiculous words in his ear.

His tail bangs against the porch loudly, his butt shimmying in excitement, but he doesn't pull away. Not until the sound of gravel crunching snags our attention. Clearly as obsessed with Fisher as I am, he spins, nearly knocking me over, and bounds toward his daddy.

I push to a stand, brushing at the dog hair that clings to my sweatshirt and legs. With a hat shading his eyes, Timberlands— surprise, surprise—a white T-shirt, and jeans, Fisher looks just as he always does.

He looks like mine.

The possessive word imprints itself on my heart, and as he comes closer, my body sags in relief. Just being in his presence comforts me. When I catch sight of the white bakery bag and iced coffee in his hand as he ambles up the driveway, I grin. "Do you ever make breakfast?"

He stops at the steps to the porch. He's so tall that from there, he only has to tilt his head slightly to make eye contact. "No."

He holds out the iced coffee.

"What's this?"

"One of those gross sweet coffees. Sutton thought you'd like it."

My mouth falls open. I haven't had a fancy iced coffee since I arrived on this island. I didn't think I could. "Where'd you get it?"

"The bakery."

I bite back a scowl. It really was sweet of him to pick this up for me, even if the evil baker is the one who made it. With any luck, she doesn't know it's for me and it's poison-free.

"Ah, and you got flirty donuts." I snatch the bag from his hand and spin on my heel.

Behind me, Fisher follows, grumbling something along the lines of *Ruckus Donuts. There's nothing flirty about them.* I temper a smile.

Inside, I hold up the donut bag and get Sutton's attention, then head for the kitchen. As I tear paper towels from the roll and set them on the table, Fisher pulls the chocolate milk from the fridge and pours two glasses. One for himself and one for Sutton.

Once we're all seated, with Fisher on one side of me and Sutton on the other, I take my first sip of iced coffee.

There's no point in even trying to stop the moan that escapes me. Not when this drink is everything I've been missing. "I'll pay you to pick one of these up for me every morning." Like a fiend desperate for another hit, I suck on the straw until my cheeks hollow.

"Told you she'd like it." Sutton grins at Fisher, and he winks back at her.

Their interaction warms my chest. The two of them schemed in order to give me something they thought I'd like. They wanted me to feel comfortable. Both of them. The warmth turns into the best kind of ache as I study them. Their thoughtfulness makes me feel like I belong here with them. Just like this. With Sutton on my left and Fisher on my right. I can envision myself doing this every day. That thought doesn't scare me in the least. It does the opposite, actually. It makes me crave the possibility.

Even more than this stupidly delicious iced coffee.

"Will Putt-Putt be fixed in time for the parade?" Sutton asks.

Fisher grunts. "Maybe."

Frowning, I look from him back to her, knowing she'll give me a more thorough answer. "What parade?"

"For the fourth. People decorate their golf carts and some walk their animals in it too." Her eyes snap over to Fisher. "Oh, we can totally put pink lipstick on Bing. And maybe sunglasses. He can sit between us in the front of the cart, and I'll make him wave to everyone."

I giggle at the image I've conjured in my head of poor Bing being done up. Also, everyone? There are barely enough people on this island to make a parade. Who are the spectators?

Unsurprisingly, Fisher answers with a single word. "No."

With a wink at Sutton, I pick up my phone. "I can order Fourth of July stuff from Amazon. We can dress him in that."

"Oh, yes!" She bounces in her seat, her messy blond hair swaying. "Can we do that?"

"No," Fisher growls. "My dog, my decision."

Phone unlocked, I pull up the Amazon app, tilt closer to Sutton, and scroll.

"Is anyone listening to me?"

I look up and catch Fisher's lips twitching. He can pretend to be annoyed—it's our thing—but so long as I keep catching those little smiles, I'll push right back. Holding my phone out to Sutton, I give her permission to go crazy with her selection. Then, with a hand on Fisher's thigh, I lean into him. "What's on the agenda for you today?"

"Work," he says gruffly as he peers down at my hand.

"But you don't have a job," I tease.

With a sigh, he tips his head back. "And yet I do all the jobs."

"Can we come with you?"

"Yes! I want to come," Sutton says without looking up from the phone. I can't wait to see all the things she's added to my cart. "But only if you promise to take us to the puffins."

I sit a little straighter. "Puffins?"

"Yeah, they kind of look like penguins," she explains, nose still buried in the device.

"Oh, I know what a puffin is." *Sort of.* "I read a book where the characters had a pet puffin, but I thought the author came up with a fictional kind of bird."

185

Fisher frowns. "A fictional kind of bird? What kind of book was it?"

"A romance." I shift in my seat, smiling at the memory of the story. It was one of my favorite reads last year. "The male main character was a major league pitcher. During a game, he threw the ball and it hit the puffin." I hum, head tilted, thinking of how best to explain the next part. "I have to start at the beginning in order for it to make sense. First the pitcher met this woman at a bar and then there was this great se—" I bite my lip. "He scored that night. In that bar. It was a total home run and—"

Groaning, he drops his head into his hands. "Stop. Please. I get it."

Sutton quirks a brow, apparently done with the Amazon cart. "Why would he score a home run in a bar?"

"Because he was a bad boy," Fisher grits out.

I giggle. "Yup. Anyway, I thought the bird was fake."

"Nope. Puffins are adorable, and Fisher knows all the best spots to find them."

"They're birds," he says like he's told her this before. "We don't live in a zoo. I can't promise we'll see one."

Sutton shakes her head resolutely. "You'll see."

Libby
Chapter 28

OUR DAY STARTS down at the docks. Fisher gets out of the truck to pick up packages, telling us to stay put. There's no way I can sit here and do nothing while he works, so naturally, we don't listen.

"Hi, Bob!" Sutton yells.

"I thought his name was Cank," I mumble as we walk over to chat.

"Ah, Libby," the older man calls. "Glad to see you're doing okay since your accident."

"Wasn't an accident." Sutton cups her mouth and does that loud whisper thing again. It's pointless but absolutely adorable. "Someone cut her wires."

Cank's forehead creases with concern. "Who would do that?"

I shrug. "Fisher's working on figuring that out. I'm still betting it was the goat."

His face morphs into a scowl. "Betty would never."

"Betty is a boy, and his name is Fred," Sutton says like Cank just made the most ridiculous error.

"Betty is a goat," Fisher growls, then shakes his head. "I mean the goat is a goat. And I thought I told you to stay in the car."

Betty is a boy whose name is Fred? That makes so much more sense, if I'm honest, since Betty is very clearly a male goat. Sutton is clearly the smartest on the island. With a huff, I frown at Fisher, who's loading packages into his truck. "What are you doing?"

"Delivering the mail," he grumbles, like it's obvious.

It would be if he was the mailman.

"But why?"

"How do you think you get your mail, Princess?" His tone is teasing this time.

I shrug. "I thought you were being nice. I didn't know this was another one of your *jobs*," I sing. Oh, now that I know he's the person I'll be annoying with purchases, a whole slew of ridiculous orders crowds my mind.

"While he's dropping off this mail," Cank says to me, "could you run into the grocery store and ask Doris to add bacon to my order this week?"

I shudder at the mere thought of dealing with Doris. That woman despises me. And she's mean.

But I'm nothing if not neighborly, so I paste on a smile and head toward the truck. "Will do."

"Will we be seeing you at the Fourth of July parade?" he calls after us.

Sutton spins and walks backward, grinning. "Yup. We'll be riding Putt-Putt."

"I said no," Fisher grumbles from the back of the truck. "Does no one listen to me?" With a grunt, he hops down and stalks to the driver's side.

Sutton and I giggle as we strap ourselves in.

"Cank asked—"

Fisher's phone rings, cutting me off.

He creeps along the path, nodding in a silent request for me to answer it. I think. Grimacing, I pick it up and put it on speaker.

Before Fisher even says hello, the line crackles, and a nasally voice says, "Oh, Fisher, I need you."

My skin crawls. This woman *needs* Fisher?

Sutton crosses her arms and grunts.

What the hell is that about?

"What's the problem now?" Fisher asks in that no-nonsense tone of his. It's kind of hot.

Okay, who am I kidding? It's very hot.

"The squirrel is in my gutter again."

He presses his tongue into his cheek, then sighs, his body deflating. "Okay, I'll be over in a few."

"Oh, thank you," the caller gushes. "I've got lunch laid out. Why don't you stay and eat? Let me show you my appreciation."

Oh my god. This woman is shameless. The voice is a dead giveaway. I know exactly who's hitting on my man.

"Thanks, but I've got the girls with me today, so I'll just take care of the squirrel."

"Oh, I'd love to spend time with little Sutton and Lindsey. I've got enough food for all of us."

Without bothering to explain who the girls he mentioned are, he snatches the phone from my hand and hits End.

It wouldn't surprise me if the woman on the other end doesn't flinch at Fisher's abruptness. From what I can tell, the people on the island have come to expect this type of behavior from him.

Besides, she's probably still talking in that nasally tone, believing he's there.

"What did she mean that the squirrel was in the gutter *again*?" I ask.

Fisher shakes his head. "Damn squirrel keeps getting stuck in her gutter. It's ridiculous."

I nod. Can't say it really surprises me, though. There's a lot of ridiculousness going on here. A male goat named Betty, an old man who paints in the buff, a man who goes by the nickname Cank but whose name is really Bob. "Do you think she stuffs the poor thing in there?"

Sutton giggles from the back seat.

"And how would she do that?" Fisher doesn't look at me, but there's a smile there, I swear.

I curl my hand into a C shape and give my fake squirrel a shake. "Come here, little squirrelly," I say, mimicking Flora's nasally tone. "Don't worry. You just gotta stay here"—I shove my hand forward like I'm stuffing the squirrel into the gutter—"for a little while so I can spend some time with *Fisher*." I drag out his name and really dig into that New England accent.

Behind me, Sutton's giggles turn into full-on belly laughs.

Fisher comes to a stop in the road and squints at me. "And why would anyone do that?"

"For your attention." I bat my eyes, hands clasped in my lap.

Scoffing, he rolls his eyes. "Would you do that for my attention?"

A smile plays at my lips as I lean closer. "I don't need to. I've already got it, don't I?"

He reaches across the console and slides his hand into mine. "Every bit of it, Princess. Every damn bit of it."

I bite my lip and lean back against the seat, unable to look away from him.

"So are we still going with that spider story, or are you ready to admit you're dating now?" Sutton says from the back.

Lips pressed into a line, I fight a smile while I wait for Fisher to take this question.

He points into the distance. "Oh look, a Puffin. And a reindeer. Oh and there's Santa too."

Sutton giggles again, the sound as light as ever.

Fisher's eyes flash with amusement as he rolls forward again. Flirty Donuts has nothing on this.

"You two coming in?" Fisher says as he parks. The baker is already standing out front, her red hair teased high, screaming for attention just like the low-cut too-tight shirt she's got on. Shameless, truly.

"We'll wait here. I'm hungry, so don't take too long," Sutton says without looking out the window.

Fisher nods as if Sutton's response is normal—*when it absolutely is not*—and disappears.

I turn in my seat and study her. I've never seen Sutton so snarky before and while I'm all for her hurrying this situation along, I'm concerned about what's going through that pretty little head of my favorite girl.

Before I can drum up the words to ask, she beats me to it. "Do you wear a bra?"

I rear back, caught off guard. If I'd had time to ponder all the things that could be bothering her, that would not have made the list.

"Um, yeah."

Lips twisting, she looks out the window.

"Do *you* wear a bra?" I ask slowly, keeping my tone neutral.

Sutton lets out a laugh far too sardonic for such a young person. "What do you think? Fisher would lose his mind if I asked him to get me one."

Suddenly, I get it. At least partially. I straighten, feeling more confident about being a confidant for her. "Yeah, it was totally awkward talking to my dad about it, but it wasn't as bad as being made fun of for not wearing one."

Sutton shifts, her lips tugging. "People made fun of *you*?"

"Everyone gets made fun of at some time or another, pretty girl. Some people are just mean."

With a sigh, she sinks lower in her seat. "Ben said he could see my nipples."

I picture the scrawny ten-year-old and decide I'll knock a paint can onto his foot—a full one—at the next rehearsal. "Believe me, one day he'll be begging to see them." I slap a hand over my mouth, but it's too late. Cringing, I exhale harshly. "Please, don't tell Fisher I said that."

Sutton laughs, the tension leaving her body.

I relax a little too. Despite clearly struggling with keeping my conversations with her appropriate, it feels good to know I can put her at ease. "But seriously, boys are jerks sometimes. And if someone tells you a boy is picking on you because he likes you, that's crap." I huff. "A boy who likes you should be nice to you. He should do nice things for you—"

"Like when Fisher bought iced coffee for you?"

Cheeks heating, I rack my brain for how to respond without stepping on any other landmines. Fisher and I haven't even discussed what's going on between us, and Sutton is his, so it's up to him to decide when he wants to talk to her about what we're doing. Whatever that may be.

"Or how he delivers all your packages?" She raises her brows.

My heart flutters, but I play it cool. "He delivers everyone's packages."

"Yeah, but he goes all the way to Boothbay to get yours, and he definitely doesn't dance with anyone else." Her expression goes thoughtful. "Before you, he never smiled."

The weight of those words slams against my chest with a powerful thud, knocking me back. "*Sutton*." I grasp her hand and squeeze, hoping she understands just how much that truth means to me.

It's bittersweet. I hate that before this summer, he never smiled, and even more, I hate that she noticed. But I can't help but be thankful that now that it's a relatively regular occurrence, she's around to witness it. Joy is a powerful thing. My hope for her is that she can emulate that and not the sadness that's settled around the two of them like a fog for so long.

"I'm really glad you're here." Her voice is so quiet I almost miss the admission.

"I'm really glad I'm here too."

Fisher comes stomping back, his friend on his heels.

"Sutton," she calls. She's wearing a smile, but it drops the moment she sees me in the front seat. Seeing as how there are no doors, it's not easy for her to ignore me, but she does a decent job. "Hi, baby girl," she coos.

"Hi, Flora," Sutton replies, her voice far more monotone than usual. She kind of sounds like Fisher, if I'm being honest.

"I was just telling Fisher that you two should come over for dinner. You could even have a sleepover."

"We've got to go," Fisher grumbles as he slides into the driver's seat. "Maybe one day next week. I did promise Libby I'd take her out on the water." He grabs my hand and brings it to his thigh.

I don't know what the hell he's doing, but I don't exactly hate it.

Flora's gaze cuts to our hands and she winces, though she recovers quickly and smiles with her teeth. "Right. Well, let me know, Sutton. I'll see you soon."

Fisher hits the gas, and the truck takes off with a bit of a jump.

"Driving like me now?" I tease.

He side-eyes me, but he's smiling.

"Please don't make me sleep over there," Sutton murmurs from the back seat.

I tense at her words, and my hackles rise at the discomfort in her tone.

As a child, I uttered those words on more than one occasion, yet no one listened. And I had a good reason. The thought makes me sick.

Fisher purses his lips like he's mulling over what she just said. I'm gearing up to go to battle for Sutton, when he says, "Whatever you want, sweet pea."

He meets her gaze in the mirror. She gives him a nod, and he returns the gesture. That's that.

That conversation—that simple moment where he acknowledged her request, respecting her wishes, and didn't even push her to explain why—has me reeling.

Unbidden, a single tear slides down my cheek. I turn away, focusing on the passing scenery as we go. On the tiny houses, each with its own personality. A blue shutter, a peach rocking chair, red flower boxes.

A warm hand settles on my lap and squeezes.

I can't look at him or I'll cry.

I can't look at him or I'll tell him how I think he's healing me this summer. He's doing it without even knowing it, probably. Because he cares, just like Sutton said.

And god, does that feel good.

"What do you say we stop at the inn for lunch?"

"Yay! Can I see if Lindsey is around?" Sutton asks.

"Course," Fisher says as he pulls down the drive to the inn.

As soon as the truck is stopped, Sutton hops out and takes off, running right past the two women sitting in rocking chairs on the porch.

I move a bit slower, taking my time unbuckling. Fisher doesn't move at all.

"Princess..." The softness of his tone, the openness, tugs at my heartstrings, and I can't help but turn to face him. "We all got demons. I'm not asking you to spill yours, but just know I'm here if you ever want to."

I duck my chin in acknowledgment and leave it at that. It takes everything in me not to throw myself at him. But if I let myself go back to that place for even a moment, I'm afraid I won't break free again. I want to stay here. In the present. On this island. With Fisher and Sutton. Here, I'm safe. Here, I'm happy.

I don't ever want to be anywhere else again.

By the time we approach the long bar top where Wilder's playing barkeep, Sutton's already settled with a Shirley Temple, a pack of crayons, and a coloring page. The picture on it is of a lobster and a bird that looks like a penguin.

"Is that a puffin?" I ask.

On the other side of Lindsey, Blue leans forward. "She's never seen a puffin before?"

Sutton shakes her head. "Weird, right? Almost as ridiculous as these two telling me Libby moved in because she's afraid of spiders." She grins back at us and then looks at Wilder. "Uncle Wilder, why don't you ask Fisher who he's dating?"

Wilder, who's wearing a shirt that says *I am the fun*, grins as he slides an iced tea in front of me. "Oh, I don't have to ask, little darling." He gives her a wink.

"That's what I said." Sutton plucks the cherry from her drink, far more confident than she was a few minutes ago.

It's a relief, seeing her like this. Even if the confidence comes at our expense.

Fisher drops an arm around the back of my chair, his fingers tangling in my hair. I glance over at him, wondering if he even realizes he's doing it. The man wears an easy expression, his posture relaxed. He doesn't even look my way, like he's set on ignoring my looks of confusion.

"But she has read about a puffin before. In a book about a baseball player who scored a home run in a bar. I don't understand how he could run all those bases inside a bar, and Fisher won't explain it to me. Will you explain it, Uncle Wilder?"

Wilder covers his mouth and coughs, fighting a laugh, his eyes jumping to Fisher's.

"I've never gotten a complaint when I score a home run in the kitchen," Blue says. "Or the bathroom. Or the bed."

I have to hold my breath to stifle a giggle. Fisher groans, and Wilder lets a loud laugh free, no longer restraining himself.

Sutton shakes her head. "I don't get it."

"And you shouldn't, because you're a good girl," Fisher grumbles.

Sutton blinks, her expression genuinely innocent. "Libby's a good girl too, right, Fisher?"

The horror that flashes across his face is almost enough to send me over the edge, but by some miracle, I hold back my laughter.

Blue lights up. "Yeah, Fisher, tell Libby what a good girl she is."

That does it. I officially lose the battle, and as my laughter rings out, Fisher cuffs the back of my neck and tugs me close. "The best girl," he whispers. "*My* best girl."

Fisher

Chapter 29

"YOU REALLY THINK WE NEED THESE?" Libby holds up a hand, blocking out the sun, and peers up at me. We've already hung two of the three cameras in the trees around her house, yet she's still asking the same damn question. "It feels so LA; not Monhegan. And nothing's happened since Putt-Putt's accident."

A sigh escapes me before I can stop it. "Lib," I pull back and glare down at her from my spot on the ladder. "Someone cut your brake line. Nothing about that is an *accident*. With all the hills on the island and sharp turns on the paths, you're lucky all you got was a bump on the head."

She shifts on her feet. The telltale sign that she's nervous, and a sigh breaks loose. But she doesn't argue.

I hop off the ladder and wrap my arms around her. Loving the way she melts into me, I pull her tight. Her pink tank top is just short enough that my thumbs meet the strip of bare skin above her waistband. I brush slowly back and forth, urging her to relax.

Though it's important that she take this situation seriously, I don't want her living in fear.

"No one can get to you when you're under my roof. Not only do I have cameras on every angle of my house, but the windows and doors are wired," I remind her.

When she discovered those details, she tossed out words like *paranoid* and *over-the-top*. But it's my job to keep Sutton, and now Libby, safe.

"I know," she mutters into my T-shirt.

"But while you're safe with me, I do not want someone fucking with your house. So let me get this last camera up, and we'll make sure that no one snoops around there either."

Her shoulders droop. "Again, very LA."

It kills me, the way this person is stealing away the freedom Libby has found here on the island. Even if she doesn't stay, I want her to always associate this place with happiness. With comfort. Because as pathetic as it sounds, if she loves it here, she might come back. And I desperately want her to come back. I'd be ecstatic if she never left, but that isn't a realistic hope.

"Only you and me, Princess. No one else is watching them. This is your power, not your prison."

She smiles against my chest. A sensation I've felt more and more over the past few weeks.

The summer, and my time with Libby, is passing way too quickly.

The Fourth of July parade was as ridiculous as I expected. Libby and Sutton decorated the damn golf cart so that it was red, white, blue...and pink. They put poor Bing in an American flag top hat, and blue star sunglasses. The two of them, decked out in matching blue Boston Revs baseball caps and sunglasses like Bings, led the charge down from the dock to the beach, honking that high-pitched horn and tossing candy to the vacationers along the path.

We might only have four carts, eight bikes, two dogs, and a goat, but the parade is always a spectacle. And this year didn't disappoint. Halfway through the route, Betty chased Lulu, Star and Ivy's Cavalier King Charles Spaniel—the most anxiety-ridden dog in existence— past the pack of bikes and through the crowd. The damn goat wouldn't stop, and the dog, who apparently has more fear than sense, jumped onto the roof of the Monhegan Brewery's golf cart, causing it to tip sideways into a mud puddle.

Poor Rip. Although Maggie, who was in the cart with her father, laughed so hard she was in tears, Rip looked more like his head might explode as muddy water dripped slowly off his gray beard.

Libby and Sutton turned back to help, and the little pink cart that could saved the day by pulling the brewery's cart back onto its wheels so the parade could go on.

At least the fish fry and the fireworks went off without a hitch. As long as we're not counting the errant firework that put a hole in Wilder's kayak. Since he was the one setting them off and he seemed happy enough about not having to take it out with Nicole the next day, I can't be sure that it really was an accident.

Yes, the woman is still here. Wilder is losing his mind.

I chuckle.

Libby lifts her head, her eyes narrowed. "Are you laughing at me?"

"No, Princess. I was just thinking about Wilder's beard."

Her nose scrunches up. "I don't know what he's thinking. It's the patchiest, most awful-looking facial hair I've ever seen."

My chuckle turns into a full-on laugh. My best friend has never been able to do facial hair. He knows this. But in a desperate attempt to get rid of the cling-on from the mainland, he's chosen to engage in a no-shave summer.

"That one chunk on the left side looks like a dead mouse." Libby shudders. "And what's up with that perfect circle of smooth skin next to his lip?" She runs a hand along my jaw. "You need to give him a lesson. You have the sexiest beard."

Stupid male pride causes my chest to puff. Fuck, I love it when my girl calls me sexy.

She pops up onto her toes and brings her mouth to my ear. "I especially love it when it's tickling my thighs."

With a grunt, I tighten my hold on her hips, my fingers biting into her flesh. "Is that a request?" If so, then fuck the camera. I'll finish it later. After I make Libby come on my tongue. And then cock.

With Sutton helping Maggie paint sets for the play, we have the afternoon to ourselves.

Giggling, she steps out of my grasp and wags a finger at me. "Nuh-uh. You said we had to finish this."

"Tease." I chuckle as I climb back up the ladder. A warm breeze blows off the water, rustling the branches around me as I pick up the drill I left at the top.

"It's such a pretty day." Libby sighs dreamily. "We should take the boat out. It looks so sad over there, stuck in the grass. Boats need water to be happy."

I shake my head at her nonsense. Only Libby Sweet would attribute thoughts and emotions and opinions to boats, golf carts, and houses.

"Plus I want to see a puffin," she chirps. "So can we?"

Once the last screw is in place, I clip the solar panel onto the camera and switch it on. Done. Now I have every angle of the house on lockdown. No one is getting near my girl or her house without me knowing.

"Can we?"

"See a puffin?" I glance down at her.

"Yeah, go out on your boat and see a puffin."

Lips pressed together, I shake my head. "That boat is winterized."

Blue eyes bright, she blinks at me. "It's summer."

I rest my forearms on the top rung of the ladder next to the drill. "According to the lobster laws on Monhegan, we can only set traps October through April, so I don't need the boat in the summer."

Frowning, she looks from me to the boat and back again. "I can't see you being a fisherman."

I almost correct her. Lobstering and fishing aren't the same thing, but that's not the point. "That's probably because I hate it."

She tips her head, assessing me. "Then *why* do you *do* it?"

"Obligation." I shrug. "Hunter worked hard to get the lobster license and even harder to acquire all the traps. It seems like a waste of his memory if I don't use it all."

"Hmm." She turns back to the boat, studying it for a minute.

It's nothing special, just a standard white and black dual motor Eastern boat. But it looks huge like it is, towering on the stilts in the yard. Especially with the black wire traps piled next to it.

Damn thing is so much work.

"There are only, what? Twenty of the metal box things? And maybe twenty-five of those teal and white floating parts?"

She's so very scientific in her description.

"Traps and buoys."

"Right." She nods. "Traps and buoys. Couldn't someone else use them? Or at least take a few off your hands so you didn't have to spend so much time doing it?"

Setting twenty traps really does take quite a bit of time. Hours, in fact. Asking anyone to take on the extra work doesn't sit right with me. I open my mouth to tell her so, but the truth is, I could give them away. I just don't. Besides... "What would I do all winter?"

She spins back to me. "Your computer stuff. What is it you say you do? Make people's lives miserable by wrecking their day?"

Chuckling, I jump off the ladder. "Hack, baby. I hack through firewalls."

"Yeah, of course." She nods as if she gets it, but she's far too nonchalant to really understand. Before I can explain it to her, she goes on. "Surely there's someone on the island who'd be happy to throw those traps into the water and then pray they don't lose a finger when they haul them up."

"Wilder loves it." Nothing makes that man happier than being out on the water. Being a fifth generation lobsterer, it's in his blood.

"Oh." Face lit up, she claps. "That's the answer. Let him do that, and you do the other thing."

She makes it sound so simple. Give the job to someone who loves it. Give up what I hate. And it should be simple. But here I am, three years after my brother died, still doing all his jobs.

"So can we *un*-winterize that thing?" She tips her chin at the boat.

"No."

Her lips turn down.

"But," I sigh, "I'll borrow Cank's boat and take you out to see the damn birds."

"Yay! Oh." She turns, only to spin back to face me. "While we're at it, can we stop on the mainland and get a bra for Sutton?"

Her words are casual, thrown out there like nothing, but when they register, my body locks up tight. That word—*bra*—rings in my ears. I must have misheard her. A pit forms in my stomach. That word and Sutton do not belong together. "W-what?"

"Yeah, a few of the other girls have them, and she really wants one."

I blink. *Not yet.* The words play on repeat in my head. I'm not ready for this girl stuff yet. "My daughter is not old enough for a bra," I grit out before I can process the words.

Libby's eyes widen and her body stiffens.

I replay the phrase in my mind and as soon as I hit the word *daughter,* I flinch. I've never called Sutton my daughter. She isn't my daughter. But at the same time, she is. Maybe it's time to break into that box full of things and people that are *just* Hunter's.

A sharp pain radiates through my chest and I slam my eyes shut. If I do that, it feels like a finality. Like acceptance that he's really gone.

A warm palm rests on my arm. Comforting me. Reminding me that I'm not alone. Not anymore.

"It's okay to call her that," Libby whispers.

My heart fractures a little more. "She's Hunter's daughter."

Slowly, she nods. "She was, yes, but that doesn't mean she can't be yours too."

"I feel like she's mine," I admit, the words almost inaudible. "Like a piece of my heart lives with her."

"Because you love her."

I nod, then quickly shake my head. How would people react if I claimed a role that never should have been mine? "But everyone will—"

"Everyone will know Sutton is lucky because she has you. And for every milestone moving forward, you'll be her parent." She shuffles around until we're face to face and squeezes my hands. "We all know you aren't trying to replace Hunter, but she deserves a parent who can do all these things with her. Things like buying a bra."

I swallow past the boulder in my throat. She's right. Sutton deserves a father, and by some twist of fate, I'm what she's got. And apparently that means I'm the one who has to get her a bra.

My insides still shake at that idea. "Hell, Princess. You're giving me chest pain." I rub at my sternum. "She's only eight."

"I know, but it would be fun for her to see an actual store, don't you think? And there is this boy..." Libby goes on to relay the details of the story that Sutton told her.

After I suppress the need to pummel the ten-year-old boy who mocked my girl, I begrudgingly agree to the bra trip.

"I need a drink." I rub a hand over my face. How the hell am I going to manage puberty and the teenage years if I can't even take her to buy a bra? "Want to take the damn cart to the brewery for lunch?"

Libby shakes her head. "That's not her name. Call her Putt-Putt."

"No." I might think it sometimes, but I've yet to say that stupid name aloud.

"I'll give you a kiss if you do," she singsongs, stepping up in front of me and batting her lashes, looking so damn cute it's almost impossible to resist. *Almost.* "You know you want one."

Oh, I do. Fighting both a smile and an eye roll, I shake my head.

She leans in so close her warm breath skates across my cheek.

The sweet scent of her perfume fills my nose, and just like that, I no longer care about the beer. All I want is time with Libby.

"Come on," she urges. "Say it with me. Putt-Putt." She kisses the corner of my mouth, teasing me. "Putt." Her sweet, warm breath hits my lips with each enunciated word. "Putt."

My dick twitches, and there's no stopping my grin.

Instead of playing her game, I snake an arm around her neck and pull her to me.

When I press my lips to hers, she squeals. "Cheater."

"Maybe so, but don't worry; I have plenty of ideas for how you can punish me." I toss her over my shoulder and carry her straight up to my bed.

Libby

Chapter 30

"ARE you going to buy something pretty for me if I take you shopping?" Fisher asks as he tosses me onto the bed.

It's been like this every time since that first night. His eyes full of hunger, an easy smile on his face. The teasing. It leaves little time for me to worry about much of anything. I'm too damn happy.

"Strip," I tell him, twirling my finger like a magic wand.

Even as he obeys, he growls. "Answer the question."

Inches of sinewy muscle come into view as he grips the back of his collar with one hand and pulls his shirt over his head the way only men can do. His abs flex with each move, drawing my focus to the dark hair that leads to the magical V that a man who works on computers shouldn't have.

He must work out a lot in the winter when there's nothing else to do on the island. How else would he look this good? He's not overly chiseled like the men in Hollywood. It's clear he works for it, but also that he works for a living. I could stare at him for a very long time if he'd allow it.

"Libby," he growls again, yanking his belt from the loops around his waistband.

"I didn't think you were the kind of guy who really cared about what his woman wears." I sit up on my knees and help him pull down his pants. His boxers go with them, and then his cock is springing free. Fuck, I wasn't prepared. I'm never prepared. The man is beautiful. The way his dick strains to get closer to me makes it impossible not to wrap my fingers around it and revel in the smooth contrast between the silken skin and the rock-hard length.

I roll my thumb over the tip, spreading his pleasure over his crown, and he hisses air through his teeth. "I've never given two fucks about anyone else."

Pausing, I peer up at him, waiting for him to finish the statement. He doesn't add to it. That's the statement. It's not about my clothes. It's not about my touch. It's me.

Even so, I can't help but goad him. It's what we do, after all. "What kind of pretty things do you want me to wear for you?"

He grunts and his eyes fall shut. "Naked. Need you naked now."

"Now, now Fisher. You asked for something pretty. Be a good boy and tell me what you want." I give his cock a squeeze.

When he opens his eyes again, they're molten. He curses and sucks in a sharp breath. "Something pink."

"Why?" I whisper.

His responding smirk is wicked. "Because that's what you like, Princess, and I like anything that makes you smile. Now take off your clothes, because you're right—I definitely prefer you naked."

I shake my head. No, I've got my mind set on something else. I want to taste him. Pushing him back slightly, I splay one hand on the mattress to steady myself and roll my tongue across the head of his cock.

Fingers tangling in my hair, he tugs gently.

Sparks ignite and zap through me at the sensation, pulling a groan from deep within my chest.

"You like that, Princess?" He tugs again. "Like when I use you for my pleasure?"

"God, yes," I mumble, my lips brushing his crown.

I lick up the underside of his length, then take him into my mouth again.

He thrusts gently, letting out a low groan. "Can I fuck your throat, sweetheart?" His words are smooth, his tone deep as he works himself in and out of my mouth.

My body hums with the promise of an orgasm. I never thought I'd enjoy pleasuring a man like this, but the sounds he makes spur me on and send heat pooling low in my belly. I've never craved anything the way I crave making Fisher lose control.

Everything he does is for the benefit of others. But me? I'm just for him. Those were his words. And I ache to please him. Ache to take care of him.

It's empowering, knowing I'm the only person who can do that for him.

"Need you naked and my tongue on your pussy," he says as he pulls back and releases me.

Bereft at the loss of him, I deflate. "Fisher."

"Don't worry, baby. I'm still going to use you. I'll still fuck this pretty throat," he says as he wraps his fingers around it and squeezes. The pressure is gentle at first, like he's easing me into trying the things he desires. Only when I moan or preen for him does he push it a bit farther. First asking, then, once he's got my permission, taking.

He may not know all my secrets, but he understands me. He's discovered my tells, and he doesn't do a thing until he knows I'm comfortable.

But with him, I'm not sure I could ever be uncomfortable. I'm safe with him. Always.

"But first I need you completely bare for me." He meets my eyes, his hand still wrapped around my throat. "Can you do that?"

I nod, and he releases me. He takes a single step back, waiting for me to undress, never looking away. There's nothing slow about the way I undress. I don't make a show of it. No, I need him now. I toss my spandex to the floor, followed by my sports bra, and then I crawl back over to him.

"Flip over," he says gruffly.

Once I'm flat on my back, he drops one knee to the bed near my head and presses a kiss to my lips. "I'm going to crawl down this perfect body, so spread your thighs, baby, and relax your throat."

The way he talks me through everything is sexy as hell.

"Okay." I arch up and steal one more kiss before willing myself to relax.

With a hand on the mattress at my hip, he drags his mouth across my breast, swirling his tongue around the stiff peak, nipping at it, sucking it into his mouth. Once he's released it with a pop, he moves to the other side and repeats the movements. He eases his other knee to the bed so he's straddling my head as he licks a path down my stomach. At the apex of my thighs, he presses warm, open-mouthed kisses and slips his arms beneath my ass, tugging my hips up. He brings that hot mouth of his to my clit and sucks, drawing a long moan from me.

Mouth watering, I grip his thighs, pulling him closer so I can swallow his cock.

We're nothing but thrusts and grunts, whimpers and pleasure. He spears me with a finger, fucking me slowly as he licks and sucks until I'm unraveling beneath him. As a wave of pleasure washes over me, warming me, he rolls off me. I'm still out of sorts when he settles himself on top of me again, this time so we're face to face, his knees pushing my thighs apart, his cock filling me in one swift thrust and his mouth stealing my loud moan. He kisses me until I'm panting for breath.

"Do you like how you taste, Princess?"

Whimpering, I lick at his lips.

A slow grin slashes across his face. "You do, don't you?" He muses. "You love it just as much as I do." He drags his tongue over his lips, then pulls back and ducks his head so he has a clear view of his dick as he sinks inside me over and over again. "Look at us."

I do. I arch up and zero in on where we're connected. I couldn't look away if I tried. The sensation of watching like this while he rolls his hips, dragging the head of his cock along my inner walls, is unlike anything I've ever experienced. "Fisher, please," I beg, my words coming out as a breathy adjuration.

"Please, what?" He fists the sheets and lowers himself, kissing me again.

"Please come. Please fill me."

"You want my cum, Princess?"

Another moan. "Yes."

With a grunt, he rises up on his knees and pistons his hips, setting a grueling pace. I lock my ankles at the base of his spine, grinding my clit against him until I shatter again. With one hand on my throat and the other on my ass, he squeezes and unleashes inside me, growling my name as he fills me just like he promised.

As our movements slow, he releases my throat. He lowers himself and cups my cheeks, pressing sweet kisses to my lips. "Are you okay?" he murmurs, his mouth brushing mine. The kisses don't stop. We stay like this for a long moment, his lips pressed to my cheek, my chin, my neck, my shoulder, dragging out the blissful sensation.

When my breathing has returned to normal, I gently push against his chest and grin. "So about that shopping day..."

He chuckles as he pulls me close. "I'll talk to Cank."

Fisher

Chapter 31

THE WARM SUN beats down my shoulders as I survey the Boothbay public dock. There's a man standing on a Grady White, yelling at the two kids on the dock to untie the lines. With what has to be eight kids on the boat with him, the poor guy probably needed a minute to get going. Especially since the two women with him are chatting without a care. I pull back on the throttle, reversing out about ten feet to give the guy room.

Two hours ago, I pulled up to the yellow-lined area and did the drop-and-go with the girls. Now, I zero in on Libby, whose blond hair is blowing in the breeze. She sends me a quick wave and a smile from where she stands by a pink and white Bayliner, chatting away with some old guy.

Fuck. I can tell already that this will not be a simple pickup.

I try not to sneer at the idea of talking to people. For Libby or Sutton—who both need people—I can do it.

I opted out of the bra shopping, because shit, I still shudder at the thought that my little girl is big enough for a bra. Thank fuck Libby is here. With any luck, she used the card I sent with her to buy herself something lacy and pink.

Just the thought of the fashion show I dream she'll put on behind my locked bedroom door has my blood pumping.

I look from her to Sutton and back again.

The difference in my feelings regarding bra shopping for Libby and for Sutton is remarkable.

My jaw locks as I realize one day some fucker is going to feel about Sutton the way I do about Libby. My hands tighten on the silver steering wheel as I idle in the harbor. If I'm lucky, Libby will be the calming force I need when boys come calling on Sutton in ten years. If not, there's a good chance I'll end up hacking into their accounts and sending all their money to charities across the country.

Fuck. I shift on my feet and pull my Boston Revs hat low, blocking out the sun. It's stupid, hoping that Libby will be around in ten years. She probably won't make it the ten weeks between Labor day and Halloween.

My heart pangs at the idea of her leaving. But since the beginning, I've known that I can't force her to stay forever. I care about her too much to hold her hostage. Her bright spirit needs to be free.

Libby's reaction to the puffins was adorable. I don't know what it is about the bird that makes people so giddy, but both Libby and Sutton squealed as soon as Puffin Island came into view. And when they saw the hundreds of birds, they giggled and smiled and took picture after picture for a solid twenty minutes. Even if I don't understand the excitement, their happiness fills me with peace.

At the dock, the Grady finally gets the last fender in and pulls away, leaving a space for me. The move is routine, and I need no adjustments as I slip in and tie the lines myself. After killing the motor, I hop onto the dock and head for the girls.

I smile at Sutton and give Libby a quick kiss. Just in case this old guy has any ideas. I trust my girl, but I want her status to be obvious to him. "How's my girlfriend doing?"

Libby's eyes light up but she doesn't call me on the title I've just stolen like a thief.

"Today was so much fun!" Sutton interrupts bouncing in her pink Nikes. "There's a taffy store here. They make it behind these windows so their customers can watch. And Boothbay ice cream is so much better than ours. And Libby took me to Sherman's bookstore too. We got the first five Baby-Sitters Club books. We're going to read them at bedtime."

"Sounds fun." I tip my chin to the pile of bags on the dock. "These it?" It looks like there are about six or seven bags in a variety of colors, but I wouldn't be surprised if they say no and point to another ten bags they haven't dragged down the ramp yet.

Libby nods, though she cringes a little. "Just these. Well..." She averts her gaze, scratches at her arm.

I knew it.

"These and the boat."

"What boat?" I turn slowly, looking along the wharf to the area at the top, where tourists sit along the pavers and benches, enjoying the view. Maybe she got one of those huge sailboats for her mantel, the kind so many small stores in Boothbay sell.

With a shake of her head, she points to the pink Bayliner. "This boat."

My stomach bottoms out. Surely I heard her wrong. "What?"

"Yeah, this nice man was selling this one. His daughter doesn't need it anymore." Sutton hops onto the boat clearly made for water skiing and tubing in the harbor. Fuck. The thing isn't at all ocean-worthy. It sits low, with padded seating and even a rug. This boat wouldn't make it a minute in the ocean. I inhale, searching for the right words, then snap my mouth shut. I'm not sure which of the seventeen fucking questions going off rapid-fire in my brain to start with.

I run my hand over my face. Holy hell. Who goes bra shopping and comes home with a freaking boat? She doesn't have stilts. She has no boathouse for winter storage. She doesn't have a mooring.

"How are we getting this home?" I finally manage.

Her face lights up. "I thought you could do that trick with ropes."

"Lines," I grit out. Pretty sure I'm having an aneurysm. I cannot possibly have accepted already that I'm towing this thing twelve miles out into the ocean.

"Right. Lasso it with the lines." She bounces on the balls of her feet, her every cell charged with excitement. "We'll make a train. You know, choo-choo." She lifts a hand and pulls like she's a long-haul trucker blowing a horn.

She has to be messing with me.

The man, who's been silent during this exchange, looks like he's fighting a smirk as he holds out a key attached to a foam keychain in the shape of pink glittering sunglasses. Fucker. Tonight, my mission will be to discover his identity, hack into all his accounts, and change his passwords. Make my life hard, and I'll repay the favor, buddy boy.

In one jerky motion, I snatch the key from his hand.

"Sutton and I can ride in the pink one."

"Absolutely not." I whip around and glare at Libby. I will lose my fucking mind if either of them gets hurt, and the ocean isn't exactly calm today. Shit. I run my hand down my face. Even if I get this thing back in one piece, what the fuck do I do with it then?

Libby just shrugs. "Okay, we can go with you." Like that's the only issue.

"And what are we doing with it when we get there?"

Her eyes light up. "Oh, that's easy. I was thinking you could make me a...what's this thing called?" She taps her foot on the wooden slats beneath us and peers over at Sutton, who looks far too at home sprawled out on the pink cushion.

"A dock." She bites back a laugh. She knows exactly how ridiculous this is. I can't build a dock in the ocean. The waves would take it out in a week.

"Or we can put it next to yours in the lawn. You know, since I'm your girlfriend now." Libby bites her bottom lip. She's fucking teasing me and I love it. And damn do I like the sound of her being mine. I'm silent for so long, fucking smiling like an idiot, that she tilts her head back and bats her lashes, likely confused. "Please?"

"Oh hell." As absurd as it is, of course I'll drag the damn boat back. I'll do anything to keep this girl happy. Anything to keep smiling.

Libby

Chapter 32

Dad: Call me. Please.

Robin: Libby, I need you to stop avoiding me.

Brad: This is fucking absurd. You? How the fuck could they nominate you?

Dad: Congrats, Libby! Please call me back.

Robin: The calls keep coming. We have a lot to discuss. Call me!

Robin: Libby! This is huge! Call me!

MY PHONE WON'T STOP. It's been like this for weeks, but this morning, everyone is extra determined to get my attention. Too bad my only concerns are here on this island. Hollywood can wait another day.

"The biscuits go to Ivy, and the lasso is for Farmer Todd, right?"

Cank shakes his head. "The lines, Libby. Not a lasso."

"Hmm, that's not what Fisher calls them." With a shrug, I drop the *lines* onto Putt-Putt's back seat. She's been busy helping me make deliveries all week. My goal has been to give Fisher a break with the hope that he'll start working on my dock so I can take the *Pink Lady* out on the water.

No such luck yet. When he's not busy doing his hacking stuff, we're spending time with Sutton or locking ourselves in his room and getting lost beneath the sheets. It's been the best summer of my life, and there's no way I'll let thoughts of the real world ruin it.

"Ivy needs the lines and *Farmer* Todd needs the *muffins*." Cank emphasizes the nickname I came up with, like he thinks it's comical.

But listen, there may only be sixty-eight people on this island, but if I don't focus on descriptions, I'll forget their names. It works for me for now, but if I plan on staying here, I'll have to drop those soon. Also, he can call them muffins all he wants, but he's wrong.

Maybe the biscuits are for the animals. They're not fit for human consumption, that's for sure. I learned that the hard way.

"Okay, Cank," I call as I get into Putt-Putt.

When I put her into reverse, she makes a loud beeping noise the islanders have come to call my warning beep.

"Have a beautiful day."

Cank's laughter floats on the breeze as I putter away from the docks.

The late July days are nearly endless, and the weather has been beautiful. Maybe it's time I convince Fisher to allow Sutton and me to finally do the Monhegan Goodbye.

My phone buzzes again, a call this time, but I ignore it as I pull up Spotify and navigate to the Summer People playlist. It's full of songs that remind me of my time here. Some of the islanders still call me summer people, but they're *my* summer people. My time with the folks of Monhegan is bringing back the joy I felt when I was here with my mom.

When Noah Kahan's "Maine" starts, I can't help but smile. I take the path toward the library at a steady pace, waving to my summer people as I pass.

"Hi, Libby," Kennedy calls as I pass the inn. She's outside with

Lindsey, who's wearing rain boots and jumping up and down in a kiddie pool.

Putt-Putt veers to the right as I peer over at them. Whoops. I grab the wheel with both hands, and when I try to straighten out, I over-correct a little and almost veer into a fruit stand.

"Hi, Libby." Maggie laughs as she jumps out of the way.

"Sorry!" I yell as I continue on.

Determined to make it to my destination in one piece, I force myself to keep my eye on the path in front of me and my hands at ten and two on Putt-Putt's wheel like Fisher taught me.

He, of course, drives with one hand on my thigh and the other on the wheel. I won't point out his hypocrisy, though, because there's nothing I love more than Fisher's touch.

An hour later, all my chores are done, and I head home. As I pull up the path to our houses, Sutton runs out the front door, her blond braids bouncing, her face covered in pink goo. "Libby!" she calls as I come to a stop. "What took you so long?"

"Sorry, pretty girl. I had to make some stops for Cank. What's on your face?" I hold out a cookie that Cank's wife sent along specifi-cally for her. By some miracle, these are nothing like the biscuits, so I'm not concerned that she'll break a tooth.

Sutton takes a bite of the black and white cookie. "Have you seen the news?" she asks, crumbs spraying from her mouth. She clutches my hand and pulls me into the house.

"Ah, hell." Fisher turns away, reaching for a towel.

He's not quick enough to hide the pink goo smeared all over his face too.

Lightness takes over, making me feel like I might float away. "What's going on?"

He looks absolutely adorable. His messy, floppy brown hair is pulled back with a pink scrunchy so it doesn't get stuck in what I'm guessing is one of the face masks Sutton and I ordered last week. It's got hibiscus oil in it and smells so freaking amazing, and because it's for sensitive skin, it's safe for kids.

Sutton grins. "We're doing face masks."

As Fisher dunks a towel in a bowl filled with water and flowers, like in a fancy spa, Sutton holds up a finger and glares at him. "It needs to stay on for five more minutes."

Fisher's jaw ticks, like he wants to react one way but is holding it back because he loves his little girl. It's the most adorable thing I've ever seen.

"Do you do this often?" I survey the room. A handful of pink and purple pillows from Sutton's bed are set up on the floor, and the coffee table is pushed back and covered in all of her spa goodies.

Fisher sits on one of those pillows, peering up at me like he's begging for help.

I want to kiss him so badly. This might be the sexiest he's ever looked. Covered in goo, showing his love for his girl. The smile that takes over my face is so big my cheeks ache.

His pathetic expression morphs into one of adoration, though his voice is rough as he mumbles, "Once a month."

"Four more minutes," Sutton reminds him.

His face falls in defeat, making it nearly impossible not to drop to my knees to cuddle him.

I turn my focus to Sutton so I don't ruin their special moment. "What's the news, pretty girl?"

"You can't tell her yet," Fisher says, his eyes narrowing.

Sutton drops her head back, groaning. "Why?"

"Because I won't be able to kiss her with all this stuff on my face."

My heart thumps against my breastbone. God, I love him.

Shit. I really love him.

I suck in a breath to keep myself from saying it. It's too soon. But it's real. I know without a doubt that I love them both.

Sutton scrunches her nose. "Ew. Why do you have to be like that?" With a roll of her eyes, she dunks a towel in the water. "You can take it off."

Rather than pass the towel to him, she does the most adorable thing. She stretches forward and cleans the pink goo off his face for him. The way he sits patiently, eyes closed, allowing her to give him this facial, breaks me wide open. It's mind-boggling, knowing he has even the smallest doubts about how good he is for her. I've never seen such devotion. My dad is wonderful, and he's done a lot for me, but never has he let me give him a facial.

Monthly facials. I'm just...wow. Yup, I love the guy.

Once she dries his face, he pulls the scrunchie off his head and tosses it at me. "Crying over there?"

I shrug my shoulders and feign indifference. "Just got something in my eye."

Sutton cups a hand to her mouth and whisper shouts, "Your nose is growing, Libby."

Fisher washes Sutton's face just like she did his, taking his time, with his tongue pressed into his cheek as he swipes the washcloth delicately around her eyes, careful not to get any of the goo in them. After he pats her skin dry, he gives me one of those warm smiles again.

He looks good wearing a smile. This one is full of pride. Like all he's got—Sutton and me and this place—is enough. I really hope it is. My life is a disaster, but by some miracle, just being me and being here seem to be enough for him. It's a heady sensation. Addictive. I've never been enough on my own. I've always taken on a role. Quiet. Effusive. Bright and shiny. Whatever was needed at the time. Whatever role I was thrown into. I'd make work. But being me? That's a role I've never had the opportunity to explore thoroughly, and I'm rather enjoying it.

He's dressed in his typical jeans and flannel, white shirt untucked. A little messy and unkempt. Completely cozy-looking. My body itches to go to him. To lean into his chest. To feel the brush of his lips against my forehead. To close my eyes and just inhale. This feeling. His scent. This summer.

"You can tell her now," he says to our girl as she takes another bite of cookie.

219

I'm not sure when I started thinking of her as ours, but in that moment, with her attention fixed on me, her blue eyes so bright, a cookie crumb clinging to her lip, one overall strap falling off her shoulder, I'm desperate for it to be true.

"You were nominated for an Emmy!" She bounces, her braids swinging.

"Don't jump while chewing." Fisher pushes to his bare feet and ambles toward me. With a yank, he pulls me into his chest. "Congrats, Princess."

Bewildered, I look back and forth between them. "What are you talking about?"

Fisher frowns down at me. "I'm sure your phone's been going off."

He knows I've been ignoring everyone. He's seen me silence enough phone calls and dismiss dozens of texts. But he never presses. Instead, he reminds me that he's here when I'm ready to talk.

That time is fast approaching. If I want them to truly be mine, Fisher deserves to know what brought me here. He needs to know what the real world will be saying once they find out where I'm hiding.

Though it doesn't feel like I'm hiding. Not anymore.

It feels like I'm finally living.

"Libby!" Sutton drags me from my thoughts. "Did you hear me? You're going to win an Emmy!"

I throw an arm out, signaling for her to join our hug. She settles against my stomach, squeezing me tight. "Thanks, pretty girl. I did hear you; I'm just trying to understand. Where'd you hear this?"

"It was on TV. Everyone's talking about it because no one's seen you for months. Kind of silly. You've been here the whole time; it's not like you're hiding."

I smile. She gets me. "You're right, pretty girl."

Eyes closed, I soak in the feel of the two of them, but within seconds, my phone is buzzing in my pocket again.

Fisher presses a kiss to my forehead and looks down at me, his expression almost pained. "You should probably get that."

As much as I hate to pull away from them, he's right. I'm no longer hiding, and that means facing the real world.

When *Dad* flashes across the screen, I can't help but smile. "Hey, Daddy."

"Oh, could this possibly be *the* Elizabeth Sweet?" he quips.

"Ha ha." I step out onto the porch and settle on the top step.

"You're harder to reach than the damn governor. I'm being serious. I talked to her an hour ago. She doesn't even screen my calls the way you do."

I roll my eyes but bite back a smile. "I get your point, Daddy. Is there a reason you called?"

"I wanted to talk to my daughter. It's been a week since I've heard your voice. Does a father need any other reason?"

"Oh, it's not because I've been nominated for an Emmy?"

He chuckles, the familiar sound a comfort. "Oh, you don't say?"

"I haven't even seen the reports. Sutton just told me."

The door opens behind me, and Bing bounds out. Fisher and Sutton are next, but they follow the dog to the yard without stopping, Fisher shooting me a wink as they go.

"In the best supporting actress category, Libby. Congratulations. You deserve it." My father's voice cracks.

That's when the gravity of the moment finally hits. I've been acting since I was a kid, but this is my first nomination. Though my performance this season couldn't even be called acting. Every emotion the academy saw on the screen was one I felt during those last few months on set. The irony of that is not lost on me.

"Thank you."

"You'll have to come back to California. Robin has a plan to get the win." That's the funny thing about awards. Acting is only part of the process. Lobbying the judges is where the real work is.

"I'm not leaving, Daddy."

Though he's trying to give me privacy—sticking to the other side of the yard while he tosses a ball to Bing—Fisher's eyes cut to mine when I make that declaration.

I blow out a breath as my dad launches into all the reasons I need to come back. Casting agents have been calling. Producers are vying for me. Apparently disappearing from the limelight has everyone talking. "And with this nomination, you'll have even more offers," he finishes.

"Daddy." With a sigh, I reiterate all the reasons I'm not coming back. This is not the first—or second or even fifth—time I've explained that I'm not sure if I ever want to act again. I can't imagine constantly being surrounded by the narcissistic people on sets again. Hollywood is toxic. Or at least the version I saw day in and day out for twenty years.

I needed a break, and the eight weeks I've had so far haven't been nearly long enough.

"At least fly in for the awards show. See how it feels to be back."

"I can't," I whisper, my chest tightening so painfully it's hard to breathe.

"Libby, this is a big deal. Huge. Your mother—" He stops himself. He never talks about her. He's never once used her memory to guilt me, and thankfully that remains true even now.

"Always wanted this," I finish for him.

It's the truth. My mother's dream was to win an Emmy. She never got the chance. But that doesn't mean I should live my life for her. Like I told Fisher, we need to live for ourselves, not for the ones we've lost.

"For you, Libs. She wanted this for you. She'd be so proud of you. And you deserve to tell your truth. To control the narrative. This is the perfect opportunity to put the production team in its place. *You* have been nominated. Not the show. Not Brad."

I suck in a breath. He wants me to control the narrative, but he has no idea what the narrative actually is. I doubt he'd be telling me to come back if he did.

"I'll think about it." I pull the phone away from my face and put it on speaker.

As the topic changes and we talk about my life on the island, I scroll through emails about potential projects from my agent.

Each pitch, one after another, makes me shake my head. I'm almost ready to give up and ignore my inbox again when one catches my eye.

Boston Theater... *Wicked.*

As I read the details, excitement bubbles in my chest.

I say goodbye to my father and focus on Fisher and Sutton. She's laughing as she and Bing race for the ball.

Boston isn't that far...

Fisher

Chapter 33

I GUIDE Libby down the row, then slip into the chair beside her and sink low in my seat. These town meetings aren't my thing, but she loves them, so I'm here week after week, and after each one, I've got a new honey-do list put together by the people of Monhegan.

Lucky me.

Libby grasps my hand and gives me a small smile, and that phrase—lucky me—takes on a whole new meaning. Because, damn, am I a lucky bastard.

"Oh no." Wilder angles forward, leaning around Libby. "Don't fall under this spell. You and me, we have to talk." He beats his chest, right over the image of a harried rooster. Its eyes are bugged out, its beak is open in a full squawk, and its feathers ruffled. Above it, the shirt reads *I'm fine. Everything is fine.* "Switch with me, darling." Wilder stands and points to his seat.

Libby releases my hand and then gives Wilder a pointed look. "You've got five minutes, then I get my seat back."

"Deal."

Libby scoots over so she's seated next to Maggie, and he flops down beside me.

"Nicole still driving you mad?" I cock a brow.

I swung by his place a few days ago to borrow stilts for Libby's boat. It has a name, but much like Putt-Putt, I refuse to use it. I haven't seen him since, which is unusual. Typically the guy is everywhere.

"No. First, the elephant in the room. You have a pink lake boat."

No shit.

I nod but force my lips into what Libby would claim is a smile. What else am I going to do? The *Pink Lady* now resides in the yard next to Hunter's boat. I want to be irritated. I've tried, but I gave up after I pulled up yesterday and found Sutton and Libby, clad in bathing suits, lying out in the boat, reading the second Baby-Sitters Club book together.

The boat will never putter around in the ocean. It barely made it to the island as it is. But it could be fun on a lake. Maybe I could rent a slip on lake Sebago. Or maybe buy a lake house. We could leave the island for weekends sometimes.

It's so easy to picture the three of us on the lake. I don't know about water skiing, but the girls would love tubing.

"You're smiling about this?" Wilder's voice jars me from my daydreaming.

I swallow. More and more, I find myself lost in the idea of a future for us. It's a topic I need to bring up to Libby soon. Because it's already August.

Which reminds me... "When are you sending Nicole home?"

Groaning, he runs his hand over his patchy attempt at a beard. "Dude, I've tried. But she's a teacher and she doesn't go back to work until just before Labor Day. She just keeps staying. She's been in and out of the inn and rented two different cabins. Even my beard doesn't scare her. She thinks it's cute."

I wince. I wish I could say the beard had filled in over the last month. It has not. It's still as ratty and awful as it was on the Fourth of July.

"Something's not right there." He slumps back in his seat.

"Your five minutes is up," Libby says, tapping Wilder on the shoulder. "The meeting's about to start, and I'm sitting next to Fisher."

With a deep sigh, my best friend shifts over.

"All right," Cank calls from the front of the room. "Who wants to start?"

Libby raises her hand, and when Cank nods her way, she says, "I have a suggestion."

"Oh yeah? What is it?"

"Well, I have a list."

I run a hand over my face and stifle a groan. Here we go.

She clutches my thigh. "Shush, you. It's for your own good." Straightening, she affixes that bubbly smile to her face again. She's always excited, and although I'm wondering what she's getting me into now, I can't fucking stop smiling.

Wilder glances past Libby and cocks a brow at me. I ignore him, choosing to focus on the front of the room rather than allow him to silently give me shit for being happy. Who's he to talk, anyway? He's wearing the crazy rooster shirt.

Libby clears her throat. "I think we are over-utilizing our sheriff."

What the fuck? I whip my head around and gape at my girlfriend.

Without even looking my way, she pats my leg. "We don't pay him. And yet we use him for pretty much everything." She takes a deep breath and stands. "We need a mailman."

All around me, people shrug and nod.

As my face heats, I sink lower in my seat.

Worrying her lip, she eyes Doris. "And the grocery store needs their own delivery person."

Doris tuts and crosses her arms. "Well, maybe people should stop ordering difficult stuff."

I straighten instantly and glare at the older woman. I've warned her more than once to be nice to my girlfriend. Maybe the diet ginger ale and the sherbet are items she can't order in bulk since they likely won't sell well to the rest of the island, but nothing Libby has requested has been extravagant. Sure, Doris doesn't make much money off Libby's orders, but she'd do it for others without complaint.

The older woman shifts nervously in her seat, realizing she has now earned my ire.

Libby's shoulder drops just a bit and she swallows thickly. But then Flora giggles, and my girl's back straightens.

She cocks a brow in the baker's direction. "And clearly we need an exterminator for Flora's squirrel problem."

Cank chuckles, though he quickly covers it up with a cough. "Anything else, Ms. Sweet?"

"Yes." She nods crisply. "We also need a dock for the *Pink Lady*."

Eyes squeezed shut, I blow out a breath. I could build a dock for Libby, but it wouldn't make it through the waves caused by a single storm.

"Since when are we taking requests from uninformed summer people?" Flora calls out.

The crowd breaks into chatter, one person talking over another, and Libby seems to deflate, slinking back into her chair. When I spot her lashes fluttering rapidly, I realize she's trying not to cry.

Fuck. What I'd give to throw Flora off the dock that I will now have to build.

It's unrealistic, yeah, but if it makes Libby smile, then I'll do it. Fuck it, I'll build ten. And they can all wash away.

Voice wobbly, Libby says, "I'm gonna go."

She stands and I move to follow her. My chest fucking aches for her. Flora could have said all kinds of nasty shit, but she didn't have to. All she had to do was call Libby *summer people* to take all the wind from her sails.

I'm on my feet without hesitation. "You should all be ashamed of yourselves," I say over the chatter. One by one, people turn toward me. "I, for one, have never been so embarrassed to be from Monhegan Island than I am today. Since when do we treat people like this? All Libby has wanted since the day she arrived on the damn trash boat was to fit in with this island. She was kind. Quiet.

227

She didn't ask for much. Just some sherbet and diet ginger ale and even that was too much." I glare in Doris's direction. "She's helping with the town play, she put all that time and effort into the parade. Hell, she's running errands around here for all of you." Chest heaving, I glare at them all, every last one of them, and point back toward the door where Libby rushed out just moments ago. "That woman went without cable, hot water, clothes. She had her cable wires cut, she's been hurt and shunned. Yet, day in and day out, she's had a friendly face for all of you. No matter what. *Do better.*"

I move to push past Wilder to go after Libby when Cank calls after me. "Sheriff, you're right. So is Libby. Come up here. What do you think about bringing on a mailman?"

I stop, hands balled into fists, but I don't turn. I don't give a shit about the mailman, especially when my girl is upset. With a long exhale, I shake my head, ready to rush off, but Wilder slams a hand to my chest.

"Dude, you can't just leave. Especially when everything Libby said before makes sense. Come on. Give them some truth. You don't want to be the errand boy anymore. It was Hunter's thing. Not yours. And that's okay."

I sigh. "Five minutes." Eyes narrowed, I stomp to the front of the room.

For the next ten minutes, I answer question after question from Cank, as well as half the people gathered. Most of them demand I keep one job or another. They all think they need my help, which is why normally I don't push back.

But when Farmer Todd says, *"I want to keep Fisher on goat duty, no one else can get the damn beast out of my green house, he has a magic touch. And what else do you have to do?"* I'm done.

Glaring, I growl, "I still have a job in Boston."

Are these people so goddamn self-centered that they've forgotten that? How else am I going to make a living since they don't pay me?

The room erupts again, and I take the opportunity to get the fuck out.

"I'm leaving," I mumble to Wilder. "Let me know what they decide." I've only made it a step or two when I'm stopped by a hand on my arm.

The red nails come into view first, and on instinct, I pull away. "Yes?" I ask Flora as I shuffle back a step. Out of respect for Marissa's memory I've given her cousin a lot of leeway over the years. But knowing that Sutton is uncomfortable around her is all the encouragement I need to put a stop to her antics once and for all. And after the way she was rude to Libby today, well yeah, she's used up every bit of my patience already.

"I wanted to invite you over for dinner tomorrow night." She drags her teeth over her lower lip, lashes fluttering. "I thought we could talk about Sutton and plans for the fall."

I blink. She's invited us to dinner a few times, and I've gone out of obligation, but never alone. And fall plans? What's there to discuss? Sutton will go back to school in the fall and be part of whatever island activities are available, just like always. And frankly none of that is Flora's business.

"I don't think that's a good idea."

"But it would be nice. To have a break from everyone." She reaches out but before she can touch me I cross my arms over my chest and take another step back. "We've never had the chance to hang out, just the two of us."

"Why do you think that is? I'd never spend time with someone who refuses to serve someone because she doesn't like her. Your attitude towards summer people is awful but with Libby you crossed a line. If you haven't figured it out yet, I'm *with* Libby."

Sending me a patronizing smile like she's heard not a single word I've said, she nods. "For now. You and Wilder have your summer fun." She chuckles. "But she's leaving. Summer people don't stay."

The statement is like a dagger to the heart. I might know Libby's leaving, I might understand it, but my heart hates it. But my anger over her treatment of Libby is stronger. "And yet I'd still choose her over you anyway."

Her mouth falls open and on a parting glare, I add, "Oh and Flora, you know all those fancy iced coffees and extra donuts I've been adding to my order? Yeah, those have been for Libby. My *girlfriend.*"

Flora's face is beet red but before she can even formulate a response, I stride away.

Walking out the back doors of the school, I head straight home. I should stop by and pick up Sutton from Mrs. K, but for now, talking to Libby is my first priority.

Her expression as she walked out gutted me. I should have followed her rather than staying around to answer questions. Yes, I might be important to this town, but Libby is important to me.

The second I step into the yard, Bing is at my heels.

"Stay," I tell him on Libby's front porch.

I tap on the door, but I don't wait before I stomp inside. Only when I've got eyes on her do I slow. She's standing at the counter, focus fixed on her phone. I brace myself, ready to be hit with a devastated look. Instead, when she looks up, her blue eyes are sparkling with excitement.

"Guess what?" She runs at me and jumps into my arms.

Damned if I know. I'm just glad she's smiling. Instantly, my muscles relax, and I breathe her in.

"What?"

"I got an audition for the play," she practically squeals.

"What?" I rear back so I can look her in the eye. They're making her try out? She's been part of the group all summer. Fucking hell, Maggie is the one person I didn't think I had to talk to about being nice to my girl. I swore they'd become friends, so what the fuck is this?

"Yes!" She bounces in my arms. "The Boston theater called. They want me to come in this weekend."

My heart plummets to the floor, but I keep a smile on my face.

Boston. Of course she's looking for acting jobs. But damn, the reality of her leaving once again smacks me hard in the face.

"Wow. Congrats." I swallow back the pain creeping through my chest. "Can I take you out for the audition?"

Excitement radiates from her as she nods. "Maybe Sutton can come too."

I shake my head. "She'll stay with the Knowleses."

If my time with Libby is almost up, I want a weekend alone. Time to take her out and spoil her. The opportunity to tie her to my bed and make her scream my name. I want to show her, and maybe myself, what forever would look like, if only it were possible. Even if doing so will make it harder to say goodbye.

Libby
Chapter 34

"WHY CAN'T I COME? I've never been to Boston." Sutton gives me the saddest puppy dog eyes.

Guilt consumes me. We're sitting on the edge of the porch, legs dangling, waiting for Fisher to gather supplies for Bing. Wilder is keeping him while we're gone, and Sutton will stay with Mrs. K. Fisher is adamant that just the two of us go to Boston. He didn't tell me why, and I'm too afraid to ask. I'm too afraid to push him when it comes to her. I may be his girlfriend, but she's his entire world. If he's drawn a hard line anywhere, it has to do with her.

"I'll talk to Fisher about bringing you next time."

Sutton rolls her eyes and drops her head back. "Yeah, right. He's never once taken me to Boston."

I frown at her. Really? He lived in Boston before his brother passed away, yet he's never taken her there to visit? He's never wanted to experience the sights with her? Or just get off the island?

"Nope."

Maybe he doesn't want her to see what he left behind. Doesn't want her to feel any kind of guilt over what he gave up to raise her. I get that, I guess.

Sutton scoots closer to the edge, swinging her feet and kicking up gravel. "Can I tell you something?"

"Anything. Always." I set my hand on top of hers and squeeze.

She sucks in a breath, and when she exhales, words escape along with the breath, as if she's been keeping them in for a while. "I don't want to live here anymore. I want to meet more kids. Make friends. I want to live on land. The winter here is so dark. It's cold and lonely. And Fisher hates it. I know he does. He won't say it—"

"He doesn't say much," I interrupt.

She nods, her shoulders falling like the weight of all her thoughts is too heavy for her little shoulders. My poor sweet girl is being crushed by this secret.

"Sutton." I shift so I'm facing her and wait for her to look me in the eye. "There is not a single thing that Fisher wouldn't do for you if you told him you were unhappy."

She shakes her head. "Anything but this. I think he wants to stay because of my parents."

I nod. She's right. But Fisher would be devastated if he found out she feels this way but is afraid to tell him. "I could talk—"

"Please don't." She grasps my arm tightly, her nails digging into my skin.

I place a hand over hers, uncurling her tiny fingers.

Sheepishly, she looks at me, realizing I've got scratches from her wild nails.

"I won't say a word. I promise. But you should. Tell him your truth. If there's anyone in the world who would move heaven and earth for you, it's him."

Her small body relaxes a fraction. "Maybe," she says softly.

I fight the urge to sigh. She won't tell him. And I won't betray her trust. But maybe I can find a way to get Fisher to figure it out on his own. Looks like I've got my work cut out for me this weekend.

The porch creaks as Fisher steps outside. "Ready to head to Mrs. K's?"

Sutton throws her arms around me. "Promise you'll come back?" she whispers.

Behind her, Fisher eyes us cautiously.

I force a smile and press a kiss to her hair. "Of course, pretty girl. We'll be back in two days."

Sighing, she pulls back. Then she hops off the porch and heads to the truck without looking back.

"She okay?" he asks, his attention trained on her back.

I nod, lips pressed together. This is the first time I've lied to him. I don't like it. That means I have to get these two to be honest with one another, and soon.

Two hours later, Fisher picks up both our bags in one hand—my pink carry-on and his dark green canvas weekender—then holds his hand out to me. "It's only a few blocks. You okay to walk, or do you want me to grab the car and come back and get you?"

I pause, frowning. "Grab what car? Did you rent one?"

Fisher wiggles his fingers, reminding me that he's waiting, and I slide my palm against his.

"Nah," he says, guiding me toward the street. "My Range Rover is here."

I pull up short. "Your what?"

He glares at where my feet are firmly planted. I'm not moving until I get answers.

"My truck. It's a Range Rover. Ever heard of it?"

I roll my eyes. "Of course I've heard of it. I'm just wondering why you have a Range Rover *here* when you live *there*?" I throw a thumb over my shoulder, gesturing to the island so far out it can't even be seen on the clearest of days, which today is not.

"Can't bring it there," he grumbles, as if that actually answers my question.

He tugs on my hand, and I allow him to steer me through the droves of people swarming the small town. Sutton and I explored the town the last time we were here, so I know there's a small boutique just up the hill, nestled between tourist shops. In every window, T-shirts and hats emblazoned with puffins and lobsters are on display. Plush versions of the creatures are easy to come by, and we even found Lego sets. I was tempted to buy the puffin set, but figured the boat was a big enough purchase. I'll save that one for another day. Maybe on our way back to the island. As we round the street corner and start toward a hill, Fisher slows down a bit so we're walking side by side. "Are you ready for the audition?"

No. Yes. Maybe? With a sigh, I settle on "I don't know." Nerves skitter through me like they do every time I think about the upcoming audition. "I took voice lessons as a kid, but once I got my first movie role, that kind of fell to the wayside."

"You sing in the shower," he says with a smile.

"Oh, are you standing outside the bathroom and listening? That's a little stalkery, Hacker."

He lifts one shoulder. "I like watching you."

Eyes wide, I scoff. "Fisher Jones, do you have a camera in your bathroom?"

Fisher chuckles. "Nah, just yours."

I pull my arm back and hit him in the shoulder.

"I'm kidding, I'm kidding. It's aimed at the side of the house, but if you don't close the blinds..." He waggles his brows.

I hit him again. We're both laughing when we reach the parking lot. There are about a dozen cars here. Halfway across the lot, he releases my hand and pulls a fob from his pocket. When he taps it, the lights of a hunter green Range Rover in the back flash.

Though he continues on, I stop and turn in a slow circle, looking for the parking lot attendant.

"What are you doing?" he asks as he holds the door open.

"Isn't there someone you need to talk to?"

"Talk to?"

"Ya know, to pay? Or to tell them you're taking the car?"

Fisher frowns. "You want me to report to a stranger that I'm taking my own car?"

Well, when he says it like that... "Fine, but isn't there an attendant? How do all these people pay?" I ask, scanning the other cars.

"There's a box over there. We put ten bucks into an envelope, write our license plate number on the outside, and drop it through the slot." When I still don't move, he sighs and tosses the bags in the back seat. "What?"

I shake my head. "People in Maine must be so much nicer than people in LA."

With a shake of his head, he snags my arm and guides me to the passenger door. He hovers until I'm buckled, one brow cocked. "Maybe, Princess. Though I'm pretty fond of this one girl from LA."

"Yeah?" I beam up at him.

Smirking, he bends down to kiss me. "Yeah."

"Explain this to me again," I ask an hour later as we're hitting Boston traffic. "You won a bet by hacking into the Revs' firewall, and your prize was tickets to tonight's game?"

Fisher nods. "That about sums it up."

I shake my head. And people say Hollywood is strange.

"Want to go to my apartment first and drop off our stuff, or should we grab an early dinner before the game?"

"Let's go to the game." I lace my fingers in my lap. "Once I get you alone in your apartment, I probably won't want to leave."

His brows lift, along with one side of his mouth. "I wouldn't mind that, Princess."

Warmth pools in my belly at the thought. "It's been a long time since I went to a baseball game. And you love the Revs."

He hums, not taking his eyes off the traffic. "How do you know that?"

"You wear a Revs hat just about every day."

"I like you more." He winks at me as he presses on the gas. "I could wear you on my cock instead."

Head dropped back, I cackle, and the rest of my nerves fall away.

Fisher
Chapter 35

AS I PUT the Range Rover in park in the VIP lot at Lang Field, Libby pulls a pink quarter zip over her head. I'm not sure which of the ten packages that came yesterday contained the Boston Revs gear or how she knew that the pink puffin design was an option, but Libby's shopping talents are astounding.

"What do you think?" She pulls a ball cap on, flashing me a smile.

"You look beautiful, as always."

Her mouth flattens into a thin line, and although I can't see her eyes behind the sunglasses she's slid into place, I feel the eye roll. "Charming. However, I meant are people going to recognize me?"

Between the high collar on the quarter zip, the baseball cap pulled low, and the sunglasses, I hardly recognize her.

I unbuckle my belt and peck her lips. "I think you're safe."

"Perfect." She beams. "So do you know where we're going or do you need to ask?"

A chuckle escapes me at the idea of having to ask for directions. "I've been here hundreds of times, Libby."

"Really?"

I nod. I've held tight to most things from my old life, but I did

238

give up the Revs season tickets. I miss watching the game from ten rows behind home plate, but spending money on tickets I couldn't use became depressing. "Used to come to games all the time."

"With Hunter?"

My chest tightens painfully, but I swallow back the emotion. "Sometimes. Not often." My brother only came out to Boston once a year or so and always alone. I really only ever saw him and his family when I made the trek to the island. "Marissa didn't like bringing Sutton off the island. And Hunter was busy. You know how it is. Always one more thing to do at home."

She nods. "So Sutton never came to a game." It's not a question. She's sure of her statement.

I shake my head and clear my throat. "Actually, I was going to bring her to a game the weekend of the accident."

Libby slips her glasses off her face, her expression serious. "What happened?"

I run my tongue over my teeth, giving myself a minute to rein in the hurt. Otherwise I don't think I can get the words out. "Hunter and Marissa planned a weekend in Boston. Sutton was going to stay with me for the first time. I had stayed with her on the island a few times so they could get away, but she'd never stayed in the city with me." I flex my hand into a fist on the console between us, already more emotional than I'd like.

Gently, Libby wraps her tiny hand around mine. The pressure allows me to release a modicum of the viselike tension in my muscles.

"Wednesday night, Hunter called and said Marissa was panicking about the idea of Sutton in the city. She's always been a wanderer—no fear, no concern about strangers. So they were nervous." I spent most of the conversation telling Hunter the city would be good for Sutton, that we'd work on stranger danger, and maybe she'd acquire at least a little sense of caution. "He asked me to come to his house instead. So I did. Rather than waiting until morning, they left that night. It was late by the time they got to Portland.

And some guy jacked up on heroin was driving the wrong way down 295. Head-on crash. They both died on impact."

A quiet gasp escapes her. "I'm so sorry."

I shake my head and swallow back the tears. "It was three years ago. But their wish to keep Sutton safe and on the island still feels big." So big it's crushing sometimes.

"Do you ever think that she might like to see more places?"

Of course I do. When I was her age, I felt trapped on that tiny rock when there was an entire world to experience. But before my father retired and Cank stepped up, my dad was the harbor master, and that was a year-round job. Leaving for more than a quick boat trip to the mainland just wasn't possible.

But I don't say any of that.

"She might love to see a game," Libby adds.

I nod, ready to end the conversation. I don't want worries about whether I'm doing the right thing with Sutton to cast a shadow over the day.

"Come on." I push my door open, and by the time I meet her on her side of the car, she's got the glasses in place, and she's back to incognito.

Not one person recognizes her as we make our way inside.

"Oh my gosh, how fun is this?" Libby's head snaps from one direction to the other as we walk through the kids' area along the harbor. Just inside the gate, there's a baseball-themed play structure and climbing tower. Kids are lined up for the forty-yard dash and waiting somewhat impatiently for their turn in the batting cage. There's a bar set up along the water where parents can sit and enjoy a drink while they watch their kids play.

"It's such a cute setup. Kids must love coming here."

I nod, imagining Sutton running around, shrieking and laughing. Our girl would love this. Guilt and worry swirl in my gut, but I swallow down the racing thoughts and lead her to the escalator.

"This way. We're going up to the boxes."

"Fisher Jones," a familiar British voice says as we step off. "You didn't tell me you were coming today. What kind of dodgy shit are you pulling?"

I come to a halt at the familiar lilt and turn.

My college roommate and forever friend Cal Murphy strides my way with his cousin Zara Price at his side.

"You live in New York." I shake my head, but I can't help but smile at the asshole.

"I texted a few weeks ago. Remember? Told you I was coming up this weekend." Brow arched, he assesses Libby.

My mood sours instantly. Cal is the biggest player I know. The last thing I want is for him to hit on my girl. "Although I see why you might not want me mucking up your plans."

"Don't be a shit, Cal." Zara shakes her head and steps closer. "Fisher."

"Zara." I release Libby's hand as Zara leans in to peck one cheek, then the other. "This is Libby."

Zara reaches out, though she stiffens with her arm half extended, her eyes going wide. "Bloody hell, Elizabeth Sweet. The entire world is looking for you, and you're hiding out in Boston with our Fisher?"

Anxiety courses through me, but beside me, Libby smiles, as if she doesn't mind that her cover has been blown.

With a massive grin, Zara embraces her.

When she pulls back, Libby turns to me. "How do you know my favorite fixer?"

Her favorite fixer? I guess I should have realized that the Hollywood star and the woman who fixes image crises all over the country would know each other.

"Oh, love. Fisher is my computer man. When I need a photo to disappear, he's who I ring." She flings a hand at her cousin. "Cal and Fisher went to Harvard together"—Harvard sounds more like *Havad* in her British accent—"so Fisher's been my secret weapon since long before the rest of the world was after him."

A small wrinkle appears between Libby's brows just above her glasses.

"It's a hacking thing," I assure her quietly.

"However, Elizabeth, you have wounded me." Cal rocks back on his heels and clutches his chest. "How many times have I begged for a date over the years? And now you've passed me over for this bugger?"

I glare at my friend. Pretty sure I hate him right now. He's with a new woman every week. Without thought, I drape an arm over Libby's shoulders, tucking her into my side.

Cal's eyes dance with delight as he locks in on me. "Who would have thought you would fall?"

Zara whacks him on the arm. "Don't be a wanker. You're the one we all say that about, not Fisher."

Libby and Zara fall into a conversation about the upcoming Emmys. Libby is still waffling about whether to go, though as they talk, her demeanor is casual, her mood light. The two women are clearly friendly. For weeks, I've thought about how incompatible our lives are, only to realize we have mutual friends. The realization is as odd as it is nice. This moment feels like the evidence I need to believe we can continue to be an *us* past Labor Day.

"Mum!" Zara's daughter calls from down the long corridor. She's a couple of years older than Sutton. "Dad says hurry up. We don't want to miss the first pitch."

Asher Price, Zara's husband, played for the Revs until he retired two years ago. But they still go to all the games.

Zara raises one finger to Clara. "Elizabeth, if you're in Boston, we must do lunch. And Fisher, be better about keeping in touch. We really must get Sutton and Clara together." She yanks on her cousin's arm. "Come on, Cal."

Cal peers back over his shoulder. "And the both of you should reply to my texts more often."

"Don't respond to his text," I mutter. I'm half tempted to block his number on her phone right now.

Libby giggles. "Oh, I know all about Cal and his playboy ways.

I've been telling Zara forever that he is primed and ready to fall hard for someone. I can't wait to watch it happen."

Fuck, I love the idea that we have mutual friends. Even if I never see mine anymore.

"This way." I pull her down the hallway to the owner's box.

"Mr. Jones, Mr. Langfield is expecting you." A large man dressed in black tips his chin to me and pushes open the navy blue door behind him.

The second we're inside, Beckett Langfield stands and crosses his arms over his chest. "Well, if it isn't the bane of my existence."

Next to him, Cortney Miller, the Revs' general manager, chuckles. "Aren't we dramatic today?"

Beckett, clad in his pin-striped double zero Revs jersey, whirls on his best friend. "Not even close, Man Bun. And I haven't forgiven you for hiring this guy. People are still talking about the purple picture he sent to the entire organization."

The deeper his scowl, the bigger my smile. Damn, I love riling him up.

"You really did look like a giant grape." Cortney smirks.

I've done work for Cortney's family over the years, and after one of Cortney's interns clicked a link he shouldn't have, he called me to run checks on the Langfield Corp system.

"I'm not the one who made the bet with him." Cortney, the calmer of the duo, rolls his eyes as he steps behind him.

"What?" Libby, who's been silent beside me, finally chimes in.

"This one"—Beckett thumbs over at the blond six-foot-six giant towering over him—"hired your guy to do a network security check." He frowns. "That I didn't think we needed. So I made a bet that he couldn't hack into our system."

Cortney brings a fist to his mouth and chuckles. "Not only did Fisher get in, but he sent the entire company a photo of Beckett from back when the kids and I put purple dye in his soap and turned him into an eggplant for two days."

"We got you back good, though. Your face when your car started burping bubbles was priceless." Beckett laughs.

"Not so priceless, really, after the cost to fix it," Cortney grumbles.

These two are something else. Though if I'd understood their dynamic beforehand, I might have turned down the job. The two of them have been blowing up my phone nonstop for weeks. Apparently they like me enough to have created a group chat between the three of us.

"Make yourself at home, but I'll be watching you." Beckett puts two fingers to his eyes and then points at me.

Libby blinks up at me. "I'm so confused. Do people pay you to hack into their own stuff?"

"Wait..." Beckett squints at her, then me, arms crossed again. "You don't know what he does? Is this a new relationship?" The way his voice lifts hopefully at the end is weird as fuck. Why is he so interested? From what I dug up about him online, the guy is happily married.

"Oh, here we go." Cortney flops back onto the sofa.

"He says he makes people crazy by ruining their days. And he mentioned hacking." Libby shrugs. "I guess I didn't ask many questions. All I really see is the work he does as the island sheriff."

I sigh. Libby should probably know the truth. "I'm a network security specialist. People hire me to find the weak spots or holes in their firewalls and to upgrade their systems."

Cortney snorts. "He created the best software in the industry. He works with 90 percent of the financial community, half the airlines, and a handful of your big ten. The guy's a computer genius."

I pull at my neck to relieve the unease growing inside me. "I wouldn't go that far."

"I would. And I need to know, is this a first date?" Grumpy Beckett has vanished. I swear the man is almost giddy now. "A first date because of my bet?" He claps his hands. "I am the ultimate matchmaker."

I scoff, at a loss for how to respond to the nonsense he's spewing.

Cortney angles forward, resting his forearms on his knees. "Let him have it. Trust me, it's easier than arguing about it."

"Hey, Man Bun, you can't complain. I found you the perfect wife."

The blond holds up both enormous hands. "I have zero complaints about Dylan."

As the two men bicker back and forth, Libby looks up at me. "They're a lot, but I kinda like them."

Head hung, I sigh. "At least one of us does."

After two innings, my head is about to explode. The guys have yet to shut up. Libby, my hero, suggests we sit in the open-air seats for a while. God, I love the woman. Even the humid August air is refreshing after so much time stuck listening to their never-ending conversation.

"This is fun," Libby says as we sit hand in hand.

I have to agree. The only thing better would be if Sutton was with us. Looking over at the woman beside me, a woman that can't possibly be stuck on an island twelve miles from land forever, I think about the possibility of a lake house. And the boat. Maybe it's time for a change. Guilt and responsibility collide in my mind, making my head pound. With a deep inhale, I will my racing thoughts to settle. For now, I want to just enjoy the moment.

As if reading my mind, Libby gives my hand a squeeze. "Don't think about it now."

By the top of the sixth, the Revs have taken a six-to-nothing lead and the energy emanating from the stands is contagious.

"Look at your dad throwing the fire." On the other side of the brick half-wall separating the boxes, a dark-haired woman appears. The toddler in her arms is sporting a number thirty-five jersey. "Oh, sorry," she says. "I didn't realize anyone was out here."

"That's okay." Libby leans over and grins. "Aren't you the cutest? How old are you?"

With a bashful smile, the toddler tucks her head into the woman's shoulder.

"Eighteen months old and driving her parents crazy. I'm lucky I'm just Meme." The woman tickles the girl's tummy. "So I get to give Delaney back to Mom and Dad after the game."

The little girl holds out a stuffed puffin to Libby.

My girl runs a finger down the soft fabric and smiles. "I love puffins."

"So do her parents."

My heart thumps oddly in my chest as I watch Libby bop the little girl's tummy with the puffin, making her giggle. She's so good with kids. It's easy to imagine her with one of her own down the road. And Sutton would be a great big sister.

My lungs seize up at that thought. Is that what I really want? Watching Libby in this moment, I know it is. But is it possible to make that happen while still honoring all the things my brother wanted for his daughter?

The little girl snakes a hand out and pulls on Libby's pink hat.

"Oh." Libby tips her head, and her sunglasses clatter to the concrete.

Delaney keeps the hat firmly in her grasp, yanking it toward her.

"You like my hat, huh?"

The murmur of the crowd turns up a notch, then another. Only when I hear someone nearby whisper-yell "Elizabeth" in a way that makes her sound like Sutton do I scan our surroundings and realize Libby and Delaney are on the Jumbotron.

"Oh, shoot. Sorry. I should have warned you. This is Christian Damiano's daughter. The fans love to see her. So she ends up on the big screen all the time."

Libby's eyes go wide as she searches for her glasses, but it's too late.

"Oh my god, it's Elizabeth Sweet."

It's a known fact how quickly a celebrity can be mobbed by fans, but until this moment, I didn't understand just how jarring it is.

Within thirty seconds, people are moving in the aisles below us to get a better view and calling up to Libby.

"Are you signing autographs?"

"Can we get a picture?"

Libby plasters a smile on her face and waves like she's used to it.

"I'd keep her away from the baby. She might lose it on the poor kid and throw something."

I frown down at the man who makes that comment.

"Can't share the screen with a toddler either?" This from another person nearby.

Next to me, Libby's body has gone rigid.

"You going to demand that we air-condition the great outdoors, princess?"

"Thought you were too good to grace us with your presence anymore."

What the fuck? One after another, the nasty comments pummel her.

"Finally over the coke problem?"

I don't understand. How are these rumors still floating around? And why the fuck has she not done anything about it? Especially if she knows people like Zara Price.

I move to stand up, but Libby grasps my thigh, her nails biting into my flesh through my jeans. "Go inside."

In one quick move, I pull her to her feet and rush her through the door. Once safely inside the box, I pull her into my arms.

"I want to leave." She blinks back tears, her body trembling.

"I'll get you out of here, but then we have to talk." Because I want to know exactly what happened to her before she showed up in Monhegan.

Libby
Chapter 36

A HIGH-RISE IN BOSTON. The man lives in a high-rise in Boston. As we pull into the underground parking garage my thoughts are a jumbled mess and my heart is racing. I have to tell him everything tonight, but I'm still trying to wrap my head around all that he hasn't told me.

He has a freaking apartment—a whole life here—that he just walked away from.

He went to Harvard. He knows Beckett Langfield and Zara Price. Cal was his college roommate. The stoic man beside me is best freaking friends with the least serious person I've ever met. Honestly, he makes Wilder look settled.

He's a hacker. A genius hacker. Not a grumpy small-town sheriff.

None of it makes sense.

He's frozen in this life. Maybe we're similar that way, both unwilling to completely let go of the past. Though for completely different reasons.

I think he's holding on to this old life, scared to let go because maybe then he'll have to admit that he's taken over his brother's existence. Keeping his apartment, his car here, means this facet of who he is still exists. It allows him to believe he's just doing the right thing rather than giving up everything.

But who the hell am I to talk?

Because I've spent months hiding from my problems.

We're silent as Fisher gets our bags from the back seat and leads me to the elevator.

If I speak now, anything I say will come out wrong. A jumble of thoughts that could sound judgmental. And that's the last thing I want. I'm struck by the differences between this Fisher Jones, the one who lives in a high-rise in Boston, and the Fisher Jones who drives a beat-up truck with no doors around a tiny island and wrangles a stubborn goat at least once a week.

I can see what his life used to look like. I can see him hanging out with Cal, flirting with women at an upscale bar. Laughing. Smiling.

Was that who he was?

Did he smile more before?

A painful jealousy floods me. I'm jealous of nameless, faceless women, of the people in his old life. I want to think I'm the one who makes him smile. Even still, I'd rather imagine that his life was full before Hunter's and Marissa's deaths.

There's a whole other side of Fisher I don't know, and that's throwing me for a loop.

I thank my lucky stars when the elevator stops on the eighth floor rather than going straight to the penthouse. The hallway is nondescript. Gray walls decorated with unremarkable images of Boston. Neutral carpet and four identical black doors. It's not homey like his house on the island. I'm trying to rectify the two versions of Fisher when he stops in front of one door and types in a code.

"Fancy," I mumble as I step into the apartment.

Instantly, I'm hit with the smell of Lysol and...is that a vanilla Glade air freshener?

Yup, I clock one in the wall in the corner.

Fisher says "lights on," and the living room is illuminated. The space is mostly taken up by black leather couches and a fancy La-Z-

Boy. The only decorations are generic, as if the place was staged by a designer.

The kitchen and dining room are all one big space. The charcoal-colored island and the bowl of fruit on top of it really throw me. I clutch the back of one of the chairs pushed up to the slab of granite to steady myself. "I feel like I've stepped into the Matrix."

With a chuckle, he heads for the hall. "Make yourself comfortable. I'm going to put our stuff in my room. You want a glass of wine?"

I frown at his back until he disappears. Then I suck in a deep breath and spin in a circle. When I spot the bar in the corner, I peer inside the wine fridge. Then scan the rack beside it. Both are filled with expensive bottles. Caymus, Opus One, Screaming Eagle. Who the fuck is this man and what has he done with Fisher?

I walk away, still too stunned to even fathom what I'm seeing, and pull open the fridge. It's the fancy kind that displays what's inside while the doors are still closed. And it's fully stocked. In the center, there's a row of cans of diet ginger ale, and when I pull open the freezer, I hiss a breath at the sight of my favorite flavors of sherbet lined up.

Fisher Jones...this man...he's *ruining* me.

I slide it shut and go for a bottle of water.

"So wine?" Fisher reappears and heads straight to the wine rack. He dips lower, as if studying what he has.

Better question is what doesn't he have?

I shake my head. "Fisher, you have a damn wine collection over there. Of course I want wine."

From his crouched position, he looks over his shoulder, shooting me a smirk. "Red or white?"

"Dealer's choice," I mumble.

He grabs a bottle of Opus One, and I squeal a little inside. That's exactly what I hoped he'd choose. He returns with two glasses and sets them on the counter. And as his forearms flex while he removes the cork, my mouth waters.

"I don't get it."

The cork comes out with a pop, and he quirks a brow. "Get what?"

"Why do you keep this place? It's like a mausoleum. A shrine to your old life." A life I'm realizing I know little about.

He scans the sterile space, then, with a shrug, pours the first glass. "Tonight we're talking about you."

I blow out a breath and nod at my wine. "Then keep pouring. I'll need more than that."

He smiles, but it's a gentle one. Empathetic. "I've got you, Libby. You know that, right? There's no scaring me off, and there's nothing you could say that would change how I feel about you. I just want to know you. I want to be here for you. I want—"

I press my finger to his lips. This man. The freaking man. "So many words, Hacker."

His lips twitch beneath my fingers. I think he likes showing me this other side of him. It's got to be a relief to be himself rather than the sheriff. The passion in his tone makes it clear that this is a larger part of who he is than I thought. But at the heart of it all, there's no doubt he's still the man I fell for.

He nips at my finger and settles beside me. "Only for you."

I take a slow sip of wine, trying to postpone the inevitable, but he watches me, waiting for me to swallow, and then grasps the seat of my chair and tugs until I'm wedged between his thighs. Maybe it's intentional, maybe it's not, but somehow that gesture, his closeness, gives me the strength to speak.

"About six months ago, I was on set early. I did that often. I'd been on the show for twelve years, so the people behind the scenes, my room there—it all felt more like home than my actual home. I'd go in and snack on my favorite foods and coffee and go over the script. Maybe scroll social media. Mindless stuff, really." I shake my head. My chest hurts just thinking about that day. There are so many things I wish could be different, but I can't go back, and I wouldn't anyway. Knowing what was going on, I'm glad I was there. "Anyway," I take a sip of wine. "Brad's character had just started dating a single mom on the show and we'd cast Reece as her daughter. She's sixteen, but she was playing a thirteen-year-old. Honestly, I thought she was too old for his tastes. I never thought he'd be that brazen. But when I realized what was happening, it was obvious he really wasn't even hiding it. They were running lines, which there was no reasonable explanation for since they had no scenes by themselves. Lydia, the actress who played his girlfriend, was always in their scenes."

Realizing I'm throwing out a lot of facts, I pause to give Fisher a minute to catch up and to clarify if needed. But he only waits patiently, dark eyes locked on my face.

"He set his hand on her thigh, like this—" I mimic the move, resting my palm high on his inner thigh, and trail my fingers against him the way Brad did with Reece. "She flinched when he made contact, but he kept going with the lines, and his fingers kept traveling higher until his hand was practically up her skirt." I close my eyes and breathe deeply. "That's when I interrupted them. She practically jumped, though he didn't even flinch. Nope. He smirked. Then leaned back on the couch and acted completely innocent of any wrongdoing. But I know exactly what I saw because he did the same kind of thing to me years ago."

Fisher goes rigid and hisses a "fuck."

I force a smile, but it's pointless. Fisher's face is a mask of fury mixed with disgust. He's not looking to be placated. He's tortured, but he's holding himself together for me. So that I don't have to hold it together on my own.

Even so, a tear slides down my cheek unbidden.

He cups my face and swipes the moisture away gently with his thumbs. "Keep going."

So I do. While he continues to wipe away my tears, I tell him the truth. "I called him on it immediately, and, of course, he denied it. Said I was seeing things." A sob breaks free. "He said the same thing years ago. He told me I'd made it all up, and I know this sounds insane—if I hadn't experienced it, I'd believe I was nuts too—but I think I wanted to believe I made up all the inappropriate touches. It was self-preservation. It hurt too much to think about the way he'd put my hand in his lap and grind against it until he groaned. Now I know he was coming in his own damn pants with a child's hand forced against his dick. But then?" I shake my head. "His mother and my mother were best friends. His family was my family. My father was busy working, so his mom helped get me to rehearsals and auditions."

Fisher's jaw ticks and his eyes blazed, and not in a good way. "Libby, you are not to blame for any of this. He was an adult and you were a child. You don't have to explain—"

My chest shudders. "But I do. I do because the producer didn't believe me when I told him what I'd seen. And he didn't believe me when I told him what had been done to me. According to him, if I'd experienced that, then surely I would have spoken up long ago. And it'd been years since he'd had the audacity to touch me.

"The older I got, the less the touches occurred. Maybe he was no longer attracted to me, or he worried that I'd realize how sick he was and say something. Either way, I did my best to forget about it. To tell myself that I'd imagined it. And I was ashamed. So ashamed. *Like my mind was dirty for thinking it.* I'd even say we were friends until that day. We attended award shows, arm in arm. How could I explain that I did all of *that*—spent holidays with him and his family for years—even after he'd done this horrible thing to me?"

"He groomed you," Fisher grits out. "You were a child, and he touched you and made you believe it was normal. *He* is the one who is in the wrong, Libby. Not you. Never you." He drags me to his chest.

A sob bursts from deep in my chest, surprising me, but I focus on his pounding heart and force the rest of the details out. How Brad denied it. How Reece acted like nothing happened. How they created this narrative where I was jealous because the focus of the show was shifting from not just the connection between my character and Brad's, but to his character's potential new family.

But that couldn't have been farther from the truth. My character was in college. It was a given that she was the future of the show. What our audience really wanted to see. There were plans in place for Brad's character to fall in love and for the show to spin off into a college dramedy of sorts. I can't even imagine what that would have been like. At the time it was just what was next, but looking back, I can see how little say I had in my own life. And when I demanded Brad answer for what he'd done, they killed off my character.

"I only went quietly because they created a policy that required the presence of a third-party for any extra rehearsals, and minors must be accompanied on set by a parent or guardian."

Fisher rubs my back in soothing circles. "What did your dad have to say about all of this?"

"I never told him," I say quietly.

"Libby," he chides.

Stiffening, I back away. "My father would be devastated. He'd blame himself. He'd—" I blink back tears. "He'd kill Brad."

"He should," Fisher grits out. "You shouldn't have to face this alone. You should never have faced *any of this* alone."

"I'm not alone," I say honestly. "I've had you."

Face crumpling, he hauls me to his chest again. "You have me," he rumbles in my ear. "You always have me."

"But what if I get this part?" I sob. "I'll be in Boston and you'll—" I pull back and swipe at my cheeks. "Would you come here? With Sutton?"

His eyes dim and his face falls. "Libby, I—"

I see it. The explanation he's searching for. He's trying to let me down gently. It was selfish of me to even ask. Shit. Worst timing ever.

I shake my head and give him a facsimile of a smile. "I can go back and forth. There are ferries," I say. "Or maybe it's too soon. I don't have to do the play. I can stay on the island."

He shakes his head with fervor. "No. You're not giving up anything else."

"You're the one thing I don't want to give up." God, I sound desperate, but it's true. My career could tank—hell, it already has—and I'd survive. But losing him? Losing Sutton? I can't do it. I won't let them go.

"No," he grinds out, his jaw working back and forth.

I'm scared to death, worried he's working up the nerve to say we were just a fling. That he'll push me away and break my heart.

"I can come back and forth too," he finally says. "I can't lose you either. If you get the part, I can come out at least once a month. Maybe bring Sutton for a weekend."

Relief hits me like a freight train, but all I can manage is a simple sentence. "I think she'd like that."

He looks off toward the window, to the city beyond, maybe. Boston is lit up, an entire world out there buzzing with excitement while we're here in our own little bubble. Trapped within the confines of our own struggles. I don't want him to feel trapped with me, and I don't want to push him beyond his comfort limit when he's been so careful to work within the lines of mine.

"Let's not worry about it right now." I blow out a breath. "Who even knows if I'll get the part."

His head snaps back in my direction, like he's only now realized that he disappeared on me. Tortured brown eyes meet mine. "*Libby.*"

I shake my head. I refuse to let our time go to waste. Whether we only have the summer—which I refuse to believe—or not, I want this weekend with him. I want *him.*

"Please, Fisher." I press my hand to his heart, taking comfort in its steady beat. My greatest hope is that it beats for me in the same way mine has begun to beat for him.

I don't know when it happened. Maybe in the moments beneath the stars as he held me while we danced. Or maybe when he carried me through town after my accident. Or perhaps when he believed Sutton without question about her unease with Flora. Or maybe it wasn't until now. Until he believed me without hesitation, without judgment. Or maybe it was the culmination of all his thoughtfulness, his care. Through every act, he's shown me time and again that he's someone worth loving. Even more beautiful than that, though, is how he's shown me that I am too.

I lean closer. "I need you," I whisper against his mouth.

With a thoughtful frown, he studies me like he's trying to determine if I truly want this or if I'm trying to hide behind my words.

I don't move.

Our breaths tangle together and the air grows charged. I trace the lines of his face with my eyes, waiting for him to realize what I know.

"You've got me, Princess." He angles in and his lips crash into mine.

Fisher

Chapter 37

THE DULL BUZZ perforates my state of concentration, the sound getting closer, but I won't stop until this is done. I finished the hard part—getting into the account—five minutes ago. Now I just need to leave the gift. I type out the number quickly, then click the box. Half a heartbeat later, the voices are close. Just down the hall.

In the week since Libby and I returned to the island, I've been singularly focused on my mission. I've never felt the desire for violence before. However, when Libby poured her heart out, along with her tears, opening up about what Brad did to her, I wanted to end him. I wanted to track him down and beat the shit out of him. I want him dead.

But that isn't possible.

Libby and Sutton need me.

This way, they can still have me while I seek a modicum of vengeance. While I silently make Brad Fedder's life a living hell.

On our first day back on the island, his security alarm malfunctioned. Ninety-nine percent of the day, the system doesn't work. But every morning at 3:06 a.m., the alarm blares for seven minutes. No matter how many times he types in the code to disarm it. All emergency personnel report to his house. Police, fire, and ambulance. For no reason. Not one of the many people from the alarm company who have been called to service the system can figure out why.

Day two, his phone reset. All the data just *poof,* gone. Oddly enough, his iCloud has no history. He's just shit out of luck.

Day three, his password key went nuts, suddenly populating the wrong password for every account and on every site.

Day four, all of his bank accounts were frozen by Homeland Security. Although no one can explain why, it will take time to sort through the channels to release the funds.

My time spent torturing this bastard has been the highlight of my week. It's also ensured that he hasn't had the time or ability to fuck with Libby. And, thankfully, no one has bothered her at all in weeks. With any luck, the fucker has given up.

"*Hacker.*" Apparently *Sheriff* is no longer fitting, so Libby has taken to calling me Hacker.

"Yeah, Princess?" I black out my screen and swivel around, leaning back in my chair.

"Was that Instagram?" She narrows her eyes on the screen behind me.

"You know I don't have Instagram." I stand and pull her out of my room. She doesn't need to know what I've been up to. Plausible deniability and all that. Although typically, when someone is paying me to break into their network, it's all above board, these side projects with Brad fall into a gray area.

"Maggie, Sutton, and I were thinking..." she says, her lips tipping up.

"That right there is enough to scare me," I tease as we head down to the kitchen.

Libby shakes her head. "Look at you suddenly learning how to joke."

"Oh my gosh!" Sutton bounces on her toes as she looks up from my laptop. It's set up on the counter for her to use with supervision. "Did you see what Logan posted?"

Expression neutral, I watch her, waiting for what comes next.

"Logan?" Maggie asks.

She lifts her hand and stage whispers, "That's not his name. That's his name on the show."

"Oh." Libby's eyes cut to me. With everything that's been reported this week, it's possible that she suspects I'm up to something. "What did Brad post?"

"Right, Brad." Sutton spins the computer, and Libby's eyes widen.

Maggie gasps. "Holy heck. He gave the world his cell phone number."

Yep. Day seven is officially taken care of. Now Brad will be sorting through millions of texts and phone calls. He'll have to change his number. Too bad he lost all his contacts and has no way to inform the people he wants to communicate with.

Under Libby's scrutiny, I cross my arms over my chest and blink.

"That man must have earned himself some bad karma." Maggie shakes her head. "It's been one thing after another for him. The news reported that first responders keep having to go out to his place because his alarm has been malfunctioning. And then his Tesla shorted out in the middle of Rodeo Drive."

Day five. I couldn't plan where it would happen, but I set the virus that would kill the computer system of his beloved car to kick in after five miles. Now it's just a pretty brick.

"And that video of him freaking out on the alarm people? The alarm that no one can seem to fix," Maggie adds.

Day six.

"And now he's doxing himself?" The way Libby's tone gets higher says she doesn't believe it.

This isn't even half of what this asshole deserves, but at least it's something.

I turn away to hide the smirk threatening to overtake me. Though I pull up short when I catch sight of my best friend. He's lying on my sofa, arms crossed over his chest, legs crossed at the ankle. "Wilder?"

"Don't mind me. I'm hiding." He doesn't even bother to open his eyes.

"You should be, looking like you do," Maggie teases, coming up behind me. "You really need to trim that thing on your face."

"I did. Yesterday." He sits up and straightens his T-shirt. Today's reads *Battery Life 1% Help me*. He glares at us. "I'm being stalked and not a single one of my friends cares."

"Because you could fix the problem easily if you'd just tell her it's over and ask her to leave you alone." The man isn't a child. This is beyond ridiculous.

Wilder flops back on the sofa. "I can't be mean."

"Just annoying," I mutter.

"Hey, Sutton," he calls. "Cover your ears, sweet pea."

With a giggle, she cups her hands over her ears.

Libby places her hands over them for good measure. "Okay," she calls.

With a sneer, Wilder sticks both his middle fingers up at me.

I scoff.

"Wilder!" Libby chides as she slides her hands to our girl's eyes.

"Shit." He drops his hands. "Sorry. I meant eyes. Cover your eyes," he mutters. "See? I'm losing my mind."

"It's not the first time," Sutton giggles.

Libby glares at my best friend.

Wilder chuckles. "You're not helping my case, sweet pea."

"I know what you can do." My little girl scoots around the counter, heading for the sofa. "It would be the best thing ever."

"You name it."

She plops down next to him on the tweed sofa and looks up at him from under her lashes. Whatever this is, he's going to agree. He's a sucker when Sutton and Lindsey break out the puppy dog eyes. "Convince Fisher that we can do the Monhegan Goodbye today."

Head tipped back, I groan.

"Oh." Wilder sits up. "Let's do it. I'll jump with her."

"Hey," Libby chimes in. "Maggie and I were going to do it with her."

"We'll all do it." He's suddenly all smiles. "This is great. I can be outside and have fun and still avoid Nic. There's no way that prissy woman is jumping in ice-cold water. This is a win-win."

Six hours later, I am absolutely not winning. Both of my girls are ready to plunge into the icy water behind a moving ferry. The line of summer people getting ready to board the boat runs down the dock and up the path toward the bakery, and piles of luggage have been loaded onto the boat for the twelve-mile trek back to Boothbay.

"You're sure you want to do this?" I ask Sutton as the waves crash against the rocks on either side of the dock.

Her entire body droops under the black wetsuit I insist she wears when she goes in the icy waters. She sighs, the sound one of pure annoyance. "Yes, I really want to. It's high tide, so the jump is only, like, ten feet, and it's warm today."

Warm is a relative term. The temperature is currently hovering at seventy degrees, and there's a decent breeze. At least the sun is out.

Libby gives my hand a quick squeeze. "We've got this."

When I focus on her again, all I see is skin. So much skin. Damn, she looks hot in that bikini and cut-offs. Every inch of her. Even her feet are hot. Pink toenails and rhinestone flip-flops and all.

There is no denying how gone I am for this woman.

"And you've got our towels. I'm sure you'll do a great job warming us up when we get out."

I angle in so my lips brush her ear. "I'll warm you up tonight, Princess."

She rolls her lips together, but there's no hiding the flash in her eyes. My girl likes that idea.

"Who's ready to do this?" The high-pitched voice claws at my ears a second before Flora steps onto the dock next to the line of people now filing onto the ferry.

"Oh no, it's Flora," Sutton mumbles as she steps closer to Libby. "You're not jumping, are you?"

261

Judging from the wetsuit pulled up to her hips and the towel in her hand, she is. "Yes, I heard from Mrs. Knowles, who heard from Blue, that you're jumping for the first time. I thought it would be fun to join you. I can hold your hand."

"Sorry, Flo." Wilder steps into our little circle on the dock, and with a thunk his large hand lands on my shoulder. "I've got dibs on our little sweet pea."

Wilder understands his role. His job is to make sure Sutton surfaces quickly and gets safely to shore.

"We're going to race Maggie to the rocks." Sutton's blue eyes brighten as she looks up at my best friend. "I climb on your back, and you swim like the fishes."

"Exactly!" Wilder holds out his fist and Sutton pounds it.

"Well, I swim like the sharks." Maggie steps up next to Wilder, wearing a purple bikini. "So good luck beating me."

Wilder turns, and I swear he stiffens. He blinks once, twice, and his mouth opens, but nothing comes out. Like he's forgotten how to speak. Eventually, he clears his throat. "I like the purple, Mags."

"Thanks." Maggie's cheeks go pink. "Libby's been helping me with shopping."

"See." Libby nudges her. "I told you this one would be amazing."

"Yeah." Wilder shakes his head. "Looks good."

I look from one friend to the other, eyes narrowed. Are they...? Do they—

"You should have told me you wanted help." Flora's grating voice pulls me from my thoughts. "I would have gone shopping with you on the mainland. We need to have more girl time. Just islanders, not summer people."

Maggie doesn't even look at Libby.

"Libby and I went shopping on the mainland a few weeks ago," Sutton says. "You should come with us next time, Maggie."

"Absolutely." Libby gives Sutton a sweet smile.

Flora frowns. She's always tried to join in with us, but she has a way of constantly insulting people that makes everyone uncomfortable. Any interaction with her is awkward, though it's gotten worse lately. Even Sutton avoids her now. Which I prefer. I've never liked the woman.

"We should line up," Wilder suggests.

I watch warily as they move toward the edge of the dock. They only stop when they're standing closer to the ferry than I'd like. I run my hand over my beard as Blue and a few other regulars step up too.

"Her first time, huh?" Cank asks from beside me.

I nod. "Both of them."

"Oh, Sutton will be fine. She's got the wetsuit and years of Maine living."

"It's Libby," we say at the same time. And we leave it at that. There's no need to finish the thought.

For the next two minutes, we watch as the ferry slowly moves away from the dock. The boat's speaker crackles, and the captain says, "And as we pull away, turn and give a wave to the islanders as they perform the Monhegan Goodbye."

The horn blows, and all twelve of the islanders participating launch themselves off the pier. Shrieks and screams and giggles ring through the air, followed by a series of splashes as the ferry speeds away.

Sutton and Wilder surface first, and Maggie pops up two seconds later. Then the trio races to the rocks, splashing wildly and yanking on each other. A few more heads appear before I see the blond hair I've been watching for.

"Oh my god." Libby pops up and sucks in a huge breath before submerging again, thrashing her arms wildly.

My stomach bottoms out. What is she doing?

Her blond ponytail comes up again, only to vanish once more.

Does she not know how to swim?

Pulse thudding in my ears, I run the three steps from my spot next to Cank to the edge and jump.

263

I drop quickly, and then my body hits the icy water. Although it's been at least ten years since I've punished myself by getting into this ice bath, the shock of the cold sends a familiar rush through my body.

My head breaches the surface quickly, and I spin, looking for her. "Libby," I call, panic seizing me.

Her head pops up two feet from me, and I lunge, latching on to her and pulling her tight to my chest.

She sucks in a big breath and blinks, her lashes wet and clinging together. "Fisher?" Her eyes are wide and her teeth chatter as droplets of water run down her pale skin. "Wh-what are you doing?"

Relief floods me. "Apparently saving you." With one arm firmly wrapped around her waist, I turn and use the other to swim to shore. My heart is still pounding when I step onto the rocks and stand in the waist-deep water. "Why would you jump in if you can't swim?"

Maybe it's pointless to ask. Honestly, it seems like something she would do. Jump and then learn to swim when she hits the water. Why worry until she has to, right? I tighten my hold on her. I'll do the worrying for her, I guess.

"I can swim. But the cold water was a shock, so I guess I panicked a bit, and I swear something pulled on my leg." She snuggles into my chest. "But you jumped in fully dressed."

"You needed me," I whisper into her wet hair. "And if you need me, I always come."

I pull her back a fraction and tip her chin. When her blue eyes meet mine, my heart skips in my chest. There's no hiding the truth at this moment.

"Hell, Princess. Don't you know by now that I'm head-over-heels in love with you?"

Her lips form the most adorable O. "You love me?" she whispers. Those crystalline irises brighten as she studies me, as if she's trying to comprehend how this could be true. "Really?"

Does she seriously have to even ask? Who couldn't love this

woman? She's daring and kind, fun and caring. She makes every fucking day of my life better. She makes me want to live. Makes me want to jump in and experience everything, but only if she's at my side, doing it right along with me.

This might not have been the time or place to make my confession, but I don't want her to doubt how I feel for even one second. With a smile, I tuck a wet lock of hair behind her ear. "I love you so damn much, Libby Sweet."

Her quivering purple lips pull up in a pretty smile. "I love you too." She says it like it's the most wondrous thing. Like it's mind-boggling that we're only now voicing the sentiment. Because we both know that it's been true for a long time. She's in awe, thrilled. As if she believes we could have missed out on this. Or maybe that's what I'm thinking, because, fuck, I worked so hard not to fall for her. And if I'd succeeded, then I would have missed out on this. I would have missed out on living.

"Thank fuck," I mutter. Swamped with emotion, I drop my lips to hers.

All too soon, whistles and the cat calls erupt around us. As much as I want to live in this moment, soak up the warmth of her mouth, savor her sweet taste, I pull back.

"I love you," I whisper against her lips. Then I scoop her into my arms and carry her over the rocks. There's no way I'll take the risk that she'll slip and fall.

"Libby!" Sutton calls.

I trudge through the seaweed to the grass, where my little girl is standing and set my girlfriend on the ground.

"We did it!" She wraps her arms around Libby, hugging her tight.

"We did," Libby says breathlessly, hugging her back.

I scoff over our girl's head. Libby barely did it. "Sutton, you are free to do it again. However, Libby, you're a one-and-done participant when it comes to this goodbye." I shake my head.

"Fisher." Sutton tilts her head, water dripping from her braids, as she takes in my soaked clothing. "I thought you said you'd only go in when pigs fly."

Wilder chuckles. "Turns out the pigs are flying all over lately."

I wrap a towel around a shivering Libby and engulf her in a hug to warm her the best I can. "Ready to go home, Princess?"

Libby

Chapter 38

BY THE TIME the sun went down tonight, my cheeks were pink and my heart was full. After early morning play practice, Maggie, Sutton, and I met Kennedy and Lindsey at a tiny beach carved out between rocks. We spent hours lying on the craggy shoreline, and now I'm paying for it. And not only because of the slight sunburn, but because the little pebbles left tiny bruises all over my ass.

Fisher will have a fun time laughing at me, I'm sure. He spent the day helping Wilder and Blue work on something at the inn. I can't remember what, since I tuned out when he took off his shirt.

No matter how many times that man undresses in front of me, I'm taken by him. The hard edges that soften when he catches me. The light that reaches his eyes. The cocky smirk that plays on his lips. He's smiling more and more lately, but that smirk undoes me every time. Who am I kidding? *He* undoes me. No matter what expression he wears.

I take my time applying lotion to my body, knowing he'll be the benefactor of my smooth skin shortly, then slip into my robe. I came home to pick up more clothes and figured I'd shower while I was here. After our day at the beach, we met Fisher at the inn for dinner, so when we returned, I was more than ready to rinse the sand from my body. Fisher planned to get Sutton cleaned up and in bed. Then he had to get some hacker work done, so I'll take my Kindle over and sit on the futon in his office. It's become our routine. While he works, I curl up and read until I fall asleep. Then he carries me into bed. It's silly, since the futon isn't the most comfortable spot by a long shot, but I feel most at ease when he's close.

The hair on the back of my neck tingles, and I spin and peer out the window. Is he watching me? Someone definitely is. I step closer and pull up the pane, breathing in the fresh summer air. Sea salt and a distant fire. Probably a bonfire on one of the beaches. There's a group of bachelors here this week. Wilder is taking them out on his charter boat in a couple of days. When he teasingly asked Maggie and me to come out with them and be their entertainment, I thought Fisher was going to knock him sideways. I chuckle to myself as I survey his house. The light in his office is out, so it must be the cameras I felt watching me.

With a shake of my head, I shut the window.

In my bedroom, I disconnect my Kindle from its charger and slip it into the bag I've filled with more clothes. I've made a habit of doing my laundry here, and I don't ever keep too much at Fisher's place. I don't want him to think I'm trying to move in or anything. Though if he asked, I'd say yes.

I hate every minute I spend away from the two of them. His house feels far more like home than any place I've ever occupied. Even if it simultaneously feels like the three of us are living in someone else's space.

Nothing in that house fits Fisher's personality. Now that I've seen his apartment in Boston, it's obvious that he's living within the confines of his brother's memory. His job, his decor, his life.

Even so, within those walls are the two people I've fallen head-over-heels in love with, so I'll stay anywhere they are if that's what they need.

Though the more time I spend with them, the clearer it is to me that neither of them actually do need it. In fact, it's keeping them from moving on. Sutton especially. But my role in their lives is new, so I'm careful not to step on any toes and point out what I think she really needs.

Giving Fisher a little more time to get Sutton settled, I sit at the edge of the bed and pull out my phone. I've got several emails from my agent, but one in particular sticks out. The one with the word *URGENT* in the title.

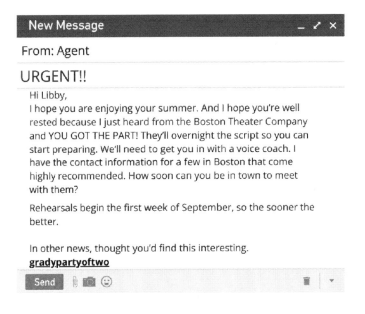

I click on the link at the bottom of the email and am redirected to the web browser and an article about *Grady Party of Two*. According to the report, they've paused filming in the wake of the release of Brad's texts and emails. Little by little, an unknown source has dropped bombs. The most damning are the threats he sent me and an email to his agent about the lovely million-dollar donation to the charity where he's adamant that he wasn't behind it. All the good press that garnered is gone, as is his money. Now the public at large is wondering why he was promising to destroy me.

Can't say I'm not happy that he's being exposed for the slimy snake he is.

I also have a feeling I know who's responsible for all of this, but I've yet to confirm it.

I close out of the email and will my heart not to pound at the idea of having to leave the island. The *Grease* performance is this weekend. I guess I'll have to head to Boston once that's over.

Though the thought fills me with trepidation, there's pride there too. Because I did it. I got the part. Another new beginning. Another chance to discover who I am now that I'm no longer the Hollywood starlet who arrived on that trash boat almost three months ago.

Light on my toes, I collect my things and rush out the door, determined to enjoy every minute I have left with my two favorite people.

When I walk into the house, Bing doesn't run to the door, which means Sutton is asleep and he's curled up in bed with her. Fisher must have his headphones on too, because he doesn't peek out to greet me. I take my time putting my bag in his room and then head for his office with my Kindle in hand.

I peek into Sutton's room, and when Bing catches sight of me, he lifts his head, on guard. Though an instant later, when my identity registers, he settles at the foot of her bed. Like I thought, she's fast asleep, the rainbow moon lamp beside her bed bathing her innocent face in a soft glow. I stare at her for a few seconds, a smile on my lips. I love this little girl something fierce.

When I push the door to Fisher's office open, he turns, his lips hooking into a smile. He pulls the headphones down around his neck and motions for me to come closer. "You have a nice shower?"

I drop my Kindle onto the couch and climb into his lap. "So

good." I snuggle into his chest, inhaling him. He's wearing one of his old Boston Revs shirts that's so soft because of how worn in it is.

He runs his hands up and down my back, inadvertently hitting the tender skin caused by my time in the sun and causing me to wince. Hands coming to a stop, he studies me, and when I smile, his expression relaxes. "I've got a little more work to do, but then I want you in my bed so I can inspect your sunburn."

"Oh, you want me naked?" I say, all tease and innocence.

Fisher shakes his head. "You aren't getting rewarded for not taking care of yourself."

"Oh, are you going to punish me, Hacker?" I tease.

He chuckles, the sound deep and dark, vibrating through me. "Wouldn't you like that?"

"Actually." With my lip caught between my teeth, I slide off his lap and onto the floor. The hardwood bites into my knees, but I relish the pain as I press my palms against his thighs. "What I'd like more is this."

I tug at the waistband of his sweats, but he grasps my wrists, stopping me.

"What are you doing?" Even as he asks, his dark eyes go molten and he spreads his thighs a bit.

"Playing." I tug out of his grip and pull on the drawstring at his waist.

The sweatpants come off easily, partially due to the way he lifts his hips to allow me to take control.

His cock grows under my gaze, and by the time I've pulled his slippers off and he's naked from the waist down, thighs spread wide, bracketing my shoulders, he's completely hard.

I grin up at him. "Go back to work. I can keep myself entertained." I lean in and press my lips to his crown, kissing gently.

He hisses out a "fuck" and shifts, causing the chair to roll backward and bump into the desk.

"Shh," I tease him. "If you're going to be noisy, I'll have to find another way to keep you quiet."

I suck him into my mouth and hollow my cheeks, suctioning with force, and I don't release him until he's groaning loudly.

"I think I'd like that," he grumbles.

I pull back and wiggle out of my pink panties, then ball them up and shove the damp fabric into his mouth. When his eyes widen in surprise, a thrill races down my spine.

With a final grin at him, I get back to work, sucking and jacking him. All the while, I can't decide what I want to focus on more: his gorgeous wet cock or his heated gaze. He looks unbelievably hot with my panties stuffed into his mouth, his brown eyes eclipsed by blown-out pupils and a hazy desire.

I'm sucking hard again, one hand cupping his balls, when he spits my panties out. "Fuck this." He yanks open the drawer beside him and pulls out a set of metal handcuffs.

I gasp, and heat pools low in my belly. He promised weeks ago that he'd use them on me, and now he's finally following through.

I'm still giddy at the prospect, lost in a haze of lust, when he lifts me and lumbers toward the futon.

"You're not the only one who gets to play," he rasps as he lowers me onto the cushion. With one knee planted beside me, he flips open one cuff with a single fluid flick, unlocking a new kink inside me. Then, with a kiss to my pulse point, he locks it around my wrist. "Too tight?" He searches my face, a hint of concern creeping into the lustful look.

I shake my head. "Nope."

Smirking, he lifts my arm and loops the handcuffs around the frame of the futon. He gently forces my other arm up, and with another click, I'm secured to the couch. "Now stay while I go back to work."

Jaw dropping, I gasp. "Fisher Jones!"

He drops his head back and lets out a laugh. "I'm just teasing, Princess. I would never get any work done with this perfect pussy, wet and ready for me, only a couple of feet away." He presses a kiss to my lips and slides down my body, pushing my thighs apart.

"Don't be too loud, or I'll have to stuff your panties into *your* mouth."

God, why is that hot? I squirm, bucking against him.

The warmth of his lips hits me as he chuckles against my sensitive flesh, then his tongue licks a trail from my entrance to my clit. "Fuck, you taste good," he grumbles before diving in for more.

I'm thrashing against the futon, half desperate to touch him and half thrilled to be restrained like this.

My orgasm comes on so quickly I have to bite down on my cheek to keep from screaming in surprise. "Fisher, please," I beg.

As if possessed, he tightens his hold on my thighs and pulls me even closer, lifting my ass off the futon as he sucks my orgasm from me.

"Fuck me, please." I'm a panting mess by the time he finally lifts his head and licks his lips. "Please."

"Your hands okay?" he asks, hovering over me to inspect them.

Impatient, I scowl. "Yes. Now fuck me, *please.*"

With one arm resting beside my head, he lines himself up and pushes inside me with a low groan. The guttural sound has my toes curling. His heavy weight settles on both sides of me as he rolls his hips and sets a rhythm. His lips meet mine, and we silence one another by kissing, devouring each other's moans. Like every time we're like this, it's the best I've ever had.

"I love you," I say as emotion washes over me.

He pulls back, his eyes flashing. Then he's scrambling for the key he dropped on the desk and unlocking the cuffs. He pulls me onto his lap and holds me close. "Needed to feel your hands on me."

His admission tugs at my heartstrings. I run my fingers over his chest, back and forth, back and forth, keeping time with the roll of my hips. I'm so full of him. He's everywhere. Inside me, holding me, kissing me.

"I love you, Libby. Love you so damn much," he growls, every word sharper than the last, as if he's moving dangerously close to the edge of reason.

He pistons his hips, fucking up into me, and the moment he falls, I wrap my arms around him, bringing my chest to his, reveling in the way our hearts beat in time. For each other.

His heavy breath is in my ear, his hot cum filling me when I join him in the abyss, my body going limp as our orgasms wane.

Fisher's arms tighten around my waist and he squeezes me to his chest.

"I got the part," I whisper.

He goes stiff beneath me.

I straighten so I can get a better read on him and poke him in the ribs.

"Jesus, Lib." He flinches and bats my hand away. "Give me a minute to breathe. You just stole the life from me."

I press a kiss to his jaw. "And I'm going back to LA."

His hand tightens on my hip. "What?" His voice is rough, but not in a good way.

Realizing how easily my words have been misinterpreted, I shake my head and cup his cheeks. "Not for good, just for the awards show."

"Jesus fuck. Seriously, you've just stopped and restarted my heart at least a couple of times. Like a damn defibrillator." He blows out a breath and his face lights up. "First, congrats, baby. Of course you got the part. I'm so proud of you."

"Thank you."

"Now talk to me about LA. When's the event?" He looks around like he's searching for his phone, probably to check his calendar.

"You don't have to come."

"If you think I'm letting you deal with Brad yourself—"

I shake my head. This isn't up for debate. "I don't want the media to get wind of us. If they do, then they'll know where I've been and they'll never leave us alone."

"Libby," he says, his voice low and filled with frustration.

I roll my hips over him and press a light kiss to his lips. "Did you release Brad's emails and texts?"

He nods, his expression solemn. "It was that or fly out there and kill him."

I can't help but chuckle. "He's not worth it."

With a hum, he runs his hand through my hair and settles it on my cheek. "I know that, but you are."

My heart floats like one of those buoys offshore. "I'm happy right here, Hacker."

"Obviously." He smirks, already hardening inside me.

I roll my hips and shudder, my clit still sensitive from the first two orgasms he gave me.

"Fuck," he mutters.

"Yes, Hacker. Fuck me like you love me."

"I do, you know." He cups my other cheek too. "I love you so much."

"I love you too. Now less talking, more fucking."

With a laugh, he bucks up into me. Who woulda thought that I'd be begging for this man of so few words to shut up?

Libby

Chapter 39

GOOD NEIGHBORS' "Home" blares from my phone as Putt-Putt bounces over a rock on the path toward the theater. Laughing, I veer to the right, waving in apology to Farmer Todd, who's crossing the street to the town meeting. Oh shoot, I'm supposed to meet Fisher there.

With one hand on the wheel, I pause the music and hold the button on the side of my phone down to dictate a text so he knows I'm going to finish up at the theater and plan to meet him later. The play is in two days, and the car needs one more coat of pink paint.

Gotta make *my* Pink Lady proud of her car counterpart.

I smile at the thought of the boat on stilts in Fisher's yard. We have yet to get it out on the water, but it makes a great spot to lie out in the sun and read with Sutton. It's become vital to our new afternoon routine.

I peer at the church where they're holding today's town meeting since the theater is a bit of a mess, but I don't see my man. He's probably still taking care of things around the island. The meeting doesn't start for another hour or so.

As I open the door to the theater and inhale the familiar scent of new paint and old, worn chairs, I smile. This place brought back my love for acting, and I don't even have a part in the play. Like everything else on this island, this simple building has helped me discover another facet of who I am. Next week I'll head to Boston to begin voice training, but I'll be bringing more than a piece of Monhegan with me.

And because my two favorite people will still be here, I'll be back often. This island holds my heart.

"Libby!"

I spin at the sound of one of my favorites.

Sutton's dressed in a pair of jean shorts and a peach T-shirt that says *Island Girl* on it. I have one that matches. It's hanging in Fisher's closet. We got them in Boothbay. I don't know why they don't sell them here.

Behind her, Kennedy and Lindsey appear. Kennedy's long blond hair is pulled up in a messy bun and she's got on a pair of ripped jean shorts and a tank top. Her daughter is in a bathing suit, her little tummy popping out, revealing the most adorable outie belly button. Every time I see it, I want to poke her like the Pillsbury Dough Boy.

"No peeking!" I shout. I want *someone* to be surprised by the set, and Kennedy might be the only resident we haven't dragged into painting because she's always busy working.

She throws her hand over her eyes and laughs. "Sutton wanted to come help you rather than go to the beach with us. Is that okay?"

I prop a hand on my hip and eye my sweet girl. "You'd rather work than have fun? Who are you?"

She lowers her head and toes the dirt, obviously not interested in explaining herself. She doesn't need to. It's been hard on her, knowing I'm leaving soon. It's been equally hard on me. I will physically ache when I pull away from the dock.

I wave off Kennedy and Lindsey. "Go have fun at the beach. I got my pretty girl."

Sutton's lips lift, joy once again radiating from her as the girls say their goodbyes, Kennedy still shielding her eyes.

When it's just the two of us, I wave, signaling Sutton to join me on the edge of the stage. I sit, letting my legs dangle, and when she drops to her butt beside me, I rest my head against hers, watching as she kicks her smaller legs beside mine against the stage. Back and forth, smack, back and forth, smack.

"You want to talk about it?" I ask.

Focus still fixed on our feet, she says, "Not really."

"I'm going to miss you too," I tell her.

She lets out the loudest sigh. "I don't understand why you have to leave so early."

"I haven't sung in a long time, pretty girl. I have to train my voice for the role." I only got the part because my name on the marquee will guarantee a crowd, but I'm determined to prove that I'm more than just my name. I'll do my part, and I'll do it well. "But I'm not leaving for good. This will be my home eventually. I just need to work for a bit." It's important to me that she and Fisher understand this. I'm not running anymore. This island is my solace because they're here. Wherever they are will be my home. I nudge her with my elbow. "You know you can come visit me whenever you want. If you talk to Fisher—"

A thunk near the doors catches my attention. When I look up, though, we're alone. "Did you hear that?" I say, jumping off the stage.

"Yeah." Frowning, she scans the theater.

"Hello?" I call out, taking another step forward.

When no one responds, I shrug and turn back. "Must have been the wind."

"Or a squirrel." Sutton giggles.

I roll my eyes. "Only if Flora's around."

She screws up her face, making me laugh.

"So like I was saying." I shuffle back toward her. "You should talk to Fisher. Tell him how you feel about living on the island."

Sutton eyes me, her lips pressed into a firm line. "Will you do it with me?"

Affection blossoms in my chest. "Of course, pretty girl. I'll do anything you want."

For the first time today, she gives me a truly joyful smile. "Okay, so what do we need to do?"

I glance around the set, seriously impressed with all we've already completed. "The car just needs one more coat of paint." I turn the music on again, and we get to work, jamming out to Taylor and Gracie Abrams, Lake Paige and Melina Rodriguez, dancing every time we hit a really good chorus, laughter and smiles our companions as we work.

"Gosh, it's getting hot in here." I yank off my sweatshirt.

Sutton swipes at her sweaty forehead. "Yeah, maybe I'll go open a window."

"I got it." I drop my paintbrush into the tray and head down the aisle, but with each step I take away from the paint, the scent of it dissipates and another fills my nostrils. "Is that..." I inhale again. "Sutton, do you smell smoke?"

The second the words are out, I catch a flash of orange in the corner. Blinking, I take a step toward it. The orange light at the side door dances, casting shadows on the floor in front of it.

I almost shake my head to clear my vision, but when I look back, the orange blazes forward, and I realize there's a fire coming from the side door. Fuck. We need to get out of here.

Fisher
Chapter 40

"I'D BE HONORED." Bill beams as his wife pats his forearm.

I don't know how being nominated as the island's new mailman and delivery guy is an honor, but at least Doris's husband is happy. And more than that, the task is no longer mine. Maybe I should feel sad about the loss of the jobs I've held for the last few years, but all I feel is freedom.

Though the sensation is dampened by concern, because Libby still isn't here.

Wilder elbows me and glares at my leg, which I only now realize is bouncing. I don't know why, but I can't ignore the unease that nags at me over Libby's absence.

I reread her message.

> My Princess: Hey, Hacker. I forgot that I need to…oh, here we go. Yes, we got it. Good girl, Putt-Putt…ooh, good girl. I'd love you to call me good girl later…but after painting, okay?

> Me: English, Lib.

> My Princess: Oh sorry. I was dictating the message. You know how I cheer Putt-Putt on. If I don't, she doesn't take the curves well. But we made it. You're probably already at the meeting. I'm coming, I promise. Just doing a little painting at the school first. I'll meet you there. Stand firm. No more jobs for my hacker.

Even her clarification makes little sense. But I love the *my hacker* part. Every time she claims me, my chest swells. And then I do dumb shit. Like attend a meeting I used to avoid at all costs because she wants me here.

> Me: Everything going okay?

Her response will probably be nonsensical, but just hearing from her will calm my anxiety.

"Fisher?" Cank's voice pulls me from my ruminations. "You approve?"

I blink. Approve what?

Wilder elbows me in the side and hisses, "Just say yes."

"Sure." I nod and once again force my leg still.

"Then it's settled. Fisher will maintain his role as acting sheriff. Bill will take over the mail and grocery deliveries. And since Star lives close to the farm, she'll help Todd keep Betty out of the strawberries."

Eyes narrowed, I search the crowd for Flora, certain she'll pipe up and insist I'm still on squirrel duty. Oddly, the woman isn't here. My muscles tighten with unease again. She never misses a town meeting.

I force myself to relax, rolling my shoulders out. Jeez, I need to chill. This could be a good thing. Maybe she's found something to keep herself entertained.

Next to me, Wilder clears his throat. "And my petition?"

Cank nods. "Yeah. We took a vote. You can take on the teal and white buoys. You'll now have sixty traps. Teal, yellow, and white, per the union."

Wilder pumps his fist.

"Did the mainland approve too?" I whisper.

Lips pressed together, he nods. "Two weeks ago."

That means I no longer have to go out on the water in the frigid New England winter. An instant sense of relief makes me feel buoyant. Mixed in with the sensation, though, is a hint of guilt. Hunter loved getting out on the ocean, even when the mercury dropped below ten. Me? I hate it. I shake off the guilt and take solace knowing that Hunter's legacy will continue through Wilder and his own passion for the open ocean, while I get to be home and dry.

And warm.

I glance over my shoulder again, but still no Libby, and she hasn't responded to my text either.

"What about my issue?" Blue calls from the first row. "I've petitioned twice and gotten two hundred and twelve signatures this summer."

On the other side of Wilder, Mrs. K groans.

Her son, naturally, chuckles. "He's my hero."

"We cannot put up nude sculptures that point the way to each landmark!" Doris exclaims.

She's not wrong. The island is full of children all summer. Really, even if it was just Sutton here, I'd veto that without a second thought.

"This is censorship. You're taking away my freedom of expression. It's communist," Blue rants.

"These are the days your father should be here," Mrs. K huffs, eyeing Wilder.

"Art shouldn't be censored," Ivy says. "But maybe we can use mermaids and mermen instead?"

"We don't need more fish. We got enough fish forever." Blue pushes to his feet. "I'm telling ya'll, them young people are on the phones. We need something that the Instagram will go nuts over. And that's naked pointers."

"There are kids here," Todd says. He himself has a fifteen-year-old son and a ten-year-old daughter. "We can't have porn statues pointing to the farm and brewery."

Wilder chuckles, his shoulder shaking.

"It is not funny," his mother hisses.

They continue their back-and-forth, but I lose the conversation when a light dances outside the window, catching my eye. A bright orange glow coming from up the hill.

I lean forward, squinting. For a heartbeat, I watch it flicker before I understand, and my gut plummets.

"Oh shit." I jump out of my chair. "*Fire.*"

The whole room is up and rushing to the door or window to get a look. With as dry as this summer has been, any fire is a potential for disaster. But this fire is coming from up the hill by the school. The school where Libby is painting.

I push through the crowd, heading for the door in a rush.

My heart stops as I step onto the church's wooden porch. The fire isn't near the school. No, the school is fucking ablaze. A loud pop makes me flinch, and then a window bursts, sending flames licking up the front of the building. The entire entrance is engulfed in large flames and thick smoke. All the bushes around the red schoolhouse are burning red and orange and even blue.

Fuck. Libby has to be out of the building. She *has* to be.

Heart hammering and gut churning, I jump off the steps and sprint down the path. I hurdle the gate rather than stopping to open it and pick up my pace.

"Fisher!" Eddy screams from behind me.

"Keep Sutton back," I call without turning. I can't look back. I can't slow down. Not while the flames continue to overtake the once perfect schoolhouse.

"*Sutton's with Libby.*" Her voice bleeds desperation.

I stumble, and my knees almost buckle.

283

No.

Not both of them.

I swallow hard, fighting the urge to retch, forcing my legs faster. The gravel flies behind me as I run up the hill. I can't lose both of them. I can't lose *either* of them.

"I'll get them," I promise, but my heart pounds wildly and my mind reels at the possibility that I might be too late.

"Fisher, wait," Wilder calls from behind me.

I don't even slow. Up ahead, through the smoke, a figure appears. A person stepping out from behind the building. Only one person. Too tall to be Sutton. My breath comes faster, but I'll get Sutton out too. I'll get them both out.

As I come up even with the front of the school, the woman's red hair is visible. Fuck. Not Libby.

"Fisher." The voice that normally sends a shudder down my spine has my heart lurching right out of my chest. "Stay back. The fire is out of control. It got too big too fast."

I don't have time to even consider why Flora is here or worry that she's too close to the schoolhouse for her own safety. But as I dart past her, she clutches my arm.

With a rough shake, I break free and push past her. "Sutton and Libby are inside."

"Sutton!" she shrieks, grasping for me again. "It was only supposed to be Libby, not Sutton. I didn't know. I just was getting rid of..."

Every muscle locks. Every nerve goes on high alert. Higher than they have been.

What the fuck did she say?

"If there is even a single scratch on either of them, I'll kill you." I yank my arm away.

"I would never hurt Sutton!" Her screams are drowned out by the roaring of the fire as I turn the corner to the back of the school. The fire isn't as bad here, but the brush around the base of the building has already caught.

Fuck.

"Libby! Sutton!" I yell over the blaze. My heart pounds wildly, blood whooshing in my ears. Smoke stings my eyes as sweat starts to trickle down my brow. "Sutton? Libby?" My throat burns with the force.

"Fisher!"

At the sound of my daughter's voice, I snap my head up. She's balanced on a window ledge about five feet off the ground at the far corner of the building. Her face is flushed and covered in soot. Behind her peach shirt, the fire glows hot, and smoke billows out around her. All I can see of Libby are her hands. They bracket Sutton's waist, holding her steady as the fire creeps along the ground below them.

"Jump, Sutton," Libby says. "You can do it. Jump. It's not as high as it looks."

She's right, but I'll be damned if I don't catch them when they jump.

"Fisher!" Sutton calls again.

"Jump," I order as I dart over. "I've got you."

With a choked sob, she flings herself out the window, over the flames and into my arms. The feel of her warm body hitting mine is the greatest sensation in the world. I give her one quick squeeze, then set her on her feet.

"Okay, sweet pea. I need you to run up the hill and get away from the fire. I've got to get Libby out."

As tears pour down her cheeks, she turns back to Libby, who's waving at her to go.

The sight of the fire, already burning brighter, surrounding Libby has my heart racing.

"Go, Sutton. Now!"

She startles at the command, but finally, her little legs start moving.

Libby has climbed up onto the ledge now. She glances back, then zeroes in on me. A loud crash sounds behind her, and her eyes go wide.

"Your turn, Princess," I coax, trying like hell to keep my voice even and my fear at bay. She doesn't have time to hesitate.

I hold my arms out to her, beckoning her to me. If I could walk through the fire and scoop her up, I would. But that's not how this works. She needs to trust me. She needs to jump.

"Come on, Princess. I've got you."

Another loud crack has my heart hammering and terror slamming into me.

Without another second of hesitation, she jumps. The force with which her body crashes into mine almost knocks me off my feet. As I teeter and work to keep my balance, I hold her tight to my chest. Her face is covered in soot, her hair damp with sweat. She smells like smoke, and her cough sounds painful.

When she melts against me, her body going limp, relief sinks deep into my bones. She's alive. She's here. They're both okay.

"You saved me again." She heaves a deep breath, then presses her lips against mine.

I kiss her back, then help her to stand and hold her at arm's length, inspecting every inch of her. "When you need me, I'll always come," I promise.

Between one heartbeat and the next, her body goes taut again, and her voice breaks. "Sutton?"

I scoop her up, then spin and move toward our girl. When the three of us are together, I drop to my knees and pull my daughter into my arms too.

Both. I've got them both. Shaking with a mixture of fear and adrenaline and abject relief, I hold them tight to my chest. Thank God.

"Are you okay?" I pull back, frantically assessing Sutton the way I did Libby. Their clothes are covered in soot, and so is their skin, but neither looks hurt.

"I'm okay." Sutton tilts away from me, eyeing Libby, but I'm making it hard, since I can't release either of them. I can't even loosen my hold.

"Me too, pretty girl. I think." Libby swallows. At the sound of a loud crash, we turn. The roof of the school caves and lands with a devastating clatter. The crackling of the fire intensifies, and the flames lick up over the walls.

In unison, the girls gasp. My heart damn near splats on the ground in front of us, but I remind myself that both girls are right here with me. It might have been close, but they're safe.

"I don't know what happened." Libby's voice shakes. "We were painting and singing along to music. Then all of a sudden, smoke was everywhere."

I know exactly what happened.

Teeth gritted, I set my sights on the woman up the road who's glaring back at us. The girls might be fine, but Flora Henries will pay for this.

Fisher
Chapter 41

IT TOOK an hour and a half for the one small truck we have to put the fire out. Thank goodness for Ryder, Star, and their two volunteers. They kept the blaze from spreading while the building burned to the ground.

The south pump on the beach had just enough pressure to get the water up the hill and save the church and surrounding houses. The schoolhouse will have to be completely rebuilt.

After Eddy looked over both of my girls, I insisted they go home, but neither would budge, both watching with tears in their eyes as the school crumbled under the intense heat.

Now, from my position on the dock, I can just make out Ryder's and Star's forms as they track through the rubble, making sure the embers are doused and there's no risk of the fire reigniting.

"Sutton shouldn't have been there."

It takes everything in me not to whirl on the woman who's cuffed to the chair behind me. These aren't the play cuffs I used on Libby. No, these are the ones that are kept locked in the safe at the harbor master office. The ones used to secure criminals until the coast guard arrives to take them into custody.

I've never arrested an islander before. Here and there, I have to pick up a tourist for drug possession or shoplifting. Rarely anything more serious. I don't feel even an ounce of sympathy for what this woman will be facing. Not after she almost killed my girls.

"Stop talking, Flora," Cank warns.

"But it isn't fair." She pounds her feet against the wharf, the sound mixing with the lapping of the waves beneath us.

Apart from Flora's ranting and the rhythmic sounds of the ocean, it's quiet. Cank shut down the harbor to all incoming traffic until Flora is picked up. My truck is parked across the dirt road leading to the wharf to stop curious tourists from getting too close. That doesn't mean they're not watching from decks and windows all over the island.

"If Libby had just left, then everything would have been perfect." Her manic green eyes are locked on mine, pleading. "We would have been happy. You and Sutton and me. We could have been a family."

Nausea roils in my gut at the idea. There is no happiness for me without Libby.

I keep my mouth shut. I can't even speak to this woman. It's hard enough reining in the urge to toss her into the sea while she's still handcuffed to that chair.

"This is all her fault," she sneers. "If the little Hollywood princess had given up when she had no cable or hot water, then none of this would have happened."

None of it would have happened? She acts as if this was an act of God. Something impossible to stop. When in reality, she's at fault. She tried to kill Libby. And she almost succeeded. She almost killed my little girl along with her.

None of what she's spewing is new. She ranted about all of it as I dragged her down the hill in cuffs, screaming about how Libby doesn't belong here. As furious as I am at the woman, as heartbroken as I am about the schoolhouse, I'm relieved to know this is the end of it. To know that Flora was behind the cut brake lines and the pilot light. Because once the state police show up with the coast guard, I can rest assured that Libby is finally safe.

"But she kept running to you. Even the night I threw the rock through her window to scare her, you showed up before I was even out of the bushes."

With a huff, I shake my head. I should have searched Libby's house more carefully that night. But I was focused on getting her safely out of there, not on the idea of someone hanging around.

"It should be me beside you. I spent years waiting for you. *Years.*" The chair creaks as she pulls on the cuffs. "Even when the other kids were mean, you never teased me about my frizzy hair or my glasses."

Had she not tried to kill my girlfriend and my daughter, I might pity her. I do understand the feeling. I get how lonely life gets for a kid who doesn't fit in. How isolating. It's apparently enough to drive a certain kind of person mad. Luckily for me, a princess came to my rescue before I lost my mind.

"You were always nice. I knew you'd come back for me. And then finally you did. It was fate. We were meant to be," she pleads. "I'd do anything for you. I cut her brakes and pulled her under the water, hoping the current would force her toward the ferry. Do you know how many times I had to trap that damn squirrel and shove him into the gutter?" she screeches.

I blink. That last confession is a new one. Poor rodent. At least he's finally free.

"I don't understand what happened to you." Cank shakes his head. "Your mother raised you better than this."

"Elizabeth Sweet happened to me. She shouldn't be here." She kicks her feet wildly, causing the chair to tip one way, then the other. "I will kill her."

Cank looks up at me and sighs. "How much longer until the coast guard arrives?"

I look up at the camera mounted just over his head. One of the many I installed around the island over the years. The footage goes directly to a NAS drive in my office, where it's saved for sixty days. So not only will this confession be on tape, but so will the fire.

"Oh." Cank nods. "Look at you. All that computer nonsense is gonna be useful."

Head bowed, I give it a shake. "Who would have thought that all those skills people gossiped about when I was a kid would come in handy?"

Just as the coast guard pulls up, Cank grins and adjusts his floppy hat so the puffin and whale are centered over his face.

This better be quick. I want to get back to my girls.

Libby

Chapter 42

"I CAN'T BELIEVE it's all gone." Maggie sniffles.

While the people of Monhegan did their best to get the fire out quickly, the paint acted as an accelerant, and there isn't a thing left that's salvageable.

Sadness engulfs me. All the work we did. The kids, the town. It was all for nothing. And all because Flora was *jealous*. I can't believe she was responsible for all the mishaps: the golf cart, the window, *the hot water heater*—honestly, that one almost put me over the edge. Hell, she tried to drown me during the Monhegan Goodbye. I knew something was pulling me down. Now I know it was *someone*.

I'm both relieved and bothered by the truth.

Relieved because it means that Brad had nothing to do with any of it and is likely still oblivious to my whereabouts, leaving this island as my respite from the rest of the world.

Bothered, though, that Flora hates me so much she nearly killed me and Sutton today. Thank god we noticed the fire before we were totally trapped.

I pull my girl into my side again, needing her close to remind myself that she's okay. "I'm so sorry, Maggie."

Maggie's green eyes widen, and her twin braids swing as she

snaps her head in my direction. "Why are you apologizing? We should all be apologizing to you. You moved here to escape the crazy, only to find another breed of it. This isn't who we are, Libby. Swear it."

I hold out my arm and pull my sweet friend to my other side.

She sniffles against my shoulder, then a sob breaks free. This theater was her everything. Maybe her only thing. Yes, it was used as a theater and meeting place during the summer, but it's also the schoolhouse. Her schoolhouse. Where she spends her days shaping little minds.

"We'll rebuild." Though Fisher told us to stay out of what's left of the building, Wilder has been wandering through the debris. He steps out of the charred mess, his dirty blond hair darker than normal from the soot, holding up a sign. The *Grease* sign. "And we got this."

There's a low buzz of conversation around us as neighbors discuss what to do next. But I focus on that sign.

"Yes, we'll rebuild," I say louder.

Maggie nods against my shoulder and straightens, inhaling a steady breath. "Yes. We'll rebuild, and next year, we'll put on the best version of *Grease* ever."

Smiling, I shake my head. "Not next year. We'll perform on Sunday."

Wilder tilts his head and regards me, though his expression is thoughtful rather than disbelieving. And if I'm not mistaken, there's a gleam in his eye. Yeah, he knows precisely what I'm going to say.

"We've got no set. Nowhere to perform," Maggie says glumly.

I release Sutton and take the sign from Wilder. "We've got a sign." I point to the park in the distance. "And in the words of William Shakespeare, all the world's a stage."

Maggie blinks at me, then squints at the sign.

"No one was hurt," I tell her, holding out my arms as proof. "And like you said, this is community theater. Participatory theater. It'll be a little more participatory now because the people in the audience will need to use their imaginations, but we can do this," I say, my energy and mood lifting.

Maggie bites her lip, her dark eyes watery. "I don't know."

Wilder steps up beside me and drapes an arm over my shoulders. "It could work. I'll get some chairs from the inn—"

"I can provide flashlights and popcorn," Doris offers.

Maggie frowns. "Flashlights?"

"For the car." I give Doris an appreciative smile. "Fisher and Wilder could hold them on stage and pretend to be our Pink Lady."

Wilder waggles his brows. "I make one hell of a loud engine, Maggie." He lets out a loud vrooming noise.

"That line belongs on one of your shirts." She giggles, wiping at her tears. "You'd really all do that?"

"We're islanders," I tell her. I feel it in my bones. I may be new to Monhegan, but this is where I belong. "Of course we would."

Maggie surveys the crowd. The people gathered talk over one another with suggestions and offers to help.

Finally, she pulls her shoulders back and nods. "Okay. Let's do it."

—

The next twenty-four hours are a whirlwind. Fisher doesn't let me out of his sight, and he holds me extra tight when we fall into bed late that night. But we're up early to help get the park ready for the play.

"I've got eggs and bacon going," he says when I come down, dressed for the day.

I waggle my brows. "Making breakfast? I like it."

At the table, Sutton talks around a mouthful of toast. "Well, he couldn't get donuts."

Fisher spins and points at her with the spatula. "Too soon."

Chuckling, I step up behind her and drop a kiss on her head. "Morning, pretty girl." From there, I make my way to Fisher and sink into his hold, relishing the comfort he gives me. I kiss his chest first, then tip my head back and purse my lips, silently asking for a smooch. "Leave her be. She's right. You'll just have to come visit me in Boston for donuts now."

Fisher's eye twitches. He hates that I'm talking so openly about leaving.

I get it, but it's happening whether any of us are ready or not. "Kiss. Me." I say the words slowly and then dramatically pucker my lips.

With a sigh, as if he's being put out, he brings his mouth to mine. "Go sit." He swats my ass with the spatula. "I'll bring your coffee and breakfast over."

Squealing, I scurry to the table. "He's really trying to get me to come back," I say as I slide into the seat next to Sutton's.

She nods, brows lifted. "Maybe you should ask for that dock again. I'm pretty sure he'd cave."

Fisher grunts as he sets a cup of coffee in front of me. It's iced and frothy and the perfect beige color that signals he used just the right amount of creamer. "Not you too." He squints, looking betrayed.

Sutton shrugs innocently. "Just trying to see what else she can get out of you."

Hovering in close, he kisses the bare skin between my neck and my shoulder and whispers, "Everything. You can get everything out of me."

A delicious warmth floods me, from my chest to my fingers and toes and all the way up my neck and into my cheeks. I pick up my iced coffee and take a sip to cool myself down.

When Fisher returns to the table with our plates, he slides his hand onto my lap. And he leaves it there all the way through breakfast.

God, I'm gone for this man. He doesn't have to worry about whether I'll come back. When I'm gone, I'll be counting down the seconds until I can hop on a ferry—or helicopter or trash boat—and get back to him.

—

We spend the rest of the morning and early afternoon getting the park ready for the show and rehearsing. Then Mrs. K allows us to use the private dining room at the inn for hair and makeup.

Just as we're headed out, ready to walk out onto the figurative stage, Maggie squeals. "Oh my goodness! Our Instagram post about the show change is blowing up!"

There's a knock on the door, then Fisher's deep voice. "You guys ready?"

Maggie opens it and steps out, her focus glued to her phone. "One of the summer people must have posted about your help with the show. The page has tons of new followers, and they all want to know if it's true that Elizabeth Sweet is performing tonight."

When she lifts her head, beaming, I choke back the urge to wince, instead faking a smile. Once she's engrossed in her device again, babbling about how this is going to be great for the school, Fisher and I glance at one another nervously.

At the sound of a throat clearing, we turn in unison.

"It's true," Cank says. "There was a whole slew of people getting off the ferry this afternoon. Normally the incoming ferry on Sundays is mostly empty and the outgoing is full."

A rumble of a growl rolls up Fisher's chest.

With a sigh, I place my palm flat against his racing heart. "It'll be fine."

His jaw clicks, his dark eyes swimming with concern. "I've got a bad feeling about this."

So do I. But what choice do we have? Besides, more tourists means more money for the island, and we need that money more than ever now that the schoolhouse will have to be rebuilt.

I've already called my financial planner and instructed her to make an anonymous donation that will cover the rebuild, but there are a thousand other ways this town could use the extra income. The brewery, the inn. They can all use the business. If they benefit from the chaos that's sure to ensue, then it'll be worth it.

Ten minutes into the show, it's clear Fisher was right to worry.

It's hard to hear the opening number over the shouts.

"Give us Elizabeth Sweet! Where's Libby?"

Those types of demands come from every angle. I'm hiding out in the tent we set up as our backstage area so that only the characters on *stage* are seen. The stage being the grass in front of the tree.

Fisher gives me an apologetic look, and I know what he's going to say before he says it. "We're getting you out of here. Wilder can take Sutton back to the house."

As much as I hate to miss the show, this is the right call. So I follow Fisher out of the tent. He takes his hat from his head and puts it on mine, then he and Wilder flank me to keep me from being seen until we're out of view. Once we're a couple hundred feet away, Wilder heads back to the show to stay with Sutton.

The walk is tense. I'm caught between wanting to apologize and knowing he'll be mad if I do. I know this isn't my fault, but I can't help but feel bad that the hard work the kids and Maggie put into the show is being overshadowed by my stardom.

As we crest the hill, a group of people standing outside my house comes into view.

"Fuck. They found me."

Fisher shakes his head. "I'm going to arrest every one of them for trespassing."

I grasp his arm lightly, hoping to imbue a little calm. "You can't arrest everyone."

His chest puffs. "Watch me."

"*Fisher.*" My heart thunks heavily as I peer over at him. I know what I have to do, no matter how much I hate it.

His eyes narrow, and he shakes his head sharply, like he knows what I'm going to say. "No."

"Come on, Hacker. You know how to get into the house. Sneak me in through the back door so I can get my stuff."

"*Libby.*" His lips pull down in a tortured frown. He knows I'm right.

"I planned to leave this week anyway. We knew this was coming." I loop my arm through his and press my cheek to his bicep. "Let the excitement die down. I'll head to LA and do the whole Emmy thing. Then when I'm back in Boston, maybe you and Sutton can visit?"

I'm confident about every facet of the plan except that last part. I worry that once I'm gone, he'll change his mind about bringing Sutton to see me.

But I don't have a choice. I can't stay here. At least for now. I can't bring more chaos to this island. Sure, the income from tourism is great, but people love Monhegan because it's a place to escape to. Its anonymity is its superpower. People come for the quiet, untouched beauty. Not in hopes of seeing celebrities.

I won't ruin that.

Fisher gives me a singular nod and pulls me to his chest, hugging me fiercely. "I'm not giving up on you, Princess."

"That's good." I hold him tight and inhale his scent. "I'm holding you to that."

Fisher

Chapter 43

"SHE'S BETTER AT THE VOICES," Sutton pouts as I stick the bookmark in *Kristy's Big Day*. Book six of the Baby-Sitters Club is apparently one of Libby's favorites. Can't say I love the series, even if the girls gush over it.

"Libby does a lot of things better than I do, sweet pea." I wrap an arm around her and pull her closer. Her little head drops to my shoulder and she sighs.

Bing looks up from the end of the bed and whines. Even the dog misses our girl.

She left this morning. The sun had barely crept over the horizon when the three of us snuck down to the beach and took the dingy out to *Glory Days*. Cank was more than happy to let us borrow his boat for her escape.

The rest of us? There was no happiness to be found as we dropped Libby off at the Boothbay dock and watched her slide into the waiting limo.

All day my skin crawled. It hurt, sending her off on her own like that. There are moments in life when it's important for one's partner to be present, to be supportive. And for Libby, this is one of them. I should be with her, holding her hand. Staring down Brad Fedder and memorizing reporter's names so if even the slightest negativity about my girl is published, I know who to exact vengeance on.

"Why can't I come?"

I sigh. "I never said I was going."

But I am. I've already talked to Mrs. K about keeping Sutton.

"It's like you're half gone already." She sinks farther into the mattress, her little lips tugged down. "You're moving on, and you're leaving me behind."

Those words slice through my chest with so much force I have to press a hand to my sternum. I'm worried I'll bleed out if I don't.

"Sutton." Once I can breathe again, I place my index finger under her chin and tilt her face up, forcing her to look at me. "Whether I go support Libby or I stay here—or if I visit her in Boston—I am *never* leaving you behind."

She blinks rapidly, her eyes pooling with tears. "Are you sure?"

God, this kid is gutting me. T "You and me, sweet pea." I grasp her hand. "We're family. We're a package deal. You're mine and I'm yours. Always."he words stick in my throat, but I'm determined to get them all out. "I loved your mom and dad. They were two of my favorite people in the whole world. And I will always make sure you remember them. I'll make sure you know where you came from. But Sutton, as far as I'm concerned, you are my daughter, and nothing —*nothing*"—I swallow past the lump in my throat—"will ever change that."

A tear slips from her eye and she launches herself at me.

"I love you, sweet pea."

She sniffles. "I love you too." For a minute we stay like that, but it isn't long before her little body tightens. "Can I tell you a secret?" The words are so soft I barely hear them.

I pull back and nod, holding eye contact. The seriousness of her expression makes my anxiety spike. But I inhale deeply and exhale slowly, forcing a calm I don't feel.

Sutton picks at her quilt. "I like it here. But sometimes..." Her voice trails off. With her lip caught between her teeth, she drags her focus up to my face. "Sometimes I wish we didn't live here. I wish we could be like Grams and Gramps. I wish we could live somewhere else and come here just to visit." She heaves a breath, and her words come faster. "Where I could go to school with lots of kids my own age and see a movie in a movie theater. And go on an airplane and try McDonalds."

The idea doesn't shock me. I figured she felt this way. But she's never voiced any of this before.

"Do you ever wish that we didn't live here?" she asks.

I could lie, but she's giving me her truths, and I owe her the same. "All the time, sweet pea."

"So why can't we leave?"

I wish there was a simple answer to that question.

She drops her gaze and goes back to picking at her quilt. "Maybe we could leave for a visit. Go see Libby, then see how we feel?" Her little voice holds so much hope.

I sigh, and her shoulders slump.

"I'm not saying no."

She straightens, her eyes lighting up.

"I'm not saying yes either," I warn.

Like a balloon losing air, she deflates again.

How the hell do I explain this situation to an eight-year-old? Part of me wants to avoid it, but I can't. Not if Libby is in our lives. "You've read about the emails that Brad Fedder sent Libby, right?"

A little line forms between her brows. "He wasn't as nice as Logan is on the show."

"He's worse than not nice," I say seriously.

She purses her lips, her chin dropping.

Fuck. I struggle with the words. This isn't easy. As I sort through my thoughts, I can't help but be even more impressed with Libby, because she lived it and came out stronger.

"Libby was young. Barely older than you when they started working together on the show."

Sutton nods.

"And Brad." I clear my throat. "He did things, touched her, said things that made her uncomfortable. And instead of stopping when she told him to stop, he did it again and again."

For a minute she just stares straight ahead, but her eyes move back and forth as she processes the implications. Finally, she swallows and peers up at me. "No one made him stop?"

Fuck. Pain blooms in my chest. Because no, no one made him stop. All those fucking adults around, people who should have protected Libby, and no one made him stop.

But I don't want to scare her, so I take a breath. "She didn't have anyone she trusted enough to talk to. She was afraid. But Sutton." I wait until her eyes meet mine. "Listen carefully to me." I clear my throat. "If you ever feel uncomfortable, if someone touches you in a way you don't want, you tell me, and I'll take care of it. You should never be afraid to tell me anything."

She nods solemnly, the expression far too serious for such a sweet, innocent child. It hurts to see it, but she needs to know.

Lips turned down, she studies my face. "You listen to me," she says, like it's so simple. "Like with Flora."

"I will always listen to you," I promise.

"I'm really lucky I have you," she whispers. "Libby didn't have a *you*. She had a *Logan*." Her tone turns harsh when she says the name.

Though I hate that I might have ruined one of her favorite shows tonight, I'd rather she didn't idolize a person like Brad Fedder.

Sutton takes a deep breath. "Libby needs you."

"That's what I'm worried about, sweet pea."

She nods. "You should go." She's resigned. She knows I can't take her. Although the melancholy lingers, the anger is gone. "I'll cheer really loud from here. So loud Libby will hear me and know how proud I am of her."

The words suck the breath from my lungs. I haven't looked at the situation that way. I haven't thought of the moment as one where Sutton will see Libby shine. A moment Libby might want Sutton to see.

Guilt claws up my throat.

I smooth a hand down her hair and kiss her head. "Go to sleep, sweet pea. We can talk in the morning."

Once Bing is settled on the foot of her bed and her moon lamp has been turned on, I shut the door and stomp down the stairs.

It's too fucking quiet with Libby gone. I hate it.

"Want a beer?"

Wilder. He's been here all day. Dealing with the constant flow of reporters who've come knocking and sending them all away. He hasn't complained, and he hasn't left my side.

"Thank you," I say as he hands me an amber bottle. Though my appreciation is for something else entirely.

He clinks his bottle against mine.

"Elephant in the room?" I smirk. "Thank fuck the beard's gone."

He chuckles. "Dude, so many people have taken my picture. I couldn't stand looking at it. It had to go."

"Smart choice."

He rests his forearms on the counter. "Elephant in the room?"

I hum in assent.

"Libby's endgame."

I nod. No doubt she is my forever.

"And she's gone..." The words trail off like he's expecting me to deny it, but we both know it's true. "So...*what the fuck are you still doing here?*"

I rear back like I've been punched in the gut. Once I've caught my breath, I drop my head into my hands. "Sutton."

"Is very portable," he jokes. "She's what? Sixty pounds? Easy enough to pick up and move anywhere."

I fight an eye roll. He's ridiculous. "I can't just *go*."

303

"Why?" He says it like the idea is simple.

He, of all people, should get it. I can't abandon the citizens of Monhegan. Hunter isn't here anymore. That's why I've slotted into his role. If I leave, then what happens?

"What do you mean why?"

He sets his beer down and plants his palm on the counter. "I mean why can't you go? We've all been trying to get you to leave for a year now."

I scoff. What the hell is he talking about? Every day, I swear this island needs me more, not less.

"Man." He shakes his head, ruffling his messy blond hair. "Why do you think we keep piling on more shit jobs? We did it hoping you'd see that this life is not what you want."

I sputter. Is he saying that all the deliveries and errands and goat herding nonsense—

"I don't understand."

With a chuckle, he slaps my shoulder. "We all love you. But after a year on this island, you were miserable. We all see it. You're not meant to stay here, so we started giving you shit to do, thinking you'd get fed up and say enough is enough. Instead, you just kept taking it."

The air slowly leaks from my lungs. "Are you telling me Hunter never did all that shit?"

Wilder laughs. "No way he'd have put up with being the island errand boy. And that goat made him insane. That's why when Libby finally brought it up, we all happily took over the jobs we're capable of doing. We've just been waiting for you to realize that you're meant for more than this."

I rough a hand down my beard as I process what he's saying. "You're saying everyone wants me gone."

"No." He shakes his head resolutely. "If you were happy here, then we'd be thrilled to have you. But you're not. And we just want you to be happy. Sutton too. There's no reason to stay unless it's what you want. And it's not. We're not saying jump ship and never come back. I expect you to visit all the damn time, or spend summers here, but your life has always been in Boston."

For three years, the possibility of leaving has felt just out of reach. But if what he says is true, if the islanders would accept us if we became summer people, then maybe...

I blow out a breath. There's still one big issue.

Scowling, I bow my head. "I can't. You know what Marissa and Hunter wanted."

"Yeah." He nods, spinning his beer on the island. "They wanted their kid to be happy and loved. Don't you remember how they talked about being mainlanders during the school year once Sutton started first grade?"

Yeah, but when Marissa changed her mind about bringing Sutton to Boston, my brother thanked me for understanding, and all that talk seemed like just that: talk.

"Dude." He shakes his head. "I'm going to be morbid here, but if something happened to you, what would you want for Sutton?"

Fuck. The girl can't lose anyone else. My gut twists. Because if we stay here, won't she be losing Libby?

Wilder sighs. "Just work with me."

The words slip out easily. "I'd want her to be happy and loved."

"Exactly. That's all your brother wanted." He gives me a long look, his expression far too serious for his always easy-going nature. "And he wanted you to be happy too."

I shake my head.

"And I'd bet my boat that he'd love for Sutton to have a dad *and* a mom." He tips his beer in my direction. "Even if that means living in Boston."

I take a slow sip of my beer and mull over everything he's been saying, knowing, deep down, that it's all true. Marissa and my brother were wonderful parents. Putting myself in their position now, looking at Sutton as my child, makes it all so obvious. So easy.

Fuck, Wilder is smarter than he looks. And maybe a little smarter-looking now that the damn beard is gone.

Hunter and Marissa would want Sutton to be happy. They'd want her to be surrounded by people who love her. But there's one thing I'm still not 100 percent sure of. "I don't even know if Libby wants that kind of responsibility."

Wilder breaks into a wolfish grin. "You won't know if you don't ask her."

Libby

Chapter 44

RETURNING to the place I called home for nearly all my life felt like anything but a homecoming. The sterile scent of washed floors and scrubbed bathrooms hit me the second I stepped inside, instantly making me miss the musky, sweet smell of Fisher's house. On the island, I usually woke to the aroma of coffee and bacon, maybe something sweet. Here, it's nothing but cleaning supplies and a killer view of the ocean.

Even the panoramic view has nothing on the one I'd find each morning on Monhegan. There's nothing more beautiful than the sight of Sutton curled up on the couch watching cartoons and Fisher leaning against the counter, arms wide open, waiting for his morning snuggle. Even Bing. What I'd give to watch him dance around my feet again.

LA is no longer home, and I can't wait to get this last part of my life over with so I can return to the family I found back east.

Step one: get through the next few hours.

I study my reflection, appraising the work my stylists have done, and second-guess my plan another four times.

The Emmys are tonight. Win or lose, I'll face all kinds of questions on the red carpet.

And I haven't figured out exactly how I should handle it all. Should I tell my story? All of it? It's unlikely Brad will be there. He's not nominated, and I can only imagine he's in hiding after so many of his transgressions have been leaked. Maybe allowing Fisher's punishments to be enough is the right thing to do.

But there's a part of me—and it's not even the petty part, though that's surely there too—that believes that if the world finally knows the whole truth, then maybe my story will open eyes and remind people that monsters like Brad exist. If I don't come forward, I worry the cycle will just continue. Maybe it's naive to think that what I have to say will even matter. I wouldn't be the first Hollywood star to speak up, but damn do I wish I could be the last.

Either way, my biggest fear is that if I don't use this opportunity, the production company will get away with dismissing me, dismissing my truth, and sweeping the controversy under the rug. If that happens, then who's to say another child won't be hurt under their watch?

After all, it's entities like the production company that allow men to continue to do these things. They provide the cover-ups. The money. And they'll gladly destroy anyone who speaks out against them.

They can try to destroy me. I couldn't give a fuck. Hell, they already did. They used gossip rags to convince the world that I'd had a mental breakdown. They killed off my character and blamed my mind.

What they didn't count on was that I no longer care about that career.

My identity in Hollywood as Elizabeth Sweet doesn't matter nearly as much as the Libby I've discovered during my time on the island. The Libby I've come to be to Sutton. For her, I want to be stronger. I want to do the right thing.

I want to be someone she can be proud of. I want to love her the way my mom loved me. Even though I didn't have my mother for long, she left the most astonishing impression. My mother's strength in those last few months of her life still inspires me. The big moments aren't what I remember about her. It's the little ones. The smiling through the pain. The way she always showed up for me.

I want to show up for Sutton. And I intend to do it with a smile on my face.

Which means I have to tell my father the truth, and since he's currently standing behind me, waiting to leave, it looks like there's no time like the present.

So I swallow back the trepidation and clear my throat. "Daddy, I need to talk to you."

Eyes drifting to my face, he slides his phone into his jacket pocket. He's dressed in a tuxedo, prepared to walk with me down the red carpet. So debonair with his gray hair slicked back.

Does he ever look back and wish he'd done things differently? We both missed so much of my childhood. Maybe he didn't know better. Maybe his grief was just too big. But I can see all the ways he tried. Just like Fisher, he was stuck. I hate knowing that I'm about to hurt him. This truth will be torturous for him, of that I'm sure. But I can't lie to protect the feelings of others anymore.

"You've met someone and you want to stay in Monhegan," my father says with a knowing smirk.

There's no stopping my smile. "Well, yes. But that's not what I need to say." I inhale, searching deep for the strength I'll need for this conversation. "Could we sit for a few minutes? I think we'll both need it."

———

My father is red and shaking by the time I'm finished. By some miracle, I haven't shed a single tear. Telling Fisher and then my publicist first probably helped.

My father, on the other hand, swipes tears from his eyes, begging me to forgive him.

That's when I finally break.

"Oh, Daddy. You didn't know."

"I should have. Dammit. I should have—" He hangs his head. "Why is he still standing? Why hasn't he been arrested?"

Plans have been put in motion. After tonight, Brad will be living in the same kind of fear I've lived in for years. Maybe he won't be convicted, but I won't go quietly. When I'm done with him, everyone will know how sick he is. He'll face what he did, and with any luck, he'll never work in Hollywood again.

I grab a tissue from beside me and dab under my eyes. "Everything is being taken care of, but we have to go."

"No." He straightens, his expression hardening. "We aren't going. You aren't going to give this industry even another second of your time," he growls. "I was wrong to push you, Libby. I never would have if—"

I hold up my hand. "You were right to push me. And I deserve to say my piece."

He shakes his head. "I'll kill him if he shows up."

With a long breath out, I nod. "Let's hope he's not that stupid." With a squeeze of his hand, I stand and head for the mirror by the door. I dab at my eyes, thankful my makeup held up through the tears, then nod to my reflection. "I have to do this."

I spin as he steps up behind me and straighten his tie.

He heaves out a breath. "I'll do whatever you want."

A genuine smile tugs at my lips. "Thank you, Daddy."

He holds out his arm, motioning for the door. "On the way, maybe you can tell me about this man who's stolen your heart."

My chest warms at the thought of Fisher and Sutton. "I'd like that."

Outside, he helps me into the limo, then sits beside me. At the gate, the car stops. It's not unusual, but after we don't continue on right away, I crane my neck and peer out the window.

We sit for a good five minutes before the driver's voice comes over the speaker. "Sorry, Ms. Sweet. We have a bit of a situation at the gate. Someone was trying to breach the fence. Security is dealing with it, though."

Instantly, my body goes on high alert. While this isn't the first time we've had a security breach, it's been a while, and after all the ways Flora terrorized me, I find myself more than a little unnerved by it. Knowing that Brad's life is going up in flames doesn't tame my worry either. It's quite possible that he got wind of my plan and is trying to stop me. I wouldn't put it past him.

"Call the police," my father grits out.

"*Daddy.*"

"No. We aren't taking any chances. You've already come close to death once this summer."

"Flora's in custody." Even as I say it, my voice wavers. Because is she? Could she have made bail? Would she know where to find me?

The questions hit me one after another. Yes, she most certainly could. The woman is determined to have Fisher all to herself, and clearly, she's deranged.

My heart races as I search our surroundings. The limo no longer feels like a safe place. It feels like a death box. Visions of being trapped in the burning theater pummel me. The heat, the terror, the fear that we wouldn't make it out. What if she used some type of gas this time? My lungs sting, making it hard to breathe.

"Daddy," I gasp. "Open the door"

"Libby." He squeezes my hand. "Breathe, hunny." Though his words to me are gentle, in the next breath, he bangs on the ceiling of the limo. "Call the police!"

"I just need to talk to her for a second."

The words barely permeate my frazzled brain. The blood roaring in my ears is too loud.

"Tell her it's Fisher. She'll want to see me." The angry voice gets louder, this time washing over me in a way that instantly drowns out the panic.

"Fisher!" I yell, pushing the door open.

My father grasps my arm and pulls me back. "Stay, Libby."

Barely able to catch my breath, I shake him off. "That's Fisher, *my Fisher*." I say as if that means anything to him.

I peek my head out and immediately spot Fisher on the other side of the black gate. Though he looks so different from my Fisher. In a black tuxedo with his hair perfectly done, he glares at my security personnel.

"Libby!" The sound of Sutton's sweet voice has my heart lurching.

It only takes a minute to find her. She's wearing a pretty pink dress that matches mine almost perfectly.

"Sutton Jones," I call, my heart racing. "What are you doing here, pretty girl?"

The fury in Fisher's expression evaporates when he hears my voice, and when he spots me, he sucks in a sharp breath.

"Wade, you can let them in. They're family."

My security guard shakes his head, his lips turned down. "They're not on the list."

Fisher arches his brows in a teasing way.

"My mistake," I say as Wade finally releases the lock on the gate, allowing Fisher and Sutton in.

"Hell, Princess," my man practically growls. "You look gorgeous."

Sutton giggles, her head tipped back. "That's a bad word."

He mumbles an apology, but he never takes his eyes off me.

"What are you guys doing here?" I ask as I hold out my arms.

Without a moment's hesitation, Sutton runs into them and hugs me tight.

So much for my makeup still being intact, because, on contact, my eyes flood with tears.

"We needed you," Fisher says as he wraps both of us in a hug.

That's when I officially lose it. "I needed you," I whisper. "Both of you."

Fisher puts two fingers beneath my chin and tilts my face up, then presses his lips to mine. "I know. That's why we're here."

"You're here. You're *both* here," I say through a sob.

He nods, his cheek pressed to mine. "Both of us."

"This is *the* guy?" my father says behind me.

I pull back and turn. "Dad this is—"

"Fisher Jones." He holds out his hand.

Confusion swirls through me as he smiles at Fisher, his expression softening. "He's been taking care of the cottage. And he's the one I asked to get the place ready for you. Cank gave me his number. Says he does everything on the island."

The two of us let out matching laughs. "Not anymore," Fisher says, shaking my father's hand.

"No?" I say, questioning him.

With a smile, he peers down at me. "No. From now on, the only people I do everything for are you two." He squeezes Sutton's shoulder.

"I can't believe you're here." I'm still blown away. Still confused about how they got here. About why they're here.

"We couldn't miss your big award." Sutton grins.

"Oh." I glance at my father. He was supposed to be my guest tonight.

He gives me a warm smile. "Take them." Quickly, his expression morphs into something far more serious. "But if Brad so much as looks at her—"

Fisher tenses beside me. "I've got her."

Straightening his jacket, my father nods. "Good, because if I see him, I'll kill him."

Sutton squeaks and I glower.

"Sorry," he says sheepishly.

Fisher shakes his head. "I'm with you."

"No one is hurting anyone," I say, looking back and forth between them.

"Right," Sutton says proudly. "She's going to decimate him with the truth."

Smiling, I bend down and hug her again. "Exactly, pretty girl."

—

Between our encounter at the gate and the phone calls I made to ensure we secured a third seat, we missed the red carpet. I may not have had the opportunity to speak my truth there, but I promise myself I'll find a way.

Sutton sits between Fisher and me. It was more difficult than I expected to magically come up with a third seat, but my publicist is a saint who was more than willing to give up her spot.

Every few seconds, Sutton grabs my arm and points at another celebrity she recognizes. She knows more people here than I do since I've always been too busy to watch anything other than *Dancing with the Stars* regularly.

We're not seated with anyone from my show. Probably on purpose. Maybe my people arranged it. Maybe the production team did. Either way, I can't say I'm not happy about it. I've yet to spot Brad, but I won't breathe easy until we're back on the East Coast.

The award for best supporting actress is announced near the end of the night, and when Joey Berkshire—the heiress and winner of *Dancing with the Stars*—says my name, I break out in goose bumps.

The audience cheers, but the sound fades as I stand and lock eyes with Fisher.

Holy shit. This is actually happening. I won. I *won*.

Fisher reaches across Sutton and squeezes my hand. "Proud of you."

Sutton throws her arms around my waist, vibrating with excitement. With a steadying breath, I hug her tight. "Thank you, pretty girl."

Her blue eyes meet mine, so full of wisdom and trust. So full of belief in me. "Now go tell your truth."

I walk up to the stage in a daze and accept a hug from Joey before turning toward the now quieted crowd.

For a moment, my mind is blank. But then I spot Brad, seated in the third row, with a smug smile on his face, and the words spill out.

"You all watched for months as my character fought a battle that many people face in real life. Depression. Drugs. The loss of the will to live. The truth is, I didn't even have to act in those scenes."

I meet Brad's gaze, and he lights up like he thinks I'm going to admit that I had a drug problem like the producers alleged.

More determined than ever, I look away from him. "I had been fighting a similar battle for years. An internal one. But it had nothing to do with drugs. I battled with myself because I felt dirty within my own body because of the way someone else touched me." I look back at him. "Because of the way *Brad Fedder* touched me."

The auditorium room breaks out in a collective whoosh of air.

Brad jumps up, his hands balled into fists. "This is bullshit!"

Security starts down the aisle because, fortunately, the Emmys take their ceremonies seriously, and a rowdy member of the audience won't get to stay.

"Sit down, Brad. You never listened when I said no, but you are going to listen to this."

Music plays, signaling that my time is up. Or maybe it's a way to gloss over what's going on. To silence me. But I won't be silenced any longer.

"I was eight the first time he touched me. *Eight.*"

Murmurs break out throughout the audience, and Brad shuffles toward the end of his row, but he's stopped when several people refuse to move out of his way.

"He was sixteen," I continue. "Many of you might wonder why, if he'd molested me, I auditioned for a show. You may wonder how I could have worked with him for years without speaking up. The answer is complicated. I was a child, and his family was my family. I was scared I'd lose more people I cared about."

I look at Sutton and smile. "But I'm not scared anymore."

"This is bullshit!" Brad yells as an older gentleman holds him in place. The woman on his other side stands with her arms folded, her face a hard mask of fury. "She's making things up," he rattles on. "It's been twenty years"

"Eighteen, actually," I muse. "And funny thing," I say, though this is absolutely the least funny topic I've ever discussed. "But in the State of Rhode Island, a victim of sexual assault has twenty years to press charges. And while we may be in California now, Brad's family had a house on Block Island."

I stare him straight in the eye and force myself to breathe, to hold tight to my strength.

"I have my own family now. I'm not scared of you anymore. You have no power over me."

When the clapping starts, it's just a single person. Immediately, I search for the source. Sutton is standing, clapping as loudly as she can. Fisher's holding her shoulder, his face full of emotion.

The woman beside them stands and joins in. And like a stadium of fans does at a sporting event, they stand, creating a wave, until my peers are all on their feet, applauding. The music is still playing and Brad is still screaming, but it's all drowned out by the cheering of the crowd. This is it. The sound of me taking back my truth.

I'm finally stepping out of the shadows and into the sun.

But I don't want to be here anymore. So I rush off the stage, award in hand, and when I return to my seat, Fisher and Sutton are there to greet me. Fisher pulls me to his chest, and without having to ask, guides us out.

"You realize you're going to be on the cover of every gossip rag and celebrity magazine now, right?" I grin at him as we step out of the theater.

With an arm draped around my shoulders, he kisses my forehead. "We're in this with you, Libby. It's the three of us from here on out. So what do you say? You ready to go home, Princess?"

I squeeze my eyes shut and let the words that once irritated me wash over me. They hit different now.

"Yes," I say as an overwhelming sense of peace settles within my bones. "Take me home."

Epilogue
Fisher

I HIT return and sit back, smiling as I survey all five screens. I don't know what I get more joy out of: hacking through somebody else's firewall or building an unbreakable one.

My focus drifts to the framed photo of Libby and Sutton on opening night of *Wicked*.

The real joy comes from the two of them. The rest is just icing on the cake. Libby is two months into her run as Glinda, and she loves every minute of it. She's finally giving her understudy a chance to perform so she can have a few days off.

She might have to be back for the matinee on Sunday, but she won't get any complaints from me. I'll take what I can get.

I attach my full report to the email, confirming that the client's firewall is up and running, and I've just hit send when my phone vibrates on the desk.

Cal's name appears on the screen. I smirk, knowing exactly why the hot shot New York attorney is calling me.

"Hey, man, what's up?"

"Why me?" he whines, his British accent only making him sound more pathetic.

"You clicked the fucking link." I laugh.

I've been managing Murphy & Macon's network security for years. They were one of my first clients, and yet fucking with my friend never gets old. One of my network checks involves sending emails with just a link or a shared drive to see who will click. The person who does is then required to take a network security refresh class.

"Of course I clicked. It was from you, you wanker," he mutters.

"They always come from someone you know." I pull my phone away from my ear to check the time. Sutton will be home from school soon.

He groans. "Can you give me a pass?"

"Nope. You'll be at the class with all the other clickers." I smirk. "But think of it this way, when you come up to Boston, you'll get to hang with Libby and me."

After the Emmy's, Libby, Sutton, and I moved into my apartment in Boston. For the first few weeks, reporters and paparazzi followed Libby's every move, but by the time September rolled around and Sutton started school, things had settled.

From there, we fell into a comfortable routine. Every morning, Libby takes Sutton to school, then heads to rehearsal while I get a few hours of work in before Sutton comes home. On the nights Libby has a show, Sutton and I swing by for an early dinner with her.

Libby shines on the stage, like she was always meant for live performance. And Boston is good to all of us. We eventually need to upgrade from my three-bedroom apartment, but for now, we're all content.

Bing lifts his head and peers around, then hops off the sofa. That can only mean one thing. Day after day, he greets Sutton the second she's home. The door to our apartment slams shut, and a heartbeat later, she calls my name.

"Sutton's home. Gotta go. Stop clicking the links." I hang up on my friend, laughing at the creative curses he throws out.

My girl flies into my office, braids bouncing, and tosses her pink backpack to the floor.

"Are you done? Ready to go?" Excitement spills out of her as she dances from foot to foot. She might have wanted to leave the island where she was born, but that doesn't mean she isn't dying to visit. "You said we were leaving right after school. And Maggie said she'd meet us at the wharf."

Since it's November, I wanted to take a chopper, but Libby insisted on returning the same way she arrived the first time. So Cank managed to get us first-class tickets on the trash boat.

"Libby's on her way home, sweet pea. How was school?"

"You know what Addie did in art today?" Sutton launches into a story about Beckett Langfield's stepdaughter, who has become her best friend. The two of them attend Bridgeworth Academy and play offense for the girls U9 soccer team. Now that the season is over, Beckett has been pushing hard for them to play softball. But since we plan to spend most of the summer on the island, Sutton isn't sure. Going back and forth so often could get tricky, but we'll do it if that's what she wants.

"Did Libby pack my rain boots?" Sutton says, jumping straight from her story without even a breath. She tilts her head, and her braids fall over her shoulder. "Wilder said I could pull up some traps before Thanksgiving dinner tomorrow, and I need my water boots."

"I'm pretty sure we left them there the last time we went out." Although Libby hasn't been back to Monhegan this fall because of her busy show schedule, Sutton and I have been out a few times to check on the houses.

Since the idea of taking over Hunter's old room still sits like lead in my stomach, we decided to renovate Libby's house. Although fine for spring and summer, the structure hasn't been updated for the cold Monhegan winters. We added a woodburning fireplace and remodeled the kitchen and master bath. They finished this week, and I can't wait to show Libby how it turned out.

"Hello!" Libby calls.

Bing yelps happily in response.

"Yes." Sutton jumps up and down, then darts from the room. "We can leave now!"

I stand and stretch, then trail behind her. At the mouth of the hallway, I prop myself up on the doorframe and watch the two of them.

With a smile, Libby brushes a hand softly over Sutton's blond hair. "Someone is excited, I see."

"I can't wait to go back. Eddy said there's already snow. Lindsey and I are gonna make a snowman, and Mrs. K said I can help her bake the pumpkin pie tonight if we make in time. And I get to have a sleep over with Lindsey, and—"

Libby cuts her off with a chuckle. "No wonder you're so pumped. Sounds like fun."

"Get your backpack. Everything else is loaded in the car."

The second Sutton takes off down the hall, Libby moves to me.

I hold my arms out and engulf her, breathing in her sweet scent. "How was today? They gonna make it three days without you, Princess?"

"Haha." She pinches my side.

"Who said I was kidding? I couldn't make it three days without you." I tilt her chin up and press my lips to hers. My intention is to steal a quick kiss, but I can't ever get enough of this woman, and I find myself cupping her cheek and diving in for more. Our tongues tangle for a minute before she pulls back.

"Mmm," she mummers against my lips. "I couldn't make it without you either, Hacker."

"Stop standing on top of each other. We need to get moving." Sutton rushes down the hallway with the backpack designated for travel rather than school. "Come on, we don't want to miss our ride."

She bolts past us, heading to the apartment door, with Bing hot on her heels.

"You heard the girl." I smirk and swipe a thumb beneath Libby's bottom lip. "Our trash boat awaits."

She giggles. "Ready to go home, Hacker?"

That's the thing I've learned over the last six months. Home is Boston, or Monhegan, or wherever Sutton and Libby are. Because these girls—they are my home.

bonus epilogue

LIBBY

"I don't understand why we can't take that boat. It's nostalgic." Forming a perfect pout that I know Fisher finds impossible to say no to, I wait for him to cave.

Beside me, Sutton grabs Fisher's hand and tugs. "I agree. It's tradition!"

"We're not going on the freaking trash boat," he growls.

Sutton rolls her eyes, and I huff at the grump. For the most part, the man gives us whatever we want. That's why Putt-Putt is currently being loaded into Big Daddy. Oh, excuse me. I forgot that he didn't like the name. So now the truck Fisher bought for the sole purpose of transporting Putt-Putt from Monhegan to Boston is called Putt-Putt's Ride. We even had the name painted on the side—in pink lettering—as a surprise for him.

His exact reaction: "Ah, hell, woman. What did you do to my truck?"

Yup, it's been a year since we met, and he's still just as exasperated with me as he was back then. But he loves it. And he loves me, which is all that really matters, right?

"It's not my fault that you wouldn't let us bring *Pink Lady* too."

I tried to convince Fisher to get an additional parking spot for our boat so Sutton and I could hang out in her during the winter. Bringing Putt-Putt was our compromise. She has her own parking spot and everything, and I take her to run errands in Boston. As long as it's not snowing, it's not a problem. She drives great, and aside from the random Massholes who like to honk when I can't keep up with traffic, it's the perfect way to get around my new favorite city.

"Boats need to be winterized, Libby. We've talked about this."

"But it's summer."

Fisher drops his head back and counts slowly. His therapist suggested he try it when he gets annoyed. It's worked wonders for his blood pressure.

We all see a therapist these days. After finally facing the truth of the abuse I suffered from Brad, it was a necessity. Fisher was the one who suggested he and Sutton see a therapist as well. It's helped them both work through the trauma of losing Hunter and Marissa.

Pride fills me as I take them both in. It hasn't been an easy year, but it's been the best of my life.

"Are you done counting yet, Dad?" Sutton asks. "I have something to tell you, but I want you to be completely calm when I do."

Fisher tenses, but his voice is gentle when he says, "What's up, sweet pea?"

She takes a deep breath. "I told Addie we were renting out our house this summer, and she told her dad. Now he wants to come to Monhegan and stay there."

"Beckett Langfield wants to rent our house for the summer?" Fisher's expression turns into one of horror.

I, on the other hand, try to fight a laugh but fail miserably. Sutton and Addie have become close, and according to Beckett, that means we're family now, and apparently families text a lot. Fisher's phone lights up all hours of the day with messages from Beckett.

Most of them include ideas for how Fisher can propose. Beckett seems oddly fixated on the idea that he should make an honest woman out of me. He's desperate for us to get our happily ever after. According to him, it would make a great story.

He's not wrong. I've read a lot of scripts over the years, and I'd say our love story tops them all.

But I'm happy to continue at the pace we're going. I like calling Fisher my boyfriend. He says it sounds ridiculous at his age, but I catch him smiling every time I do.

And we all know how I live to make that man smile.

Speaking of my boyfriend...

Fisher shakes his head. "He can rent another place. I already have a renter booked for the whole season."

"You do?"

His responding smirk sends a thrill through me.

"Fisher Jones, what did you do?"

His face lights up. "Remember Nicole from last summer?"

Sutton frowns. "*Wilder's* Nicole?"

He dips his chin. "Apparently she loved her time on the island so much that she wants to stay from Memorial Day to Labor Day this year."

"Shut up," I hiss, giggles overtaking me. Wilder's schemes last year were entertaining. I can only imagine he'll have to get more creative to get rid of the stage-five clinger this time. "You're evil," I tease as I tug on Fisher's shirt and pull him close.

"Ugh, you guys are doing it again," Sutton whines.

"Close your eyes," he grumbles.

She complies quickly. She's used to this by now.

Once she's safely shielded from the offense, he grabs my neck and pulls my mouth to his. Every kiss feels like the first one. It's like we're breathing life into one another. It's a straight hit to the heart that catapults me right back to when I was discovering who I was— and he was learning how to be true to himself while filling the parental role he'd taken on.

I love this man and I love this life.

Arms wrapped around his neck, I deepen the kiss. When I pull back, I give him my most winning smile and whisper, "Please, can we take the trash boat?"

"I woulda picked you up if I'd known you missed the ferry," Cank says as we disembark. "No need to take the trash boat."

With a grumbled curse, Fisher hoists another one of our suitcases onto the dock.

"Oh, we wanted to take it," Sutton explains. "Tradition and all."

Cank nods like it makes perfect sense.

"See?" I grin at Fisher. "He gets it."

"Oh, your new renter got here last weekend," Cank says.

This has Fisher smiling. "I know. I checked in after she arrived. She said you helped her get all her things to the house. Appreciate it."

Cank nods. "That's what islanders are for. Right, Libby?"

Even though we're officially summer people these days, it feels good to know they've accepted me as one of their own. They're certainly all mine.

"Wilder should be here any minute with your truck. That'll make getting your luggage to the house easier."

As if on cue, the old truck with no doors comes round the bend, Wilder and Maggie bouncing along with it as it hits ruts in the dirt path we use as a road.

My heart swells at the sight of them. The last several months have been busy, and I've missed my friends desperately. Both Maggie and Wilder have been out to visit on occasion, but the winter weather makes it hard to travel back and forth. Early spring weather too. So we never see them enough.

The truck comes to a stop and Wilder gets out. The usually jovial man is glaring, an expression I'm not sure I've ever seen on his face, as he rounds the hood, never looking away from Maggie. When he reaches her, he holds out his arms and helps her to her feet.

My heart practically stops when he ensures her body slides down his in one slow, sensuous move.

What the heck is this?

Wilder dips his head and brings his mouth to her ear.

An instant later, her cheeks go crimson.

"Holy shit," I whisper.

Sutton gasps. "That's a bad word, Libby."

"Sorry. But seriously—holy shit."

This time she giggles.

"What's happening?" I ask far too loudly as Wilder wraps an arm around Maggie and guides her our way.

As they get close, she breaks into the strangest smile.

"Why does it look like you've been kidnapped?"

Wilder glances down at her with this look that I can't quite figure out. Half adoration, half annoyance, I think. "I guess now's as good a time as any."

"As good a time as any to what?" I look from one friend to the other and back again, feeling like a pinball machine.

Wilder beams at me. "Maggie and I are dating."

"What?" Sutton and I squeal at the same time.

Maggie smiles, this one just as strange and, if I'm not mistaken, forced. "Yup. Surprise."

Head tilted, I study them. Something is off. The fake smile. The over-the-top way Wilder helped Maggie out of the truck. It almost feels fake.

"Congrats," Fisher says, clearly not sensing the same thing I am. He hugs Maggie, and when he and Wilder do the bro hug thing, I snag my sweet friend's wrist and pull her away from the group. "Blink twice if you've been kidnapped."

With a laugh, she rolls her eyes. "Not kidnapped. But god am I glad you're back."

"Another summer on Monhegan Island." I hum as the anticipation begins to build.

Fisher holds out a hand to me, his eyes warming. "Ready to go home, Princess?"

I squeeze his hand and grin, letting him tug me against his chest and press a kiss to my forehead.

Lucky for me, as long as I'm with these people, I'm home.

acknowledgments

A huge thank you to the real town of Monhegan Maine who welcomed us last year after a truly harrowing ferry ride–no we did not take the trash boat though we did see it!--as soon as we stepped off the ferry, ideas began sprouting into our heads and Libby and Fisher were born. While the town is absolutely gorgeous and some of the business names have been used, the story is complete fiction. The staff from the donut shop are lovely and certainly would never terrorize anyone.

This book would not have come together without the help of some truly amazing people. Tiffany, Glav, Bri and Jess, who were with us when this story was born, thank you for listening to our ramblings, helping us plot and surviving that ferry ride. More importantly though, the sincerest of thanks to Tiffany for helping us navigate our FIRST multi-cast audio production.

To our beta readers, Sara, Kristie, Glav, Andi, Becca and Jill for your sensitivity read, this book is better because of you. To our lovely editor Beth, thank you for loving Fisher and Libby as much as us and making the book better as you always do.

To our incredible street teams who help promote our books day in and day out, every release gets better because of you! We are in awe of your friendship and support.

A huge thank you to Elin for the gorgeous cover image and the drawings you did for this project and to Sara for creating the gorgeous covers and special editions, formatting, graphics, and the million and one other things you did weekly to keep this book on track.

Finally, none of this would be possible without you, our amazing readers. Thank you for all of your messages, your Tiktoks, your dms, your posts and your rants. There is nothing we love more than hearing from each of you how a character affected you, or a storyline made you laugh. We love your reviews, your anecdotes, and the notes you send.

This is only the beginning of our co-writing plans for this year. So make sure you follow us on facebook, instagram, and tiktok (and join our patreon) to keep up to date with our next project: The Dadcoms!

also by brittanée nicole

Bristol Bay Rom Coms

She Likes Piña Coladas

Kisses Sweet Like Wine

Over the Rainbow

Bristol Bay Romance

Love and Tequila Make Her Crazy

A Very Merry Margarita Mix-Up

Boston Billionaires

Whiskey Lies

Loving Whiskey

Wishing for Champagne Kisses

Dirty Truths

Extra Dirty

Mother Faker

(Mother Faker is Book 1 of the Mom Com Series, but is also a lead in to the Revenge Games alongside Revenge Era. This book can be read as a Standalone, or after Revenge Era and before Pucking Revenge)

Revenge Games

Revenge Era

Pucking Revenge

A Major Puck Up

Boston Bolts Hockey

Hockey Boy

Trouble

War

Playboy

Standalone Romantic Suspense

Deadly Gossip

Irish

also by jenni bara

Want more Boston Revs Baseball

Mother Maker - Cortney Miller

The Fall Out - Christian Damiano

Back Together Again - Mason Dumpty

The Fake Out - Emerson Knight

The Foul Out - Kyle Bosco

Finding Out - Coach Wilson

The Freak Out - Asher Price

Curious about the baseball boys from the NY Metros

NY Metros Baseball

More than the Game

More than a Story

Wishing for More

Made in the USA
Coppell, TX
22 June 2025

50998802R00190